WAR OF THE MYSTICS

Riders of Dark Dragons Book V

C.K. RIEKE

Books by C.K. Rieke

Song of the Ellydian I: The Scarred

Riders of Dark Dragons I: Mystics on the Mountain
Riders of Dark Dragons II: The Majestic Wilds
Riders of Dark Dragons III: Mages of the Arcane
Riders of Dark Dragons IV: The Fallen and the Flames
Riders of Dark Dragons V: War of the Mystics

The Dragon Sands I: Assassin Born
The Dragon Sands II: Revenge Song
The Dragon Sands III: Serpentine Risen
The Dragon Sands IV: War Dragons
The Dragon Sands V: War's End

The Path of Zaan I: The Road to Light
The Path of Zaan II: The Crooked Knight
The Path of Zaan III: The Devil King

This novel was published by Crimson Cro Publishing
Copyright © 2023 Hierarchy LLC

All Rights Reserved.

Cover by Get Covers dot com.

All characters and events in this book are fictitious.
Printed in the United States of America. No part of this book may be used or reproduced in any manner whatsoever without written permission except in the case of brief quotations embodied in critical articles or reviews.
This book is a work of fiction. Names, characters, businesses, organizations, places, events and incidents either are the product of the author's imagination or are used fictitiously. Any resemblance to actual persons, living or dead, events, or locales is entirely coincidental.

Please don't pirate this book.

Sign up to join the Reader's Group
Click here to Sign Up

PART I
THE BATTLE OF VALEREN

Chapter One

There were no words for what he felt.

His blood-shot eyes glared out at the awestruck battlefield, darting around feverishly for a sign of Gracelyn—but she was nowhere to be found. In the few moments when the Great God who Stone never actually knew to be real had arrived and vanished with Gracelyn, Rosen, and Arken—everything changed.

Stone clutched his chest with his free hand, dropping to a knee while his Masummand Steel sword's tip slid into the mud. Beads of sweat mixed with warm raindrops dripped down his brow and eyelashes, stinging his eyes. He felt the hot blood beating thickly through his heart and the veins in his neck bulged.

Murmurs flooded through the thousands in steel armor behind him, back within the city of Valeren. The tens of thousands of readied soldiers, eight thousand plus cavalry, and the mighty royal elite guard of the crown—the Vlaer all shuddered in the aftermath of the brief fight with Arken.

Stone looked back and saw Queen Bristole Velecitor frozen in a dreaded statuesque pose upon her mighty steed. Within the clear blue ice, her entire flesh, bone, and heart were rendered to little more than a memory. Her mouth was agape in horror, her pristine silver armor with gold tips was transformed to sparkling ice, and her massive steed was left frozen in a half-stride of panic. Her Masummand Steel blade was the only thing that was undamaged.

The five mighty, massive Neferian before them roared and snapped their black maws with long sharp teeth toward the dragons behind Stone. The Neferians' spiked necks curled, their long arms dug with strong claws into the ground with spidery ashen wings hinged behind, and their serpentine-devilish yellow eyes glaring madly down upon them.

Arken's great Neferian roared louder than the others, with its crimson head easily twice the size of the others'. While the other four Neferian were quickly remounted by their Runtue riders, armed with thick swords and tridents, Arken's dark dragon was left riderless—as the Dark King had been taken away in the blink of an eye by the one god Crysinthian.

But he wasn't the only thing taken from the battlefield…

Gracelyn was gone. Rosen too. Stone gritted his teeth as Adler and Ceres called out uselessly for them as Stone saw the spot where the red gemstone had been after it had fallen from his pocket, as it was taken too. Crysinthian had taken the three of them—and the stone Arken called an Adralite.

Stone felt a pit in his stomach at the resentment that he hadn't tried to use the power of the Adralite while it was in his possession. But he didn't know the power it had—the power that Crysinthian had appeared for to keep it from Arken's grasp.

How could I have been so stupid? I could've stopped all this had I used it, but I didn't know how—I don't know how. Maybe I could've stopped him, maybe I could've stopped them both! And Gracelyn and Rosen would still be here with us, with me.

He looked up into the unnatural yellow snake eyes of

Arken's Neferian rising high before him, roaring so loudly it shook the stone walls of the city behind him.

Where'd he take you? We sure could use your magic right about now...

He heard the familiar snap of bowstrings, but it was by the hundreds, and the sky darkened as a wall of sharp arrows plowed into the dark dragons, but ricocheted off, only enraging them.

Just beyond the dragons, Salus Greyhorn stood before his own frozen steed, whirling his sleek, metallic staff with a shining white jewel above his crown of twisted bone and ivory that fitted over lifeless, dark eyes. His tan, bald head and crooked nose were pattered by the thick rain as his robes dangled below his elbows, and his one handless arm emitted a dark, blackish-green glow.

Paltereth Mir, the dark sorceress, had led the over three hundred Mages of the Arcane down from their attack upon the northern city of Verren and was casting a spell of her own as it spun above her in large arcs of gassy green magic. Her pale face and dark eyes glowered with wicked delight as the Arcanic Magic emitted from her fingertips.

Kellen Voerth, who'd led down the darker Mages of the Seliax from Verren, lay on his side with a murky pool of mixed blood and rain underneath with a sharp spear sticking through his abdomen. He was unconscious, or hopefully dead, Stone thought.

The army of the Vile King and Arken's Neferian readied themselves for the greatest battle of Valeren in over a thousand years, and the three-thousand-year-old city had never fallen... yet it had already just lost its queen...

General Joridd, the wide-shouldered, strong-armed soldier in black leather armor with slivers of gray metal adornments, yelled out orders behind him with his baritone voice as more arrows flew out into the army of mages, with most being struck away by spells, but a few striking hard into the soft-bodied, armorless mages. Joridd's thick, black braids whipped behind his bald, ebon-skinned head with shaved sides as he yelled out his orders. A thin violet cape tussled behind him in the strong winds. He was the most kingly soldier Stone thought he'd ever seen.

Vandress Constance, the mage and Dream Walker, rallied to Joridd's side. Her tan skin had streaks of tears from her amber eyes that she hadn't wiped away. Her dark hair was pulled back into a bun, yet her bangs fell to just below her thin chin, framing her plump lips, and her teeth gritted in rage. She held a staff of curved wood with veins of violet and white gemstones. A blue aura emanated from the staff, and as it glowed, Stone saw other lights flare up on the walls of the city —thirteen, to be exact; the mages of Valeren.

The Neferian took to the air as their riders pulled hard on the reins. Perhaps to get out of the storm of sharp-tipped arrows, but most likely to begin their attack on the city, Stone worried.

Stone ran to get up on Grimdore's back, as Ceres and Adler both hustled over to the teal-winged dragon as well. Corvaire got up on the old dragon Zênon's body, with gray scales and deep, dark gray horns that ran down the length of his wide back. The gray dragon roared thunderously as the hundreds of scars on its face wrinkled. Drâon Corvaire's cape flapped behind him as the dragon lifted up into the air after the dark dragons—a rare sight as Stone had never seen him wear a cape before and assumed it was a sign of the significance of this battle.

Marilyn the Conjurer got upon the ivory-scaled dragon Belzarath. Her long, wet silver hair blew back behind her as her dark eyes narrowed on her tan face. The white dragon flapped her mighty wings as she stood powerfully back on her hind legs, then leaped up into the air after the dark dragons.

The thin, dark green dragon Īzadan snarled as she flew up

behind the other three. Her sandy wings flapped more sporadically than the larger dragons as her long body unwound from a corkscrew shape to a thin majestic one as she flew up into the air.

Four dragons to fight five Neferian—including Arken's monstrously giant one.

Not the odds I want. But hopefully those Dead Bows the queen built prove to be more than expensive decorations for the city. We sure could use you right now, Y'dran... you're sorely missed, friend...

Conrad the Guild Master was back in the city with his ranks of assassins, and there were the other mages of the city up upon the walls at the entrance of Valeren: thirteen who wielded the Elessior and three who dealt in the dark arts of the Seliax—a weapon none of them in Stone's party found comforting.

As Grimdore hovered above, with the three of them upon her back, Stone looked down and saw a dog run out of the front gate and to Joridd's side—barking wildly, although his anger was drowned out by the sound of the roaring and hissing dragons, the heavy rains with booming thunder, the bustle of the army of Verren, and the electric sounds of the dark mages' spells being cast.

All was in motion for the biggest battle in Valeren in more than ten lifetimes of men.

In an explosive burst of magic below, and a plume of green smoke, Salus blasted up a burst of his magic that caused every arrow in the sky to incinerate to ash, even the ones still readied in the hands of the archers, burning their hands and causing many to fall to the ground in agony.

Joridd led the charge, running with his sword held ready over his shoulder. Vandress unleashed a spell that shot out in three directions toward Salus, Paltereth, and Kellen while spells were hurtled from above down in arcs as the mages beyond.

The battle had begun as the queen stood frozen in bitter

ice atop her steed and Mud ran out beside Joridd into the fray. The legions of Valeren rode out behind Joridd, as the cavalry of thousands poured out of the many entrances of the northern walls of the city. Infantry ran out behind, and a smirk crossed Stone's face, which Ceres caught.

"Wouldn't smile yet," she said from behind him. "They may have the numbers below, but we sure as shite don't up here!"

Chapter Two

Grimdore's wings flapped wide at both sides of her long body with the muscles in her back and tensing beneath Stone, Adler, and Ceres as the winds bit coldly at their faces and the rains made her teal, thick scales slippery as they held on tightly.

The teal dragon rose high above the city center as Belzarath flew toward the sea, and Zênon and Īzadan flew west together. The five Neferian followed with their eyes gleaming in rage and the riders in thick, gray armor whipping at their reigns wildly. Each of the dark dragons had riders except Arken's—with its blood-red head and serpentine yellow eyes—flying swiftly after Grimdore.

"You think it remembers her?" Adler asked in a loud voice in the whistling winds. Arken's Neferian snapped its jaws in a seemingly meaningful response.

"She did kill one of its kin," Ceres said, her blond hair rustling behind her neck. "I'd be pissed as all hell, wouldn't ya?"

"C'mon, Grimdore—fly!" Stone said as the massive dark

dragon behind was catching up at blinding speed with its giant wings outstretched behind its long, scaly arms.

Grimdore twirled over, with its right wing flipping it completely over, making each of them cling on tightly as the dragon glided upside down back toward the city. Through his narrow eyes, Stone glimpsed the magical explosions that were rocking the entrance gate of the city and saw battalions of soldiers and cavalry funneling through the gate out into the lands beyond—and the mages.

The Neferian followed behind, not as agile as the smaller, teal dragon, but in straight flight, it would beat her nearly every time. Stone heard a dull thud from below, followed by a brief, thick vibrating sound. The dark dragon pulled its wings back, slowing its descent, barking out a loud, glass-shattering roar as the steel bolt whizzed past its neck, flying upward into the sky.

"Damn," Adler said. "Nearly got the devil!"

Stone looked down to see the soldiers upon the tower with the Dead Bow scrambling to set another bolt inside it. There was good reason for them to scramble so, as the mighty Neferian had its monstrous eyes set upon the tower.

"Back around, girl," Stone said, tugging at Grimdore's scales. "Now's our chance." With a swift turn that pulled their bodies harder onto her back, the teal dragon curled around and dove at the beast.

Stone's fingertips warmed as the fire within grew hot, and just before the dark dragon sensed her behind, Grimdore shot a plume of wicked dragonfire upon it. It blasted into its rear legs with hot smoke smoldering back into Stone's eyes. The Neferian roared and turned its mighty head back and snapped its jaws with sharp teeth and its muscular jaws tensing. Grimdore pulled back, out of the way, but continued to trail after the dark dragon—who was still gliding down toward the tower.

Another low buzzing sound snapped from the east, and

another bolt of steel flew at astonishing speed past the dragon, missing by a good twenty yards. Though it missed, the dragon shrieked and tucked its wings in to fly faster down at the tower, whose soldiers were quickly abandoning their posts, scurrying down into it for their safety.

But the dragonfire of a Neferian cared little for men hiding behind rock.

The dark dragon spewed a thick, raging blast of black fire upon the top of the tower, blowing the top two floors of it to smoking rubble as the Dead Bow fell far to the ground below, engulfed in dark flames. There were no screams, and perhaps there'd be no bodies to find later either.

The dark dragon crashed into the blazing tower with its claws sinking deep within, and with a burst flew back off, sending the rest of the tower breaking to the ground. Its blazing golden eyes were fixed upon Grimdore and those on her back once more.

"Uh oh," Adler murmured, with his eyebrows raised.

"Fly, girl, fly!" Ceres yelled.

Grimdore whipped around and flew back up to the sky with all her might.

"Ceres," Adler said, tugging her pants at the knee. "Now'd be a good time to use some of those spells o' yours!"

To the southern shores of the city, while spells exploded, and the battle raged at the northern entrance to Valeren, Belzarath flew frantically with two Neferian at her tails. The riders had wide-eyed, maniacal grins on their faces as they chased after the ivory-scaled dragon.

Marilyn was atop her, casting down spells of bright red back at the two ensuing dragons. She herself was wild with her silver hair flowing behind her and a look on her face of the huntress. Marilyn the Conjurer was a warrior through and through. Perhaps it was the blood in her veins, Stone thought, along with the help of the spell the Aigonic Mages cast on her to bring her back to her old self. She was revived—reborn like the Phoenix—and the spells she cast were all the more proof of that.

To the west, her brother Drâon was mounted upon the old, gray dragon Zênon. Īzadan slithered behind with her long green body flying like a serpent. The last two Neferian flew after them wildly, hissing and growling. Below, the soldiers manning the Dead Bows had their bolts locked and ready. They'd seen what had just happened from Arken's dark dragon, so they knew whatever shot they took had to count. No bolts flew through the sky after the dark dragons that were so far up in the clouds; they remained locked tightly back in their bows.

Corvaire shot down sizzling spells at the two ensuing dragons, but even with the old dragon's great body and wing size, he was no match for the speed of the Neferian. Īzadan's slender frame jutted around their air with seemingly impossible angles and movements, as she could curl her body around Zênon's with ease. This frustrated the dark dragons as they gnarled their teeth and flapped their wings after the green dragon with sand-colored wings.

An icy spell bit into one of the Neferian's eyes and sent the rider covering his head, crouching back down into the dragon's thick scales. Corvaire looked like one of the heroes of tales of old. Stone watched him and Marilyn casting down ancient spells from the backs of dragons and he thought about the tales and songs that might be told of that moment for centuries to come... if only they could live to tell the tale.

Suddenly, Arken's Neferian caught up with Grimdore while they seemed to be watching the other dragons, and it flew past, hitting her side, nearly knocking the wind from her—and Stone.

"*Infernus!*" Ceres said, sending out seething flames at the dark dragon, but they blew past, flowing off its scales like water over slick stone.

The red-headed dark dragon sunk its teeth ferociously into Grimdore's shoulder like a crocodile and didn't let go.

"Argh," Ceres said, holding on with a powerful grip while the enormous dragon shook its head with its teeth sunk in deep. Grimdore turned her head around and bit at the neck of the Neferian, causing it to release its jaws and they turned their claws toward one another, slashing as they fell toward the city.

"Hold on," Stone said as the winds blew past the two dragons who plummeted, clawing and biting at one another. He turned his head to evade the winds and saw that Grimdore's shoulder was leaking blood in streaks behind them.

"Use your spells!" Adler said. But they all saw Ceres was clinging on with both hands so tightly she couldn't.

Stone thought about trying to use his own spell, but he was in the same position she was in, clinging on for dear life, and tucked his chest into Grimdore's back. The Neferian growled in rage as a whistling sound shot past, cutting through the webbing in its right wing. The bolt rose high into the sky until it was out of sight. Fumes rolled out of the angry Neferian's mouth as spots of blood trickled down its scales and flicked off into the winds, and Grimdore's teeth glistened in its blood.

Another bolt flew past, this one nearly hitting Grimdore's neck.

"Watch it!" Adler yelled. "Wrong dragon, wrong dragon!" They continued plummeting together in a tangle of tooth and claw as another bolt darted past, this one coming mere feet from the Neferian's throat. It snarled and roared. "Much better," Adler said under his breath.

They'd flown so far down entangled with each other that they were only seconds from the ground when the dark dragon roared loudly, causing Stone and the others to cover their ears. Each of them did their best with one free hand, but while they did so, the Neferian flapped its wings, separating from Grimdore.

During the commotion, another bolt whizzed by, yards away from either dragon, but caused the dark dragon to shudder, making its way back to the sky. Its wide, dark wings flapped, and its long tail slithered behind like a thick tree trunk. As Grimdore got her wits about her, the tail of the dark dragon slammed into her and slid up her back.

"Get down!" Stone said with his knuckles whitening from his grasp on the scales. The enormous tail bounced off the teal scales and rose over Ceres as she hunched down, but as it came back down, it slammed into Adler, knocking the breath from his lungs and flipping him completely over.

The tail bounced off again, rising just over Stone, and whooshed away. But Adler had been toppled from the teal dragon's back and was clinging to the side of Grimdore with his feet dangling below her torso.

"Adler!" Ceres cried.

"Hang on," Stone said. "I'm gonna get you. Hold on!"

Adler's eyes were wide with fear.

Something struck the dragon's belly hard then, and Stone saw it was one of the other Neferian's dark scales flying past. He reached back with all his might to grab Alder's hand. But the teal dragon was rocked to its side in the air, causing Adler's grip to loosen, one of his hands falling to his side, as he held on for his life.

"Hold on!" Ceres yelled from behind.

"I'll get ya," Stone said. "I've almost got you…"

Stone's fingers were inches from Adler's as he hung completely off, dangling to the dragon's side.

"Turn, Grimdore," Ceres said as Stone stretched out his arm as hard as he could. "Turn back."

The Neferian knocked into Grimdore's stomach once

again, and Stone watched with life slowed as Adler's grip on the wet scales slipped and he fell free from Grimdore.

"Adler!" he yelled. "No!"

Grimdore's body was rocked again by Arken's Neferian and as her body was shocked by the hit, Adler was out of view in an instant. He fell. His body fell back down into the city.

"Adler!" Ceres cried. "No!"

Chapter Three

Soldiers in gleaming, clean armor poured through the mouth of the front gate of Valeren—the last unscathed city of the Worforgon. The rains hit their silver plate armor in sharp tinks, but as a whole, it was drowned out by the ravaging dragons blazing through the sky above.

The soldiers came so quickly out of the city they appeared to not only thread through the walls themselves, but they seemed to come wholly out of the ground. An army of thousands was coming out to meet the legion of dark mages before the gates. With only a small group of their own mages at their backs, the massive army would need more than luck to get within striking distance of one that commanded the power of the Arcanica or the Seliax.

Joridd and Vandress led the charge. Vandress let out a vast spell with a blueish aura that cascaded out in a funnel shape toward the vanguard of mages, including Paltereth Mir and the Vile King. The mages of Valeren cast down spells from the walls behind that shielded the two from the maelstrom of dark green, cloud-like spells that pummeled into them as they led the charge.

The loud pounding of hooves on dirt quickly came about their sides as the cavalry rode with great speed at Salus and Paltereth's mages. They rode past with the vigor to enact redemption, defend their homes, and defeat evil.

While the mages of Valeren's spells were concentrated upon Joridd and Vandress, their spells were weaker upon the cavalry—and as the spells of Salus' mages blew through the cavalry's ranks, shrieks of agony poured from the men and horses' mouths. Sharp spells tore through flesh, black magic caused skin to boil and tear, and red mists blinded and scorched. Dozens died instantly.

Paltereth Mir stood wide under her black robes, letting a purple-veiny pale leg slide out of the long slit in them. Her reddish teeth showed as she gritted her teeth and hissed. The green flames that had been building along her arms slung forward as she shot her sharp fingertips toward Joridd and Vandress. The two leaped apart, diving in opposing directions into the mud, trying to hide behind even the slimmest blades of grass. The green flames hit the mages' shielding spell and rolled overhead, but many of the flames tore through, flaming overhead, and singed some of the hairs on the tops of their heads.

Salus stood tall and held his long metallic staff out at the two on the ground. The air sizzled as a bolt of darkened magic from the staff's white jewel at its tip shot like black lightning at the mages' of the city's protective spell, searing a great hole in its center. The Vile King's spell faded as he readied another. The mages of Valeren cast more energy down to repair the damage, but the hole closed slowly, knitting itself back together. Joridd was quickly back up to his feet, urging Vandress to follow him, which she did.

With a wave of her hand, Vandress quickly repaired the missing patch of the shielding spell with a sparkle of light—as Paltereth and Salus slung another barrage of spells upon them.

The infantry was running in droves past them on both sides as the two dark mages squared off with Joridd and Vandress. The causalities were so catastrophic so quickly that the pile of dead at the ring around the army of mages was proving to become its own challenge. The army and cavalry were slowed so much that the archers began unleashing more swarms of arrows onto the mages as they continued casting their dark spells.

This wasn't how this battle was supposed to go. Queen Velecitor had worked out the finer details with her council. The Majestic Wilds were supposed to be there on the front lines to use their Elessior to fight Paltereth and Salus and to aid the infantry to gain ground to reach the Mages of the Seliax. The mere mages of Valeren were no use against the strength of their sheer number. The dragons could incinerate the lot of Arcanists in minutes if they were able, but the same could be said of the Neferian if they were able. As Stone watched the battle unfold in brief glimpses from the sky, he cursed Crysinthian's name. *Did he know he'd completely changed the tide of this battle? Or did he not care?*

The dragons fought as they soared through the overcast sky above the battle as thin-looking spears shot up toward the heavens like needles puncturing thin cloth. Flames erupted in huge swaths, illuminating the clouds like a storm of its own. Reds, oranges, and golds blew from the maws of the dragons, met with flames of black from the Neferian, causing the sky to darken further.

From within the city, chaos had stirred awake. With word of the queen's death, and the Majestic Wilds gone from the battle, hope had faded and panic stirred within the city streets. Small fires burned and people ran in disarray, with babes in their arms and their meager wealth clanking in their pockets and bags.

In surprise, Arken Shadowborn, before his removal from

battle by the Great God, had offered a parlay. But with him gone, all knew there would be no mercy given from the Vile King and his witch. If they took the last free city, they would not leave it in a place to rebuild a force that would match their own—not after the bloody battle that ravaged on.

Joridd gripped his sword's grip tightly in his hand, letting the leather squeal with the mud that lubricated beneath his strong fingers. His teeth gritted and his brow furrowed as the explosions of magic burst before them repeatedly. He wanted nothing more than to cut the head from the snake, but the back and forth of the magical shield before them continued, and he had no way of getting through it.

At his elbow, a tuft of fur scratched him, drawing his gaze. The dog growled as it snarled its teeth.

"That's it, boy," Joridd said. "I hear you. We just need to trust in our mages' magic, and wait for our turn to strike."

"I don't know when that time will be," Vandress said, from the other side of Mud. "Those two show no signs of slowing. If anything, I can feel their magic getting stronger."

"You're stronger than they are," he said. "You show them what coming to Valeren means! Show them the strength of our people!"

Heavy streams of magic erupted from her hands as her eyes dazzled a wild blue—causing the shield spell to double in size. Mud barked, showing his teeth as Paltereth sneered in anger.

To Joridd's left, three soldiers rushed by, braving the fray before them. Pain tore through them as a black mist cut through their armor, searing their skin and pouring into their open mouths, sending them falling to the ground in lifeless heaps before even a scream could be muttered.

There was death all around—it filled the air with its stench of iron-rich blood, and the feeling of overwhelming, gruesome horror hung thick.

"I'm not going to die here," Joridd said, barely managing to get to his feet in the frenzy of battling magics before them. "This is not the day I die."

"We'd better find another way out of here then," Vandress said. "Or, we need to find some other way to die beside right here, like this… Because if we can't find a way, the sorceress and him are going to overtake us."

Mud growled low and the fur on his neck straightened.

Joridd looked up to the sky. "We need those dragons! C'mon, Stone, c'mon, Drâon. Hurry up now…"

IN ONE CORNER of the city, with no discerning features over any other drab one, smoke and soot rose from a torn, thatched roof structure. A calico cat bounded from a windowsill to the dirt ground, slowly approaching its curious new visitor.

A beam of sunlight glowed through the thin smoke, shining onto an eyelash covered in ash. The cat's scratchy tongue licked the man's fingers as he groaned low. He sat up, dizzily looking around at the four walls not so widely spread apart. A soft purr came from the cat before it bounded back off out of the window.

Adler was on a broken bed with a mattress a mere two inches thick and thatched roofing strewn all around him. His head pounded, and his fingers rolled over a lump the size of a strawberry on the back of his head. His other hand then nervously shot down to his hip, wrapping his fingers around the grip of his sword.

"Thank the heavens." He sighed. He moaned as he got to his feet, dust and ash falling from his clothing and hair as he did so. "Where am I?" He stumbled out of the cracked side of the structure where a hinged door once was. A small boy ran by, holding a smaller girl by the hand. They had panic set into their reddened eyes as tears streamed down their cheeks.

The familiar roar of breaking glass broke through the commotion of the people rushing through the roads. Adler looked up to the sky and saw the long dark tail of one of the Neferian slinking through the clouds, and as the dark dragon emerged out the other side, he could see Zênon's gray wings and Corvaire upon its back with his cape flowing behind.

"Salt in slash," he said. "I should be up there! Which way to the front gate?"

He yelled out to those rushing by, but none paid him heed.

An older woman ran past him and he grabbed her by the arm. "Which way to the front gate?" She paused but looked at him as if he were the enemy and tore her arm free and ran off.

There was an explosion of light to his right, with a green hue glowing above the buildings.

"Guess that answers that question…"

He ran through the crowd on the main road, pushing past and in between those who were trying to flee the northern section of the city.

"I don't know what going to the gate is going to do for Ceres, but it's not like I can fly myself back up there… Guess I'll just have to go kill a couple bleedin' mages to get the dragons' attention."

Chapter Four

"**D**id you see where he landed?" Stone asked as hot dragon smoke bit at his nostrils and flowed along Grimdore's scales.

"I can't see a thing." Ceres bowed her head low under the smoke. "I can't see a damned thing with all these clouds and rain. I don't even know how high we were when he fell." Her voice was quick and panicked.

A red spark flickered below, and Stone caught a glimpse of Marilyn directing one of her spells at a quickly ensuing Neferian.

"I don't think we were that high up," Stone said, only half-sure of his own words. Inside, he was pleading with some god to make sure Adler was all right.

"We need to go back," she said, causing a low grumble from within Grimdore's enormous chest, seemingly hearing the request. Not but thirty yards behind, the red-headed massive dark dragon of Arken flew angrily behind as another bolt zipped up into the sky far behind it.

"Don't think she wants us to turn around," Stone said. "If he's all right… it looks like he's on his own for the moment."

She sighed. "If he's all right…"

"Well, while we're stuck up here," he said, with his own wet, black hair whipping into his brow and neck, "we've got to figure out something quickly. Letting these monsters chase us around like this wasn't part of the plan."

Black fire erupted from the ensuing Neferian's maw and Grimdore pulled her wide wings in close, darting back down toward the city.

"None o' this was part of the plan," Ceres said, knocking her fist onto Grimdore's thick scales with a wet thud. "Who knew He was real? Who knew that a god actually was real?"

"I don't know," Stone said. "It's my fault. I shouldn't have let the red stone fall from my pocket. He sensed it. That's why he came."

"He came because Arken almost got it. He almost got the Adralite you found."

Grimdore spun back up, rising high up into the sky again as the dark dragon's fire faded and he let out a loud grumble as it followed behind.

"He was right there," said Stone with a sigh. "The Dark King was right there in front of me. I should've been able to end it right there, right then. My sword cut him; I saw his blood. If only I'd been able to kill the devil, then… She'd still be here if I'd been able to do that."

"Gracelyn can take care of herself," said Ceres. "Don't worry fer' her yet. Worry fer' her after we get out of this mess."

"It's my fault," he said, clutching on tightly to Grimdore's scales as she widened her wings and curved toward the sea. "But you're right. There will be time for that later. For now, we've got to figure out how to even the fight so that we're not the ones being chased."

"There." Ceres pointed ahead to above the sea. "There's Corvaire. Let's see if we can't at least give him a break from bein' pursued. What do you think, girl?"

Grimdore growled, causing more black smoke to flow from her mouth, and she flapped her wings mightily toward Zênon.

The dark dragons that followed Zênon were so caught up in their pursuit of the old gray dragon and the man on his back casting down powerful, surging lightning spells at them that they didn't notice, as Grimdore had flown high above them. She'd gained some space between her and Arken's Neferian by the time she began her attack.

The teal dragon's sharp teeth bit deeply into one of the dark dragon's necks as its rider pulled his legs up into his saddle to avoid the vicious attack. The Neferian had long streaks of dark blue down its back. Stone recognized it from the battle in Dranne.

"Infernus!" Ceres said, casting a swirling cone of fire upon him. The attack seemed to be so unexpected that the rider was completely caught unaware, and the searing flames burned his clothing as he held up his arms to cover his face.

"Again!" Stone said. "Quick!"

The nearby Neferian's rider pulled her reins to help the dark dragon under Grimdore's attack as it roared and tried to shake free. Fire brimmed in the oncoming Neferian's mouth as Arken's red-headed dragon was quickly approaching.

"Infernus!" Another blast of fire ripped into the rider as he became fully engulfed in flames and he screamed as he tried to extinguish them.

The incoming dark dragon had red-tinted wings, and Stone knew from Corvaire's tale, that was the one that had burned the city of Hedgehorn to the ground.

"We've got to get out of here," Stone said. "Grimdore, get us out of here!"

She loosened her teeth from the Neferian and pulled back to fly away as there were now three Neferian upon them. The other two were surely chasing after Belzarath and Īzadan.

As the red-winged Neferian and Arken's one came flying in

from both sides, a buzzing filled the air, and a new dark cloud formed overhead.

"Move!" Stone yelled. "Fly!"

Grimdore dove down as the buzzing grew louder. Their attack had worked, seemingly… for in his brief respite from being chased, Corvaire had the time to summon his spell that the red-winged Neferian surely remembered all too well. As the swarm of large hornets engulfed the three dark dragons, Grimdore flew up and around to join Zênon up above.

The three Neferian thrashed about, wailing and roaring to get the thousands of stinging hornets off them. The riders were covered in the insects that stung their bodies relentlessly.

"Serves 'em right," Ceres said.

Grimdore and Zênon flew closely together as they watched the three dark dragons disperse.

"That won't keep them at bay long," Drâon Corvaire said, sitting mightily, kingly upon the back of the aged gray dragon with the many years of scars upon its face and body.

"What should we do?" Stone asked. "How do we fight them? They outnumber us."

"One of those Dead Bows has to land home once," Ceres said.

"They don't have an unlimited supply of them," Corvaire said. "And the dark dragons are swift and cunning. But yes, we need the queen's contraptions to land home."

Corvaire shifted in his seat to look back at the northern gate to the city, where the heavy fighting and maelstrom of magics were lit bright enough to be seen even that high up. "They won't hold the mages back much longer."

Stone looked down at the battle far below, and the pit in his stomach returned. So much death was surely down there upon the brave soldiers of the city, and all he was able to do was keep the Neferian from making the devastation that much worse.

"If we weren't outnumbered up here," Ceres spat, "we could get Grimdore down there to burn every last one of those devils."

"The dark dragons are regaining themselves," Corvaire said. "We should split up again and regroup for attacks like that one."

"Killed those two riders, I think," Stone said. "Thanks to your spells."

"A small victory," Corvaire said. "Now fly swift. Stay ahead of the dark dragons, and swing in low to get them close to the Dead Bows below. One has to find a home, eventually."

Pushing through the crowd, his head pounded from the fall and the array of dizzying commotion. People yelling out to run, calling out to loved ones, soldiers barking orders, and the explosions at the front gate that were growing louder the closer he got. His elbows and wrists ached, and his right hip popped when he walked. But he continued pressing through the crowd.

In the square he was in, only a few streets down from the main gate, the entire plaza was brimming with people. Those being carried back from the battle were shoved through with great force on stretchers or carried upon soldiers' backs. Occasional steeds marched through anxiously, making those in the square shove themselves back out of the way of them.

"Got to get through this," he said, shoving himself between two soldiers, barking orders up to some unseen person farther ahead. He gripped his sword as he knew this was a thieves' paradise. "There's got to be a better way than this to get to the front." The arch of the end of the square was finally visible, with two flags of the city just ahead. But he was at a standstill. It was worse than a standstill even, because he found his feet moving backward. "Hey. Stop shoving."

"I ain't shoving, I'm getting shoved," one of the men before him said back.

It was quickly apparent to Adler this wasn't the place he wanted to be. The men in front of him were pushed back into him, crashing into his arm and chest, and the two soldiers behind him barely budged. Adler wasn't a big man, young and trim, but nothing like the other men surrounding the square. Then the shouting started. He heard the shouts from under the arch, but couldn't make them out, but as the soldiers behind began yelling back, he knew he needed to move.

The men in front of him were forced back into him, nearly knocking the breath from his lungs. Lines of people were behind him, farther than he could see. One of the soldiers behind him yelled to him to move, but there was nowhere to move to. Adler felt his chest squeeze as the groups of men before him were being pushed back by something, but he knew not what.

A dragon soared overhead, but he couldn't look up in time to see if it was one of his—or one of the Dark King's.

"Move," he said to the soldiers behind, who didn't like his tone at all by the grimace on their faces. "Can't ya see we're not getting anywhere? We've got to get back. I think they're drawing back from the battle."

"Shut yer mouth, you twit," one of the soldiers said, smacking Adler on the back of the head, hitting the knot that protruded from it like a hammer to a nail.

"Fer fucks' sake," Adler fumed. "I fuckin' hate soldiers!"

"Say that again, you twat," the soldier said, mere inches from Adler's nose. "I'll break that pretty nose o' yours."

"If I wasn't stuck here with you two slug-heads, I'd make you two bow down and apologize... but I've got more important things that need my attention."

"I'd cut you down right here in the middle o' this," the

other soldier said, "and not a damned soul would know or care what happened to ya."

Adler's hand still clung to his Masummand Steel sword. "I'd like to see you try."

"I—" the first soldier steamed, ready to unleash perhaps one last threat before steel flashed.

Then a light caught their eye. A blue hue that Adler recognized immediately, but which made the two soldiers raise their eyebrows and their noses scrunched.

The pale-bodied fairy waved her thin arms between them and pointed to Adler to move back farther from the arch and the main gate.

"I can't move," he said, squirming, knocking into the two soldiers and the men before him. Another shove came from the front. "Ugh!"

She waved her arms more frantically, but he couldn't fight the tight spot he was in. He closed his eyes and tried to squeeze between the two soldiers, but they couldn't move either. The air grew thick, and his breaths became labored.

"I'm trying, Ghost, but I can't get even my arms free." He saw her then, not waving her arms but pointing down with both hands as her long violet locks drifted down her torso. "I can't. There's no air down there!" She took a deep breath and held it with puffed-out cheeks. "Well, fine then. You lead the way. I'm not getting anywhere this way."

He took a great inhale, filling his lungs full, and shimmied his shoulders, sliding down to a crouch. The blue light of her wings shot down from a few feet away, and he made a quick effort to crawl on his hands and knees toward her.

Crawling between the two soldiers, he got a quick knee to the ribs but maintained his breath. Ghost waved her arms for him to follow as he pushed his way between another tall soldier's legs. It was chaotic underneath the giant crowd of people, and he had to exhale after going a dozen feet, and took another long draw of thin air.

For what felt like an hour, he crawled through the hundreds of legs, eventually coming to where he saw Ghost hovering between a group of people far enough apart so that some sunlight beamed onto her glittering wings. He made it over to her and got to his feet, taking in a great inhale. Looking back at the crowd, the ranks were being shoved back farther and farther, and many shouts and cries came from it, screaming out that they couldn't breathe, or they were being crushed.

"I've got to get to the battle," he said to Ghost, who nodded back. "Do you know a better way?" She quickly nodded again and flew off to the side of the square toward a row of small shops and large piles of boulders. She turned and beckoned him to follow with her skinny arms. "I'm coming, I'm coming. Not all of us can dart around like a damned bird."

Chapter Five

Chilling winds mixed with foggy breaths of warm bursts from the battling mages as the bodies piled higher and higher. The rains pattered the lifeless as the rows of mages walked over them. The army of three hundred was finally beginning their offense.

"We can't stay here," Vandress said behind a shield spell of chaotic nature. The spells of Paltereth Mir, the Vile King, Vandress herself, and the thirteen mages of the Elessior behind shuddered back and forth violently in different arrays of greens, golds, blacks, and blues.

"Hold just a little longer," Joridd said, holding up his arm in an attempt to drown out the blinding colors. "They are losing their strength. I can see it." There was a hesitation in his voice, an inkling that perhaps he didn't believe even his own words.

"We are losing the battle," Vandress said with grit in her voice and fiery blasts of golden magic shooting from her fingertips. Strands of her black hair rose in spidery tufts from the electric power of the spells. "We need to pull back."

Joridd looked past Paltereth's wicked glare and the Vile

King's looming presence with his metallic staff lifted high to the encroaching mages behind in the slinking, wet, dark robes.

Mud let out a rare whimper.

Joridd was lost in thought as Vandress put her hand on his shoulder.

"We'll regroup within the city. It's no use out here. A full assault is costing us too many." She turned her head and looked into his eyes. "You know what I say is the truth. We'll die out here."

He clenched his teeth and looked all around him, and then at the sullen dog next to him, slowly stepping back. With a wave of his hand, he motioned to his generals behind, pointing back toward the gate. Horns quickly blew from high up on the city gate, and Vandress stepped back slowly as Joridd sighed, but did the same.

Motioning up to the mages upon the high gate, Vandress let her spell dissolve, and they both ran while the mages fortified the shielding spell that nipped at their ankles as the sorceress and the Vile King lunged their powerful spells harder.

Mud darted through the city gates.

Horses neighed in shrill pain, soldiers groaned as they lay with blood pouring from their bodies and the lifeless lay in the rains, their voices silenced forever.

As Vandress and Joridd got back behind the front gate, it was closed solidly behind them with a *clunk*, like two immense tree trunks being knocked together. The remaining cavalry and infantry slid back into Valeren in the many ways they'd come out; hidden to the naked eye.

The army of mages made their way over the semi-circle pile of corpses that was nearly ten feet high at its highest. From behind Paltereth and Salus, they halted their approach, and the mages above ceased their spells for the moment. Three of the Aigonic Mages tended to Kellen's wound in his torso, into which Mogel had plunged a spear through.

Kellen moaned and his head flopped to the side as the three Mages of the Seliax looked grievously at one another.

The Vile King and Paltereth looked dismayed looking at the leader of the Aigons on the ground with blood soaking his tunic. Salus turned his back to Kellen and hefted his long, sleek silver staff into the air with his one hand.

Vandress and Joridd climbed the eastern tower of the gate quickly and stood by the mages and archers on the gate. Joridd's two generals followed.

"Your command?" one of them asked.

"Arrows won't work," Joridd grumbled.

"Our thirteen cannot match their number," Vandress said. "Especially with those two leading them."

"Only a handful of them have fallen," one mage said, "and we've lost so many."

"This is only the beginning of the battle," Vandress said. "They will get theirs."

"What can we do with the Majestic Wilds taken from us?" another younger mage asked with his brown hair cut at his brow line. "Our power is no match for such a force."

"No, it is not," Vandress said. "But we have other forces far stronger than them." One of the dragons screeched far overhead in the clouds. "We just need to free them to fight at our side."

"If we had but the two of the House Corvaire with us," the young mage with the auburn hair said.

"We need to trust in them," Vandress said, wiping her sweat and rain from her cheeks and brushing her hair slicked back on her head.

The Vile King took long strides forward.

"Is that all your force could do?" he said in a chill voice. Paltereth's dark eyes narrowed, and her reddish teeth showed behind a wicked sneer. "Now you pull back behind your wooden gate? You think that will protect you?"

Joridd and Vandress scowled down upon the Vile King, but made no rebuke yet.

"Throw down your arms," Salus said. "You've naught but more death should you proceed in this meager fight." His lip seemed to involuntarily curl. "You're leaderless, and your dragons are outnumbered and outsized."

"We will never surrender to you," Vandress said, winds whipping past her, blowing her black collar-length hair to the side. "Valeren has never fallen to wicked hands, and it surely will not fall to your perverse kind."

"You act as if you have a choice," Paltereth said, slinking forward with her circular bone earrings in her ears and nose swaying. "It's not so much an offer of surrender we offer, but a quicker death."

"Remember those words when my sword's tip sits ready at your neck," Joridd said, "and you're groveling for mercy."

"Hollow words from a hollow man," the sorceress said. "You couldn't even defend your sacred queen. How can you defend an entire city of nearly a million souls?"

"Her sacrifice will not be in vain," Joridd said. "And it will be avenged one-hundred-fold upon your heads."

A green spark lit in Paltereth's white staff with green veins of emeralds. "Oh yeah?" she said. "Good." She lifted her staff suddenly and aimed its tip at the queen and her steed, frozen in a solid block of ice.

"No," Vandress muttered and Joridd lurched forward, gripping the large blocks of stone on the walls, gritting his teeth as they watched helplessly.

"I hope you put up a good fight," Paltereth said. "All the more pain to extinguish when your souls fade into the dark…"

A bolt of shocking green burst from the tip of her staff and shot at the queen, causing the ice to crack with streaks of the same green hue, and in the booming explosion, the ice broke apart into thousands of tiny shards.

The queen was already dead, but that act sent a new vigor of anger and torment into the many that watched from the city.

"All your kings and queens are dead now," Paltereth said in a loud, shrill voice that echoed behind even the walls of the city. "A new age has come. An age where magic rules the lands. The meek will fear the powerful, and strength will be the new currency of the land. Your old cities will crumble, and new ones will be erected. Fear not for your lives, for the weak will not be slain, but given a new purpose—new meaning. You will not need paltry gods to pray to anymore, for you'll have new saviors to lead you into the new world." Salus stood tall and proud in his old age next to her, as if a new king and queen were proclaiming their right.

"Surrender or not," the Vile King said. "By the end of this day, you all who fight for this fallen city will be in chains or together in the Dark Realm. But I'd much rather you put up your final stand. My mages thirst for your souls. They will become more powerful than the winged ones that soar the heavens above us all."

"Prepare to cast the protection spell upon the front gate," Vandress said to the other mages, cracking her knuckles on both her hips.

"Get all of our troops pulled back," Joridd commanded to his generals, both nodding back. "I want everyone in place for the defense of the city now. They'll start their attack any moment now."

One of the generals ran down the stairs, hollering out orders as Joridd turned his attention back toward the two below and the pack of mages standing just behind.

Commotion fluttered in behind the city walls while the hundreds of dark-eyed mages stood behind Paltereth and Salus. A chill wind gusted sideways, blowing their cloaks' tails at their feet. The aged old wizard and the younger sorceress of cunning deception glared back at Joridd and Vandress. Their stares were cold and piercing, as if looking deep within, and with an overwhelming rage—as if thirst or hunger were driving two predators mad.

"Begin," the Vile King muttered, and at once, like many rows of candles being lit in a long cathedral, colors of a dizzying array lit in the hands of the Mages of the Arcane and Seliax behind them. Once lit, the mages strode forward toward the city, fully revealing the mounds of fallen men, women, and horses behind in a massive half-circle nearly a quarter mile in diameter.

"Brace the gate," Joridd yelled to those below.

The mages upon the walls with Vandress chanted their incantations and a glowing aura of blue enveloped the front of Valeren's entrance.

The remaining general whispered behind his hand to Joridd's ear. "They won't be able to hold the dark mages off."

Joridd groaned but nodded slightly.

"Just have our troops ready to strike, and strike hard and quick," he replied, unfolding his muscular arms and letting his hands dangle at his sides with his fingers ready to curl. As the rain fell harder then, he scowled down upon the Vile King—his eyes never leaving the old wizard. "Valeren has never fallen. And today is no different than the thousands of years before. You enter my city? Fine. But this will be the last sun you will ever see this day. By all that is holy and good, you will draw no breath once you enter through that gate."

Seemingly as if he heard Joridd's low voice, Salus Greyhorn smirked, and then with a flash of his tan, bony hand slid forward with his fingers facing up—black, thin smoke flowing out of each fingernail.

All at once, the mages shot their hands forward, ejecting each of their glowing spells in a high arc at the front gate, like a river pouring over a large boulder, and smashing into the sheer rock wall. The magic shot off back in a shocking effect that the entire front wall of the city shook under their feet.

"Loose," a woman's voice yelled to the side, and the archers upon the walls shot down in the rows of mages, hoping to catch the mages in a moment of lapsed defense, but the arrows quickly burned away to blackened coal, and spells were cast at the archers in thin, red streaks and gassy black clouds, but they were pushed back by Vandress pulling her own magic from the front gate to deflect them.

"That's it," Joridd said, watching the young mage quickly focus her spell back to the front gate. "Just like that! You're too powerful for them. Your magic's as strong as Gracelyn's and Rosen's.

"No, it's not," she said behind clenched teeth. "But I'm giving all I've got left."

Another assault was laid upon the front gate, harder and stronger than the last, and the resulting deflection was weaker. The ground itself shook from the rocking explosion.

"We won't hold them much longer," Vandress said. With wide eyes, her gaze shot to Joridd. "Get your forces ready…"

Chapter Six

❦

Arken's Neferian was spewing black flames and brimming with wild rage as it flew after Grimdore and her riders. Grimdore showed no signs of fatigue as the alpha predator herself was in the unusual place as the prey in their chase.

While the teal dragon had speed and agility on her side, the dark dragon nearly twice her size held a rage within, unlike any other beast—perhaps the rest of the world—known and unknown.

In their chase, Stone's focus had been solely upon the encroaching dragon, Ceres' spells cast back upon it, and the fleeting sights of the other dragons and their pursuers.

It was the second spell cast upon the front gate that turned his gaze back down to the city.

"Stone?" Ceres said, whipping her attention back down, too.

"Could you feel that too?" he replied.

That blast was so strong I felt it rock in my chest. What in the Dark Realm caused that?

They were above the southern coast of where the city met

the sea, and the blast wasn't visible, but the rising smoke always signaled where the main fighting was.

"North," Stone said to the dragon. "Fly swift."

He didn't know if the dragon understood or simply had the instinct to head toward war, but she flapped her powerful wings and flew at an exhilarating speed toward the rising towers of smoke. The red-headed Neferian followed.

"Fighting on these two fronts isn't of use to anyone," Ceres said.

"Well, it's keeping these monsters from the city," said Stone, leaning his chest down to the dragon's scales.

"I know," she sighed. "But I'm just sayin'. We're getting nowhere. Just not dead is all."

"If we could get rid of a couple of these Neferian, then we could use Grimdore to fight off the mages," he said. "But we're not there yet."

"Their swords and spears are no match for the magic of the Arcane and Seliax," Ceres said. "Dragons and spells will decide the victor of this war. Not steel."

"Get that thing off our tail," Stone said, turning his head to look back at her, "and then we could have Grimdore do what she does best. But with him back there, she can't do squat."

"He's too strong. My spells don't do nothin' but push him back at the best."

"Well, we've got to figure something else out then," said Stone. "Think. We're wasting time."

"I wish Gracelyn was here," she said, casting another spell back at the dark dragon.

Me too.

"Whoa," Adler said, stopping in his tracks as he was running along a high wall after the fairy. "Did you feel that?" Small pieces of rock chipped off from the gray wall and crumbled down onto his head, falling into his hood behind.

Ghost hovered in place, seeming unsure of what had happened. She looked all around, and to the rocks tumbling down and the smoke rising to the northeast, toward the front gate, and then she zipped up high into the air with speckles of blue fairy dust trailing behind.

"That front gate is going to hold against a power like that," he said to himself. "What am I doing following her? I should be on the front lines." He turned to walk between a couple of structures back toward the explosion, but stopped and exhaled. "When's she ever been wrong?"

Ghost flew back down and pulled him farther along the wall.

"What did you see?" he asked, even though he knew she wouldn't respond in any tongue he could understand. She only pulled him forward more, finally finding a wooden ladder tall enough to reach the top of the wall. Motioning for him to set the ladder and climb up, he did so without hesitation.

Anchoring the ladder's bottom at the base of the wall, he ran to the far end and pushed it up, little by little until it was set, and then he quickly climbed up as Ghost's little arms moved quickly—ushering him up.

"I know. I'm going as fast as I can."

Once at the top, he quickly turned to face the front gate as another explosive cascade of spells rocked into the spell protecting it, sending sparks and magic high into the air and he had to spread his feet to stabilize himself with the wall shaking beneath. Bigger rocks broke free from not only the wall before him, but all around, including sending an entire two-story structure to the east crashing down in a plume of dust.

From his vantage point, thousands were scurrying through

the city, mostly scattering away from the front gate, but he knew that might only save them from the current fighting. There was nowhere to run from the war, though.

"Where to now?" Adler asked, but before Ghost could answer, a second burst of spells from the dark mages blasted into the gate, and as he braced low for the oncoming quake, he gasped. "Oh no…"

The blast didn't ricochet off the front of the wall but instead broke through. The dark grays and blacks of the mixed spells boomed out of the gate like an hourglass on both sides, blasting back the dozens of soldiers that were bracing the gate.

The quake hit then, and the stones under his feet broke apart and swayed, with one giant block of stones under his right foot sliding down from the wall. He shifted his weight to his left foot and stood back as half the wall slid and crashed to the ground.

At the front gate, the spells shot through readily as chaotic spells were cast down like a spider's legs onto the mages from both sides. Adler's hand covered his forehead and his mouth fell agape. Ghost was buzzing by his ear but then landed on his shoulder and her shoulders slunk as her head hung low.

"All those people are going to die down there," he muttered. From the gate, he could see from his vantage point the Vile King and Paltereth Mir walked through the shattered wooden gate, casting dark magic upon the lines of infantry that ran at them. Arrows flew down from above but were burned away by spells. Bolts flew high into the air from the Dead Bows —missing their targets—and scattered fires burned throughout the city. "We should be down there."

Ghost's violet hair fell past her pale face and bare body as her tiny fingers clutched the back of her head.

"Why'd you bring us up here?" he asked, but any answer he'd receive was drowned out by the magnificent, yet terrifying roar of Grimdore as she was falling with her back to the city, as the red-headed Neferian bit and clawed at her front.

"Fly away, Grimdore!" he yelled as the two giant dragons plummeted toward the front gate, but would land a few hundred yards short of their trajectory. A bolt flew up from a Dead Bow a couple of roads away to the east but missed the dark dragon far behind its tail. Adler watched as the men scrambled to get another bolt set into it.

"Ceres!" His hands were out wide, and Ghost had flown back to life, buzzing around him frantically.

The two dragons bit savagely at one another's faces and necks as they plunged toward the ground. Their wings wrapped around each other and their tails flailed as Grimdore fought frantically to break free from the stronger dragon's claws.

From her back, Ceres shot spells at the Neferian's wings, but they seemed to not dissuade the ferocious dragon from its attack.

In the distance, he saw Zênon, Īzadan, and Belzarath were all flying from different parts of the city toward the two falling dragons, but they were far off, and they had Neferian on their tails, too.

"What can we do?" Adler said in haste, spinning to face Ghost. "You always know what to do. What can we do to help them?"

She watched the dragons descend at a terrible speed, and then glanced back to the army of mages pouring through the mouth of the city. Ghost looked as if she was in a trance.

Adler cupped his hands around her, stopping her fluttering wings, and her soft feet fell into his palms. He brought her up to his face, which was the size of her body from tip to toe.

"What do we do? Why did you bring me here?"

She sparked to life again, flying from his hands, and

pointed away from the dragons and the front gate of the city, where all the fighting was.

Scratching his chin with an eyebrow raised, he said. "That's it? That's your plan?"

THE SHARP TEETH the size of a stout man's arm sunk into her skin only feet from Stone's hands. He had to pull back his right hand, momentarily only leaving his left grip on Grimdore's scales as they fell through the air. Grimdore let out an ear-ringing roar of pain as she bit into the dark dragon's neck near where Arken's saddle was fastened.

"Get 'em!" Ceres said. "Bite the worm's head off!"

Stone had an idea in the turbulent struggle, but he didn't have much time. From his hip he unsheathed his sword with his right hand, and with it held awkwardly in the rain behind his hip, he swung it into the dark dragon's lip, knocking into the hard tooth too.

The biting dragon didn't seem to notice as it bit harder into Grimdore's thick scales—with its fiery amber eye then fixated upon him.

"Hit the fucker harder!" Ceres cried out.

He pulled the sword back to a high pitch over his shoulder and swung it hard into the same scaled lip and tooth. The Masummand Steel rang as it cut, like a falling nail hitting clean iron. The sword's edge cut cleanly through the lip, leaving two bloody flaps, and cut two-thirds through the thick tooth.

The Neferian's eye grew wide, and its mouth smoldered with black smoke as it pulled its teeth from the teal dragon and roared loud as the flaps of its lip split like linen pulled apart. Grimdore took the chance to claw wildly at the larger dragon's chest and push herself free.

Ceres cast a ball of fire into the dark dragon's face, blinding it long enough for Grimdore to spin out from under the Neferian, gliding to the west as the larger dragon spread its wide wings with its long arms and slowed its fall, trying to regain its composure.

"The other dragons are approaching," Stone said, wiping the sweat from his soot-covered brow. "All five of the dark dragons will be together soon."

"Stone, look," Ceres said, pointing down at the gate—which burst wide open.

"We're too late," he said as Grimdore flew back up higher into the sky.

A bolt whizzed past the red-headed Neferian, and that seemed to be enough to draw the beasts' attention. It roared with the fire still brewing from within its chest. The Dead Bow's attendants scurried to run down the tower and prepared to repel from ropes down its sides, but the black fire from its maw blasted over a hundred yards down onto the tower, knocking the tower of stone to the ground upon impact.

Stone sighed as he watched.

"No one could've survived that," Ceres said in a somber tone.

"I hate these dragons," Stone said, gritting his teeth. "I hate them with all my heart."

"The mages are in the city," said Ceres. "It's gonna be tougher to get Grimdore to kill many without hurting others with them in such a tight spot."

"Look at all the bodies," he said, looking past the gate.

Ceres didn't reply. She only stared at the calamity and death sullenly.

"We're losing this battle," Stone said. "We could use a miracle right about now…"

Chapter Seven

The air surged with power, raw, unhinged, unbridled power. It was the most terrifying thing the young soldiers of the city of Valeren could face. Beams of light mixed with dark clouds erupted from the mouth of the shattered gate of the city.

Beams singed armor and broke blades. Clouds passed into nostrils and tore holes in organs, causing the hundreds who inhaled the dark magic fumes to convulse in a most savage way. The sorceress who led the charge sent out green spells in fanning motions with both hands, causing those in their path to lose control of their bodies. Most of them slowed to a crawl, making them easy prey, or fell to the ground where their bodies forgot how to control their lungs, so they gasped for air as they choked to an excruciating death.

The Vile King led a charge up the stairs to the mages above—still fighting with all their might to keep the dark mages away even though they'd busted through into the city. Dark mages climbed both steep stairways to the high wall, pushing back the defenses of the mages of Valeren.

Joridd held his sword out, with his shoulders square and his feet spread, ready to fight. Vandress continued lashing spells down upon the mages as they fought their way through the soldiers with ease, casting dark spells that made the men topple from their posts to the hard ground below.

"Is it just you now?" Salus said with his thin lips as his eyes narrowed above his crooked nose. "The last line of defense of the great city of Valeren."

"We are not the last," Joridd said down to him in the pouring rain. "We are the first."

"Well, when you fall, who will be left to stand against the strong?" Salus sneered.

"There are more than enough to fight your kind off," Vandress said, with her arms fully enveloped in a violet hazy spell. "Without Arken here, you're just a bunch of street magicians, pretending to be so much more than you are. You're vermin."

Salus scowled. "How I'll love to cut that nasty tongue of yours out!"

The mages pushed hard through the last line of soldiers holding them back, only six steps until they'd come to the high wall of the city. As the brave soldiers fell to their deaths below, Joridd ran to the front of the eastern stairway, sword in hand, ready to strike down any who dared come farther.

Vandress ran over to the western stair, as the thirteen mages of the Elessior huddled together in the center, many with heavy beads of sweat running down their brows and cheeks.

"You'll never take this city," Joridd said, shaking his sword as spit flung from his lips in his anger. "You will *not* take this city!"

"Look around you," Salus said, slinking up the last couple of stairs. "Look down there. It's lost. You've lost. Your queen is dead. Your dragons are outnumbered and outmatched. Your entire army can't stop my beautiful children."

"We'll stop you," Joridd said as the Vile King ascended the last stair with a blue shielding spell separating the two.

The other mages rose from the other stairwell and Vandress turned to say, "This is the end of the road for you."

With a sparkle in his dark eyes, Salus sneered one last time, and then his face instantly went cold and stiff with angled bones in his cheeks. "Kill them!" His staff spun and blasted an enormous rush of energy at them, as his mages did the same.

The spells flew into the shielding spell, causing it to bob back and forth like a ripple in a cove. Joridd leaped through the spell before any seemed to know he had.

"Joridd!" Vandress yelled, still pushing her power into the shield. "Push the shield farther!" The mages followed her lead and tried to expand the spell as the mages blasted into it even harder.

With his leap, he landed on the outside of the spell, surely knowing he didn't have more than a few flutters of a hummingbird's wings to make his action count. He landed, took a large lunge forward, and drove the tip of his sword at the Vile King, whose wide eyes and slow reflex showed his surprise. The sword tip slid past the shaft of the sorcerer's staff and cut into his robe, but missed flesh.

Salus twisted sideways as the thrust barely missed his abdomen, but Joridd didn't stall in his movement as he grabbed the staff with his free hand, causing a hissing sound, yanking it into him, pulling the Vile King in close—whose meager physical strength was no match for the soldier's. Joridd turned the sharp edge of his sword into the armpit of the Vile King, and while pulling him into him by the staff, sliced through the soft skin of the aged man, cleaving his arm off at the shoulder.

A hand grabbed Joridd's cape, yanking him back.

"No," Joridd said as the Vile King let out a devilish roar. His hand was smoking where he held the staff.

"Get back," Vandress said, pulling him back harder.

"No," Joridd said as he pulled his blade back to strike Salus again. "I've got to finish this!" Sparks spattered from his hand on the staff, causing more dark smoke to rise.

"Get back here or you're finished!" Vandress said, pulling him harder.

Seemingly seeing the gathering spells shooting at him, Joridd gave in, releasing the Vile King's staff and falling back into the spell, falling on top of Vandress. The spells zapped the shielding spell, causing a loud *boom*.

Two mages ran to Salus' side quickly, wrapping his wound in their own robes, and pressing hard on it. Salus' eyes were red, as red as a ruby's. His teeth gritted, not from the pain, but from pure hate as the mages pulled him back, and the other mages ran up the staircase to stand between him and Joridd.

"You see that?" Joridd yelled. "We're just taking you a piece at a time. Your head is next!" Joridd pulled his hand shaking back to his side, with his fingers curled as if holding an invisible ball. His face winced in pain.

"Joridd, your hand," Vandress said.

"Pay no mind. It's fine."

Salus writhed in anger and hate as they pulled him back. Joridd, Vandress, and the others faced a new threat, though.

"We're surrounded," Vandress said. "And outnumbered." There were more than two dozen dark mages on the wall with them then.

Joridd looked around as they got back to their feet. He had no answer, but he still held his bloody blade up, ready to fight, but not yet ready to die.

"This is the end," one mage hissed. "Our Arcanica will feed on your deaths. Grow stronger while your souls fade."

"Come and try," Joridd said, flashing the blade stained with the blood of their leader.

Vandress turned to the thirteen. "We'll have to attack. All

at once, though." Her voice was calm, but strong. A born leader through and through. "This will be our only chance. Make them strong. Make them hurt."

"If this is our last hoorah," Joridd said to her quietly. "Know that…"

She cut him off. "Save it for later. I don't want to hear you getting soft on me right now. You're the one who's gotta cut through this lot."

He winked and faced the dark mages. "Yes, ma'am."

In that long moment, which felt like ten minutes, but was perhaps more like a half of one, Vandress seemed to change her mind. "But if this is our last moment in this life, I reciprocate whatever you were going to say."

"Ready?" Joridd asked.

"Ready as we will ever be."

The dark mages spread out, each trying to get a clear view of their targets. Their spells were readied, and their gruesome faces were like that of a cobra, ready to strike and consume their prey.

"Now!" Vandress said, followed by an incantation that sent a plume of fire out at the dark mages before her. Joridd lunged forward with his sword at the ready. Everything spun into chaos within that moment. Violent spells whirled and collided, sending huge pillars of sparks and smoldering smoke up into the air.

The thirteen unleashed their greatest offense in a deafening roar of different spells, and the Arcanic Mages did the same. Only this time, without their full force to protect themselves, the thirteen mages were left vulnerable, and one was hit instantly with a crippling spell that caused her to paw at her throat as she gurgled for air. There were none to care for her, as another took a blow to the leg, sending him to the ground groaning and praying.

Joridd flung back through the air ten feet by the nearest

mage who'd spoken to them before. Salus was gone from the fight, but the remaining mages held their ground and began their inching forward. Two of the thirteen were down, and Joridd lay on his side with his sword firmly in one hand, but his other seemed to be rendered useless at the moment.

Vandress was the only mage who was powerful enough to not only unleash spells that permeated the Arcanic Mage's ranks, but always was able to protect Joridd, who she'd put behind her.

"Get them," Joridd said, struggling back to his feet, hunched over on his knee. "Kill them all."

"I'm trying," Vandress said, with her amber eyes glowing a golden hue and her black hair flying back behind her as she sent forth powerful, blazing spells.

An orange spell washed along the stones at their feet and climbed up the unsuspecting legs of two of the thirteen, sending them reeling in pain and screaming out for help.

"There are too many," Vandress said. "I can't stop them all."

Joridd got back to his feet with a deep groan. "I'll not go down like this." He raised his sword out. "If I die, then I die fighting!"

He ran forth past Vandress, past her flurry of spells with his sword held over his shoulder, ready to strike the first of the pack of then twenty mages on that side of the wall and cut through every last one of them.

Vandress sent a fresh blast into the mage, hoping to distract it enough for Joridd, as he swung into the dark mage. As the sword's sharp edge approached the mage, two mages behind appeared from the shadows below and grabbed onto Joridd. They had an unnatural strength about them and each gripped one of his arms, holding them to their chests.

"Let me go, you demons," he said, fighting to break free.

"Joridd!" Vandress said, but her spells were repelled by the many mages behind.

The dark mage before Joridd, with pale, wrinkly skin and large, reddened charcoal eyes reached out and grabbed Joridd's sword, and as much as Joridd fought it, the mage pried it from his hand with ease as the two mages held him easily back.

The mage held the sword, eyeing it as the spells erupted about them, and as if there was no war going on around them, it casually put the tip of the sword up to Joridd's throat.

"With your life," the dark mage said. "Our powers will grow, and the fear will spread further throughout your city. Know that your death will be in vain."

Joridd spat in the mage's face, who recoiled in anger, and wiped his face with the sleeve of his robe.

"You done?" Joridd said, holding his neck out in the pounding rain, as the light of a shimmer of the sun's rays hit the blade, causing a ripple of light to glide along it.

"Joridd, no!" Vandress cried, trying to press forward, but the combined spells of the Arcanic Mages pushed held her at bay.

"Do it, snake," Joridd said through gritted teeth.

The dark mage grinned, moving to push the sharp tip into his neck. But something strange was happening, as the dark mages looked around at each other. Something was off.

His grin turned to a contorted frown as a bloody arrowhead cut through the side of his neck, and another cut into his ear, and out the back of his head. The two mages holding Joridd pulled back into the shadows at his feet quickly, as Joridd's sword clattered onto the wet stone.

He grabbed his sword quickly and looked back at Vandress in shock, or some sort of answer, as the dark mages shuffled around in confusion, and faint cries of pain happened from the back of their ranks.

"What is it?" he asked.

"I—I don't know," she replied, as the last of the thirteen tended to their fallen.

Arrows then zipped through the air from strange angles. Men in dark gray cloaks and hoods suddenly appeared, crawling out of the walls themselves, it seemed.

They fought in a savage, yet methodical manner against the mages, using surprise as their greatest weapon as they swarmed the Mages of the Arcane. They spun with dual daggers, cutting deep into calves, wrists, and arms as they moved from one mage to the next, attacking from all angles. The mages at the back fled back down the stairwells on both sides.

"Who are they?" Vandress muttered.

One man from their ranks emerged, after striking down one of the mages who'd been hurling the strongest spells. He walked up to Joridd and Vandress, sheathing a dagger, but still holding his bloody sword at his side. His wide, beady eyes were clear as his curly silver hair wove out from under his hood. A wry smile lit his familiar face.

"You always were one for the dramatic." Joridd laughed.

"You were supposed to stall longer until I could get my men in place," the man in the gray hood said.

Vandress ran and wrapped her arms around him. "Thank you for coming, Guildmaster. You saved our lives."

"You would've done the same for me," Conrad said. "Now let's go hunt those bastards down…"

PART II
BROKEN, BATTERED, AND BURNT

Chapter Eight

❦

The rains pooled in the grass and muddy plains before the kingdom and streamed between the cracks in its stone pathways. A high sun hid behind thick clouds as the early morning battle had pushed into the early part of midday. The flickering of torches and candles throughout the city were extinguished—for none wanted to be seen by the coming army, or the most fierce force in all the land—the dark dragons and their riders.

Conrad and his assassin's guild pushed the intruding mages back down from the high parts of the gate, but surprise was their ally, but waned quickly. The last of the thirteen, nine healthy mages and Vandress bombarded the retreating mages as the assassins cut deep into them. Lifeless bodies in dark robes were scattered upon the high wall. It was a victory, but the war still waged on.

The Guild Master led the charge, regrouping as the first soldier to press down the rows of mages on one stairway as Joridd led the other, fighting tough with his one good hand. The Vile King was nowhere to be seen, but down below, the remaining mages were still flooding into the gate, pushing their way easily through the ranks of cavalry and soldiers of young and old who were brave enough to stand their ground and protect their home.

Paltereth Mir was the head of the snake, striding through the city's entrance with a confidence and destruction that caused panic and dismay with her every step. This may as well have been her army. With every move of her hand and spell she cast, dozens were sent into excruciating pain or directly to the Dark Realm.

The mages that crawled back down from the high wall slithered back into their ranks, pouring out into the city. Arrows cascaded down in sheets with the rain from above, but they were rendered asunder by only a handful. The three hundred mages of Salus, Paltereth, and Kellen may number less than that, but they numbered well over two hundred and were tearing the city apart.

Rock crumbled from their spells. Men crawled over one another in agony, and all the while the dark dragons still hovered overhead. Bolts from the Dead Bows shot sporadically from below, but with nothing to practice on prior, the Neferian proved too swift for the men and women working the giant crossbows.

Fear spread like an icy wind. The roars of the dragons overhead sent waves of terror throughout the city, as the dark dragons that all in the Worforgon feared—were at last at the city of Valeren. Even with their queen dead, though, there was still hope. The city not only had its own brave—fighting off the horde of mages, but the destined destroyer of Arken Shadowborn was up in the sky atop the only dragon to have killed a Neferian. Stone, born from the dirt, was still fighting the dark beasts, and while he still drew breath, then his destiny was still alive.

"What now?" Ceres asked, with winds ripping through her completely damp clothes. "Stone…"

He heard her say his name, sort of, only as if it was in a distant dream.

"Stone." She nudged his shoulder blade hard.

"Huh?" he said over his shoulder.

"What do we do now? They're stormin' into the city."

He watched far below as the mages spread like a disease into Valeren. He didn't know what to do. He knew he wanted to fly down there and burn them all to the Dark Realm, but with the Neferian on their tail, it might end up far worse.

"Should we burn them all alive?" Ceres asked. "I'd love nothin' more than to see that."

"We need to shake that beast," Stone said. "Besides, there are far too many Valerens down there. They're all mixed together."

"Might be worth it," she said in a non-sarcastic tone.

"Let's regroup with the others," Stone said. "Maybe we can sneak attack one of the dragons again." His fingers slid into a deep gash in Grimdore's scales on her back. He sighed. *We've got to figure something out. We can't just keep running around like this. She's going to get more hurt...*

Grimdore lowered her right wing and twirled back around to the south, with the great red-headed Neferian looming behind, hot dragonfire ready to burst from its maw. Ceres readied her Elessior, focusing on her Indiema, gathering her strength for the next collision with one of the dark dragons.

I wish Gracelyn was here. She'd know what to do...

༺༻

SINCE CONRAD and the Assassin's Guild's arrival at the front gate, hope had come. It was a warm welcome to those who fought against the impending evil. But hope alone doesn't save cities.

Paltereth burned through the city with wicked fires and

poisons, crushing all those in her path. She was fully down an entire city street with mounds of scorched bodies in her wake. The mages that followed her as a swarm following the queen protected her. Free to cast her wicked spells, a blackness spread of despair and misery.

Conrad, Joridd, and Vandress struggled to get back down the main gate as the dark mages had fortified their position and numbers. They halted their retreat not even half the way down the dueling stairs before they began their climb again, pushing the three back up, higher back, to the last of the thirteen.

"We'll need to regroup," Conrad said, with the rain making his silver hair slick and showing the angles on his lean cheekbones and sharp chin. His wide shoulders for his lean frame backed up behind the spell erected by the mages above—they were yet again on the offensive, and surprise had faded from their fortune.

"Where?" Vandress said, shouting so her voice could reach both of them over the booming magics crashing all around them. "Along the wall? East?"

"We need to get to the sorceress," Joridd said, holding his injured hand slightly behind him, out of view.

"Impossible now," Conrad said. "We're out-manned. Got to regroup. We have a place we're going to fall back to, hidden deep in the walls."

"We can't retreat now," Joridd said, spit flinging from his lips. "We're only just starting."

"We'll die here," the Guildmaster said, shaking his head with his brow furrowed. "Swords against magic alone won't do enough." He looked to Vandress, who nodded back. "Fall back. I'll lead the way."

Joridd was gruff as he folded back up the stair, rejoining the last of the thirteen—seven then.

"Follow me," Conrad said, as Vandress and the seven

remaining mages protected the last of the guild, which surprisingly had halved in size, but not half had been slain.

"I'm beginning to see how you arrived when you did," Joridd said, "as you did from the walls themselves."

"It's an old city," Conrad said, "with lots of secrets."

A discreet section of the stacked rock wall with thick lines of mortar shifted back and up, revealing a hole just big enough to crawl through.

"I see," Vandress said with a wink. "You all go first; I'll hold them back as long as I can."

Conrad followed behind two of the assassins in their wet gray cloaks. Joridd followed after. The dark mages noticed their thinning ranks and pressed hard at the seven and Vandress. A spell broke through of sparkling white light that tore into one of the mage's chests, causing the same-colored light to glow in her mouth, eyes, and ears. She stood briefly, mouthing Vandress' name, but then fell to the ground.

The seven was then six.

"Go, go!" Vandress said as the mages rushed into the hole, climbing down unseen footholds on the front side of the chasm. She was the last to slide her boots and legs into the hole, sending a bright flash of blue from her hand, knocking back one of the Arcanists enough to send him reeling off the high wall, falling far to his doom.

They were all in the narrow wall that was no more than two feet thick and they had to shimmy their way down from side to side, dropping down four feet to one side, and then the other until they got down to what appeared to be the main floor of the hidden passage.

The stagnant air echoed from the explosions just on the other side of the walls and from the far battle going on where Paltereth was surely leading the attack.

"We need to get back out there," Joridd said. Beads of

sweat were streaming down his brow and his arm was shaking behind him.

"Let me see," Conrad said, as Vandress ran up to his side.

"It's nothing. Let's get going. We've got to..." his words trailed off as Vandress took his upper arm.

"Joridd," she said, and he slowly held his hand out for them to see. He also watched with his head pulled back and his eyes squinted.

His fingers were white with ash and contorted. His knuckles bulged, and the fingers were withered and bony.

"I got him good, I did," Joridd said with a half-laugh.

"Get him to a medic," Conrad said to the assassin woman standing near. She nodded.

"No," he said in a stern voice. "Absolutely not. We are going to stop that witch first." His gaze met Vandress'. "Then I'll see whoever you want me to see."

"You can't keep your hand from shaking," Conrad said. "I know you're tough, but I can't imagine the pain you're..."

"You going to talk all day, or can we get moving?" Joridd said.

"Here," Vandress said. "I can't mend it, but with your stubbornness, we will be here all day." She cupped his trembling hand in hers. "*Trancillian Caln.*" A cool frost washed over their hands, and a frosty breath came from both their mouths as they exhaled.

He looked down with wide eyes as his hand's shaking slowed.

"It's only temporary," she said. "Doesn't heal anything."

"Pain's gone," Joridd said. "That's enough. Now, where to?"

"This way," Conrad said, as he grabbed a torch from an iron sconce on the wall. "Our best option is to corner her—get in close; real close."

"She's cutting through them like wolves hunting sheep," Ceres said, ripping winds flying by her and heavy raindrops hitting her already-soaked clothes.

A Neferian's roar resounded from the south, and they both saw a jarring bolt of red light shoot down from the white dragon Belzarath's back as the spell plunged into the ensuing dark dragon. Stone's mouth fell open as he watched the rider atop the great Neferian's back plummet, tumbling toward the ground.

"That's the last of the riders," Ceres said. "Marilyn got 'em."

With a barking roar, the monstrous red-headed Neferian chasing them swooped to the south—after Marilyn and Belzarath.

"Where's Corvaire?" Stone asked, his gaze darting around in the cloudy, wet sky. "I don't see him."

"Neither do I," Ceres said, and her tone turned serious as she grabbed Stone's wrist. "Now's our chance." Her green forest eyes were wide.

"You know what that means," he said. She nodded. "We're leaving both of those beasts to Marilyn."

"They're dying in droves down there," she said, releasing his wrist and scratching her forearm.

"Let's be quick," he said, patting Grimdore's scales. "They'll be after us. We need to be swift, and deadly. You hear me, girl?" He leaned into her back. "The sorceress needs to be stopped. We need your dragonfire."

Grimdore shrieked and growled low, pulling her wings into her body, and their descent began.

Chapter Nine

❦

The leather boots squealed by on the wet cobblestone road. Dark linen dragged, torn and tattered, along behind them. Conrad slunk through the tunnel with his torch left behind, so as to show no light as the top left corner of the tunnel showed the road and the dark mages trampling by.

Joridd and Vandress walked behind, along with the last seven mages of the Elessior. A handful of assassins held the rear of their small platoon. The other assassins had filtered out into other corridors beneath the city.

An explosion ahead rocked the road and caused dust and debris to fall from the stagnant ceiling of the long, straight tunnel only a couple of yards wide. Rainwater fell into the tunnel, further draining into the sewers below.

"That's her," Vandress said quietly.

"She's not far," Conrad said, turning his head to the right side of the tunnel, away from the mage's ears to the left.

"How will we get out of here?" Joridd asked, trying hard to dampen his deep voice.

"There's a courtyard near her," Conrad said, "and an alley

exit behind a row of old buildings. We'll exit there. What's your plan?"

"Distract and kill," Joridd said. "Our mages will pull her in one direction while you and I go in from the other."

"That'd need to be one hell of a distraction," the Guildmaster said. "Her mages guard her. We wouldn't get within twenty feet of her."

"You hear that?" Joridd said, turning back to Vandress.

"Yes," she replied. "We'll hit hard and fast. With any luck, they'll be so concentrated on their attack that their defenses will be weak."

"Luck, huh?" Conrad asked with a groan. "Don't like to rely on that too much."

"Well, what else is there?" Joridd asked.

"If it's gotta be luck," said Conrad. "Then luck it'll have to be."

Two roads down, they could finally see glimpses of the sorceress, and indeed she was in the courtyard he spoke of. It fanned out into Gambry Courtyard, which Joridd and Vandress had known since they were little ones. Statues hundreds of years old of famous soldiers and scholars lined the walkways of plush green ivy, with bushes and flowers coloring the walkways. Their brilliant color had faded from the dark aura of the war.

Paltereth was casting spells that filled nearly the entire courtyard with hazy dark spells that tore through the scattered soldiers as they futilely made their attacks. A fiery rock covered in black tar shot from a distant catapult, hurtling through the air at her. Paltereth continued casting her dark spell into the nooks and crannies of the stone courtyard, not paying mind to the boulder, nothing more than a mere glance. More than a dozen of her mages ran to her side, together casting a spell that shot upward in an orange dome that caught the side of the fiery stone, knocking it away to the left, and landing on the cobblestone road with a loud thud.

"You'll have to get all their attention," Joridd said to Vandress, walking just behind his right.

"We'll get it so they'll forget where they even stand," she said.

"Our path leads this way," the Guildmaster said, pointing down the part of the corridor that led to the left, directly under the sorceress.

Joridd turned to face Vandress.

"We'll show them no mercy," Vandress said. "We'll show them what attacking Valeren means."

"I know you will," Joridd said. "Don't stop your attack, even if we near your spells. This has to work."

She looked at him with unease, furrowing her brow and scratching her cheek.

He leaned in close to her ear. "I know in my heart you're the third of the Majestic Wilds. Let your magic burn free, let it erupt from within you like the hellfire I know you can."

"I don't think I am," she said. "I don't feel it."

"I know you are." He smiled, put his hands on her head, and grabbed her forehead to his lips. "You've always been like a little sister to me. My children look up to you as their own blood. Don't be afraid to unleash everything. The power of the Majestic Wilds is in you. You will save this city. I know it to be true."

She half-smiled and nodded. "I'll do what I must. But once she's dead, you need to run. We can't defend you from all those Arcanists and defend ourselves at that distance. Do you hear me?" Her intense amber eyes were feral, like a tiger's. "Run!"

"Come," Conrad said, walking down the left corridor, and Joridd followed.

Vandress led the other mages to the right, as the assassins trailed behind them. One of the assassins ran past her and led them to a wooden ladder on the ground, putting it up to the right side of the tunnel above. She climbed up and pushed the wall out, eyeing the alley, then pushed the section of wall to the side, sliding through the dirt and ash.

She crawled out, and once out and on a knee, reached out for Vandress to follow, which she did quickly. Once out she saw they were on the dirt road on the backside of the old, vine-covered buildings, she helped the others out. There were seven mages and fifteen assassins with them. She looked around and cast a spell up into the air, with a single line of smoke trailing out of her finger, and as it rose high enough above the buildings it let out a loud whistle and turned to a light blue seagull, which flew directly up into the sky before fading after a few seconds.

"What was that?" the female assassin at the lead asked. "What're you doing?"

"Calling for reinforcements," Vandress said.

"You're calling them out?" one of the mages of the Elessior asked, and the other six watched eagerly, waiting for a response.

"Yes," she said. "We need all the magic we can get."

There was an anxious two minutes that went by that felt more like twenty to Vandress—but then she saw them.

Striding down the far side of the alley were three figures in dark cloaks, and with darker demeanors. Their bony shoulders slunk as they drifted toward them with unnatural ease, as if floating above the dirt. They looked like three shadows coming to welcome one to the Dark Realm.

"Aigons?" the assassin asked with narrowed eyes.

"We've made our deal," Vandress said. "And you hold to your word and help me with this, then the prisoners will be freed, and you will be allowed to leave your service to the crown."

One of the Mages of the Seliax, with his pale skin and dark eyes, bowed his head.

"Don't even think of doing anything otherwise," she said with a sharp tone. "You know what would happen should you think of changing your mind."

The dark mage nodded once more.

"Very well," she said. "We hit them, and we hit them with everything we've got. We are going for the sorceress. You will cast from the far side of that building, and we will attack from here and there." She pointed to the alley before them that led to the courtyard and then to the other side of the building, on the opposite side.

"Are you sure about them?" one of her mages asked as the three Mages of the Seliax went to where she said.

"Not absolutely," Vandress said. "But we've got something they want. And if they want it back, then they're gonna play by my rules."

A distant dragon roared in the background, causing Paltereth's attention to veer that direction.

"This is our moment," Vandress said, gazing secretly behind the corner of the building.

"Where are they?" the mage asked, hiding just behind her.

"Don't see them, but they're ready," said Vandress. "They're just waiting for our move; we'll wait until they get a little more into the—"

Vibrant blasts of black shadow shot from the other side of the buildings, causing Vandress to scramble from her position.

"Spit and fire," she said running out from behind the building and saw the three Mages of the Seliax launching their dark spells upon the group of mages, including Paltereth, who was fully caught off guard as the spells blasted into the side of her pack of mages, sending a half dozen flying back in anguish.

"At least they're attacking them," the female mage said, "and not us."

"Thyfonus Bitternex Onum!" Vandress sent her Winds That Freeze spell at them, and the other mages sent their spells of the Elessior too—including all four sets: Wendren, Sonter, Primaver, and Utumn. Her icy storm spell mixed with all their spells, causing a whirling maelstrom of magic upon the dark sorceress and her mages. A dragon roared again; this time closer than the last.

※

"You think she's the last Majestic Wild, then?" the Guildmaster said, as the two watched the wild mix of spells flow from Vandress and the other mages' hands.

Joridd growled. "I don't think. I know."

"I can see she's as powerful as Rosen, from what I see," Conrad said, his silver hair blowing out from the gray hood. "But Gracelyn's got her beat by a mile."

Joridd's growl turned to an angry, sizzling hate—not toward Conrad, but toward Paltereth Mir.

"You're going to die for what you've done here..."

The two watched as Vandress and the mages lunged enormous spells upon Paltereth and her dark mages, causing many to die, blowing their lifeless bodies and rolling shoulder over shoulder from the oncoming spells. But Paltereth and many of the others gathered behind spells of their own, while Paltereth herself was encased in an orb of vile, translucent green with black smoke rolling over it.

"It's now or never," Conrad said, hefting his sword in his hand. "You ready?"

"I'm ready," Joridd said, as the two were ducking behind a statue, thirty yards from the pack of dark mages, with Paltereth at their center.

"You got right," Conrad said in a powerful voice. "I'll go left. Use the shadows, and be swift."

"I'll meet you over there," Joridd said. Conrad winked back.

The Guildmaster took a great inhale, and then with a deep exhale said, "Here we go then."

"May death find the bitch painfully," Joridd said, running off to the right behind a line of statues of old soldiers in stances of honor and vigor, yet many had been blown to pieces in the battle.

"Cut off the head, and the body dies," Conrad muttered as he ran in a swooping circle to the left.

He approached the fighting quickly, keeping Joridd in the corner of his vision, as he darted like the wind from shadow to shadow. All the while, Paltereth was his focus as he came upon an Arcanist, helping to summon the field around the sorceress. Conrad's dagger found his heart from under a rib quickly, and a twist of the knife sent him silently to the ground with a hand over the dead mage's mouth.

Joridd took two mages down in the same span of time, leaving their bodies slowly trickling blood into pools behind him.

Then it was time. They were both behind statues, only yards from her and a ring of mages, as the storm of magic from Vandress shot in. It was like no storm the Worforgon had seen in many hundreds of years. An army of mages fighting back the best that Valeren had to offer.

The Guildmaster and Joridd looked at one another, then at the sorceress as she shot dark, smoldering spells from her staff and fingertips. Her dark, black eyes sparked a pinprick of white light in her glee and her sharp teeth showed as her thin-lipped mouth opened wide in ecstasy.

Conrad and Joridd clutched their swords tightly to their chests as they looked at one another, and with a nod from each of them, they spun around the statues, running at her. Conrad knocked a mage from his feet quickly with his shoulder, pressing forward hard toward her.

Paltereth's attention quickly turned toward them, as did her mages. As they ran at her, Conrad could see commotion happening in the outer part of the courtyard but ran on.

They passed through the green orb as the hands of the mages moved toward them. There was no time. They only had one chance.

Paltereth spun faster than the others, with her eyes wide and her face full of surprise.

Joridd was only feet away, two strides left—Conrad, too. This was their moment to strike. This would be their only opportunity. This was their chance to end the battle and save their city.

As they readied their swords to strike hard and true, suddenly the world turned white, searing with vibrant power—blinding them to only the intense light with streaks the color of the sun, and the roar that ensued was as terrifying and deafening as anything they'd heard in their long lives.

Chapter Ten

She heaved fire from her maw that caused Stone's inner thighs to feel the cauldron that was burning inside of Grimdore's chest. The great teal dragon's neck tensed, and her horned head shook from the violent inferno. Fire raged down upon the sorceress, and Stone hoped with all his heart that the dragonfire burned deep—down to her bitter heart.

Another dragon roared from the sky behind—and as his gaze spun, his mouth flung agape.

"Stone—" Ceres cried. "He's almost here."

Stone clapped Grimdore's back as her fire calmed, and her long neck turned back to see the red-headed Neferian flying in quickly with his long teeth showing and his lips curled as he snarled.

The massive dragon flew down with frightening speed, landing with a thunderous quake on the far side of the courtyard. It fell to all four legs and slunk to the eastern side of the wide plaza. Its head was low as it growled, causing the many spikes upon its back to gyrate. It growled low but didn't ready its fire. It wanted to taste flesh. He wanted to fight tooth and claw.

Stone looked up to the clouds and saw all the other dragons flying in toward them, with Marilyn upon Belzarath's back closest to the southern sky. Corvaire was in the distant southwestern sky upon Zênon, with Īzadan flying in curling spirals behind. All four of the other Neferian flew swiftly behind, yet only two still had Runtue riders saddled to their backs.

Behind Grimdore, her fires faded from the blast, but still scorched the road black. The sorceress' green orb had faded, but the stones beneath where the orb had been remained gray and wet. Paltereth heaved breaths and sweat trickled down her brow and cheeks. Joridd and the Guildmaster both lay on their sides, struggling to regain their composure and get back to their feet. Conrad reached out and grasped his sword from the ground.

The air reeked of burnt flesh as the broken bodies of many mages lay smoldering and blackened. Their charred bones cut sharply through remnants of cloth that were their tunics. Dozens of their kin were dead, but many more ran from the mouth of the courtyard in, as did Vandress and her seven, along with the three Mages of the Seliax and the assassins darting in like shadows in gray hoods.

"He may be bigger," Stone grabbed onto Grimdore's thick scales hard. "But you're meaner and stronger. Show him your true wrath. Send that bastard to the Dark Realm in a pile of ash."

Stone's eyes and fingers flickered in a pale blue light. He'd only just recently discovered he had the power of the Elessior, and it was nothing compared to Ceres' or Marilyn's. But he felt it swell within him as he clenched his teeth.

"Show that monster what we're made of," Ceres growled. "Do it for Lucik and Hydrangea. Burn that fucker down!"

Grimdore's claws dug through the cobblestones beneath

her, knocking tall, heavy statues to their sides like they were mere toys. She lunged toward the great Neferian, as he hulked forward slowly, letting out a voracious roar, spreading its wings wide and its tail clapped sideways into a brick structure, knocking it to a heap of dust.

Paltereth Mir spun toward the incoming pack of mages behind Vandress, and the Mages of the Arcane quickly shot up their spells. Vandress' mages, along with the three of the Seliax, cast spells to deflect the Arcanic Mages' spells.

But Vandress ran at the sorceress.

Paltereth readied a spell as her staff pointed at Vandress, but the spell faded and she shot her staff behind her, and the steel of Joridd's sword clanged into its shaft. Their eyes met with wicked hatred.

"Unworthy man," she hissed. "Your city is lost to you."

"Not as long as I draw breath, witch!"

"That's the idea." She pushed his sword back, not solely from the muscles in her arms, but with unnatural strength.

Conrad attacked from the side, and with a spin of her staff and a clang of the metals, she sent him reeling backward.

Vandress cast a spell of vicious ice and snow at the sorceress.

Paltereth shot out a quick spell of green flames with one hand behind her to block the icy spell.

She was surrounded by the three, but she showed no sign of fear in her eyes.

Grimdore and the red-headed behemoth of a dragon clashed into one another viciously fifty yards off. Both snarling and biting and clawing, with their wings and tails flailing. Belzarath was only moments away, with two more Neferian just trailing behind.

A whizzing bolt from a Dead Bow to the east shot just above Grimdore's right horn.

"Hey!" Ceres shook her fist. "Look where you're aimin'!"

As the mages battled and the dragons fought—chaos reigned down upon Valeren. Lightning crashed and thunder roared from above. The rains plummeted down from the heavens; striking the ground in waves. Dragons' roars shuddered throughout the city and the sounds of magics crackling echoed through long streets and alleyways.

The bodies of the fallen piled and numbered higher and higher by the minute. Soldiers' bodies and mighty steeds lay broken, battered, and burnt. As Belzarath flew from the sky to the fighting between Grimdore and the red-headed monstrous dragon, her fire lit the sky. Golden-orange flames tore through the air, engulfing the giant Neferian as it brushed its wings up to shield itself.

The ivory dragon then flew down and entered the fray—two Neferian not long off. Corvaire's lightning spells blasted back at the two other dark dragons, hot on the aged, gray dragon Zênon's tail, still minutes away.

Grimdore, Arken's beast, and Belzarath tangled in a snarling and slashing knot—biting and clawing, leaving blood streaking down their long claws.

"Hold on!" Stone clamped his fingers down onto Grimdore's scales, as Ceres did the same as the teal dragon's back swung back and forth. Marilyn, too, with her wet silver hair flowing behind her, was unable to cast spells because she had to hang on so tightly.

Belzarath's fires blazed past the side of Grimdore's neck. Stone and Ceres tucked themselves into her, pressing their chests against her. Stone's heart beat wildly; adrenaline pulsing through him as the two other Neferian landed on the western side of the courtyard, sending ancient statues crumbling to the ground.

The two Neferian shrieked and roared. They flapped their wings hard, rustling the rain from them in fine mists. As they ran toward the fighting dragons, terror gripped the city. Many of the soldiers in the courtyard watched helplessly as the two dark dragons shook the ground beneath their boots as they ran. Another bolt of a Dead Bow whizzed at the pair, but the spell of a mage disintegrated it with a quick spell of black smoke.

Magic still flooded the air above as Paltereth fought off her three attackers. From two sides, Paltereth battled Joridd and Conrad, while deflecting spells from Vandress—even pushing the young woman back stride by stride.

Paltereth's normal grin from such ecstasy in a battle was replaced by a wicked glower. Her normal swift, playful attacks were replaced by labored, forced ones. Her spells were cast in bursts, while brushing back the attacks of Joridd and the Guildmaster, many of which sent the men reeling back, sending Conrad to the ground and Joridd to a knee.

Archers rained down arrows upon the incoming army of mages, but they were singed away by the spells of the back of the horde. The front of the Mages of the Arcane fought with the seven, while the three Mages of the Seliax drifted into their party. Suddenly, the mages of the Arcanica and the Seliax fought side by side for the city of Valeren—and their spells fought together to fend off the invading army.

Corvaire was not far off, with the dragon Īzadan just behind. Stone's mind raced as the battle had suddenly come to full intensity with the dragons in the middle of a battle that was already causing Grimdore to pour her blood to the ground, slowing her not one bit. Her muscles glistened in wet rain and as lightning struck south of them. Her powerful jaws snapped —as did Arken's Neferian's.

The two other dark dragons rushed in, but Belzarath took to the sky, flying over the red-headed Neferian, and landed on its backside—next to Grimdore.

"Marilyn!" Ceres yelled. "What can we do?"

"Keep fighting," Marilyn said, gripping tightly to the ivory dragon's back as her long, wet robes stuck to her scales. "Distract them with your spells."

Ceres flashed a fiery spell with one hand at the two dark dragon's heads, as Marilyn cast one upon the red-headed one, blinding it momentarily. Stone even, focusing hard on his Indiema, imagining his father's face as vividly in his mind as he could, cast a spell of his own.

"*Fridaras!*" His fingers cooled as icy spindles flew from his fingertips at the two Neferian, striking their heads and long necks.

Ceres gave him a quick nod, turning her attention back to her own spells.

Every ounce of his being focused on the spell flowing through him, as he felt an energy brimming cold from deep within.

"That's it, Stone," Ceres said, while illuminated in the golden hues of her fire spells and the cold blues of his own. "Don't let them regain focus. Keep them fighting us. Don't let up!"

The two dark dragons staggered and stalled, but they crashed in with tremendous force in the raging storm. Blinded as they were, they plowed into the larger Neferian. It snapped its enormous jaws at them in a fleeting moment, before they all came back to their senses—outnumbering the two dragons of Stone, Ceres, and Marilyn. Drâon was not far off.

Another bolt whizzed into the fray from the south, flying ten yards overhead before it disintegrated to smoke from a focused spell.

The mages at war blasted their spells back and forth, yet while the fighting seemed evenly matched, more and more of the dark mages poured into the round courtyard.

Out of the corner of his eye, Stone saw what appeared to be the Vile King being helped through the main northern entrance. He walked awkwardly, unevenly, as if something about him was missing. His metallic staff helped him to walk into the courtyard, before dropping to a seat on a stone bench.

"You see that?" The icy spell receded back into his fingers, causing him to breathe heavily.

"I do," Ceres growled. "Somethin's different about him, though. Looks like a stray cat more than a scary wizard."

The mages that ran into the courtyard pushed back the soldiers that stood down long roads and alleys in a ring around the courtyard. Of the three hundred which started the attack, Stone guessed two-thirds of those still drew breath and didn't seem to be slowing in any respect.

Lightning sizzled in the sky above, with Corvaire's eyes lighting gold like a god as the lightning zapped from his extended arm down to the three Neferian below, coursing into their spidery wings and slick backs.

The old gray dragon lined with brittle spikes landed with a thud, letting out a shuddering roar with its yellow teeth gleaming. Corvaire's brow furrowed, holding out his sword at the dark dragons as slivers of lightning danced upon its sharp steel.

"Infernus!" Marilyn shouted, sending cones of searing fireballs at the backside of the distracted Neferian. They turned their heads in unison, screeching. They were pelted again by more bursts of lightning from the back. The crimson-headed Neferian heaved from his chest, pushing his shoulders out wide, and then, in a quick motion, dropped his head low and let out a deafening roar.

It crackled and broke as Stone and Ceres clapped their hands over their ears. The other two joined in. Like one three-headed beast, each of them roared louder than anything Stone could imagine. It was louder than a mountain being broken in half or the sea tearing itself asunder.

Even Marilyn and Corvaire had to cover their ears as Grimdore, Belzarath, and Zênon shook and pulled their heads back.

Down below them Vandress, Joridd, and Conrad paused their fighting momentarily.

The spells faded, causing the city to dim from the intense lights they'd created. Īzadan flew in, landing next to Zênon. She writhed from the dark dragons' roars. The two Neferian were on her tails, each of them with riders upon their backs.

The mages' spells had halted, if even only momentarily.

The two Neferian beside Arken's dark dragon roared so loudly that black flames sparked from their maws. The larger of the two, with yellowish orange specks, pricked down its black-scaled back and with gray wings and three large horns upon its head, turned its serpent-eyed attention to Stone and Ceres.

It stopped its roar as the other two continued, lowering its head and preparing a plume of fire in its chest. It craved death —Stone's death. Its gaze was terrifying, and its scaly mouth brimmed with fire.

"Grimdore." Stone shook her scales. "Grimdore, fly. Fly!"

The great teal dragon flapped her wings, but it was too late —the fire poured out of the dark dragon's maw, spewing scorching hot black dragonfire at her. It forced Grimdore back, causing her to cry out in pain. It was a high-pitched squeal, more like a yelp than a roar.

The scales Stone and Ceres held onto became hot quickly, and they both closed their eyes and used Grimdore as much as a shield as they could. Stone smelled the hair on his arms singeing and the breath he inhaled was hot and burned his nostrils.

Fly, fly away! You can't take much more of this. We must...

Suddenly, the world slowed, and the flames faded. Stone gasped for air—Ceres, too. They heaved heavy breaths as Grimdore fell back to all fours with a low growl and smoke pouring up into the rain from her front side.

Stone opened his eyes back wide again, and what he saw took his breath away.

The gold specked Neferian glared back at him, but the fierceness had gone. And one long, six-foot bolt protruded from the back of his head, sticking sharply through its right eye. The mighty Neferian staggered, snarling and wheezing.

Arken's Neferian and the other with blue streaks upon its back halted their roars in confusion. The gold-flecked dark dragon staggered, turning its long neck backward, attempting to fill its chest with black fire once again. Its snout pointed toward a tower to the west, where Stone noticed something blue faintly floating over the huge Dead Bow.

The Neferian collapsed to the ground with a thud that shook the ground. It gasped for air, and in its last breath let out a flicker of dark fire. Then the light from its eyes faded.

Stone looked down at the fallen beast with his mouth agape, and then he glanced quickly back to the Dead Bow with the flickering blue light flapping its far-off wings over a familiar face.

"Adler!" Ceres gasped, covering her mouth. "You're alive!"

Chapter Eleven

Stone threw his hands over his head in exhilaration. Ceres covered her mouth as tears swelled in her eyes. Adler's auburn hair blew back, covered in ash and sweat. His eyes gleamed with hatred upon the fallen Neferian with the golden flecks. Arken's dark dragon ceased its roar, scanning its fallen kin with a sort of bewilderment. It cocked its enormous head, looking at the monstrous dragon at its side. The two riders on the other Neferians' backs pulled back their long reins—causing the dark dragons to hover in the air, flapping their wings slowly with puzzled scowls on their scaled faces.

Paltereth stood in silence with her arms still covered in green, crackling flames. Vandress and the other mages watched the huge, shadowy dragon fall to the ground. Stone looked back at the entrance to the courtyard to see the Vile King stagger as a mage helped collect him to his feet.

In that fleeting moment, where Stone could hear the rains spattering upon the ground, he could feel the tide turning. The dark dragons had another of their great evils extinguished. Grimdore and the other dragons were no longer outnumbered by the larger invading dragons from the east. Four against four they were—and the Neferian knew it.

"Hold on." Stone grabbed the damp scales tightly. Ceres pushed away her excitement and gripped the teal dragon's scales.

Adler and the other soldiers upon the tower readied another bolt.

As the mages resumed their battle, and the sounds of the rains were replaced by whirling spells and explosive blasts of flashing light, the dark dragons did not do what Stone expected —in fact, they did quite the opposite.

Grimdore was battered, burned, and bloody, and Stone readied another ferocious fight with Arken's dragon. Instead of lurching forward with a fresh attack, he let out a sharp bark of a growl—as if speaking to the Neferian beside him. The two riders whipped their reins, as if understanding, and pulled back, pulling the colossal heads of the dark dragons around.

The red-headed dark dragon rose to his hind legs, flapping his immense wings out wide, raising his long neck to the sky. He and the other Neferian flew up to the sky, while Grimdore, Belzarath, Zênon, and Īzadan growled; regrouping together.

Corvaire, Marilyn, Stone, and Adler were finally back together for the first time since the battle started.

"Where are they going?" Stone asked as the mages' battle boomed to full force once again.

"I don't know," Corvaire said in a low voice.

"After them!" Marilyn called from Belzarath's back as the dragon growled.

"Now we do the chasin'!" said Ceres.

Adler shot another bolt from the Dead Bow with a dull *thwap* of the thick bowstring. The bolt dissolved before it got halfway to the dragons rising into the air. The mages regained their senses, and Joridd and the Guildmaster were stuck hiding behind statues. Vandress and the other mages were forced back toward the structures they'd emerged from.

The four dragons took to the skies after the four Neferian with the two riders whipping the reins.

"I don't have a good feeling about this." Stone turned his head for Ceres to hear as the winds blew past.

"We're at war," she said. "At least he's alive down there. We can win this. Things are startin' to turn our way!"

"I hope so," Stone muttered as his gaze fell back to the four dark dragons.

Their ascent was cut short though by the Neferians' wings flattening, only sixty yards up. Then they dispersed from one another.

"What're they up to?" Stone asked, only loud enough for himself to hear his words.

"After them, girl!" Ceres shrieked, almost as if the chase had turned to a game for her suddenly uplifted spirits. "Go kill the rest of the bastards!"

Something wasn't right, though. *Why would they flee now? The fight is far from won or lost for them.*

The answer was stark and sudden, and it caused Stone's stomach to sink.

"Oh no," Ceres gasped. "Now I see what they're doing... They're not coming after us. They're going after *them*."

The four Neferian, almost exactly on cue, began spewing dark dragonfire below. It poured onto stone towers, knocking them to their foundations. It ripped through wooden homes like strong winds blowing through willows. It seared everything and everyone it touched; burning, scorching, killing.

Their lust for destruction had turned. They not only wanted revenge, but they also wanted to burn. So, the long streaks of the city of Valeren beneath their wings burned. Chaos tore through the city. People were no longer safe in their homes or in their cellars. Dragonfire needled through every crack and crevasse it touched.

Arken's dragon cast down its mighty, deadly fire in plumes that were fifty feet wide, and he was heading toward the queen's palace.

"After him!" Stone got from his seat upon Grimdore's back. "We can't let them do this."

Below, hordes of people flooded out of their homes into the streets. They were trying to flee, but with the four dark dragons spreading out in different directions, they ran into each other, clogging the arteries of the city, and Stone swallowed hard. It wasn't only him that noticed these crowds, but the dark dragons too, as they turned back, readying more fire to burst down upon them.

Belzarath crashed into the one with the dark red webbing, causing its head to fly back wildly; spewing flames up into the air. Its dragonfire hissed from the rains falling onto it.

The Neferian with blue streaks on its back dodged Zênon's slower flight, blasting its dark dragonfire onto a long, wide road of the city. Dozens were instantly killed. The aged, the young, and the defenseless were all burned away. Lives were lost forever in one fell swoop of the monster with the stoic rider with thick, gray metal armor upon its back.

Stone watched in horror as all those souls were extinguished and his sadness was replaced by thick, throbbing rage.

"Oh my god," Ceres said in a hollow, helpless voice. Cries rose from the city in waves. "Oh, my god."

"Fly, Grimdore!" Stone yelled in the rain as lightning cracked to the south ahead, and thunder boomed just after. She roared as she chased Arken's dragon.

"I can't watch." Ceres shielded her eyes with one arm.

Stone's fists pounded on Grimdore's scales. "Fly! Faster, faster!"

She cast a spell with a wave of her arm, sending out a fan of green mist that flew into the nostrils of five soldiers brave enough to run into the ranks of mages. Two tried to flee at the sight of the vapor-like spell. They covered their mouths and noses as they ran, but the snaking spell slid between their fingers, finding its way into their lungs, sending them choking to their knees and dying a slow death—gasping for air.

Paltereth then turned her attention to Vandress and the seven as they clung to the sides of the stone structures, hiding behind a blanket of spells they had erected. Vandress watched as the hordes of dark mages piled into the courtyard from the northern archway where Salus stood watching, shaking his one fist with his staff firm in his grasp.

Joridd and Conrad darted from statue to statue, evading shooting spells as rocks exploded near their heads. Each of them made their way to the backside of the monstrous body of the fallen dark dragon. They heaved heavy breaths with their backs to the golden-flaked scaled spine of the beast.

"What was the backup plan?" The pupils of Conrad's eyes were large and his hand shook, just enough for Joridd to notice.

Joridd sighed. "We didn't have one. Damn, we blew that one chance we had. Damned all to the Dark Realm."

"We need to take her out." Conrad took a deep breath, letting it out with a strong huff. "We could flank her when she's distracted with Vandress."

"I don't think she's ever going to be that distracted," Joridd groaned. "She's got too many watching her back. We really need those dragons."

"Or another army of wizards." Conrad peeked over the side of the dark dragon, with a spell zapping into it, cracking off part of the brittle scales. "But I think this is all we'll muster."

"Let's make our way to her," Joridd said, pointing to the west with his thumb, where Vandress was battling the mages.

"Might as well head back into the tunnel if that's the plan," Conrad said as Paltereth shrieked in the pleasure of battle on the other side of the dragon.

A Neferian swooped back overhead, incinerating the road below. Dark flames and smoke rose high instantly. Joridd swallowed hard at the sight. Zênon flew after—too slow and too late.

"We're losing," Joridd said, watching a battalion of brawny soldiers get blown back in the eastern side of the courtyard.

"Aye," the Guildmaster crouched, touching the wet stones at his feet with his bare fingers. "We've got nothin' left to fight these bastards except the dragons. And they're off trying to save what's left of the city."

"I'm not giving up," Joridd said, hefting his mighty sword with both his hands.

"Nor am I," Conrad said. "But we're not going to get far just standing here."

A faint blue light lit the tops of their wet heads. It sparkled as it dropped in front of their eyes. Ghost's nude, pale body floated before them. Her eyes were wide, and her gaze darted around—very much unlike her.

"Where do we go?" Joridd asked, familiar with the fairy.

She zipped up over the dragon, dodging red and black spells with long tails. To the east and west, she looked, flying back down after.

"Well?" Conrad asked with his hands out.

Her tiny shoulders slunk.

"She doesn't know what to do." Conrad looked up to the skies with a groan. "That's a first. Argh, I was hoping for something…"

"The Dead Bows," Joridd said, nodding his head to the fairy.

She shook her head low.

"Won't work," the Guildmaster said. "There's too many of them. They'll see it coming a hundred yards off."

"Can't attack like this," Joridd said. "Can't attack from the sky…"

There was a brief pause. Then they all three looked at each other, as if something was on the tips of their tongues. They all looked down.

"The sewers. We've got to get Vandress and others," Joridd said. "Maybe we can mount an attack from underneath."

"Don't know if it'll work," Conrad said. "They'll just follow us down."

"Well, we aren't going to live long enough up here to find out…"

⁂

"Watch out!" Vandress launched a bolt of ice to the north, ricocheting into a pair of mages in dark robes, knocking them back to their sides.

"Thanks," one of the seven said, heavy beads of sweat running down her face.

"This is so much better than being locked away," one of the Mages of the Seliax said. A thick vein in his forehead bulged as his smile rose to two sharp, curled corners. Red spells flicked out of his fingers at the encroaching army of hundreds. "So much better!"

Vandress didn't reply, but by her silence, she seemed content enough to have someone thrilled at being so outnumbered.

The bombardment of spells fell onto them like waves hitting a beach. They crashed into them in waves, and from all directions. The stone walls at their sides were crumbling and toppling over. The slick ground didn't help either as they were pushed back, inch by inch.

"Should we run?" the woman of the seven asked in a rushed voice.

Vandress glanced over her shoulder to see a pack of over a dozen soldiers. Their faces were blackened with ash and streaked with rain. Their eyes were reddened. Many wanted to fight, waiting for their chance. Many wanted to run as shown by the blank stares, trembling hands, and shock on their faces.

"We've got to turn the tide, now," Vandress said, with her hair whipping behind her from the clashing spells.

"How?" the woman of the seven asked with desperation in her voice. "We're going to die out here. We can't win."

Doubling down, Vandress said in a voice loud enough for all of them to hear. "If I die here, then I die fighting for my home and family. There's nothing worth fighting for more."

The seven seemed briefly inspired by a strong force of magic, but the sight of more mages piling into the horde, weaving between the shrubs and statues, did little to soothe their fears.

From the soldiers behind them, they heard a "Hey, hey!"

Vandress spun around, ready with magic to unleash.

The soldiers had their weapons drawn at the hidden door to the tunnel they'd emerged from.

"Hold!" Joridd called, crawling up the ladder and out onto the alley.

The soldiers withdrew their weapons, and as Conrad came up after him, many of the Assassin's Guild leaped down from the wall above.

"We've got to get under them," Joridd said to Vandress. "Attack where they can't see us."

Vandress looked around, unsure of what to do.

"Die here or hide down there, lass," Conrad said. "At least it'll give us time, and maybe give Stone and the others enough time to handle the beasts above. What do ya say? We haven't got time to dally."

"The city will be left defenseless," she said, shaking her head as she looked at Joridd.

"The queen is dead and the city's burning," Joridd said, putting his strong hand on her arm. "If we all die here, then there won't be a city to save."

"Into the sewers," she said. "You." She gave the Mages of the Seliax an icy glare. "Cover our backs while we retreat, then follow us in."

The three nodded in agreement, then turned back and hurtled massive black spells into the Mages of the Arcane.

"Hurry," Conrad said. "Everyone into the tunnels!"

Chapter Twelve

One by one, they crawled down into the guts of the city. They smelled musty from the pooling rains and irony from the blood that trickled down into the sewers. Their boots splashed through knee-high water and rats scampered away from the loud blasts above. They dispersed in different directions to confuse the enemy.

At their rear, the Aigonic Mages battled with trailing dark mages. The shivering soldiers and the stealthy assassins followed behind their leaders. Vandress was at the rear too, while Joridd and Conrad led the men down separating tunnels.

"Bring it down!" she yelled in the commotion of the battling magic. "Bring it all down!"

She, along with the three mages of the Aigon, sent up destructive spells that sent the entrance to the secret sewer path crashing down in a pile of rubble.

"Hurry, this way," she said, pulling them back to follow the line of soldiers. "Hurry, they'll be after us soon enough."

Scuttling under the courtyard, Joridd eventually came to a small gutter in the courtyard above, on the western side near a bakery building he shopped at many times for his children.

Vandress ran up the ranks of soldiers to him. Conrad and the Assassin's Guild were somewhere else—but they could not be sure.

"You see her?" Vandress wiped the rain and sweat from her face. Her collar-length dark hair was frayed, and her normally pristine clothes were tattered and singed.

Peeking through the thin, rectangular gutter, he watched the boots run by to the southwest. The mages' long cloaks stuck to the wet ground, with their tails being pulled behind them.

"No," Joridd said. "Not yet. Don't hear her either. Wait…" He turned to the left, looking north. "I don't see her, but I see him…"

He bowed his head down and Vandress peered up through the twelve-inch gutter, only a couple of inches high.

"That's him," she said in a gruff voice. "Doubt Salus is leading anything now. It's her we need."

"She's too protected," Joridd said. "At least at the moment. There's only a handful next to him."

"Well, we're not doing any good standing here," she said. "And they'll find their way down here any moment now."

"Follow me," Joridd said. Then a heavy roar boomed in the sky just above. Its sound trailed off like shattered glass. "Get down!"

His loud voice called to all in the tunnel, as they quickly dropped to their knees or clung to the side of the slick tunnel.

Black dragonfire blew down into the courtyard with a wicked fury. The red-winged Neferian destroyed a long section of the southern tip of the round courtyard, shaking the ground and incinerating everything and everyone in its wake.

Joridd popped back up again quickly to see massive dark flames rising thirty feet into the air to his right. He didn't see Paltereth anywhere, but to the north, he saw the Vile King scrambling down from his spot on the waist-high walls of the outer ring of the courtyard. He moved frantically and with much aid from the surrounding mages.

"What's happening?" one of the seven asked, a younger man in the lower part of his thirties.

Joridd's mouth curled to one side. "Just a reminder that the Neferian aren't beholden to these mages. With the Dark King gone—they're fighting two separate battles."

"Doesn't that mean we are too?" The young mage rolled his hands over his knuckles.

"Yes," Joridd said. "But it also means we can use it to our advantage. If they're busy looking out for dragonfire, we can sneak around in the shadows."

"You still thinking we travel north to him?" Vandress asked.

"No," said Joridd, coming back down from the gutter to meet their level. "We find her. If their mages are distracted, then we may get another shot at her. There are more exits from these tunnels than I'd imagined. If we find her, and distract her, then I might be able to get up there and cut her down."

"We're with you," one of the braver soldiers at the front of the garrison said. Joridd nodded with a groan.

"That means we're going back the way we came," Vandress said. "That part's caved in."

"We'll use another path. Creep along silently until we find her. Then we fight," he said.

The dark dragon roared again overhead.

※

Black, sharp fire tore into the upper windows of the palace. Bolts zipped by, flying wide of the monstrous dragon. Dragonfire ripped through walls, melted glass, and sent many hurtling down—leaping to their deaths.

Arken's red-headed beast flew around the wide tower in a large ring, burning into the queen's palace from all sides. In its rage, it had flown at tremendous speed, leaving Grimdore a full minute behind.

Stone and Ceres found themselves once again helpless to stop the dark dragon's destruction. Behind them, long swaths of the city burned, and these were no fires rains could extinguish—they burned until there was nothing left to burn.

Stone gritted his teeth, and Ceres was silent in her thoughts.

You'll pay for this, Stone thought, but he doubted his own words. There was a chance the dark dragons would burn the entire city to the ground before they could be stopped, and he knew it.

"The tower's lost," Ceres said in a forced voice, pushing past the sadness as they watched the poor souls leap from the high windows, engulfed in flames.

To the east, one of the Neferian with a rider was casting its fire down upon the city. Marilyn and Belzarath flew behind it, spewing their own spells and fire at it, but they were of little use. To the west, Īzadan was struggling to keep up with the other dark dragon and rider—burning that part of the city. Behind, Corvaire was after the red-winged one.

"Always too far behind and too late," Stone said. "The dark dragons are too swift in their rage."

"And Adler's the only one with any damned aim," said Ceres with a sneer.

"He did get one," Stone said. "He's gonna rub that in until the day we die."

"He sure will."

Arken's dark dragon flew past the tower to the south, toward another tower a mile off.

Stone's stomach turned. He knew what he needed to do, but he didn't want to do it.

"What?" Ceres asked as her blond hair blew back hard in the wind and rain.

"We need to go back," he said.

"We can't let it destroy the city," Ceres said. "We've got to stop it, or distract it, or…"

"Grimdore's injured," he said, petting her scales.

Ceres sat in contemplation.

"We can take out Paltereth," Stone said.

"So many will die," she said.

"Yes," he said. "But they'll die, us going like this."

"I don't want to leave them," she said in a soft voice. "I want to help them."

"We need to stop the mages," he said, seemingly talking more to himself than to her.

"Killing her won't stop the dragons' rage," Ceres said.

"It'll kill some of mine."

Ceres looked at him with an eyebrow lifted. "There's no right answer," she said. "I wish Gracelyn was here. I feel she'd know what to do."

The battle had been so intense, and his emotions so wild, that he'd briefly forgotten about Gracelyn off somewhere with that god. At first, it was a spike of hurt, like a nail being twisted in his stomach, and then it burned like hot oil being poured into his heart and veins.

"We need to end this fight," he said through clenched teeth. "We need to find where Crysinthian took them…"

Ceres sighed, nodding.

"Grimdore, fly back," he called out in the storm, pulling her teal scales back. The great sea dragon barked out once, seemingly not wanting to listen—only following her predatory instinct to fly off after the dark dragon. "Fly back! We need to help the others."

She roared again, causing golden fire to fly from the corners of her long, toothed mouth.

"Fly back! They need our help."

Grimdore turned her head back, as if understanding what he was saying.

"We need to go back…"

The teal dragon looked at Ceres, who nodded slowly.

Grimdore spun her head and neck fully about, and with a sharp tilt of her wings, glided back north.

The largest of the Neferian—The Dark King Arken's beast burned wildly and unhindered to the south.

Stone glared back at the dark dragon, letting out a deep sigh.

I hope you're doing the right thing…

※

THE MAGES HAD TAKEN the courtyard. It was only just two hundred yards into the city from the front gate, but it was a pivotal moment. The full brunt of their force was concentrated there, where half of the hundreds-year-old statues lay broken on the wet ground. So many soldiers had been killed that the mages filtered out into the spider-web-like roads that spread out into the city. There was little opposition then. From the tens of thousands of soldiers that began at the beginning of the battle—many had lost their lives, many drew back into the city, and many had fled in cowardice and desperation.

The queen was dead.

Their leaders were retreating.

The Majestic Wilds were taken away.

One Neferian lay dead, but four then burned the city with terrible ferocity. So many were dead.

The two who led the invading army of mages still stood, Paltereth Mir pushed forward unscathed, and the aged Vile King still drew breath.

Dread rolled around every nook and cranny of the city. Not

one citizen of Valeren didn't think that death might come at any time. There was no protection from dragonfire if the Neferian came. Many felt their only option was to flee—so the beaches and plains below the city saw thousands running aimlessly in terror—only wanting to be nowhere near the city that was falling.

Arken's red-headed dragon flew to the next high-towered palace, burning it with a roar that echoed throughout the entirety of the city. The three other dark dragons burned as well, with the following three dragons unable to keep up with their speed or match their strength. The Neferian flew as if a new power had awoken in them—and it was turning the tide of the battle.

"There she is," Stone said in a strained voice.

She walked with a stalking swagger, with her thin hips swaying under her slender dark robes. There was no magic surrounding her—at least none visible—as she looked up at the single approaching dragon. Her minions flocked to her at the sight.

"I don't have a good feeling about this," Ceres said, tugging at his pant leg.

"When was the last time we had a good feeling about anything?" he said, regretting his words as soon as they left his lips.

"She's ready for us." Ceres clung on tight as Grimdore tucked her wings in and began her approach. The teal dragon was fearless, even in her battered state, and in deep need of restoration from the sea—her inner fire knew no bounds. She'd fight until death took her; Stone knew.

"We just need one good shot." Stone clapped Grimdore's back. "Full force fire down upon her."

"Stone, you're not thinkin' straight," Ceres said. "Look, they're pulling into her."

"I don't care," Stone grumbled past clenched teeth.

"I miss her too," said Ceres in a soft pitch. "But killing ourselves won't bring her back."

Tears trickled out of the corners of Stone's eyes as he gritted his teeth.

"I'm ready to die. If that's what it takes to save these people."

"Your death won't do anythin'."

"Her death will."

Ceres sighed. "Well, I'm not wantin' to die just yet." Her apprehensiveness turned to a mean glower. "But if I'm to go, then I'll take down that bitch as well."

Stone turned his head and looked deep into Ceres' mossy eyes. "That's my girl."

Ceres clapped Grimdore's back. "Fly, girl, fly!"

Chapter Thirteen

Cold, biting winds blew in from the Obsidian Sea to the south. The rains turned hard and thick. The storm overhead grew so wild it could be named and written about for ages to come. The Worforgon seemed to sense what the battle meant and knew the tragedy of the lives it cost—and she wept.

Paltereth was the eye of the storm, and the ring of mages that encircled her was her shield. She was as important to them as the dragons were to the city, and they'd give their last breaths to protect what she meant to them. They were the full force of the magic of the Seliax—a living, breathing representation of magic that was thought so rare—fleshed into full form. It was one of the greatest forces and weapons that had ever existed, and she and Salus Greyhorn were the architects of that awful power.

At that moment, a single, legendary dragon that had rested in the sea for no one knew how many years—flew at the Arcanic Mages' champion, and hot fire brewed deep within the dragon.

Grimdore knew the sorceress and knew her as her enemy.

She'd killed her friend Y'dran, and the lord of the Dark Realm himself would surely feel the scorn of a dragon's vengeance.

Stone and Ceres' trepidation diminished. There was only their own vengeance left. They feared not for their own lives, for the battle was nearly lost, and if the city fell, then all three kingdoms would belong to the Mages of the Arcane. They would not let that happen while they drew breath.

So, they flew. They flew at terrifying speed.

Stone threw his open hand back and Ceres grabbed it.

"Here we go," he said, ducking into the dragon's back as the rains bit hard on his face.

"Here we go," she said as lightning struck just beside them, cracking down onto a tower to the east. Thunder boomed as Grimdore roared, and they felt the vibrations on their inner thighs.

This is it. Make it count. Stone felt the warmth from inside the dragon and from Ceres' own hands behind. Reaching deep within himself, he drew out the few memories of his kin, and his father—magic flames dripped down his forearms to his hands.

They approached like a torrential storm. Grimdore's sharp-toothed mouth opened wide; flames licking out.

The mages below flocked in tight together with their spells and staffs swirling above their heads.

Stone nor Ceres spoke, but their souls meshed. If this was to be their last hurrah, then at least they'd be together in the end.

Grimdore spewed hot dragonfire, lighting the entire courtyard in golden-orange light like the sun. The fire was hurtling at Paltereth as her damp, green-colored spell shot up in a thick sheet and the mages around cast similar spells. The dragon didn't stop her fast descent. Her flames crashed into the wall of magic, causing it to explode into a gigantic sphere around them.

The flames grew in intensity, as did the mages' spells—yet Grimdore didn't slow.

She was fifty yards off. Forty. Thirty. Her wings spread wide, and her claws were shown, angling down at the sorceress beyond the magic and fire. Grimdore's fire burned so hot it turned a blinding white.

Grimdore struck the wall of magic with an electric crash, causing an explosion like a strike of thick, hot lightning. The spell shuddered, her flames diminished, and her claws ripped into the smoky spell.

Stone and Ceres were rocked from the impact, being driven into her back with both their chests and the sides of their faces. Grimdore's snout was only a handful of yards from the sinister sorceress'—and their eyes met—one predator versus another.

The teal dragon clung to the magic sphere with her claws sinking through. Green smoke rose up her legs like slithering snakes, while they ripped through as if she were clawing through old wood.

She's physically fighting their magic. How can a dragon do that?

"Hang on," Ceres said as the dragon fought ferociously down, and the mages cast harder up at the clawing and biting monstrous dragon.

Clinging to her thick scales, Stone pulled himself over to the side of her back and looked down at the battalion of mages below, sending their scathing spells upward. He noticed something was off, though.

The mages on the outer ring. There was something going on. The whites of their eyes drifted away from the dragon. Their spells shifted focus, and that caused the protection spell overhead to dampen. Grimdore roared, clawed, and bit as her thick muscles tore into it with a terrifying, adrenaline-pumping vigor.

"What's goin' on?" Ceres said, noticing something was awry.

Stone narrowed his eyes, gazing through the misty green veil. Through flashes of blue light beyond, and then red and yellow—he felt the hairs on the back of his neck tense.

"It's them!" He turned back to Ceres. His smile was impossible to withhold. "Now we've got a real shot."

Vandress and the mages attacked from both sides of the dark mages. They were heavily outnumbered, but steel found its mark as masses of angry soldiers and stealthy assassins cut into the horde.

The Arcanic Mages were completely caught off guard. Grimdore had been the ultimate distraction, as the dark mages were forced to fight off not only the ravenous dragon above, but the fresh attacks from both sides.

Stone saw a look on Paltereth's face. He thought he'd never forget if he lived long enough to remember it—fear.

It was only there for a long moment, as long as it takes a candle's light to blow out from your lips, but it was there. And it was sweet.

She glowered and her reddish teeth sneered. From her emerald-encrusted white staff, a blast of black magic burst out in a fanning orb, pushing back not only the oncoming mages, but her own.

Grimdore too was forced back violently, crashing onto her side and sending Stone and Ceres from her back. The crash was so hard Stone slid on his back twenty feet, watching helplessly as Ceres rolled shoulder over shoulder the same distance to his right.

"Ceres!" He got to his feet quickly as the dragon shook off her fog. He ran to Ceres, kneeling over her. "Hey, get up, are you all right?" She moaned as he grabbed her by the upper arms and inspected her. There appeared to be no injuries he could see.

"I—I'm okay," she groaned. Her wild forest-colored eyes sparkled through the pain. "Help me up, Stone. I'm gettin' real tired of this broad."

Stone and Ceres stood behind the dragon, yet with a clear view of Paltereth just past.

Her long dress robes were tattered. Her pale head was singed, and her nose bled where the round bone piercing hung from it. She stood tall and proud, as if relishing in the challenge.

Grimdore snarled as the battle erupted all around. Joridd and Conrad were leading their forces through the dark mages.

Stone felt a tuft of scratchy fur on the side of his leg and heard the familiar snarl. "Hey, boy," he said. "Just in time." Mud growled low and the fur on his back straightened.

"Ready?" Ceres said.

"Not without me," followed by the sound of rushing boots just behind. "If you're going on this fool's errand, then you're going to need a real fool." Adler's Masummand Steel blade was sharp at his side, ready to be coated in a fresh layer of blood.

"The orphan drifters trio," Stone said. "Back together for their biggest test yet."

Paltereth scowled and readied her magic. Sparks shot from Ceres' hands. Stone held his own Masummand Steel sword before him as it dripped in flames.

Get through her, get to Gracelyn. That's all that matters.

The three ran as fast as they could, rushing at the sorceress. Grimdore roared and Mud ran with teeth showing.

The dark mages surrounding her erected a spell to protect them from the dragon's flames. More than one got an arrow in the chest or neck as they were attacked from all sides.

Time slowed as Stone ran—every stride lasted the length of a sunset. His heart raced as if it would be the last beat. His sword grip squealed in his hands as he tightened his grasp. He roared a battle cry as the three of them ran at the sorceress, with the dragon's massive head looming over with dragonfire whipping between her sharp teeth.

Paltereth glowered, spreading her thin legs wide beneath the sleek, wet dress and she bent her knees, angling the white staff with dazzling, wicked green emeralds at them.

The world spun into its most chaotic moment of the war. Stone felt deep in his heart that if the world was to end—*this is what it must look like*.

But to him, he was okay. If this was to be his last stand, at least he was by his friends' side. Mud was with him, ready to bite the witch's head off. This moment was worth it if it was to be his last. The thought of him never meeting his family was brushed aside by the gravity of this moment. It wasn't the thought of Arken remaining loose out in the world that bit at him though... The one thing that pained him was that Gracelyn was out there somewhere—and he wouldn't be able to say goodbye, and give her one last kiss.

Blue flames tore up his sharp sword, clutched over his shoulder—ready to strike down. Ceres and Adler ran on both sides of him, both with their swords ready to do the same.

They were mere yards from her, as the mages around scrambled ready to push back Stone, while others fought the invading forces from both sides. Paltereth moved to strike.

Her thin, green spell swirled like a typhoon overhead, then lurched out at them. Ceres broke the spell quickly with a fiery spell of her own with a subtle movement of her lips. The two spells collided just between the two parties, fading in a trail of sparks.

Black smoke rose as red streaks shot out at them from the dark mages, and Ceres already readied another spell—but there was no time.

Stone closed his eyes and lowered his shoulder as he ran

into the dark magic. They were so close to the sorceress that he could smell her—a musty mix of soot and iron.

Overhead, a dragon roared, not one of the Neferian, but the familiar call of the ivory dragon, Belzarath. Feeling nothing knock into his shoulder as he ran, he opened his eyes to see a glowing sphere of red and blue lights interweaving like two balls of string; knotting into each other.

Paltereth's dark eyes widened, scanning the sphere rising eight feet above and to the sides. Stone, as he ran, saw two casters on either side of them, pushing the two interwoven spells: Vandress to the left, with her arms shaking from the icy blue spell, and Marilyn the Conjurer on the right, with hands of brilliant, red fire.

Stone's lip curled.

"This is for Y'dran!" Adler yelled.

Take this, you bitch!

Stone slashed in a wide arc, but Paltereth brushed it past her with her staff to the side.

Adler and Ceres ran at her, and the sorceress' staff glowed a gloomy dark green, moving with unnatural speed. It deflected both strikes as the three attacked from her front. Her foot rose from the slit of her dress, kicking Mud in his snout, knocking him to his side with a yelp.

Stone gritted his teeth with hatred as the three of them continued their barrage at the sorceress, each of them being blocked with surprising speed.

Paltereth parried one of Adler's attacks high, knocking his sword back behind his head. She took that brief moment to send the butt of her staff deep into Stone's stomach. He reeled back from the pain, nearly driving him to his knees.

It was just Ceres and her for a long moment in a swirling battle of steel, white wood, and emeralds.

As Marilyn and Vandress' spells protected them from other mages' attacks, they also contained their battle. Wild blue magic erupted from Ceres' sword, causing sparks to sputter from each impact on the white staff dripping in dark green magic.

Stone gasped for breath, and Adler regained his composure as the two women battled. Mud got back to his paws behind Stone as Grimdore roared as she too was unable to join in the fight.

Ceres moved with elegant speed and finesse while Paltereth's blows became labored. Paltereth took a step back—something Stone had never seen when in battle like this.

Adler rushed to Stone's side. He rushed in to join Ceres.

Wait.

Stone reached out and grabbed Adler by the forearm.

"What're you doin'?"

"I—I don't know," Stone said, looking at his hand gripping Adler tight.

Ceres and Paltereth fought in a raging fight as the intensity of their magic grew in pulsing waves.

Wait.

"Let me go!" Adler's eyes were wide.

"Hold on," Stone said. "Something's happening."

Adler's frustration turned as he raised an eyebrow and turned to watch the pair fight.

"You better be right about this," Adler muttered.

Mud cocked his head.

Paltereth took another step back as a pulse of magic and sparks lit the bottom of the sorceress' dress on fire.

"You little lost child," Paltereth said, lunging an attack out wide.

Ceres parried it away.

"I'm not lost. You're the one who's so far from home. I'm tired o' the pain and misery that follows ya!"

"No parents," Paltereth hissed. "No family. You have nothing. Your Old Mothers were taken from you. Your dragon too.

The Great God has revealed himself. Why do you fight so hard to keep your world the way it is? The world is changing, and it's changing in my image!" She attacked hard, but Ceres pushed her back with a forceful blow, causing her to draw back again.

"You'll die knowing you did nothing except cause pain. You'll go to your grave knowing you did nothin' good in this world. And I'm gonna send ya there!"

Ceres crashed down her sword from above her head, striking the middle of Paltereth's staff, cleaving it in two.

Paltereth looked down at her staff with wide, dark eyes, and then, in a fiery glower of anger, her body resonated in a blackish-green spell, swirling up her arms and down her legs.

The spell erupted like a tree being struck by lightning, shattering out into Ceres, biting past her own red spell that enveloped her.

"Ceres!" Stone yelled.

Adler pulled his hand free, and he rushed at the sorceress.

Stone ran up to Ceres and caught her before she could fall to the ground.

"Ceres!"

Her eyes were thin slits, and her freckled face was covered in ash. The rains fell on her soft skin, and her dirty blond hair stuck to her brow.

Adler was a fierce fighter and berated the sorceress with quick blows as she fought back with the two halves of her staff. She regained her composure, standing in a wide stance back to her feet.

"Ceres, Ceres, talk to me. Talk to me!"

"S—Stone," she said in a raspy voice. "I—I'm all right. Just a scratch."

Stone scanned her body. Her clothing was tattered and burned. Her arm rested over her stomach and the other fell at her side.

Tears welled in his eyes as Adler and Paltereth fought.

"Hurry," Marilyn yelled from outside the barrier spell.

"Tell me what to do," Stone said. "Tell me what I need to do to fix you."

"It's all right," she said with her voice trailing off. "It's all right…"

"Ceres," he said with tears rolling down his cheeks, trickling off his chin.

Her eyes shut and her head rolled to the side.

Fight.

Stone shook. His arms throbbed and his chest ached.

The pain became too much. He'd lost too much in this war.

Fight.

Paltereth knocked Adler back with a wicked blow with one staff, hitting him back to his side. Mud growled with his front paws wide. He rushed in with his sharp teeth showing, ready to sink in. She knocked the dog away easily with a blow to the side of his neck. Mud yelped, fell away, and moaned.

Fight.

"This is over." Stone stood slowly, clutching his sword tight in his hand.

"Nothing is over," she hissed, slinking low, bending at the waist toward him. She moved like a snake on two hind legs.

"Your part in this is done," Paltereth said as her eyes glowed a smoky black. "*Mine* is just beginning. The Dark King is gone, and the Vile King is old and maimed. Valeren yearns for a new queen."

"That will not be you." The words soured in his mouth with the thought of her winning.

"It already is." She laughed in a low, hissing pitch. "Look around you." She took a long stride toward him. "Your dragons are outsized, your army is falling by the second, and your measly mages are dwindling. Look, they can barely stand."

He held his Masummand Steel sword out before her. It twinkled in the lights of the magics of Vandress and Marilyn.

Fight now!

He rushed forward, teeth-gritting, muscles surging with hot blood. His sword moved at an unnatural speed, slicing fast, just barely brushed away by Paltereth's two staffs. Her smile quickly faded to a scowl—and the fight was on.

The two entangled in a battle as neither drew back. The flashing steel whizzed by her ear, then her leg, then parried away with a clank from her staff. Each blow was thrown to kill.

She suddenly dropped the two halves of her staff to the ground. He didn't hesitate. He thrust his sword at her chest. But her thin, strong fingers wrapped around his wrists. She pulled his arms out wide with a supernatural strength like that of a bear. He fought, but was helpless to resist her.

His sword was in his hand, but helplessly out to the side. With their arms out wide, their faces were only inches apart. Her breath smelled like a burning cauldron. Her pale flesh was dry and almost scaly. Her eyes burned with wicked black fire. She looked like the lord of the Dark Realm if she had a face.

She moved her head forward as if to kiss him. He turned his head. Her dry tongue licked the side of his face. It scratched like sandpaper.

"I taste your tears," she whispered into his ear. "I'll remember this taste forever."

"You'll do no such thing," a voice said from behind Stone. He couldn't turn to see who it was. But a bright blue light lit his shoulders and Paltereth's face. Her pale, scaly skin lit in dancing blue, majestic light. She squinted from its brightness.

She pushed him away, pulling back, picking back up the two halves of her staff, and made a defensive pose like a recoiled serpent.

Stone was on his feet, finally turning back to see what the source of the light was.

The blue light hovered in the air, sending its light cascading down. The light was so bright it glowed through the entangled spells of Marilyn and Vandress. It glowed like a cool, icy moon. A face showed through it as Stone's eyes adjusted.

It's her. It's her!

The figure from within the light raised a bare arm out at the sorceress.

"What is this?" Paltereth sneered. "This is nothing to me..."

"*Fridaras.*" An enormous bolt of cold-like lightning shot out from the hand, surging at Paltereth. The sorceress held up both staffs in an X. The icy spell bolted into her, blowing both her arms back in a violent burst.

"Argh," the sorceress shrieked.

"*Fridaras*," again the emanated figure with streaks of blue flowing in large arcs up and around her said. Another bolt of magical energy shot at Paltereth, this time blowing her to the ground, with both her half-staffs flying to the side.

"This... this isn't how this ends..." Paltereth hissed.

"No," the voice said.

Stone's jaw dropped as he watched Ceres in the dancing, dazzling light. Vandress and Marilyn's spells faded. All who were in the war stopped their fighting to witness her suspended six feet in the air.

"This is how *you* end," Ceres said with her bare arm glowing blue. "*Fridaras.*"

"No!" Paltereth hissed, clawing away on the bare ground with her fingernails digging in the mud.

The bolt of ice rocked into her, bursting into her body, surging up her arms and down her legs. The glowing green light that surrounded the sorceress faded, and the smoky blacks of her eyes were replaced by an icy glow.

Her mouth filled with the blue light, as well as her ears and nostrils. She shook and fought, until her fighting stopped. She lay there like a statue with the blue magic enveloping her, glowing out of her eyes like lamps. Then the light faded, and the magic receded back to Ceres' fingers.

Paltereth's body finally fell completely to the muddy stones—lifeless and dead.

"She's gone," Adler muttered.

"Ceres," Stone gasped.

The blue light faded from her quickly, like a candle being blown out. Her eyes rolled back, and she crumpled to the ground.

Stone ran to her. "Ceres!"

Chapter Fourteen

The battle took a long, gasping breath. Paltereth lay in a pool of her own diluted blood. Ceres lay in Stone's arms; all the magic washed away from her. Adler, Vandress, and Marilyn stood in silence. Vandress had her hands covering her mouth. The seven mages stood in silence, taking the long moment to catch their breath.

Joridd and Conrad were both standing only feet from dark mages, stuck in awe of the moment. Grimdore even took long, grumbling breaths, with her serpentine eyes darting back and forth from the fallen sorceress and her friend. Belzarath's great ivory head dipped down and sniffed Paltereth's body, snorting hard after—as if purging the smell from her nostrils.

"Fight!" Salus' voice shrieked from the northern gate of the courtyard, with his one hand holding up his staff.

The dark mages looked at one another, unsure of which leader they were to follow.

The mob of mages stirred, ready to strike.

But then something happened—from farther north.

It was a low blow of a single horn. Its call echoed throughout the walls of the city, resounding deep into the courtyard. Again, the mages looked around in surprise. Even the Vile King looked puzzled by the disturbance.

The Neferian's roars from above followed quickly after.

"What're they goin' on about?" Ceres asked in a weak voice. Stone looked to see the Neferian abandoning their chase of the other dragons and driving north.

"I—I don't know." Stone watched them fly high overhead, but then watched Zênon's approach and landing just next to Grimdore.

Corvaire, straddling the gigantic dragon, pointed north with his free hand as his sword hung low in the other.

"Arken's men," he yelled for all to hear. "The riders of the Runtue are at the gates. They call for their master's dragons."

"The Runtue riders are here?" Adler gasped. "Salt in slash..."

Salus pushed a mage out of the way, running to the gate. Peering through, he seemed to confirm Corvaire's statement. Salus shook his staff excitedly, even turning gloatingly in Stone's direction.

Drâon Corvaire got down from the gray dragon's back, casually walking over to his group of friends, who huddled around him.

The dark mages behind congregated closer together in the center of the broken courtyard. They watched, as Salus did, as the four Neferian flew overhead, farther north, and over the palace walls. The mob of mages murmured, and Salus finally looked unsettled.

"They've come for their dragons, that is all," Corvaire said, looking past his friends, straight with a cold glare at the Vile King.

"They're not here to join forces?" Adler asked as Ceres slowly got back to her feet. "That doesn't make any sense. How many of the riders are there?"

"Their numbers have grown since we last saw them," Corvaire said. "At least a hundred now."

Joridd raised an eyebrow, looking down at the mud and wet cobblestones, shaking his head.

Marilyn spoke, "They're after their king. This battle matters not to them. If he falls, then their war is lost. This battle is not theirs."

"What of their fallen?" one of the seven asked, an older man. "Are they not to seek retribution in fire?"

"It seems not," Corvaire said in a low voice, stroking his short beard, looking up to where the dark dragons disappeared from sight. "A mighty casualty, one they won't soon forget. That much is sure."

"We should go after them," Stone said, trying to send an icy glare at Salus, who was returning to his pack of mages. "We should end this all now. Then we can go find Gracelyn... and Rosen." He ran up to Grimdore.

Ceres tried to stop him, tugging on his sleeves.

"Let him go," Marilyn said in a soft voice.

Adler ran to catch up with him, and both of them mounted the dragon's back. With a kick of their heels, the mighty teal dragon swooped up into the sky, and the other dragons stayed on the ground, growling at the mages.

They rose to the sky, high enough to get a clear view of the men and women on mighty, hulking steeds. There didn't appear to be one leading them, or at least from what Stone saw. The four dark dragons hovered overhead, with Arken's red-headed beast towering over the others.

"They are—they're leaving," Adler muttered.

"They're going to look for him." Stone wondered if they in fact knew where Crysinthian had taken him, or if their search was just beginning. To the right of the rows of Runtue on horses, a shadow drifted between tufts of grass.

"You think he'll follow them?" Adler squinted to see the Skell. "Think he'd be our spy for once?"

"Doubt it," Stone growled. "We don't have enough coin for him. That's all that matters to him."

"He did show us the way to get Marilyn healed, and he stabbed that traitorous dog Kellen, keeping him from the battle."

"I don't know whether to trust him or not," Stone said, scratching his cheek. "But it seems our fates are intertwined, at the very least."

"You know we can't follow them, right?" Adler said, clapping the dragon's scales. "Does that even need to be said out loud?"

Stone, though, wanted to follow them. For they might be the best chance of finding her the quickest.

Adler shook Stone's shoulder. "Those dark dragons would rip us to pieces out there. We'd have no chance. There—I said it out loud. Can we go back now, please?"

The horn blew from the rear of the two rows of riders, and as it did, their cavalry turned and trotted north. The four Neferian flapped their wings and flew ahead.

Stone sighed, but clicked his heels on Grimdore and she descended back into the city.

It was a tense standoff between the two armies. The mages were dangerous still, like cornered asps. Salus had returned to their ranks, and they still numbered nearly half of their original force. But with the presence of the four dragons that were slowly encircling them, droves of soldiers and cavalry returned to the courtyard. Even mothers and fathers came out with pickaxes, knives, and shovels.

Salus Greyhorn strode through the ranks of mages toward Stone and the others.

"He'd surely fight," Marilyn said, "if not for the dragons at our side."

"Aye," the Guildmaster said coldly. "He'd fight to the last. But he knows their spells wouldn't last longer than a mouse fart against all that dragonfire."

"We wish to return to a parlay," the Vile King said proudly and with his chest out.

Ceres spat on the ground before him.

"You've lost," Stone said. "There's no more than that."

"I've lost little," Salus said with narrow, dark eyes. "You've lost much."

In his heart, Stone knew that was true.

"Let me and mine leave," he said. "Under the guise of surrender, and mercy." There was a hiss in his voice that made the hairs on Stone's forearms straighten.

"Why in the Dark Realm would we let you live?" Adler said through clenched teeth.

"To save your lives," the Vile King said, almost boasting. "We may well fall to your dragons, but not before we'd cast spells out wide into this vast city. You've seen my destructive magic, but you've seen nothing when it comes to spells that linger and seep."

"We cannot let all your forces walk away," Joridd said. "You must surrender for the murder of Queen Bristole Velecitor, among many other crimes."

"I surrender myself," Salus said, throwing his staff to the ground. "Let my followers flee. They will pose no further danger. They'll return to their seclusion. Remember that they are not only soldiers, they are mothers, fathers, grandfathers, sons, and daughters. You feel for your own soldiers, and I love mine."

"You killed my friends," Joridd growled. His muscles tensed and bulged.

Vandress lay a delicate hand on his back.

"Will they obey your commands?" Vandress asked. "Whatever they may be?" The Vile King nodded. "Have them leave the city. They will remain there while we decide —"

An intense heat rushed up from behind Salus, blasting him into them. He fell into Joridd's arms like a feeble old man as the explosion drove them all back, covering their faces and turning their backs to the fire.

By the time Stone was able to uncover, and the heat had somewhat abated, he opened his eyes to see the damage that had been done.

"Holy..." Adler muttered.

"My children!" Salus gasped with his bony fingers covering his mouth, and as he fell to his knees, he clung to the cobblestones. His head dropped, and the old man wept.

While dragonfire wisped out of the mouths of the four dragons, and the entire center of the courtyard was filled with blackened bodies left burning. The smell was overwhelming, burning the nostrils and lungs with the irony, pungent aroma of burnt skin, hair, and bone.

"My children..." Salus cried. "I've nothing left... I'm nothing..."

Joridd undid his belt and smashed it tightly around Salus' mouth, tying it from behind; Salus didn't resist. "Take him." Six soldiers ran up and grabbed him aggressively, dragging him south, deeper into the city.

"The wrath of dragons," Corvaire said. "Quite a thing to behold. So wild, so free."

While the bodies smoldered behind him, Stone stared at Paltereth's body, unscathed by the flames, and he wondered what had happened—how Ceres was able to overwhelm her as she did, and what had caused him to hold Adler back. It was as if—someone had Dream Walked with him—but only in a whisper.

Adler and Stone walked through the tall front gate to the city. They had to step high over many broken bodies along the way. Cries mixed with cheers from within Valeren behind. They echoed like the melody of a sad, triumphant song.

The soldiers and medics came out with them. It was a mad dash to care for those who needed the most urgent care—mostly ushered by the loudest screams from the battlefield.

Stone didn't know what to do first. He'd seen many aftermaths of fights and battles, but none like this.

"Dranne doesn't even compare to this," he said, watching a medic wrap the head of a soldier who moaned in agony. Burns covered half the man's face, and his lips were completely gone.

"So many have died…" Adler said, scanning the piles of bodies ahead where the battle had first started. "At least it wasn't for nothing."

Stone didn't reply, he only continued walking over the bodies of the fallen. Gracelyn and Rosen were at the front of his mind.

Joridd and Vandress were with Marilyn, Drâon, and Conrad ahead. Joridd was organizing the troops to tend to the wounded and begin removal of the dead. Vandress led the seven and the Vlaer handling the body of the queen, and Conrad was regrouping the Assassin's Guild, who for the first time in generations were fully in the eye of the court and those who ruled the city.

Corvaire and Marilyn were standing beside each other, seemingly going over the battle or what was next. Ceres was certainly in their discussion.

"We're really gonna have something to talk about when she's better," Adler said, looking at the smoldering hill beyond the pile of bodies. Mud panted as he trotted between them. "What was that anyway?"

Stone pursed his lips, scratching his pant leg. "I don't want to say it out loud."

"You mean, you think she's the third, don't ya?"

Stone frowned, shaking his head slightly.

"I mean, she's not in the Wendren set like the others." Adler scratched his chin. "But that sure was Wendren magic."

"Shh," Stone said forcefully.

"You're afraid he'll take her if we say it?" Adler asked. "S'pose I'm too. He is a god, after all. He can probably hear us talking like this right now. I'd be surprised if he wasn't listening…"

"Let's not talk about this," Stone said. *If she is the third, and not Vandress… Well, why wouldn't he take her too?* Stone tried hard in his mind to think of something else.

Mud barked suddenly, leaping over a fallen dark mage, and then a couple of charred horse bodies.

"What is it, boy?" Stone asked, following him.

Mud barked loudly at a body with a spear sticking out from it. It wasn't just any body though. A weak groan came from the body as Adler pulled him by his shoulder, so he lay on his back, wincing in pain.

"He's alive?" Stone asked, balling his fingers into a fist.

"Eh, that's a shame," Adler said, standing back up, spitting onto the mage's thigh.

Drâon and Marilyn saw the commotion and rushed over.

The four of them stood over Kellen; whose beady blue eyes lost most of their luster. He coughed and wheezed, with the tight wrinkles on his thin skin cracking and deepening. His mouth hung open with dried blood stained to the sides of his chin.

"Who—who? Wha… Who's in the…?" he moaned, his voice was weak, and his throat strained to get out the words.

Corvaire whistled, and a medic twenty feet away came running.

"We're not going to save him, are we?" Adler asked with a scowl.

"He's been in Verren, working for the enemy for who knows how long," Marilyn said, bending down and putting her two fingers on his neck. "We could learn from him."

"We've got Salus," Adler said, standing back and folding his arms.

"I don't want to save him," Marilyn said, as Kellen muttered jumbled words. "But he's been with Arken. He may have information we need."

Stone gritted his teeth, thinking about the time his mages tried to assassinate King Roderix, and nearly killed them in the process, too. But he knew Marilyn was right in her statement.

The medic came up and began her assessment.

"He's close," she said, analyzing the wound in his stomach and the spear sticking through.

"Can he make it?" Corvaire asked in a bitter voice.

The medic in ashen, stained white clothes shook her head. "I must attend to others, if I may…" Marilyn nodded, and even the medic scowled as she left, heading toward a pack of soldiers calling out for her.

"I don't think we're gonna get anything from him in this state," Adler said. "Let him die alone in the mud. That's the best he deserves."

Stone knelt next to him. "Chancellor Kellen."

Kellen's reddened eyes fogged.

"Chancellor Kellen. It's Stone. Stone from the prophecy. Can you hear me? Are you in there anywhere?"

Kellen coughed hoarsely. His gaze drifted to meet his. He raised an arm, extending his bony fingers. "I know you," he wheezed. "Did we win? Did we…" he coughed. "Did we take the city?" A corner of his mouth curled up.

"No." Stone's hand tightened on his robes at the collar. "You weren't even close."

Kellen coughed and moaned.

"Tell me what Arken was planning!" Stone said. "Tell me how to defeat him. Tell me how I can kill him!"

Kellen laughed, causing fresh blood to trickle down his chin.

"You can't kill him. He's... he's already dead. You can't kill what's already dead."

"Well, I guess that makes two of us," Stone said coldly, inches from the chancellor's face.

"You two are more alike than you know," Kellen said, his foggy eyes suddenly focused. "You're tied together in this life. A string binds you, a string... a tiny, thin string..."

"What're you talking about?" Stone asked, shaking the dying man.

"Your soul..." Kellen said. "You weren't supposed to come back. You died. But when he returned, he... he..."

Kellen's words grew faint, and his eyes drifted.

"He what?" Stone asked, shaking him. "He what?"

Marilyn put her ear close to Kellen's mouth as his body gave way to the cold reach of death.

"He what?" Stone pressed again. "What about him? How did I die? What happened to me? Who am I? Who am I?"

PART III
THE CHURCH AND THE CROWN

Chapter Fifteen

❦

The joint in her finger popped. That was the first thing she heard. She stirred in the darkness. Her head felt like she'd been struck by lightning. There was a searing pain in the back of her head. She clutched it—feeling her thick hair matted behind her on a silk pillow. Her dry lips smacked, and her rough tongue scraped against her teeth.

Sitting up, she saw the light of a single candle flickering on the far wall, atop a brass candlestick on a wooden bench. The light danced back and forth; it was soothing to her painful head. There wasn't another source of light in the dimly lit square room.

She put her hands on her thighs to get up, but she was overcome with fatigue and that pain rattled in her head once more. She sat back down but felt the same linen pants she'd worn in the rainy battle in front of Valeren. Her clothes were dry, but that thought crashed into her like a long-distant, yet vivid and spectacular dream.

Rushing to her feet, forgetting the pain, she ran to the door, which she could barely see to the left. Before she gripped the handle, though, she reached to her side but didn't feel her sword where it should've been. Grabbing the candlestick in her index finger and thumb, she wafted it gently around the room, and to her surprise—her sword rested in its scabbard in the wicker chair next to the bed. She slipped it back around her waist, wrapped her fingers around the handle, and turned.

The door opened with a squeal, immediately opening the room up to the white-blue light of the marble-stoned walkway outside.

Slowly, things were put back in place, through her aching head.

"I—I'm in Endo. Or somewhere that looks just like it…" she said under her breath.

To her right, based between two buildings, two stories high, each with blue drapes covering the windows, was an elegant fountain with water trickling down its single spout. It looked like a sort of flower with its petals at the base of the pool and the spout was the stigma. She drove her hands into the cool pool of water and cupped it up to her dry mouth, gulping it down deeply. Once the first few gulps were down, her eyes focused and narrowed.

She was not in a safe place anymore.

Wiping her mouth with the rough cuff of her sleeve, she drew out her sword quietly.

"This is Endo Valaire. Why am I here? Why did he choose to bring me here?" Her eyes widened as another revelation came to her from her memory. "Rosen, Rosen must be here…" The light of her eyes dimmed, and her brow furrowed. "That means Arken must be here too…"

She stalked down an alleyway like a cat, creeping toward the structure she knew to be at the center of the city. The golden hue of the lights that twinkled from the tips of the marble structure that somewhat resembled an old tree glowed above the underground city.

"Or should I try to escape?" she whispered, with her gaze

darting around and a fistful of magic at the ready. "Can't hurt Arken with it, but if it comes to it, maybe it'll do something to that god. Wherever he is, he probably isn't going to let me go so easily."

"You are correct," a man's low voice pounded in her head, nearly driving her to her knees. She clutched both sides of her head with her fists. "Come to me. I'm waiting for you by the tree. We are waiting."

"Get out of my head," she said, wincing in pain. She heard no response.

She sheathed her sword, stood up straight, and pushed her shoulders back and her chest out with a deep inhale.

"No use in making anyone wait."

She strode into the middle of the alleyway, watching the crossing veins of grays and blacks streak through the dustless, white marble. Her boots pattered on it lightly as she turned a corner, walking out into the open. That section of Endo Valaire had three and four-story buildings of windowless white marble with intricately carved ornamentation around the windows and up their corners. Where gargoyles should be were creatures that belonged more to the fairy world than this one. The walkways were lined with garden beds of the same white marble with gray and black veins, and statues were carved of long-dead figures.

It was only two roads down to the marble tree where the god had spoken to her. Gracelyn walked down at a normal pace with no magic in her hand and her sword sheathed on her hip. She rustled her hair, patting it back behind her. She wiped the crusts from her eyes and licked her teeth.

"Whatever happens, be strong and protect Rosen. Stick together. You can do this."

Gracelyn turned one last corner, and the tree opened up in a wide courtyard at the center of the city. The sharp tips of the tree were still draped with the golden firefly lights. Under the tree, he sat stoically. They approached him slowly.

"Gracelyn Meadowlark of Thistleton," Crysinthian said. The wide-shouldered man in the thin silken robe sat pensively with one leg folded over the other; sitting on a solitary bench of marble. His fingers stroked his chin as he casually looked away from her, at the roots of the tree; knobbed and winding as they were. "First of the new line of mystics."

She stood where she was, forty paces from him. His demeanor was pensive. Her fingers fought hard to not ball up or beckon her spells. She made no move to walk closer to the god. For she had no idea of his true power.

"Crysinthian," she said in a firm voice from deep in her stomach.

His head turned toward her. His lightning eyes pierced into hers. The wrinkles on his face snapped together as his eyes narrowed. Long silver hair flowed down both sides of his chiseled face, some of it was in thin braids.

"Well, what do you think of it?" He sat up straight and put one hand up toward the tree and the surrounding courtyard. The veined muscles in his arm tensed under the thin silk.

"Where are my friends?" Gracelyn asked in a clear voice.

Crysinthian choked down his respite, pulling his arm down and clamping his lips down. His body seemed to shiver.

"Where's Rosen? Take me back to the battle. Take me back to Valeren!" Now her fists were clenched, and she was bent forward at the hips.

The god muttered something to himself.

"Did you hear me? Take me back there, now!"

From his hand that had laid in his lap, he outstretched it to his side, slowly opening his fingers.

"Do you know what this is?" he asked in a strained voice, fighting back something…

She swallowed hard. "Yes."

Within his hand was the red jewel. In his mighty palm, the stone rolled over itself, looking no larger than an acorn.

"Magnificent isn't it?" His golden eyes like lightning sparkled as he was in a trance over its beauty. She'd seen the gem many times in Stone's possession, but she'd never seen anyone fawn over it like he was.

"He was going to use it," Crysinthian's face grew cold and twisted—bitter even. The wrinkles on his face deepened. "He was going to try to use it… against me…"

"Stone wasn't going to—" she began, but was cut short by a thunderous tremor throughout the courtyard.

"Arken!" The god shot to his feet, clamping down on the red stone known recently as an Adralite stone. "He was going to take it. He nearly had it. It was right there, lying in the *mud*. Ready for him to use… for *himself*!"

Gracelyn took a slow step back, putting her arms up to cover her chest. She didn't reply.

"He almost took it… He almost took it for himself…" Crysinthian mumbled to himself, staring down at his closed hand.

"Where's Rosen?" Gracelyn asked in a calm voice, fighting hard not to break.

"Your friend is here."

Gracelyn took a deep breath with a sigh of relief. After that deep breath, she put her arms back down at her sides and straightened her back. "Where's Arken?"

"Arken?" he said, twisting his head to her in surprise. "Why, he's here too."

"He's here?" Her hand shot to the grip of her sword.

"Fear not, my child. He won't be doing much of anything while up here."

"Why didn't you kill him?" Gracelyn asked, eagerly awaiting his response, which wasn't quick to come. "He killed your people, burned your cities and your lands, brought the dark dragons here…"

Crysinthian sat in contemplation, rolling a thin braid through his fingers.

"He will pay for his crimes." He gazed up at the firefly lights of the tree bobbing back and forth. "His time will end. As will all of yours."

Gracelyn was unfazed by his comment. "I need to get back to Valeren. I can't stay here."

"You will do no such thing. You are my guest. Enjoy this. It's a rare treat indeed. The rarest. You can have anything your heart yearns for."

"Stone…" her lips moved involuntarily as she put her hand over her mouth.

"Yes, you love the young man." A wry smile came to the god's mouth. He rose to his feet. "Love is such a funny thing. Makes people do the strangest things. People put themselves in grave danger for love."

Gracelyn pursed her lips, seemingly unsure of what to say.

Crysinthian cleared his throat. "That, Gracelyn Meadowlark… I will not be able to give you here… Stone's fate is his own down in the Worforgon. Your fate… rests with *me*."

Her hands flashed with blue light, raising them up at him quickly.

"*Thyfonus Bitternex Onum!*"

Freezing winds and ice flew from her fingers in a great, concentrated storm. It flew like a great, whirling blizzard at him.

It shot at him at tremendous speed, with icy shards hurtling at him.

He lifted his arm and waved a finger away.

The spell dissipated into a wet glassy pool on the marble ground instantly.

His lightning eyes electrified, and his tone grew low and

gravely. "Do *not* do that again against me. I created the Elessior, and I can take it away…"

She lowered her hand, taking another slow step back.

"You… you created it?"

"I created all magic."

She swallowed hard.

"Are… are there other gods? Creations like you?"

He smirked. "Not here. Not anymore…"

A chill ran up her back.

"You said Arken was going to use the Adralite against you. If he did, would that have made him like you?"

Crysinthian's face twisted and his brow furrowed. "He'll never be anything like me. He's a fallen, bright star that grew dark in the summer night sky."

"What of Stone? What if he used the Adralite? Would he become like you?"

The god's face relaxed. "Now, him, he's quite the diamond, isn't he? Resilient and hardened. I can see why you have feelings for him. Quite the son, he is."

Her hands rolled over one another nervously.

"Son?" she muttered. "Do you know his family? Where did he come from?"

"You haven't figured that out yet?" He had a wry, snarky smile on his face. "Interesting. I give you too much credit, I suppose…"

"Take me back to him," Gracelyn said in a commanding tone.

"No. What becomes of the battle below with the dragons matters little. We have much important work to do here."

"What do you mean? Of course, it matters!"

"We are going to reshape everything. Or rather I will, and you'll assist me—you and the other Old Mothers. It will be *spectacular*."

"How can you say it doesn't matter? People are dying down

there. My friends are down there! You took me away from them. How dare you! How dare you think I would do anything to help you."

Gracelyn was panting. She hunched over with her arms tensed and her fists clenched.

"Keep the Dark King here for whatever you want, but send Rosen and me back down there now, or we'll never help you!"

Crysinthian sighed. "She doesn't see it..." he muttered. "Humans are so stubborn, and weak."

"I am not weak."

Crysinthian got up to his feet, and the silk robes cascaded down his chiseled body.

"You are to me."

"Are you going to take me out of this mountain and back down to my friends or not? If you do that, I will at the least entertain aiding you in building what it is you want. But if my friends don't make it, I wouldn't help you fend off a squirrel from your nuts."

"Gracelyn Meadowlark—you amuse me. Few would speak in that tone to their creator. But my patience only stretches like a band before it breaks. And my temper is not something you want—I assure you." His eyes sizzled in lightning gold again. "It entertains me you think you are in Elderon. Quite cute, actually."

She cocked her head, looking around, unsure then of where she was. "What do you mean? Are we not in Endo Valaire?"

"Have a look for yourself." He stepped to the side and held out his mighty arm with palm opened, beckoning her to walk past him.

As she walked toward him, with powerful strides, resilient to her fear of him, she was stricken with a sight she'd only just noticed, or what the god had revealed. The sky.

Big and pinpricked with silver stars, the sky was as open

and cloudless as she'd ever seen. The stars sparkled past the lights of the firefly lights that hung from the ivory tree that swayed in the mild night breeze.

She walked past him, who towered a full two heads taller than her. A corner of the plaza the tree was in approached, which opened up between two towers. It was no wider than a person laying down, but when she stepped up to the edge, her mouth fell agape.

Opening up around the round towers, she looked down in disbelief. Even upon the back of the great sea dragon Grimdore, she'd never seen such a spectacular view of the Worforgon below. She saw the distant peaks of sharp mountains, vast lakes were tiny pools, and saw the never-ending reach of a forever ocean.

She didn't speak to the god. Instead, she hung her head and closed her eyes.

She only spoke to herself, but was fully aware the god would be able to hear. "I'm not going anywhere. I'm stuck in this mess." Her eyes opened, and she sighed. "Fight the good fight, Stone. Win. You just have to win." A tear rolled down her cheek and dripped off her chin, falling into the abyss below the floating fortress.

Chapter Sixteen

Tied together in this life... A string binds you... Your soul... You died... Weren't supposed to come back... But when you returned...

The words filled his mind as if they were the only ones left in the world. They were clues—if Kellen was telling the truth, but with his dying words? Why would he lie then? There were so many questions, and only hints at answers. Stone felt as if he were being driven to the brink of madness.

Am I doomed to keep wondering forever? Will my friends be the ones to suffer and die? Will the fighting ever stop? Will there ever be peace while I'm alive?

"You think too much," Adler said, chomping down on an apple.

"What?"

"We won! What do ya mean, *what?*"

Stone scowled. There were too many things still bumping around in his mind, not to mention the fatigue in his bones, the aching in his legs from riding the dragon, and the overwhelming exhaustion from the half-day-long battle.

"We're going to go get some cold drinks first. I'm so

parched I couldn't spit past my lip if I tried. Ceres won't mind. Well—maybe she would, but we won't tell her. Then we'll go to see her. If she's not sleepin'." Another chomp. "Can you believe any of this? Did you see that shot? Right through his neck. I'm gonna be a hero. They're gonna make a statue of me here. A real statue where I look strong and brave. Can you even imagine what they'll do for you?"

"I don't care. I don't want it. I don't want any of it." Stone's voice was sour. "I just want Arken gone forever. I don't want any more battles, any more wars, and more death. I've seen enough. I've seen enough to last four lifetimes."

Adler threw his arm over Stone's back. "Chipper up. I hear ya. I really do. But we're gonna forget all that now. You hear? We can worry about the war after we celebrate."

Stone shook his head as he felt warmth on his brow. The light dried the sweat and rain. He looked up as the beaming sunlight made his eyes narrow. He'd nearly forgotten about how the sunlight felt. He blinked heavily and his arms grew heavy.

"C'mon." Adler pulled Stone's arm. "Let's find someplace without any soldiers. There's sure to be casks uncorked and flowing everywhere!"

"Yes," Stone mumbled. "That sounds fine."

"See," Adler said, with his gaze darting down the road they were on. People ran past them in droves, running to the gate and the plains outside the city. Stone watched their faces. Despair, panic, and desperation were trepid upon them all. They were going to look for their loved ones. They would be hard-pressed to find their kin, Stone thought, buried deep under mounds of other bodies or burned away or their eyes sunken in from poisonous spells.

He looked over at Adler's face, who wasn't paying nearly the same attention to them as Stone was. There was a sort of childlike quality in Adler that Stone admired at that moment.

That was another reason he loved his friend the way he did. Perhaps it was a survival tool, or just a way to continue through a life plagued with pain and guilt. Whatever the Worforgon threw at him; he always seemed to find a way to beam with enthusiasm for something out there—something to lift his spirits.

"Sure," Stone said, feeling fresh blood in the muscles of his legs. "Let's go celebrate for a bit. Not too much, though. Ceres might cast a spell on you if you have too much fun. Rip your legs off and sew your lips shut, she might."

"I could definitely see that." Adler laughed. The sun's rays caught his face—dirt-smudged and ashen. His brown hair was caked in blood, but his eyes gleamed.

Mud scampered along between the two, panting with his wet tongue out. He'd surely be snoring within seconds of finding something soft to lie in, and after some warm meat in his stomach.

Adler and Stone went into a tavern just halfway down the road, pouring themselves drinks in the candlelight. Mud snored as Stone expected, and Adler talked endlessly. Stone tried hard to push his worries away—act like there was time later to fix what needed to be fixed. He was excited to find Ceres after she was tended to by the medics, but Gracelyn never left far from his thoughts. She and Rosen were out there—and they were with Arken. That is… if they were all still alive…

❦

READY TO BURST through the door into the infirmary wing Ceres was resting in, Adler and Stone brimmed with excitement. Mud trotted with a grin beside them as their enthusiasm for winning the battle subsided to the stark reality of the aftermath of so much devastation.

There was no door, and it wasn't Ceres in a lone bed being

tended to by many nurses for her defeat of the invading sorceress. The hall Ceres was placed in was overflowing. Moans and cries were heard before they even arrived at the back entrance to an old monastery. Misery hung thick in the air. The dying were lost in their dismay as nurses darted from one bed to another; trying to tend to those most in need. Soldiers wept at the entrance for their ailing comrades or injured children.

It was then that Stone recognized the familiar stench of dragonfire in the wooden monastery. It lingered on every cot and soaked into the linens of everyone who was close enough for its long reach to touch. Tapestries bounced on the walls and the curtains flapped at the windowsills at two levels of the wide room. The sunlight lit the dust as it wafted through the room, twirling from the coughs and hollering from below.

Stone made his way through the double-door entrance where the doors had been removed to fit more beds in quicker.

"You see her?" Adler asked, pushing past a soldier whose armor was half removed.

"That's her, down at the end," Stone said. "Looks like she's still sleeping."

They went down the long hall, passing a good thirty beds on either side. A nurse in white was just getting up from checking on her. She noticed both the boys approaching and nodded as she made to walk by.

"How's she doin'?" Adler asked, causing the nurse to look up hurriedly.

"She's resting," she said. "Banged up she is. Bless the stars for her. You two take care of her now, you hear? She's a hero among men. Saved us all she did. Let her rest. She's earned it." She cocked her head as she looked down at Ceres, with an admiration she made no effort to hide. Then the nurse ran off to fall into the swaying sea of medics within the room.

They both looked down at Ceres as she slept. Her head was bandaged, but her loose golden hair fanned out over the pillows like soft, curling vines. One pale arm was lifted over her head, spattered with soot. Her other arm rested over her stomach, which was contorted as her legs twisted over to her right. Neither of them spoke. She looked like an angel—a savior sent by the heavens for both of them. Indeed, she'd saved their lives in more ways than one.

She moaned, stirring as the sunlight hit the underside of her arm. Moving the arm over her eyes, she smiled as she saw them. Stone's heart swelled, and he couldn't help but smile back. Mud barked, jumped his front paws onto her, and licked her face wildly as if he hadn't seen her in years.

"Okay, okay." She laughed. "I missed ya too, boy."

The three of them looked at each other for what felt like far longer than it was.

"What're you two lookin' at?" She smiled. "Ya look like you've seen a ghost."

"Maybe we did," Stone said, sitting on the bed at her feet. Adler bounded over her and sat on the opposite side. She tucked her knees up into her chest, sitting up. "I thought you were a goner."

"I—I feel like I did die," she said. "I can't believe I'm sitting here right now with you." Her eyes narrowed, and she shot glares at both of them. "You're sure we ain't dead, right?"

Stone plopped smacks on his sides and upper arms. "Pretty sure. Hard to believe, though."

"So glad you're all right," Adler said, his voice shockingly timid to Stone.

Ceres sniffed twice. "You've been at a pub!"

"What…? No," Adler said with wide eyes, shaking his head.

"Yeah, we were," Stone said, laughing.

She scowled at Adler.

"We brought you something though," Adler said, looking bashful and revealing something from behind his back. "Took quite a while to find, actually. Not many people bake during a battle, it turns out." In his hand was a tubular, flaky crust pastry with sweet fruit jam in its center and buttercream on top.

"Well, I'm not mad at you anymore," she said, taking it and setting it on the wobbly, thin wood table next to her. "That'll be for later."

"So…" Adler said, nudging her leg under the scratchy blanket. "What happened? We thought you were gone, but then you were floating. You were flying in the air—like a bird, like a dragon!"

Stone could tell that many around them were eagerly side-eying and eavesdropping on their conversation. He didn't blame them. She was the brightest star in the night sky to everyone who lived in that city. Ceres noticed too, sighing, then clearing her throat.

"I feel like everything went away, like there was nothin' there. Nothing. Nothin' but black. No sky, no sea, no grass—it was empty. I was scared, actually. Can't describe it, really. But I was really scared. But then something sparked. Like a torch being lit, but it burned real bright—like real bright. I couldn't see nothin' but the blinding light. I couldn't look away, though. It's like it was inside o' me. The light suddenly turned blue. It looked like fire. But not like fire. More like dragonfire. I wasn't scared anymore, though. It's like it was me that was burning. I could feel my lungs full of hot air, and then I started to breathe again. First thing I saw was her, and I was looking down at her." She paused.

"Go on," Stone said.

"She looked little," Ceres said, looking down at her bobbing knees under the blanket. She didn't speak loud, but her voice carried as many in the surrounding beds had stopped their moans or pleas to listen in. People were coming into the monastery from outside, surely having heard that their savior had awoken.

"Little?" Adler said with a raised eyebrow. "Because you were flying over her?"

"No," Ceres said. "She just looked… scrawny, kinda sad. But not in a way of pity. More like she was a little lost sheep, looking into a wolf's eyes."

Stone smirked, and many murmurs rippled in the hall.

"You were the wolf," Stone said.

"I didn't mean to say it like that," Ceres said, shaking her head.

"You just meant she looked scared," Stone said.

"She was scared." A light lit Ceres as she scowled. "But I was mad—fumin' mad."

The hall went quiet then, as the nurses were first in the rows to hear the story, holding back the soldiers and citizens who were flocking in.

"I don't remember what I said, or what she said, but I put everything I had into that spell. When I say everything, I meant everything. I wanted her to hurt. I wanted her to taste the pain she made us feel. I wanted her to beg for her life, and then… I killed her."

The hall was silent—stuck in a long moment of awe where a mouse scamper would've sounded as loud as a bell's ring.

"Yes, you did," Stone said.

"Well, technically *we* did," Adler said.

Ceres smiled; not what Adler was expecting. She grabbed his hand. "Yes, we did. I wouldn't have been able to do it if it wasn't for you two."

She grabbed Stone's hand with her free hand.

"We did it."

The three of them held hands tightly. It was one of the happiest moments of Stone's life.

The applause that came after made Stone shy away from the crowd. The nurses, injured, and soldiers hollered with invigorating energy. They whistled and hollered. The trio blushed but continued to hold hands happily with each other.

One thing still stung though, something that Stone wouldn't be able to brush aside, ever—

"We've got to get Gracelyn back," he said softly. Ceres and Adler nodded in serious demeanors.

"We will," Adler said. "We can't let her and Rosen stay with those bastards."

"We'll kill them too," Ceres said, clamping down hard onto their hands. "Nothing is going to stand in our way now." Her voice lowered to a whisper. "I'm the third…"

Chapter Seventeen

✦

"Let us through, let us through..." Stone could hear Drâon's voice pushing through the crowds that had filled the monastery hall.

"You sure?" Adler whispered.

She nodded. "Sure."

A mix of emotions grew in Stone, and he looked up at the high, vaulted ceiling of the room, anxiously expecting him to come and take her away too.

Corvaire and Marilyn both pushed their way through, up to the ring of medics that stood six feet away from the three of them. The nurses would've pushed them back too, but they recognized the two. Everyone in the city knew the two from the family of Darakon, who'd helped them defeat the forces of evil that had laid siege upon the city.

"Come, the three of you," Marilyn said. Her eyes, the color of oak, beamed with life. Though her tan skin was strewn with ash and blood, her long silver hair flowed past her shoulders vibrantly. She'd come alive again—literally back from the dead to Stone, and she looked like the embodiment of one of the great soldiers they sing songs about in the late-night, musty taverns.

Adler rose, and he and Stone helped Ceres from her cot. She grimaced as they did, but they all knew that even though the battle was over—the war was still being waged, and they needed to regroup.

They left the monastery with a mixture of tears, hoorays, and cries. The elation that the mere sight of someone like Ceres to the people of the city created was magical in itself. Part of Stone was glad that the applause wasn't for him—at least all for him. He was ready to go back out into the wilds—where he was just a nobody.

"We must meet with the others," Corvaire said. Drâon, in his new armor, looked like an invincible hero from tales of old, too. His smudged face did little to hide the lights of his amber eyes—like those of a wild cat during its hunt. His muscular arms and shoulders were bare, and his tensed, veiny muscles stuck out from under the gray and black armor with golden tips on his chest. His long cape rustled behind with frayed tails.

Marilyn went to Ceres' side, helping her walk and asking her many questions. Stone and Adler walked beside, listening. Mud bounded along ahead with Corvaire. Marilyn asked her specifics about the fight with Paltereth. Quickly, Marilyn cut her off. "Do not speak of that aloud. You are no more than yourself. That much will be plain to everyone in the city. Vandress has already made that a top priority in the aftermath of the battle."

"Where are we goin'?" Adler asked Corvaire.

"Mÿthryn Palace," Corvaire said. As they walked down the road, Stone watched as it brimmed with commotion: many carrying the wounded on stretchers, others tending to those with minor injuries or those wandering, shouting out the names of those lost in the battle.

Many of the soldiers they walked past, lowered their helmets and bowed. That made Stone's stomach unsettled.

"Doesn't make me like them anymore when they're nice like that," Adler said, shaking his head. "You put those helmets back on them and put a lance under their arm and they're all the same bastards."

"Those bastards helped defend the city," Corvaire said, nodding back to the soldiers.

"Eh," Adler said. "The guild did more than they did."

"Them too," Corvaire said with a smirk.

"We couldn't have done it without them," Stone said. "Whether we like them or not. This is their home. There's nothing trivial about that. They were defending children, wives, mothers, grandmothers."

He looked hard into the faces of the worn-down men and women in armor. They'd been to the Dark Realm and back. They'd lost friends, comrades, and lovers. They'd never be the same after what they saw. Stone related to them at that moment, even with his scorn of those in armor that had done him and his friends wrong. He saw them as normal people—people who make mistakes, follow bad orders, and have to earn a living from following those bad orders. He nodded back—giving a sincere satisfaction of camaraderie to those who fought beside him.

He wasn't familiar with the Palace of Mÿthryn, but Stone knew there must be a reason they weren't going to the queen's palace. They were going south—farther into the city, and he saw the magnificent palace they were heading toward. It was one of the five vast palaces of white marble and gray stone—with spidery buttresses flowing down, making them resemble intricate mountains. The myriad of reflective windows glowed with the colors of the blue sky or the dark sea beyond.

"You think the queen's palace is gone?" Adler asked, leaning toward Stone's ear.

Corvaire groaned. "Arken's Neferian cast it to rubble."

"It will be rebuilt," Marilyn quickly added.

"Yes," Drâon said, adjusting his belt. "Aye, it will."

"Valeren is strong. It will thrive again." Marilyn scratched Ceres' sleeve, smiling.

Once they reached the outer wall of Mÿthryn, the torches had already been lit. The fading sunlight gave way to a cool air that subdued the muggy warmth that followed the battle. The many gray stone slabs that built the base of the palace were six feet wide each, and just as tall. Guards swarmed the entrance as if another siege was possible, and Stone wondered how exhausted most of them must feel. He found it hard to keep his eyelids up; especially with the wine in his belly.

Much of the walk, he thought of Gracelyn. Even after their victory, he felt empty.

Entering the palace keep, the room was square and lit by many candles. The colors of the city, violet and gold, adorned the large square room with banners, tapestries, chairs, and even the engravings on the four long tables of dark wood.

"This way," Corvaire led them. They went up a stairway on the left side of the room that rose in four flights past floors of long halls. The floor they walked on held a long hall with no other rooms, and many in plain clothes were scattered about the candlelit room. At the far end, by a hearth neck high, Stone saw Joridd and Vandress.

Joridd wore slacks and a white shirt with cuffs unbuttoned. One arm was heavily bandaged and hung from a sling. Vandress wore a purple dress with white trim, and her bare arms were layered with silver and gold bands. Her head turned to see them, with her black hair rustling at her collar. He thought she was looking at him at first, but saw her amber eyes, like that of a tigress', were looking to his left at Drâon. She feigned a smile. He didn't acknowledge it, but led them toward the two.

The room parted ways as the group walked forward. The way that people looked at Ceres then reminded Stone of how people looked at Gracelyn. It made him feel uneasy—her too, with the way she sighed at such looks.

Joridd gave a brilliant grin and he and Corvaire took each by the hand and then embraced, clapping each other on the back. Marilyn and Vandress hugged, not with excitement as the men did, but with remorse—cold and quiet.

"I'm so sorry for your loss," Marilyn said, letting their hug trickle to the two holding each other's hands out in front of them. "She was a magnificent queen and leader of men. She died how she would have wanted; fighting for her people and kingdom."

Tears fell down Vandress' face as she dropped her head, nodding. She let go of Marilyn's hands and wiped the tears away. All in the room were watching.

"Queen Velecitor will be remembered always," Vandress said, after clearing her throat. She took a glass of wine from the mantle on the hearth and held it up. "To the queen!"

"To the queen!" The room vibrated from the many voices.

Vandress took down the half-full glass of wine with a mighty gulp. She motioned for one of the attendants, pointing to the glass and to Stone and the others.

"The funeral will be in two days' time," Joridd said. "The queen will be laid to rest by our other kings and queens in the Hall of Divinity below. The ceremony will be held in Gambry Courtyard."

"Fitting place to hold it," Drâon said, accepting a glass of wine from a tray the young male attendant brought over. "After it's been cleaned up."

Hall of Divinity... that name... Oh, yeah, when we first arrived in Valeren Corvaire called it the divine city. Why?

"How's your arm?" Stone asked.

"Seen better days." He sighed.

"Does it hurt?" Ceres asked.

"The medics say it may heal," Vandress said. "In time."

Joridd held out his empty glass for the young man to refill. While the boy did, the others in the room went back to their own conversations. The mood was cheerful, but there was an aura of grievance, too. The partying was out in the streets as the moon rose, and the mead flowed. The shouting could be heard through the open windows from every direction.

"We have word that Grimdore made her way back to the Obsidian," Joridd said.

"Good," Ceres said. "She needs time to recover. Poor thing was beat up pretty good from Arken's lot."

"What about the others?" Stone asked, scratching the side of his head.

"The three of them flew into the forest."

"Together?" Stone asked. "Interesting that Belzarath went with the other two. What of Ghost? Have you seen her since the end of the battle? We haven't seen her anywhere."

Vandress sighed. "The fairy you call Ghost hasn't left the queen's side. She lays there weeping. The two had been friends all of Queen Velecitor's life."

"That must make Ghost pretty old then," Adler said.

Vandress nodded.

Glancing around the room, Stone saw the remaining mages of the Elessior standing together. Seven where there used to be thirteen. That made him remember the other mages.

"What about the three mages that fought with us?" he asked, folding his arms over his chest and shifting his weight to one side. "What do you do with them now?"

"They fulfilled their obligation," Vandress said, looking into the crackling fire. Her face lit with the orange glow and her skin glistened where tears had been wiped away. "To all our surprise. They actually held to their word. As did I."

"Where are they now?" Stone asked, looking at the fire himself.

"Gone," she said, turning her head to him. "That may not be what you want to hear, but that was my promise to them."

Stone didn't know how to take that. His arms dropped to his side. There were so many things he wanted to say: *aren't they just going to rejoin the others? How many are they going to kill? What if they train others?* But all his questions were in vain—he knew she needed to fulfill her word.

"What else was part of that bargain?" Marilyn asked, her words hard. She had no love for the other mages of the world.

"They were granted freedom from their prison here," Vandress said, standing back up straight and taking another gulp of wine. "As well as their freedom, they demanded what they'd come here for in the first place. It's the reason we fought and captured them. Originally, they came with nine, but only three were spared. After the battle, I gave to them one of the Rings of Fog."

"What?" Marilyn said, stepping forward in anger. "Why would you give *that* to one of the *Seliax*?"

"We made a bargain," Joridd said, putting up his hand to ease her. "It doesn't mean we won't get it back."

"What is a Ring of Fog?" Stone asked. He couldn't help but wonder if it was anything like the Adralite he'd carried.

"The Rings of Fog were created as a pair," Marilyn said. "They're useless on their own, but together, they allow the wearers to enter the Dream World."

"They can become Dream Walkers, like us?" Stone glanced at Vandress. "Where's the other?"

"In Dranne," Vandress said. "It's still safely there."

"Arken killed them," Stone said with his arms out. "Are you sure it's there?"

"Pike Tower is being rebuilt as we speak," Joridd said. "Stronger and better. Commander Triog was steward of

Dranne until King Gregon Tritus was crowned four days ago. Firstborn to King Bolivar and Queen Angelica. He's but seventeen, but will grow into a fine king. He knows of the powers to protect in their kingdom; that is just one of them."

"Why would they want a ring to make them Dream Walkers?" Adler asked.

Ceres nudged his arm. "They could communicate over far distances easily. That's one thing."

"That is one great power of the rings," Marilyn said. "Among others."

"That must be why you keep them separate," Adler said, scratching his thigh.

Vandress nodded.

"We'll get it back in time," Joridd said. "For now, though, we need to figure out how to get the Majestic Wilds away from Crysinthian. Even killing Arken takes a back-step from saving them."

Stone agreed with a grunt.

Chapter Eighteen

"Do we have any idea where they are?" Marilyn asked Vandress by the great hearth, which cracked and popped with flames licking at its top.

Vandress shook her head. "Not yet."

"We need to go out there now," Stone said, leaning forward in the circle of those around the fire. "We've still got the dragons. Let's go!"

Corvaire put his hand on Stone's shoulder. "Not yet."

"But they need us!"

"I know," Corvaire said, clapping his back. "There are matters here that need our attention at the moment. Sleep beckons too. Ravens have been sent all over the Worforgon. All eyes will be out for the god."

"He could be anywhere," Ceres said. "He could be in the Golden Realm for all we know."

Corvaire groaned.

"I'm not the religious type," Adler gawked, "but who would've guessed that he was real? Not only that, but he comes with a bright light and wears gold? Long white hair?" He laughed. "Bit predictable, wouldn't ya say?"

"We will discuss that matter of him later," Joridd said, rubbing his temple. "There's more to all this than is known to all those who walk among us. There will be a meeting of the high council tomorrow that you're expected to attend. The heads of the high houses of the city will be there, as well as the heads of military, treasury, health, justice, education, church, and magic." He glanced at the seven.

"A lot of political drivel," Ceres said, scowling. "Bet it'll take ten times as long to get things out as it would right here with us."

"You have no idea," Vandress said. "It's not just those heads of industry. The church is most certain to be there too."

Ceres rolled her eyes. "That's not gonna be good."

"High Priest Polav III will come in person," Vandress said. "It will... complicate matters."

"Why?" Adler asked with a bitter tongue. "There's no mystery about what *he* did. He took Gracelyn and Rosen in front of everyone."

"He's a god," Stone said to him. "People are sure to be... riled up about it."

Adler bit his tongue.

"We'll see how it plays out," Marilyn said. "After rest tonight, we'll be better acclimated to deal with whatever is laid out by the council tomorrow."

"Do you have anything for us to discuss this evening?" Joridd asked. "There are sure to be questions, perhaps more than answers so far."

Stone swallowed, clearing his throat. "Who will replace the queen?"

Joridd and Vandress looked uneasily at each other.

"We are both on the council," Vandress said. "Joridd is head of the military, and I of magic. As the queen had no heirs, by choice I will add, then her chosen successor must be voted in tomorrow. If not, then another must be chosen by

Joridd, and then voted in. It goes down the list of heads until one is voted by a two-thirds majority."

"Why didn't she have children?" Stone asked.

"Queen Velecitor chose a different path," Joridd said. "She chose no single suitor either, preferring the company of many, and picking none to bear a title."

"I like her style," Ceres said with a smirk. "She preferred to choose a ruler not bound by blood."

"So, do we know who she picked?" Adler asked, looking around the room.

Marilyn leaned in to whisper. All of them did the same, eager to hear. It seemed as though the rest of the room quieted, too.

"It is not known to all," Marilyn said, looking past them to see who was eavesdropping. "But the queen chose… Joridd to rule after her. He would move from Head of Military to King of Valeren."

King Joridd? I can't think of anyone who would deserve it more. More than those other two rotten kings, at least.

"I did not ask for it," he said. "But I will honor my queen's wishes. If that is the decision of the council."

"He won't be able to cast a vote," Marilyn said. "So, there are only six left in the council, so, four of the six will need to vote him in."

"Well, you'll vote for him," Ceres said, looking at Vandress. "Will the others?"

"We know of a couple that will," Vandress said. "But the others are tricky and easier to buy."

Stone nodded, thinking he understood what was at stake, and how the powerful wouldn't necessarily want a soldier as king. They'd want someone in their pocket. Tomorrow would be a new dawn for Valeren. Stone sincerely hoped they chose Joridd, and he decided he'd influence it that way, if he had any chance at all to do so.

"What about that snake Salus?" Adler asked. "When does he get that sword in the gut he deserves? That gets decided tomorrow too?"

"The Vile King will be put to death," Joridd said, rubbing his injured arm in its sling. "No trial is needed. The information that we may get from him will depend on the timing of his entrance to the Dark Realm."

"I'd like to speak with him," Stone said, causing Drâon and Marilyn to give each other curious glances. "He came to me to offer a bargain before. Now maybe it's time I return the favor."

"His tongue has been taken, obviously," Vandress said. "But his ears remain where they were. If you wish to see him in private, you may. He'll have his one arm to write with chalk. He will be bound, though. Salus is conniving and dangerous, all the same. We'll take no risk and use every precaution."

"I don't need to see him in private," Stone said. "Ceres and Adler will be with me."

"I think we'd all like to be there," Marilyn said. "If it's all the same to you."

"If he knows where he took Arken and our friends," Stone said, rubbing his knuckles, "then I aim to get it out of him."

"I'll arrange it for after the council meeting tomorrow," Joridd said. "He's in the lowest dungeon—with the other rats."

"What about the Neferian that he killed?" Drâon asked, surprising Stone and apparently Adler by his raised eyebrows.

"What do you mean?" Adler asked, leaning back, but with a twinkle in his eyes.

"It's your kill," Joridd said. "It's yours to do with as you please, but its immense size will surely cause some deciding soon. We don't want it rotting too long. The city of Valeren will gladly take whatever you don't desire as a trophy, and for science."

"We still don't know exactly what they are," Vandress said.

"The Dark King has tainted them in some way over his lifetime."

"They didn't learn anything from the one Grimdore killed in Dranne?" Stone asked.

"Pieces to the puzzle," Vandress said. "Hopefully we can learn more here to fill in the gaps."

"Can't carry much of that beast," Adler said. "What would you recommend?" He was asking the whole group, giving special attention to Ceres.

"Make something of the horns and teeth," she said. "Dagger? Armor?"

"Armor..." he said with a dazzling look in his eyes and his fingers outstretched. "I could be the most cold-blooded killer in the shadows, wearing Neferian armor!"

Stone rolled his eyes. "How about a set of dice?"

Adler shoved him. "Get outta here... Armor is way cooler than that child's game."

Corvaire cleared his throat loudly. More people were entering the hall. It was filling and the noise from the crowds was growing. "Perhaps you can think it over, and we can come back to it later?"

Adler blushed, but nodded.

"Anything else?" Joridd asked.

There were many things to figure out in the battle's aftermath, but Stone thought many could wait. He wanted to know what was happening with the other kingdoms, how many of the Mages of the Arcane survived, and what to do about Ceres.

"We will not speak of *you* this evening," Vandress said, as if reading Stone's thoughts, or perhaps all of theirs. Ceres shied from everyone's glances. "That will be dealt with more tomorrow."

Something suddenly jumped into Stone's mind. He thought of a way he may be able to find Gracelyn!

"What if we Dream Walk?" he asked Vandress, catching her off guard. "Can we try to find where Arken is? Or at the least, see if he's alive?"

Her lips pursed, and she scrunched her nose. "We would be alerting him to the fact that you can do that. He may use that to his advantage, but it's worth thinking about."

"With you and me together," he said. "We'd be stronger."

"He's been a Dream Walker longer than you and I have been alive; combined. The Dream World is his to walk. We are no more than pupils to the master there with him. We'd have to do it without him knowing, which would be quite tricky."

"Now, we should retire for the evening," Corvaire said, bowing. "All of us. And need I remind everyone, as everyone in this room is doubly aware—we will speak naught of her. For ears listen everywhere, and I mean *everywhere*."

Stone wanted to continue staying up, getting all the details he could about what had happened in the battle and what the plans would be moving forward—but he couldn't deny he was on the brink of exhaustion. His bones ached, the bruises on his arms throbbed, and the torn calluses on his hands from his sword stung. A warm bath and clean sheets for a victory well-earned would be more than welcome.

"C'mon," Ceres said. "Let's go back. We don't need to stay out with the rest of the city. I'm more worn out than a whore before confession."

They said their goodbyes for the evening, and they made their way back to their rooms a half mile away. Joridd insisted on guards to escort them and remain posted through the night outside. Stone, Adler, and Ceres didn't have the energy to protest. Marilyn and Drâon didn't come with them, which Stone didn't think anything of until Ceres asked about it.

"You think there was somethin' goin' on between Corvaire and Vandress?"

Stone nearly pulled the muscles in his neck, jerking his head as he did.

"What?" he asked in a high-pitched tone.

"You didn't notice anything?" Ceres asked, biting her finger.

Stone's mouth fell agape.

"Sure did," Adler said. "Definitely something in the air between them."

Stone's head swung toward Adler. "Huh?"

"The spoils of victory." Adler laughed.

Stone's shock turned to laughter too, as he put his arms over his friends' shoulders, and they walked as a trio back to their rooms.

Once there, they said nothing to the soldiers as Stone popped the latch open and let out a deep sigh. He nearly fell over as a woman appeared next to the stairs. She'd been standing there waiting, but he'd just noticed her.

"Who are you?" he asked.

"General Joridd asked that I tend to you all. There's hot bath water, clean sheets on the beds, and food and drink. Whatever you need, I'm at your service, and he wanted me to assure you that I'm discreet." Her smile was sincere on her wrinkled face.

"A bath sounds lovely," Ceres said. "If all that's ready, we won't be needin' ya to stay overnight. You can come check on us in the morning if ya need." Ceres asked kindly but firmly.

The woman's gaze darted around, but she then simply smiled and nodded. "If you need me, I'll be next door. Just ask the guards and I'll be over in no time." She bowed and left.

"Yes, a bath sounds…" Adler said as he unbuttoned his shirt.

"Hold on there, you good-for-nothin' hound!" Ceres said with arms out wide, and her face flushed.

It was so forceful and loud that Adler looked as if he wanted to melt into the floor. Stone gulped.

"What... what do you...?" he mumbled.

"Don't you be spouting on like you're gonna run off to bed and we're not gonna talk about this!"

Adler swallowed hard. He looked more nervous than if he was overrun by a dozen soldiers. His mouth was agape and sweat beaded on his brow.

"You want me to...?" Stone began.

"No. You stay right where you are," she said, looking him dead in the eyes. "I was so mad and worried I coulda strangled Arken's dragon with my bare hands!"

"I... I'm sorry..." Adler muttered. "I wasn't thinkin' about anything. I didn't want to think about nothin'..."

"Yeah, we know! So, you went to a damned whorehouse to take your mind off things!" She picked up the chair beside her, hurling it across the room. It crashed into the table at the far end, shattering glasses and knocking food and candlesticks onto the floor.

"Everything all right in there?" A man's voice called from the other side of the front door.

She didn't seem to notice.

"You were out in the streets all on your own, doin' whatever the hell ya wanted while I was in here worried sick." Her freckles burned a bright red Stone had never seen. He was so afraid to move he thought if his boot squealed on the wooden floor he might be the next to feel her fury. He slid his hands into his pockets.

"And how'd we find you? Mumbling and wet as a fish. You were stoned drunk and couldn't tell your mouth from your ass. You sure as the Dark Realm was talking from your ass."

Adler's eyes were wide in disbelief. His mouth moved like he wanted to speak, but no words came out.

"You want to go out and do that again, then don't worry

about coming back! We wouldn't even let you in the door if you begged. Right?"

Stone wanted to nod, but she didn't stop to look to see if he agreed.

"We'll leave ya in the damned alley where you belong; like a dog, no—worse than a dog. You're like a rat runnin' around out there with the tarts and beggars. Thinkin' o' no one but yerself. You get to run off and not worry about nothin' while I'm in here crying my eyes out and not able to do nothin'!"

I didn't know she was that upset...

"I—I'm sorry," Adler finally got the voice to say. "It won't happen again."

"Don't you say that! I don't want to hear sorry from your mouth." She picked up her leg and kicked the other chair next to her, slamming it into the wall, nearly tearing a curtain down as it tumbled.

There was a knock at the door, and it creaked open from the outside.

"Is everything—" the soldier asked, but was quickly cut off.

"Close that damned door!"

The door was pulled shut in a hurry, with the guard's peering eye vanishing as if out of self-preservation.

"You can say sorry by not doing that ever again. You want to go out and screw loose harlots, then don't you dare... don't you *dare* come back!"

Adler put his arms out, easing a footstep toward her, perhaps for an embrace, or just to show he truly was sorry.

"You touch me and you'll be bedridden for days. I'm not playing with you. Her fists were clenched, and she heaved breaths as she lumbered over. Her curly blond hair was frazzled, and the room looked as if a fistfight had erupted. Perhaps it was about to.

"I didn't know what to do," Adler said softly, as if fighting to say words he didn't want to. "Sometimes the memories just get to be too much. I can't be in my own body anymore. I just want to be someone else, somewhere far, far away. I don't want to remember. I don't want to even breathe. I just want nothing. I don't want to be anything or anyone. I don't want to exist anymore."

Ceres stood there still heaving—fuming—ready to pounce forward like a cat of prey, but something held back her rage.

"I don't want to hurt you," he said, "ever. I just don't know what to do. It just... hurts so much sometimes. I just hide inside the bottom of a mug until it's gone. I thought about you the whole time though..."

She lunged forward with her index finger pointed at him and her lips pursed in anger. Tears were beading at the corners of her eyes.

"Don't say it. Don't you *dare* say that."

"I did. I thought about you the whole time. You and Stone, you're all I've got. I'm nothin' without ya. The guild means nothing, this war means nothing. There's nothin' worth fighting for without you. You're all I've got, and to know that I upset you, made me want to shrivel up even more."

I've never seen him so... small before. Big and boisterous Adler is about to grovel at Ceres' feet, asking for forgiveness. I love both of them so much. I don't know if I could go on either without them...

"I won't say sorry again if you don't want me to. But I need ya to forgive me," he cried. "I can't be the bad guy. I just can't with you. We've all been through so much together. The last thing I want is to add more sadness and tears to what we gotta go through. So, I'm sorry. I'm really sorry."

Her lips quivered and tears flowed down her cheeks to her chin. "No, I'm sorry."

Stone felt his eyes water, and he choked down his tears.

"It wasn't your fault," she said. Adler sank to the floor, bending at his knees, tucking into a ball. She fell to her knees, with her face inches from his. "What he did to you, you didn't deserve. No boy deserves that." Adler sobbed into his sleeve. "No kid deserves that. He was evil. He was an evil man."

"Doesn't matter," Adler said into his sleeve. "He's dead now. I killed him. I know he deserved to die. Even with him dead though, why does he haunt me? Why can't I just forget? I want to be able to close my eyes without seeing his face, or smelling his breath. What do I have to do?"

"I don't know," Ceres said softly. He lifted his head, and she wiped away his tears. "But we'll figure it out together." Stone wiped his tears away, kneeling down too. He nodded. "One thing, though. Do me a favor… don't go running off like that again, or I'll have to cut your head off."

ADLER LAUGHED, clearing his throat thick with mucous. "You're kidding, right?"

"I don't think she is," Stone said. "Better do what she says."

He nodded.

"How'd you do it?" Ceres asked.

"What?" Adler asked.

"How'd ya kill Armonde?"

Adler swallowed. "The only way he taught me to kill without too many questions being asked… poisoned his wine."

"Oh," Ceres said, covering her mouth. "That makes sense, I suppose."

"I had to get a recipe from outside the guild." Adler's demeanor grew serious. "Don't tell the others. Especially the Guild Master. They don't look kindly down on those who go to witches."

"I won't," Stone said. "You had to do what you had to."

Ceres nodded. "I've probably done worse things than that just to eat."

"Just don't tell no one," Adler said. "Promise me."

"I promise," Stone said.

"Promise too," Ceres said. "Now, go clean up that mess I made and take your bath. You stink…"

She stood up, kissed the top of his head, and walked casually to one of the bathrooms.

"I thought she was going to kill you," Stone said, standing.

"Me too," Adler said. "All the ways I coulda died these last few months. That was probably the one way I'd least expect, but most deserved."

"You're all right," Stone said with his hand out. "You know that? We make a good team."

Adler took his hand. "Glad we met." Then their hands returned to their sides, and they went their separate ways, each to the other two rooms with hopefully warm baths.

Stone turned to him just before they entered the two rooms.

"She really is frightening, isn't she?" he said.

"I'd rather be locked in a room with a *dragon* than with *her like that* for *ten seconds*."

Chapter Nineteen

Just after the break of dawn, and Ceres could get her fill of fried bread heaping with powdered sugar—they entered back into the hall of Mÿthryn. The hearth smoldered from the night prior, and the candles were extinguished. The thick smell of smoke soaked deep into the curtains that were pulled back from the windows filled Stone's nostrils, just behind the aroma of flowers that were scattered on the long table before the hearth.

Sunlight beamed down onto the long table fitted with twelve chairs on the hearth's side. Another fifty or so chairs were arranged at the back end of the room, by the entrance. They were already filled, and many more people stood along the walls and corners of the rectangular room. The sigil of Valeren tussled above the table in the morning breeze that skirted through the room—a golden squid wrapping its tentacles around a white cross upon a violet cloth. The sunlight hit it with a divine touch.

All eyes were upon Stone, Ceres, and Adler as they entered. Mud ran ahead and lay next to Corvaire after he petted the dog's head. Drâon wore a white, loose-fitted shirt with the cuffs rolled up to his elbows, was clean-shaven, and had his black hair tied back. Vandress sat next to him. Her green dress sparkled in the sunlight, twinkling like a diamond from the silver seams. Her arms were bare and her ringed jewelry hung along her forearms, her hair was down and its tips kissed her collarbones.

Marilyn sat proudly on the other side of her brother. She wore a formal dress of red with violet wings at the shoulders and down the arms to her fingers. Her hair was pulled up and had been done exquisitely by someone else as it was braided and wrapped in a fine fashion. She sat with her back straight and her arms folded on her lap.

Stone knew Corvaire and Marilyn weren't members of the council, but they were important enough to sit at their table.

Where's Conrad? Stone looked around, not seeing him in the crowd behind. *He should be here for this.*

Marilyn ushered them to sit beside her, where three empty seats rested. They sat, sensing the room rustle as they did so. He shimmied in his seat uneasily.

"We haven't had the best luck with these kinds of audiences," Adler said across Ceres to both of them.

"Shh," said Ceres. Adler sat back, crossed his arms, and lifted a leg over the other.

Down the row of chairs were Adler, Ceres, Stone, Marilyn, Drâon, Vandress, Joridd, and four others—the heads of the other institutions of Valeren: two women and two men; one with a belly that folded over the table. One seat was left empty at the far end, and Stone guessed it was the priest waiting to make an entrance. He didn't have to wait long to be proven right.

An entourage entered the room. They wielded crucifixes, were adorned in gold, wore tall hats of blue and white, and had long robes of ivory. At their center was an aged man with a round face, thick neck, thin lips, plump nose, and dark eyebrows. He wore spectacles and had an eerie calm about him. His eyes were dark behind the round spectacles, and he had no hair poking out from under his clear-seawater blue and gold hat that rose to a rounded point.

The room quieted as the man, who was quite towering, made his way to the table, and sat in the chair that was pulled and pushed in for him. A servant of the council placed a pitcher of liquid by him, which Polav pushed away with two fingers.

"That's him," Marilyn said in a quiet voice.

"Who are the others?" Stone tightened his hair that was pulled back at the top of the back of his head.

"Head of treasury Roen Nitherblin, Blithe Gould of education, Magistrate Cleon Hemeond, and Hugh Wordmoth of health. Very important people who would all like very much to meet you."

"I've seen some of them before," Stone said. "They were around when we met with the queen."

Joridd stood and Stone sat back to listen.

Joridd cleared his throat and spoke. "This is a meeting of the high council to determine the next king or queen of the greatest of cities, Valeren. All in attendance will remain quiet or will be dismissed from the room." He presented each of the members of the council one by one, and each bowed their head as he did so. High Priest Alexander Polav III did not, nor did he blink. His dark eyes pierced into Stone's.

"A majority vote will determine the next king or queen," Joridd said, sitting.

An attendant rose from the side of the room. He wore a suit of velvet purple and had a plumed hat. He puffed out his chest, unrolled a scroll, and read a lengthy proclamation in an old, long-winded dialect that made Stone's knee bob. He went through court-like decrees and said names Stone had never heard and probably would never have heard. It seemed to be a never-ending setup to what should be a quick, albeit extremely important, vote. Stone heard Ceres' loud breathing next to him, so he poked her with his elbow, and she stirred awake.

Finally, he handed that scroll to another attendant, unrolling another smaller one from the waist-high podium beside him. He walked over and presented it for each of the members of the council to inspect. One by one, they read it and nodded in approval for the next to read. Once it got to Polav, he didn't nod, but snorted and scowled at Joridd.

The attendant went to the center of the room, just in front of Mud, who lay on his side, stretching his legs out.

"That's Jarquiose Pentothine," Marilyn whispered. "Constable of the high court."

"Queen Bristole Velecitor, may her blessed soul rest well with the mighty kings of Valeren, named General Joridd of House Boulme, her successor. This document has been inspected and approved as the true word and wish of the queen."

Vandress didn't stand, but leaned forward and spoke loudly. "Since Commander Joridd is one of the council, his vote will not be counted. Therefore, a majority of four will still be required, but out of six and not seven."

"General Joridd, do you have anything to add before we vote?" Head of Education, Blithe Gould, a strict-seeming elderly woman, asked.

Murmurs echoed throughout the hall, as Marilyn had said the night before, that not all knew he was the one chosen by the queen.

"You are to remain quiet," Jarquiose said loudly from his thin frame. "Those who interrupt will be ejected from his hall." The murmurs hushed.

Joridd stood. "I did not ask to be named the queen's choice. But I loved our queen, as did all of you. Therefore, I will honor and respect her wish. I speak of my accolades if only to serve my queen in her death. I did not win the battle for us." Stone looked at his arm still hanging from the sling. "All that fought so bravely did, together. I'll fight and die for this city and its people any and every day I have the privilege to. I fear no evil that comes to sink its claws in her, and I will fight to preserve the valor of the Vlaer that honor her. I've long served Queen Velecitor, Valeren herself, and her people. I solemnly swear I do everything until my last breath to continue to serve her. If it is the wish of this honorable council, then I will accept the crown." He sat.

Many stirred in the crowd, whispering to one another.

Marilyn whispered to the three of them, "We have Vandress', Blithe's, and Roen's votes assured, but we don't know the men's."

"We only need one," Stone said eagerly.

Vandress stood. "Before the vote, I want to sternly remind all in this room of that which is not to be spoken of, even in the privacy of your own houses. This is the law and of most urgent importance."

Stone and Adler both looked at Ceres, and most gazes drifted to her. Her golden hair fell in front of her face as she shied away from those staring.

Jarquiose, with the purple plume blowing above his hat, adjusted his tight-fitted, button-up vest and said, "General Joridd, your vote will not be counted, as you are the queen's chosen." Stone saw Joridd wink at his three children in the front row—two boys and the eldest daughter, who sat with her chest nearly touching her knees, looking down at the floor. The two boys fidgeted in their seats.

"Vandress of house Constance, Matron of Magic," Jarquiose said. "Do you wish for Joridd of house Boulme to become King of Valeren, protector of our great and divine city?"

She rose and her words echoed throughout the chamber. "I do. I pledge my loyalty to King Joridd of house Boulme."

Even though Stone knew how she was going to vote, the hairs on the back of his neck straightened tight.

"Very well," Jarquiose said, turning his attention to the next at the table after Joridd. "Ministress of the Treasury, Roen Nitherblin, do you wish for Joridd of house Boulme to become King of Valeren, protector of our great and divine city?"

Roen stood, middle-aged with gray-blond hair cut to the bottom of her ears, and spoke. "I do. I, too, pledge my loyalty to King Joridd of house Boulme." She turned and bowed to him, and he lowered his head to her.

"Headmistress of Education, Blithe Gould," Jarquiose said. "Do you wish for Joridd of house Boulme to become King of Valeren, protector of our great and divine city?"

The elderly woman stood slowly with the help of her cane. "I do." She nodded to him, and he did the same. She sat as the room hummed and buzzed.

"That's three," Stone muttered to himself. He felt Ceres and Adler on the edges of their seats. "Just one more."

"Alcalde of Justice, Magistrate Cleon Hemeond," a man in the black garb that a justice would wear, with black wig hairs sticking out from under his black cap, and far too old for the dyed black hair on his chin stood. "Do you wish for Joridd of house Boulme to become King of Valeren, protector of our great and divine city?"

Stone's palms wetted. He could feel the sweat squeeze between the cracks in them.

"No." Magistrate Cleon said, sitting. Causing a ruckus in the room.

"Quiet, quiet!" Jarquiose said, motioning for the Vlaer placed around the room to stir, quieting the crowd. "Remain quiet or all will be removed from the hall. Now, Minister of Health, Hugh Wordmoth, do you wish for Joridd of house

Boulme to become King of Valeren, protector of our great and divine city?"

The man stood, lifting his belly off the table, and Stone had a sour taste in his mouth. Hugh Wordmoth wore a fine jacket of gray suede and tufts of white plumed silk rolling out from under it, covering his plump hand. His eyes were beady and sweat glistened on his brow. He had a smile he was trying desperately to cover up.

Oh no…

He glanced down at the high priest next to him.

"No," Hugh said, wiping his brow, letting his smile show, and sitting down with a plop in his seat.

A great commotion blew through the crowd.

"Charlatan!" one man yelled.

"Coward," another did.

"Traitor!" one yelled from the far end.

"Sit! Calm down or…" Jarquiose yelled as the Vlaer stirred, forming a line between the crowd and the council. "Quiet down, quiet down!"

Stone didn't know what to do as he watched Polav stand, adjusting his robes. "I vote against," he said while shifting out of his chair, seemingly ready to leave with the security of his entourage.

"What's that mean?" Ceres asked with her hand on her cheek. "Is that it, then?"

Stone looked at Joridd, who seemed unshaken, but his children standing and yelling as two of the Vlaer ushered them to the side of the room, away from the shouting crowd.

"Do something," Adler said to Marilyn, but looking for answers from any of them. She, Corvaire, and Vandress all just sat, watching as Polav moved to leave the table. Yet, just before he moved away, his towering presence bent over, pressed his knuckles onto the table, leaned forward, and with a bitter demeanor, said, "I'll die before I live to see the day *you* become king."

"He saved your ass!" Stone said, stirring from his seat. "I didn't see you out there fighting for your city!"

"Heathen!" Polav shouted back. "The battle is over. There's no war now, and Valeren needs no warmongering king!"

Stone's head swelled with anger, and Ceres rose next to him.

"He took Gracelyn!" Stone spat. "He took Rosen too against their wills!"

Polav gestured something over his chest and glanced above him. "His will be done," he said softly.

Stone was so angry and baffled, no words found their way out of his mouth.

"Easy," Marilyn said with a soft touch on his hand.

The entourage moved to Polav, to take him away.

"He can't do that," Stone said, shaking his fists. "We can't let him do that."

Jarquiose spoke, "The vote is not a majority vote, and this council will reconvene tomorrow for another vote of second in line." The room was so loud he was hardly audible.

"Wait, you," Stone yelled, but Polav paid him no attention, and started to walk away from the table.

"Hold," Vandress said, rising, with a stern voice at Polav, who minded her and turned a casual eye on her.

"This council is over," he snapped. "Joridd will not be king."

"The vote was a tie," she said. "He hasn't lost yet."

Polav looked around at the surrounding eight, and at the two heads still seated next to him. "There was no majority vote. The council meeting is adjourned until tomorrow." He smirked and cocked his head.

"There's one more head to vote," she said, smirking back.

"What's the meaning of this?" he shouted, waving his finger and pointing feverishly at her. "General Joridd is exempt from the vote, thou that is being voted upon sets their vote aside."

"He's right!" Hugh Wordmoth of health said, getting to his feet.

"I'm not referring to Joridd," she said, waving her finger back at them. The room had slowly noticed the commotion at the table and forced one another quiet to listen. The Vlaer listened eagerly too.

"The vote is over," Polav said. "There is no other vote."

Vandress turned her head and nodded to Drâon.

Stone's head tingled with swimming emotions. He had no idea what was going on.

Drâon Corvaire stood. As unexpectedly as it was, the room was so silent that a mouse scurrying in the corner would draw much attention.

"The house of Darakon has no pull on this council," Polav said. "They're lucky to have even been invited into the room!"

Corvaire pulled out a scroll from his pocket and held it out for Jarquiose, Constable of the High Court. Jarquiose raised an eyebrow, glancing at Polav and back to the scroll.

"What game is this?" Polav said. "I demand this council be dismissed." He rustled his collar and made his way to leave.

"You'll want to stay for this," Corvaire said. "High priest…"

"What're you doin'?" Stone asked. "What is that?"

Marilyn winked. "One last wish."

Jarquiose took the scroll, examining it. "It's the queen's crest," he said, causing another stir in the room.

Polav turned back. His face was fuming mad and flush red, but he held his tone, showing restraint for the fallen queen's respect.

The constable broke the seal, unrolled the parchment, and read down the list quickly. His fingers rose to his lips.

The heads of justice and health were both sweating profusely, and Hugh fanned his face with a fan he plucked from the table.

"It's from the queen," Jarquiose said, his feet in their fancy black leather boots shifting around nervously. "This letter is intended in the matter of the High Council. I scribe this with Drâon and Marilyn of the House of Darakon as its witnesses. They are trusted, dear friends from many years of trust and virtue. This is an aside to my will and testament, and only to be read in the occurrence of my death in the battle being held at our gates from the invasion of Arken Shadowborn and the Neferian dragons. Should I fall, and should the vote of faith in my chosen successor, General Joridd of House Boulme, come to a tie—I order a law that is written into my will and testament to come into law immediately upon reading."

"The queen has no authority to enact laws post-mortem," Polav shouted.

"This law would be effective retroactively to the time of its inscription and signing," Jarquiose said, looking to Magistrate Hemeond. "Is this not correct?"

Magistrate thought carefully, and not acknowledging the high priest, said. "That is correct. The law would go into accordance retroactively to the time of the document's creation."

Polav threw his hands up and scoffed.

"Continue, please," Marilyn said.

"...Immediately upon reading. That a new head of council be introduced, and their vote counted as a whole."

"This cannot be!" Polav slammed his hands on the table.

"The Chancellor of the Populous position is created and introduced," Jarquiose read, creating a stir and causing him to smile uncontrollably. "Far too long has the voice of the common people of this great, divine city been without a true vote at the table. Now the table sits with eight heads. Effective immediately, and without his knowledge..."

The room shot silent, with every ear eager to hear what was next, including Stone's.

Jarquiose's eyes grew wide and his face paled. "The position of Chancellor of Populous be given to Conrad Galveston of the Guild of Assassins."

Shock washed through the room.

"That murderer?" one man said.

"Praise him!" said another.

Conrad? He's an assassin! Not a public figure! He'll never...

A divide in the crowd parted as Conrad stood from his seat deep within the crowd, and he walked forward with many slack-jawed, unable to take their gazes away.

Jarquiose continued, "For his part in the winning, and we will win!, of the battle, I give this invaluable voice to him. He is wise and virtuous. A natural leader among men, I hope the people of Valeren grow to trust him as I do. In my will and testament, it is laid out that each successor of this position will be voted upon by the people themselves, so that they may have a say in the tidings of their great city. Queen Bristole Velecitor."

Polav fumed as his dark gaze followed Conrad as he walked to the center of the hall, and Mud ran up to him. Conrad was in clean, dark leather armor that formed well to his body, and looked like strong muscles under his dark cloak. His gray hair blew at his shoulder.

"There's a note at the bottom from the queen," Jarquiose said. "May the swinging dicks of the council be welcoming to one more."

Ceres' hands shot up to her mouth as she burst out laughing.

Corvaire laughed deeply. Marilyn looked at him as if he was a child. "I didn't know she put that in there, did you?"

Polav stormed past the Vlaer and left.

"I accept the position," Conrad said in a loud voice. "I'll serve to the best of my ability." He winked at Stone. "And I, of course, vote in favor of King Joridd!"

Stone threw his hands up above him and kissed Ceres on the cheek as Adler hollered and jumped up and down. The room erupted in hoorahs and shouts of celebration. Cleon and Hugh looked as if they wanted to melt into the floor. The Vlaer—normally stoic and strong—couldn't help but yell out in excitement.

"All hail King Joridd," Vandress said, kneeling beside him.

"King Joridd," Marilyn and Drâon said, kneeling. Cleon and Hugh did the same. Stone, Ceres, Adler, and Conrad followed. Soon the whole room shouted with hails, and many eyes were upon Polav, who was just about to reach the door at the far end. It was only Joridd, and he and his entourage left standing.

Polav snorted, dipping to a knee briefly, and then stormed off out of the room. The entourage knelt gracefully and then filed out of the room.

"You may rise," King Joridd said with his arms out and his children ran into them. "Now, we have much to do."

Chapter Twenty

He said there was work to be done, but Stone didn't think Joridd took into account the amount of celebration that was involved in the crowning of a new monarch. Word spread quickly.

Bells rang from tall towers, trumpets blew, children danced, and the streets flooded with those who could bear the bright sunlight from the prior night's celebrations. Joridd had won them the war, him and Vandress, whether he wanted to admit it or not. He was a true savior, possibly losing an arm for it, and he was loved.

Stone, Ceres, and Adler left Mÿthryn Tower shortly after they realized they wouldn't be needed by the droves of people that swarmed the new king and Vandress. The Vlaer were left to organize the room back into chaos and protect their new king. Conrad, too was bombarded, especially by the two men at the council who remained. Polav made his leave, most likely back to his cathedral—Rōthengâl.

"We'll meet back up with them later," Adler said, running backward in front of them. "You know where I want to go, right?"

"Obviously." Ceres rolled her eyes. "Any tavern."

"No! I want to see my kill!"

"Let's go then!" Stone said.

"They better be protecting it," Adler said. "If I have to fight anyone back, I'm just gonna start swinging!"

Adler had a wild exuberance in his eyes as he jumped up and down.

He deserves this. He's the first person to ever kill one of them!

"You know I'm gonna be famous now, right? Maybe not as famous as you..." he pointed to Stone. "But famous enough that I'm gonna have songs sung about me. That's for sure. Don't know about statues yet though. What's the rule? Gotta be at least a decade?"

Ceres stopped following him, folding her arms over her chest. "You going to act like this all the way there? I want to see it too, but if you're gonna act like a child, I'm just gonna go back."

He ran to her side, grabbing her arm, pulling her forward.

"C'mon, you know I'm just playing," he said.

"Sure you are," Stone said with a laugh.

"I can't help it," he said. "You know me by now. Let me have this one. It's a pretty big deal, after all. I killed one. I can kill more!"

They walked back down toward Gambry Courtyard, toward the entrance to the city—and to where the battle was fought hardest. Celebrations quieted behind, blood stains darkened, and the crows swarmed. Many of the dead were yet to be moved still, and by the time they made it to the courtyard, the smell was all but overwhelming. Stone covered his mouth and nose with the collar of his linen shirt. Dragonfire and burnt skin and bone wafted in the air that carried no breeze with it. The sun beamed down from above—hot and humid in the thick air. Many gagged and vomited.

What shocked Stone—and what never occurred to him—was

the number of people *other* than the soldiers and onlookers. Artists. There were rows and rows of busy artists. They sat behind aisles, painting with smooth brushstrokes, they carved madly at clay, and they sketched with inked quills on paper. Most wore masks to deal with the stench, while adorned in much more lavish colors and decor than the vast majority of people they'd seen in *any* city.

"They must've come from everywhere," Adler said. "They should be paying me for this…"

Apprentices rushed in and out of the rows of painters and sculptors, while the ones painting barked orders.

"They'll have to remember this the way it is while it's still fresh," Ceres said, then pointing to the other side of the dragon. "They're scribing over there; they must be the historians. That guy way over there with the lute. He's writing songs! This is wild!"

A young lad no older than eight ran up to them. "S'cuse me, sir." He said, trying to catch his breath. "My master would love to paint your portrait, should you be so kind."

"Your master?" Ceres asked.

"Jacque D'Lacey! You've surely heard of him?" The boy's eyes were wide, sincere, and inviting.

"Jacque D'Lacey wants to paint *me*?" Adler said. Stone was surprised by the amount of interest he had, but he'd also never heard the name.

"He'll pay," the boy said.

Adler cleared his throat and collected himself.

Stone and Ceres walked away while he chatted with the boy, surely bargaining a price.

"Look at it," Stone said in awe. "It's incredible."

Ceres' head spun.

"What do you mean, incredible? The thing was gonna kill us!"

"It's magnificent," he said, taking slow steps toward it.

The four soldiers guarding it bowed their heads, letting them pass.

The Neferian's head, alone on its side, was taller than Stone as he pressed his palm against its rough scales. His fingertips slid along its nostril and down its lip. Its eye was translucent, half-open and its normal brilliant red hue faded to the color of a pink pig's skin.

Ceres tugged on one of the horns on its head, not budging the heavy monster. "We're *sure* it's dead, right?"

Stone smirked.

"Four to go now," she said, knocking its scales with her fist. They both stepped onto its thick, wings' webbing that resembled a ship's sails, folding over itself. The specks of gold they'd seen from a distance then looked like the yellow eggs of a large bird with orange hues. Stone had to lift his knees high to step over parts of it. They examined its long, sinewy arm that held the wing from its underside, trailing all the way to the hand—dark with sharp scales, three fingers, and a thumb each with long claws like spikes that would hold down a great canopy over a small town.

"Four seems like a lot," Stone said, kicking the dead dragon's claws with his boot.

"We've got four," Ceres said.

Stone sighed, looking south to the Obsidian. "We're going to need her soon."

Ceres put her hands behind her back as they continued walking, inspecting the dragon. They came to the bolt protruding through its neck. Dried blood cracked in the sunlight from its sharp tip.

"We'll give her as long as we can," she said.

"I fear it won't be long enough," he said. "They're out there. Gracelyn and Rosen. They're out there with *him*. Crysinthian might be held to reason with, but Arken is too dangerous to be left with them. He killed the old Majestic Wilds; he killed them right in front of us."

"I remember," she groaned. "Still have that moment in my dreams." She paused their walk. "Why do ya think we'll be able to reason with Crysinthian?"

"Because I don't know what else we'd be able to do," he said, scratching his thigh. "He's a god. Not sure there's anything we could do about it. You saw him on the battlefield. He could've killed anything he chose, but instead, he decided to take the strongest of all and take them with him—to start whatever new world he decided. He's probably listening to this conversation as I say it."

She sighed, looking up at the cloudless, bright sky. "You think he took them up to the Golden Realm?" She shook her head. "I still can't believe it's all real—that he's real."

"He's real," Stone growled. "And it's all gotten very real."

They heard a commotion from behind, and turning, they saw not only the artists' apprentices scrambling to meet the demands of their masters, but a single emissary in ivory robes running at them. The soldiers guarding the dragon behind held a brief word with the man in his thirties, and then let him pass.

The man ran fast through Gambry, but didn't miss a breath as he came up to them.

"Lords Stone and Ceres Rand," he said in a cold, emotionless voice.

Ceres snickered.

"High Priest Alexander Polav the third invites you to a luncheon with him in the Cathedral of Rōthengâl. It will be a private affair, and casual." He put extra emphasis on that word. "The luncheon will begin at two o'clock. Please don't be late, wear nice shoes, and," he feigned a fake laugh, "don't worry about inviting others, as they've already received formal invitations."

"That means it's just us," Ceres said, crossing her arms and shifting her weight to one side. She brushed her hair behind her ear. "Polav doesn't want our friends there? Wonder why?"

"High Priest Alexander Polav the third eagerly awaits and expects your company," he said, bowing low, seeming to inspect their current footwear of choice. "I'll tell him he'll be seeing you at two, with clean shoes." He turned and made his way with a quick walk west, out of Gambry. Adler was looking over his shoulder at the man as dozens were painting him with his Masummand Steel sword twinkling at his side in the sun's rays. The dark dragon lay surely in the background of all those paintings.

"Didn't even wait for a word from ya," Ceres scoffed, spitting on the ground. "We gonna go? That's probably in an hour's time."

"No," Stone said, looking down at his boots. "They aren't that dirty, are they?"

"I think they expect formal wear," she said, kicking his boot with hers. "Tan leather isn't the most elegant thing for a *high priest*. He's not gonna look kindly on us not showin' up at all. He's a serious man."

"What's he going to want to talk to us about?" said Stone. "We've got more important things to figure out, rather than sitting around drinking fine wine talking about praising the man who took our friends."

"Well, in his defense, it's not a *man* that took them."

"You know what I mean," he said with a sneer.

"He might have some information about how to deal with him," Ceres said. "There's a tiny, *tiny* chance he may want to help."

"Any man that hellbent on trying to keep Joridd from being the successor to Bristole holds no honor to me," Stone said. "And the older I get, the more important that virtue becomes to me. We've come too far to waste time quarreling about politics with false monarchs."

"If we're lucky, ya know," she said, "there will be a time when that will be a hefty part of your life." She laughed.

"What do you mean?" He scratched his chin.

"I mean, if we don't get incinerated in dragonfire, or decapitated by some of Arken's men, or get blown to pieces by the one god who was revealed to actually be real."

"Yeah," he said in a playful voice. "We're doomed."

"We're absolutely doomed." She giggled. In the sunlight, her moss-colored eyes and golden hair sparkled. Her freckles were rosy on her clean cheeks and her smile warmed his heart.

"Wouldn't rather be riding off to oblivion with anyone else," he said.

She turned to him, reached out, and grabbed his hands in hers. "Me too. There's no way we're making it out of this alive. But we are going to save them."

He nodded, tugging at her hands. "Yes, we are going to save them. No matter what it takes. And I'm going to kill Arken. The Worforgon will know peace again when he's gone. I'm ready to give my life, if that's what it takes."

"If anyone can kill him," she said, shaking his hand. "It's you. You are the one from the prophecy Seretha spoke of. It's got to be you."

They released their hands and watched the hundreds of people then, painting, writing songs, sculpting, and scribbling away.

"I wonder what sorts of sweets we're gonna be missin' out on," she said.

"We'll find you some other stuff somewhere," he said, smiling. "I promise."

"Bet they won't be as good as pious sweets, though," she said. "Bet they taste divine…"

He rolled his eyes and nudged her shoulder with his.

"Adler would've liked that one," he said. "Remind me to tell him."

"Not sure if we'll get a word in with him today," she said. "He's going to be too busy talking about all the women he's going to get from killing this."

"Pretty sure he's only got eyes for you," Stone said.

She shoved him away instinctively, with a furrowed brow and shock in her eyes. "What are you goin' on about? Don't say things like that. That's disgusting!"

Stone smirked. "You like each other. It's okay."

She balled her fist and held it between them, shaking it.

"Careful, just because you warmed me up with buddy talk, doesn't mean I won't break your damn nose!"

"Okay, okay, forget I said anything." His hands were up as if surrendering.

"That's just disgusting." She had a forced look, as if she'd just eaten something sour.

He said slowly, "I'm just saying... I don't think I've ever seen you as mad at anything as when he..."

"You say it," she snapped, "and those might be your last words."

Hands up again, he walked beside her and didn't utter another word.

"That's right," she said with finality.

Chapter Twenty-One

⚜

The remainder of the day after visiting the site of the dead Neferian was spent hiding somewhat from those beckoning for their attendance from Polav—the door had people finally stop knocking just before sundown.

Stone didn't care about any consequences that might produce. He was far more worried about Gracelyn. Even as his bones and muscles ached, and his eyelids weighed like bars of iron, every time he closed his eyes, he thought of her. He tossed and turned in the night, and his soft linen sheets scratched against his bare skin.

They'd stayed in their room most of the night, as now everywhere they went people would come up to them with thanks, cheers, or sad stories of those they lost. It weighed heavily on Stone—even Adler didn't know what to say a lot of the time—if he could get a word in anyway. Things had gotten to the point where all Stone wanted to do was leave. Joridd was to be crowned king after the funeral, and he could rebuild and reshape his city. The forests and the plains called for Stone—and he longed for them.

As he lay with his eyes closed, facing the window in his

room with the curtain closed in front of it; blowing from the whistling breeze from its thin slit to let in the cool air—he heard a soft knock on the door.

It was so soft he wouldn't have heard it if he were asleep, and it was delicate enough that it didn't even stir Mud. That much was evident by his nails scratching along the floor as he bounded toward hares in his dreams. Stone usually guessed those were what he was chasing after.

He cleared his dry throat, took a sip of water from the side table next to him, swung his feet to the side of the bed, and went to open the door. His fingers grabbed the cool metal latch, and he twisted it open. It squealed on the hinges as it swung open. He expected to find Ceres, but she wasn't there.

There was nobody there. Leaning out the door, he looked down both sides of the hallway, seeing no one. He shrugged it away, spinning back toward the bed. As the door closed, he didn't hear a latch. Sitting on the bed again, he felt the tickle of grass blades between his toes. Next to him on the floor lay Mud, but it wasn't Mud. It was a spotted doe sleeping soundly. Its fur was silky as he petted it.

The four walls of his bedroom were replaced by a distant darkness—damp and hollow, as if in a dripping cave. There were no winds to speak of, just the stagnant, thick air. Beads of water clung to the bed he sat upon, with sparse grass protruding from its rocky deposits.

He felt deep exhaustion, yet he was alert. The doe's head popped up, and its ears shifted around. Its dark eyes scanned the darkness around, as Stone slid his hand to his hip, only to find a scabbard with no sword in it. He rose slowly. His black hair wasn't pulled back as normal. It fell loosely at his shoulders, and he had to brush it away from in front of his eyes.

"You out there?" he asked. "I know it's you. I can feel you out there."

A figure slunk in from the darkness. It was shadowy with

wisps of black smoke-like clouds wafting behind it as it slid forward unnaturally. It stopped where the door would be.

"You felt me? How curious," the figure said. His voice was low and broke like grinding rocks.

"I knew you'd show," Stone said. "Just didn't know when—Arken."

He smirked with his stretched, scarred, ashen skin tightening. His one eye glowed with an inner, faint white light in the darkness. Black hair flowed down both sides of his face, just as Stone's was. The double-horned helmet wasn't on his head, and he wore a long black cloak, only showing his strong shoulders beneath.

"Tell me, how did you kill Salus and the others? I want to know…"

"Where are you?" Stone shouted. "Where are they? Are they harmed? Did you hurt them?"

"Careful now," Arken said. "Get your heart in the wrong place, and it may distract you from what's most important."

"I don't want to hear your lying words," Stone said, clenching his fists.

"The battle was won, because you still draw breath," Arken said, scowling, "but the war rages. Forces have come I never dreamt would enter, have come. My plans have changed, and yours needs to, as well."

"I haven't forgotten what you've done," Stone said. "Just because Crysinthian has come doesn't mean you get to walk away from all the pain you've caused."

"My retribution and revenge are my own," Arken sneered, turning his gaze down, and clenching his teeth. "My revenge is nearly fulfilled, but won't be complete until all the Worforgon is rebuilt."

"How many have to die for that to happen?" Stone asked, shaking his head.

Arken's eye narrowed. "As many as it takes. None of these

people will be remembered in a hundred years. But you will... and *I* will."

"Where is she?" Stone glowered.

"I could see you had feelings for her the moment I saw you last, on the battlefield. The way you looked at her, the sparkle in your eyes. You *love* her."

"Shut your mouth," Stone spat. "You know nothing about me."

"It's not wise to love a Majestic Wild," he said. "Their duty is to protect the lands, and while you grow old, decrepit, and aged—she will remain her beautiful self in her youth. You'll die, and she'll mourn you for ages."

"She wouldn't have to be an Old Mother if you hadn't killed Seretha, Gardin, and Vere."

"As I said, my revenge is almost done," Arken growled.

"They're all dead now," Stone said. "Everyone who had to do with the Shadow Purge is gone."

"Those who attempted to wipe out my people that night are dead and gone, yes," he said. "But I can't forget that night. Every time I close my eye I see my people screaming. I see them run through by those following their king's and queen's orders. I cannot forget, and I won't let their memories fade away." He looked past Stone, over the shoulder, as if speaking to someone else. "I loved them, you know. I loved the Old Mothers." His gaze turned down and his voice soured. "But they betrayed me."

"They didn't betray you... you betrayed them!"

Arken scowled in anger at him.

"What do you know about it? You know nothing!" Dark spit flung from the Dark King's lips.

"I know that I'm the one who's going to stop you," Stone said, pulling his shoulders back and raising his chin.

"That's what the Old Mothers told you, eh? From their prophecy?" He furrowed his brow. "The dead will kill me?"

Stone scowled back, hunching his shoulders, wishing his sword was at his hip.

"You were dead," the Dark King said. "Very dead. That must plague your thoughts much… not knowing who you were before the ground, before your grave. Lucky for you that your friend came by when she did and dug you up." He turned sideways with his eye dimming from soft white to black. "So many questions. Yet I have all the answers. Come to me, Stone. I'm not this cold-hearted demon they portray me to be. My dragons are the mighty Wyverns of the Bright Isles. They are no Neferian." He spat in anger. "They mean as much to me as any of my people. Vorraxi and I have been through much together. He's grown more powerful than I could have ever dreamed."

"That's your hideous dragon? Vorraxi?" Stone said. "He's seen us kill two of his kin now. We're coming after them all."

Arken covered his face in his black leather gauntlet. "I feared her flame was extinguished. I felt it like a hot knife in my back. How did she die?" He uncovered his face and in the dimness of the Dream World, Stone felt a genuine sadness in his low voice.

"Adler shot a bolt through her neck. She died quickly."

Arken took a deep inhale, and then exhaled, muttering something under his breath.

"Now tell me, Arken, where are you? Where is he keeping Gracelyn and Rosen? Tell me!"

"Far from your reach," Arken said, looking up into the foggy dark sky above. "Your dragons, nor mine, can come to where *he* is."

Stone swallowed hard. "You don't mean he took you to… the Golden Realm?"

"They are not dead," Arken said slowly, "yet."

Stone's fists clenched and his knuckles whitened. Hot blood ran deep into the muscles in his arms.

Arken glowered over his shoulder at Stone. "You know it will take you and me to kill *him*."

"I don't care what happens to him. I'm coming after you," Stone said quickly.

"He won't let them go," Arken said. "He thinks he needs them to rebuild his new world. We can't let that happen, Stone."

"So you can build your new world? Never!"

"So we can build *our* world."

"You keep thinking I'm going to help you," Stone said. "That's never going to happen."

"If you want to see them alive again, then there's only one thing you can do."

"I'm not going to do anything to help you, ever." Stone was fuming mad and shaking. "Tell me where you are! Now!"

Arken turned back to Stone. His shoulders hulked under his dark cloak. He looked two full heads taller than him, and his presence made Stone feel quite small. "The Majestic Wilds cannot live in either his or my world."

Stone couldn't get the words he wanted to come from his mouth. There were so many things he wanted to say, but his rage burned too hot inside.

"You don't want to hear that, but it's true. They're too powerful for this world. A world with order needs a strong leader, but it needs no pack of witches."

"I'll cut your lying tongue from your mouth," Stone finally growled.

"You'll see in time," Arken said casually.

"That's why you came here?" Stone asked. "To tell me to join you and you want to kill my friends?"

"No," Arken said. "I've lost many along my path. And so will you. What I've come for is to tell you what must be done—what must be said. I have come to tell you that we must kill Crysinthian—together."

"You can't kill a god," Stone said, turning his back to the Dark King. "He took that Adralite, anyway. He has it. I should've used it. I should've used it somehow." He was holding his fist before him.

Arken's eye flickered white again. "There is another."

Stone's head whirled. *There is? Is he telling the truth? I need that other one.*

"It's there. It's in Valeren. It's the Adralite I've hunted half my life. They're going to show it to you, Stone. They're going to offer it to you. They know Crysinthian has to die, and that you're going to be the one to kill him…"

He wanted to refute it aloud, but he didn't think he had to. It was nonsense. But he was processing it within himself.

If I'm the prophesied one to kill Arken… they wouldn't think I'm also the one to kill… the Great God too?

"That doesn't make any sense," he muttered. "No sense at all. They'd give it to Corvaire, or Marilyn!"

"It's you, Stone, it's always been you."

"Why me then?" Stone took powerful strides at Arken, who gazed mightily down upon him. "Why am I the one?" Tears beaded in his eyes. "In his dying words, Kellen said something about my soul. Something about I wasn't supposed to come back. But he said my soul… Why? Why'd he say that?"

Arken took a long pause, as if waiting for Stone to answer his own question. His thick, black eyebrow rose over his one eye. His black hair with gray streaks blew at his shoulder. His head turned to the side, looking up where there would be stars if there were a sky above.

"Because you are part of me," the Dark King said. His eye closed slowly, and his head dropped. "But no. You were not supposed to come back. You were meant to be buried deep. You indeed were dead."

Part of him? What does that mean?

"You're…" Stone gasped.

"I am not your blood, and you aren't mine," Arken said in a harsh voice. "But in a way, we are the same…"

"Enough with the riddles," Stone shouted. "I want answers. Tell me what that means! Tell me who my father is! Tell me where Gracelyn and Rosen are!"

Arken turned away in the shadows. His voice grumbled as he faded away. "They will offer it to you. Take it. We will need it for our final assault. Then… and only then… all will be revealed."

"Arken, don't you leave now! You can't leave now! I need answers, damn it! I need more!"

"We will kill them, Stone, we will kill them all… and we will make the world as it should have been… you have no choice…" Arken's final words ended with a long hiss in the black shadows, and the world around him swirled. He shouted and fought to stay within the Dream World, but it was to no avail.

Stone opened his eyes to be panting and dripping with sweat in his bed with Mud beside him, looking at him with a cocked head.

Sunlight glowed dimly through the curtains.

"He…" Stone said in labored breaths. "He… wants to kill Gracelyn."

He leaped from his bed and rushed out of the room, leaving the door wide open as Mud chased after him.

Chapter Twenty-Two

"Wake up, wake up!" He knocked on Adler's door furiously, running past to Ceres'. Adler grumbled behind, laying in bed still. Stone popped the latch and swept in. "C'mon, we gotta go!"

Adler stirred, pulling his linen sheets over him. He squinted into the earliest morning rays.

"Just a few more hours," he moaned.

Ceres was stirring in the room next to them, creaking the bed enough that Stone knew she was at least up.

"Listen," Stone shook Adler's shoulder as Ceres peaked her head around the doorjamb. At least he had her ear.

"They're going to kill Gracelyn," he said, trying to catch his breath. "They're not going to use the Majestic Wilds; they're going to kill them."

Ceres covered her mouth and Adler sat up and looked longingly at Stone as he said the words.

"They're going to kill Gracelyn and Rosen." Stone looked deeply at Ceres.

"He came to you? Didn't he?" she asked, dipping her fingers to her chin and back to cover her mouth.

Stone nodded.

"We've got to go," Adler said, grabbing his sword from the side table and running to get dressed.

"Where?" Ceres asked. She was still wearing her nightgown of soft cotton. "Did he say where? Could you see?"

He shook his head. "I don't know where they are," Stone said. "But I'm tired of waiting here. I'd rather be in the sky looking."

"I'll go get ready," she said as she dipped away from sight.

"What else did he say?" Adler asked, bouncing as he put on his pant leg.

Stone pulled his ear in with a flicker of his fingers and whispered what the Dark King had told him—about the Adralite, and Crysinthian. Adler's eyes grew wide.

"There's so much wrong in there," Adler muttered. "You're… you're not going to help him, are ya?"

"I don't know what I'm going to do."

Adler seemed ready enough and nodded.

They ran to the next room, with Mud following.

"Come in," Ceres said. "I'm ready enough."

They ran in, and Stone saw she was in her brassiere and underwear, rummaging through clothes in a pile at the side of the room. Stone saw Adler covering his eyes, looking away.

"Ain't never seen a girl in her bra before?" She rolled her eyes. "What a child."

"I'm no child," Adler said, still looking away. "Go tell her what ya told me."

Stone went over and whispered to her the same as what he'd told Adler.

She thought long and hard after she pulled his lips from her ear. She put a pair of tan pants on, thinking to herself, buttoning the top at her waist.

They'll want to kill her too… There's no way that's going to happen.

"The queen's funeral is in a few hours," Ceres finally said, pulling a blue linen top on that fitted nicely, tight but not too tight. "We'll leave after."

"We need to let Corvaire and Marilyn know," Adler said.

"Yes, we do," Stone said.

"What about the…" Ceres asked. "Ya know?"

"How could Arken know that?" Adler asked, folding his arms and raising one eyebrow.

"He seems to know a lot of things," Ceres said, grabbing her sword and scabbard and tying them to her belt.

"He called the Neferian by a different name," Stone said, brushing his hair back with the flat of his hand. "The Wyverns of the Bright Isles." He paused, waiting for a response. "Ever heard of those?"

They both shook their heads, looking at one another.

"The red-headed one, he called Vorraxi."

"Vorraxi," Adler muttered to himself.

"Well, are we all in agreement?" Ceres asked. "Go to the funeral, let Marilyn and Drâon know, and then head out?"

Adler cleared his throat. "Well… what about the… ya know what? Should we wait to see if he was right?"

"I'm tired of waiting," Stone said through clenched teeth.

Ceres put her hand on his chest to calm him.

"Where we're goin'," she said. "We might need that… weapon."

He didn't want to think about it. His hatred of the two who were with his friends out there burned hard in him. But the smaller, more logical side, knew to trust his friends. He was only still alive because of them, and they were all he had.

"So," he said, calming his breathing. "We wait to see… one day…"

"Should," Ceres asked, "should we just ask Joridd and Vandress?"

The thought hadn't occurred to him in the short time since his conversation with Arken.

"If we do," Adler said, "what're we supposed to say? That the Dark King himself wants you to give blah blah blah to us so we can blah blah blah?"

"That doesn't have the best ring to it," Ceres said, scratching her brow.

"We'll speak to Marilyn and Corvaire first," Stone said. "Secretly..." his voice was a whisper. "Every city has ears that listen through the cracks."

"Polav and his dumb hat aren't gonna be too happy about yesterday," Adler said with a grin. "Best to avoid the whole lot of them."

"Agreed," Stone said. "If there is a *you-know-what* here, I wouldn't be surprised if he'd want it for himself."

"So," Adler said. "Just to be clear... go to the funeral, avoid creepy priests, talk to the Corvaires in secret, keep said secret from the king, go to funeral, get thing in secret, get to dragons in secret, and fly away to we don't know where... got it!"

"You said go to the funeral twice," Ceres said, rolling her eyes.

"I did?" He glanced back and forth between them.

"You did," said Stone.

※

CHILLY WINDS WHIPPED around the corners of the city as they made their way—escorted by a small pack of soldiers—toward Mÿthryn. Sunlight skipped in patches along the dirt and cobblestones as the thick, puffy clouds rolled above lazily. All eyes were on them as they made their way to the high palace. Ceres brushed away sweets graciously and Stone nodded and smiled at as many as he could.

"I can't wait to get away from this," Ceres muttered under her breath, while half-smiling.

"Agreed," Stone said, doing the same.

Once inside the palace, they were greeted by Jarquiose, who was talking with Roen and Blithe from the treasury and education. Jarquiose saw the three approaching and rushed over quickly. The guards eyed them from the front entrance and the stairwells.

"Greetings," Jarquiose said. His brown eyes glanced at each of them. His face was narrow with sharp cheekbones, and thin fingers fiddled with a black goatee on his chin.

The three nodded to him.

"We need to speak with our friends," Stone said, with his hands out by his pockets.

"I see," Jarquiose said, seeming perturbed by the tone in his voice.

Roen and Blithe both approached, but slower than the nimble constable in his tight-fitted blue suit of suede.

"Well, I'd be happy to escort you to their chambers," Jarquiose said as the ministresses caught up to his sides. They both glared at the three of them, and Stone couldn't tell if it was out of curiosity or—ambition, perhaps?

"You made quite the stir yesterday," Jarquiose said. "High Priest Polav is not the kind of man who likes his invitations ignored."

"Well, it sounds like a *him* problem," Adler said.

"Your," the constable chose his next words carefully, "attendance and grace may be needed to ease the situation… today."

"How about tomorrow?" Adler responded quickly, as if ready to answer before even hearing the question.

Head Mistress of Education Blithe Gould was the one to respond, which caught Stone off guard. "You may not be as clever as you think you are," she said with a straight face and stern voice. "You are formidable with a sword, and in battle, but best to leave the lies to the politicians."

"What do you mean?" he asked, trying to cover up his tracks.

She scoffed. "I've been around boys your age long enough to understand sarcasm."

Roen, Ministress of the Treasury, folded her arms with long sleeves over her chest. "You mean to leave the city. That much was evident by your eagerness this morning. Few run to a funeral."

Stone sighed and shook his head low.

"It's not what you think," he said.

"Is it not?" Roen asked while Jarquiose looked around curiously, as if he was the only uninformed one in the group.

"We need to speak with Drâon and Marilyn," Stone said. "It's important."

"Don't misunderstand," Roen said, with wise eyes examining him. "We know you're leaving, and why. We aren't going to try to stop you. We only wish to help guide you."

Blithe spoke next. "You'll need every advantage if you're to go to your next battle. Please, heed my words. If you do this, do it with a clear, focused mind. If you leave urgently in anger, you rush to your doom… and a darker world for us all…"

Her words cut him like a sharp knife in his belly.

As much as he wanted to brush her words aside, he knew it to be true. This was bigger than him—and the consequences of his actions would ripple out to every corner of the Worforgon. He hated that.

"What would you suggest?" he asked.

"We suggest you speak with Polav," Jarquiose said. "Even if that isn't deemed most pressing to you…"

Roen brushed the constable behind her with the back of her fingers. He moved with his mouth agape.

"You will do what you must," she said. "But there are things that should be done here before you go."

"And we do understand your urgency in your matters," Blithe said.

"We will speak after the funeral," Roen said. "Marilyn is

still in her chambers, I believe." She looked at a guard at the front doors, who nodded to confirm her statement. "Drâon is in miss Vandress' chambers," she said, seemingly trying to hold back a smirk, and carefully eyeing Stone's reaction.

Ceres grinned, lowering her gaze so her hair covered her face.

"He what?" Adler gasped.

"I'd speak to Marilyn first," Roen said. "If you see that fitting…"

Chapter Twenty-Three

In the gardens outside of Mÿthryn, beds of flowers and plants of all sizes rested with singed tips, and their petals withered in the planting boxes below. The air had grown stiff and warm, but the flowers weren't withering from the air—it was the scorching tips of the dragonfire from the battle.

The three of them sat as Marilyn emerged from the front gate of the palace and made her way over to them. Each of them inspected the gardens around for prying eyes. They'd intentionally gone away from the leering ears of the tower's windows and the many soldiers about. Many in the city revered them, but their trust in soldiers hadn't budged.

Marilyn smiled as she came and sat by them, petting Mud's head. Her silver hair was silky and flowed majestically at her shoulders and her face was washed and relaxed. She looked like a whole new woman from the time they'd rescued her from the dungeons in Atlius, from what felt like years ago.

"Good morning," she said, tucking her green dress under her thighs as she sat. By the brief pause in response, she knew something was awry. "What's wrong?"

"Arken," Stone said quickly. "He came to me; he appeared last night. They're... they're going to kill Gracelyn and Rosen..."

Marilyn sighed, hunching over, pressing her knuckle against her brow. "We need to go," she said, looking back up after only a brief thought.

"Here they come," Adler said, motioning with a flick of his head at the front gate.

Corvaire and Vandress both came out after he held the iron door open for her.

He wore the same white shirt from the day before, slightly wrinkled, but fully tucked in. Vandress came out in a long golden dress with a violet bodice and stitching around the hips and knees. It was low cut and left her arms bare and decorated with rings of jewelry up to the elbows.

"They look cute together," Ceres said, grinning.

"Ew," Adler said. "He's like our dad! I don't want to think about that at all!"

"Will you ever grow up?" she asked, pursing her lips.

Marilyn giggled, but Stone did not. His mind was still reeling from the talk with Arken—and of the dire stakes at hand.

"Morning," Drâon said, paying no mind to how they felt about Vandress being beside him. "What are you all doing up so early, here?" His eyes narrowed on Stone. "Something happened... tell me."

Vandress must have noticed a slight hesitation from Stone, who didn't look at her and tried to avoid any awkwardness.

She said, "Ah, well, I have issues to be dealt with concerning the wake. So, if you should need me, just alert the guards. Have a good morning." She bowed her head and went off back to the castle, but that wasn't before she kissed Drâon's cheek.

"I hope she..." Stone began.

"She's fine," Marilyn said. "Now tell us everything…"

They huddled together and Stone told them all he could remember: creating the new world, that Arken said they were the same, but he wasn't his father, that the other Adralite was in Valeren, and that they both planned on killing the Majestic Wilds.

After he was done, each of them watched Marilyn and Corvaire's expressions, who looked at one another. Stone could tell guards were stirring around as they'd seen them huddle together. Surely it wouldn't be long before people like Polav knew something was awry.

"This is ill news," Marilyn finally said.

"Why'd he appear now?" Drâon asked, scratching his chin. "It could be a trap. Get us to attack before we're ready and can gather resources."

"Could be," Marilyn said. "Or Arken could be afraid of *him*. He could be baiting us to help him."

"Whatever it is," Stone stood up quickly. "They're in trouble. I can't just sit here while they're with both of them. And what if he finds out about…" His gaze turned to Ceres, but he looked back away after only a glance. "I can't let that happen. We can't let that happen."

"Agreed," Corvaire said. "What do you suggest?"

"He wants to fly today, right now," Ceres said.

Corvaire sat back, and Marilyn looked at him.

"What if the stone is here?" she asked. "I really don't want to have to say this aloud, but we have no method of confronting *him* with any sense of control. We are like babes to the hungry bear with him."

"Don't speak such things aloud," Corvaire said, glancing up at the sky as if waiting for lightning to strike and the god to appear before them again. "I won't dismiss your urgency, Stone, for I believe you're right in your instinct. Though, I also believe things must be done here before we go off to that fight. King Joridd must be met with before we fly off."

He waited for Stone's response, which wasn't prompt.

"They can take care of themselves," Ceres finally said. "You know they're strong. Even Rosen's magic grows with every passing hour."

I know she's just trying to ease my mind, and I know they're strong, but they're like us... powerless against Crysinthian. We do need the stone. We will need that Adralite.

"Okay," Stone said. "What do we need to do?"

"First is the funeral at Gambry," Corvaire said. "Then the wake in the Hall of Divinity, and then we can speak with King Joridd and Vandress. We could leave by nightfall or morning, perhaps."

Stone thought for a moment, looking at Ceres and Adler, who both seemed to agree. Ceres placed her hand on his.

"They can make it another day," she said.

He didn't know she was right, and every muscle in his body told him to go, but he trusted his friends and told himself that patience was needed. He took a deep, trembling breath.

"We will regroup at the funeral then..." Marilyn said, each of them standing. "Treat this day as we have so many times..." her voice turned cold. "...as if it may be our last."

⁂

THE JOY that had filled Valeren after Paltereth's death and the end of the battle flushed away to a heavy sorrow—thick, like a dark tapestry cast over the city. The three of them made their way to Gambry Courtyard—again with guards trailing them—for their protection, of course. Droves flowed through the city like blood flowing through hundreds of veins to Valeren's heart—something the queen had been described as more than once since Stone's arrival.

Winds whistled around the walls, sending licks of sand swirling at their feet. Dark clouds filled the far sky beyond the Obsidian, and pockets of lightning cracked throughout. It made Stone think of Grimdore resting beneath the crashing waves and felt a great deal of pride and worry for the teal dragon. They would not be alive without her, many times over. They all hoped her open wounds were healing well in the saltwater—for she'd need to return to the sky soon.

Mud bounded happily next to Stone as he felt a raindrop on his shoulder, nearing Gambry. The courtyard was wide, wide enough to fit the army of mages, the dragons, and battalions of soldiers from the city, but Stone and his friends had to pass through two checkpoints, letting fewer and fewer people close to the funeral.

They were to meet Marilyn and Corvaire by the fallen Neferian, and once they entered the full courtyard—full of its broken statues, burnt plants and planters, and black-scorched streaks—they saw both of them waiting. They went over quickly, and Stone motioned for the guards to stay back.

Drâon and Marilyn stood by each other, talking. Vandress nor King Joridd were with them, but they'd surely see them soon enough, Stone thought. They'd be the main figures of the funeral, on top of the saviors of their city.

Corvaire explained that their presence there was formal, more than anything. The wake below the city was where the queen's remains were, and where those who most cared about her would put her to rest.

They followed Corvaire and Marilyn up to the front of the funeral, where the casket rested. It was of a fine, smooth white wood with golden hinges and nails. The sigil of the city was inlaid upon its top—a squid with its tentacles wrapped around a white cross with violet and golden gems. Stone eyed it carefully, and he thought to himself that it resembled the queen and the church—fighting each other in a never-ending struggle

—the queen as the violet squid. Ghost slept upon the queen's casket; her shoulders bobbed as she wept in her sleep.

"I don't like being looked at like this," Ceres said. "Never gonna get used to it."

She was speaking about the thousands that watched them get up to the long, wooden risers behind the casket. But Stone's gaze was upon the many from the church, many of them scowling. Polav stood behind the casket, but he paid no attention to them as they walked up and sat behind him. Stone felt the tension like a tight string connecting the two.

Ceres and Adler sped up their walk to reach Joridd and Vandress, who sat directly behind the casket. When Joridd shook Stone's hand, he was reminded of just how strong the king was. His arm was covered by a golden cloth sewn into his royal military buttoned shirt. Underneath, it was in a sling, or cast—he couldn't tell.

Vandress nodded and hugged them each, ushering them to sit. The three sat beside Vandress, and Corvaire and Marilyn sat beside them. On the other side of the king were the heads of the departments of Valeren, as well as Jarquiose, and other people Stone recognized but didn't know. Conrad sat at the end of the row—that made them all smile as he nodded to them.

Directly behind them sat the seven, more members of the church, and many more people Stone didn't recognize. The first rows on the ground below the casket were lined with the Vlaer—or what remained of them. There were less than half of the original hundred that lived before the battle. Many were bandaged and beaten, as they were at the vanguard of the battle, fighting beside their newly crowned king.

The body of the Neferian was covered in tarps and ropes, but its head was left uncovered with two soldiers next to it. Surely the circling buzzards above had come to feast.

Murmurs filled the courtyard until Polav cleared his throat

and raised his arms out wide before them. The crowds hushed. His back was round under the fine white robes as a few raindrops pelted them, hitting like water on rock, and they rolled down the fabric quickly. His meaty, pale fingers were adorned with huge rings of gold and gems, and his fingernails were without a speck of dirt underneath them. Beside him, Ceres seemed to notice and was picking the dirt from under her own.

Stone was surprised by the weight of Polav's voice in the vast courtyard, as from even behind him, it echoed back to Stone's ears. It was a long-winded, off-key, melodic mixture of words and chants. Stone crossed his legs and Ceres' knees bobbed. Ghost turned her tearful eyes to the high priest, but then fell back to quietly weeping. Marilyn pressed Ceres' knee down so her boot was flat on the ground.

Adler moved to whisper in Ceres' ear, but Marilyn stopped him. Stone felt completely out of place and wished to be somewhere else. He didn't feel safe in the presence of so many with so many different plans and aspirations. He thought about Gracelyn, and his mind shot to the many worries about what she may be going through. He fought to push those thoughts away, but he couldn't wait much longer. Time was ticking, and the more he was forced to stay, the longer she and Rosen were alone. But he reminded himself—as Ceres had told him—they were strong, and they could take care of themselves. That did little to abate his worry.

Stone scratched his neck, looking around at the droves of citizens who wept—and he felt completely emotionally disconnected from the funeral. Jarquiose wept with shaking hands, wiping away his tears, and many of the maidens to the side too. But Stone felt, as Polav led the ceremony, that the funeral was more a show than containing any real connection to the queen. In his chants, Polav even mentioned Crysinthian twice by name. Adler, Stone, and Ceres all shifted in their seats when he did.

It lasted for what felt like hours, and as much as Stone wanted to feel more present for the queen, he couldn't stop worrying about Gracelyn—and the things Arken had told him. His knees bounced as he was ready to burst from his seat and be on his way.

Polav finally finished as thick, ominous clouds rolled over, casting down shadows from the bright afternoon sun. The Vlaer gathered around the coffin, beginning the procession of those who wanted to say goodbye.

"Ready?" Ceres asked them. "That was awful."

"I thought I was gonna die," Adler said, shaking his head.

"Be more respectful of the dead," Marilyn said, brushing her hair with her fingers. "But yes, that was rather long-winded…"

Stone about leaped from his seat. Ceres grabbed his wrist. He turned to her with a raised eyebrow.

"Go slow," she said. "Don't want to look bad in front of all these people."

Polav spun and walked directly toward him. The high priest didn't have the intimidating presence that Stone thought he may, but the many watching eyes that followed the priest did.

"I see you missed my invitation," he said. His chin was raised, and he peered down at Stone from under his round spectacles. Stone went to speak, but Ceres kicked his boot. "I'll be expecting you after the wake. Your presence is requested." With the tone of the said word requested, Stone knew it was anything but…

He didn't respond, but stared back at Polav's gaze.

"We have more in common than you may think," he said, brushing the last raindrops from his white robes. "The world is changing, and sometimes it needs to be… veered in a direction, so that dark forces may not take the helm. I believe now is one of those times."

"I'm sure the king will want to be involved in those conversations," Marilyn said, politely yet in a firm voice.

"Yes, of course," he said with a growling undertone. "The council will have much to discuss. Yet for the one destined to rid us of the Dark King's marauding, I wish to share words with. If that is all right with you, although he is a grown man now, and can do as he sees fit."

Polav walked away with his entourage, but not before turning to speak over his shoulder. "After the wake."

Those in the pews behind the coffin rose and chatted, and a line formed around the courtyard, many with flowers in their hands.

"We're not going, right?" Adler asked.

"No," Stone muttered. "We need to speak with Joridd and be gone from here."

"Excellent," Adler said, locking his fingers into fists.

"Let's go get somethin' to eat," Ceres said. "I'm famished."

"How can you be hungry with that stench?" Stone asked, pointing to the dragon under the tarps.

"Noses smell, not stomachs," she said, sticking out her tongue.

"Best get some food then." Adler crossed his arms. "Don't want to see angry Ceres again."

"See," she said. "You *can* learn!"

"There's food prepared at Mÿthryn," Marilyn said.

"I'd rather not bump elbows with this lot," Stone said.

"The seven wish to have a word with you," she said, "before we go."

"Them, I'll meet," he said. "Gladly. They are true heroes."

Conrad came over, and they all embraced. "It's not only you they want to speak with," he said, shifting his gaze to Ceres.

She blushed and shied away, but Stone knew there was no hiding it, even though no one spoke of it. She'd become the last of the Majestic Wilds, but she couldn't be one… she wasn't of the Wendren Set of magic. It was impossible for her to be one.

There were so many questions he had about it, which were measured with equal parts pride and worry. He'd never seen power like that in her, as when she killed Paltereth Mir, but now she'd be hunted, even more than Stone now.

Chapter Twenty-Four

Fires blazed within the halls of Mÿthryn. Many familiar faces filled the main hall in groups, while other faces were new. Stone could feel them watching him—all of them, though not all at once. Many of them even stared. He could feel the unease with which Ceres stood with her arms folded and her swaying with her golden hair hanging down. Adler stood close to her, nearly touching arm to arm.

They were in a corner of the hall, next to a table filled with gentlemen in fine clothing with white pressed shirts. They laughed heartily as Stone sipped a dry red and Adler drank from two mugs beside him on a shelf. Ceres nibbled on crackly, nutty brittle.

Corvaire and Vandress were with Marilyn in the center of the hall, talking with the other heads of the council. They shared wine and ate small bites of cheese and fruit that were carried by servants on large, silver-rimmed platters.

The minutes couldn't fly by fast enough for Stone. He loathed the political bantering and the small talk. He wanted nothing more than to have a dragon stench upon him as he rode it back off into the sky.

"There they are." Adler pulled down the lip of his mug from his mouth.

At the far corner of the hall, closest to the front of the tower, the seven made their way into the long, rectangular room. The groups parted, and the chattering grew. There were indeed many heroes in the battle that saved the city, and they would now be revered as legends.

"Think they're here to talk to us?" Adler asked, taking a sip of frothy ale.

Stone nodded. "I want to speak with them."

The seven walked through the hall. Four women and two men, aged and young, injured and fresh. They were an eclectic lot, Stone thought. They looked as much like each other as sand does to grass.

"I wonder where they're all from," he said, brushing loose black hairs behind his ears.

"Probably like us," Ceres said. "Drifters brought together because of what they have."

"They got magic," Adler said. "What do we got?"

"That's a stupid question," Ceres said with her lips pressed together in a line. "You're baiting me, aren't ya?"

"I wasn't baiting you…"

"You kind of were," Stone said.

Adler kicked the ground, scuffing the dark purple rug with his boot's toe. "Was just tryin' to…"

"Shh," Ceres said under her breath to him. "Don't embarrass me in front of them."

The seven came up to them, each bowing, as the men at the table next to them got up and moved, making room for four of them to sit. Three remained standing before them. Stone thought they looked divine themselves, immortal even for what they'd been through. Their eyes were wise and knowing, each and every one of them. They pierced hard when they looked at you, and Stone felt uneasy, yet safe next to them. All of the sudden, he wasn't in a hurry to leave anymore.

Vandress split the room as she rushed up to join them. Corvaire and Marilyn trailed behind.

"No need for introductions, I suppose?" the oldest of the seven said. "You know us and we you, although we haven't yet had a real conversation yet."

The three of them nodded.

"Aye," Stone said.

Many in the room took steps toward the growing ring of mages. They didn't hide their prying ears.

"Back," Vandress said, with her dress whooshing along the floor behind her long strides.

The men halted their sly advances, and the clacking metal of the Vlaer's armor signaled for them to back up farther. Five of the Vlaer stood with their backs to Stone, keeping those back from whatever they were about to speak.

Vandress stood beside Stone.

"Margaret," she said to the eldest of the seven who stood before them. "It's no secret we will need to be vague about what we speak." She eyed everyone at the table, and even back to Stone, Ceres, and Adler.

"Very sorry for your losses," Ceres said, bowing her head. Stone and Adler did the same. "They fought bravely."

"Yes, they did," Margaret said. Her wise eyes wetted. "They were incredible sorcerers and our family—"

"We know that feeling all too well," Stone said. "We lost ours too, Lucik Haverfold and Hydrangea Van Heverstrom. Y'dran too."

"Our condolences. We are familiar with your friends who fell…" she said.

"Should we go to another place?" Ceres asked, motioning to all those watching around the room. Only then did their glances shy away.

"We know your time here is short," Margaret said, rolling her head and letting out a popping sound. She seemed unusual to Stone—she had a presence, much like Vandress, only much older.

The heads of the council came from behind Corvaire and Vandress. Conrad was with them. The circle widened around, but Stone, Ceres, Adler, Margaret, and Vandress were at its center.

"We'll have no time to become friends," Margaret said, causing Ceres to scratch her arm and Stone to cock his head.

What are we here for then? Are we not to be friends? Comrades?

"We have things that must be discussed before you go off on your final flight," the old sorceress said. "She is not supposed to be what she is." She looked to Vandress, who nodded in approval. "You are Sonter Set. You control fire and plant life. That which you've become is ice and animals of fur. You are a Litreon as well. These things do not change. These things cannot be one. They never have been."

There was silence. Long and daunting. Stone looked down, shaking his head from side to side, trying to figure out what that meant.

Margaret didn't speak low or whisper. It was a proclamation against nature what had come. While none argued, not that they could argue what she had become—there were far too many witnesses to the death of the infamous Paltereth Mir. There seemed a need to know *why*.

"I—I don't know," Ceres said, fumbling with her knuckles. "But I know. The same way I knew it happened with the others." She stared deep into Margaret's eyes. "I don't know why. But I do know it."

"It has never been this way," Margaret said, with each of the remaining seven on the edges of their seats, screaming inside they wanted the answer.

"If the god above created it," Conrad said from the back,

walking into the pack, past the other heads. "Then, with his arrival, he changed it."

"Not impossible," Vandress said, "but it has not been this way since the beginning of things. They have always been since our earliest writings, and always the same, but now different."

The words screamed so loudly in his mind, he had to say them. "He's going to kill them," Stone said, causing many stirs. "Arken or Crysinthian. They're both going to kill them. They won't allow them to exist—not with what each of them craves—control. Absolute control."

"How do you know this?" Margaret asked. "Speak."

"He spoke to me," Stone said, causing gasps in the audience. The Vlaer widened the circle, pushing people back. "Whoever takes their control, the Dark King told me that they'd both kill Gracelyn and Rosen."

"He could be lying," Margaret said. "Arken's mind is warped and twisted from his torturous years. He's not the same man he once was."

"I know," Stone said. "But there was truth in his words. I think he knows what Crysinthian's plans are."

"Perhaps we shouldn't be so prudent with our words," Corvaire interjected, walking into the center of the circle.

Stone bit his tongue.

"We have to take the fight to them," Adler said. "While we still can."

"He'll be expecting you," Margaret said, raising her chin, and looking down upon them. "You'll be walking into a trap with a god."

"I don't care," Stone breathed in between clenched teeth. "I don't care." He uttered through them after.

"Very well," Margaret said, nodding to someone to Stone's right. His head spun to see Joridd standing to the side. Stone couldn't believe he hadn't noticed the king's entry.

"Joridd," Adler said. "Oh, shite, I mean King…"

Ceres smacked the back of his head. "What is the matter with ya?"

Margaret smirked, covering her mouth. Others in the seven laughed.

"If you ask us to go with you," Margaret said, "then our magic is at your command."

She bowed, but not to Stone—to Ceres.

The other seven stood and bowed after, not low, but enough to be symbolic.

Ceres nodded quickly.

"We have much to discuss before then," Margaret said. "Much to uncover before the final battle—the battle to decide the fate of our world. So many questions…" Her tone turned cold. "And we have no time."

"Come," King Joridd said in a low voice. He waved for them with his good arm.

Stone, Ceres, and Adler bowed to Margaret and the others.

"Nice ta' formally meet you all," she said. They went to Joridd.

"Where we off to next?" she asked. "The queen's wake?"

Joridd stood tall, wearing kingly clothes of pressed white with golden stitches.

"In our last moments of the day, we will bury the queen's remains. But there are a few more things I'd like you to do before the final preparations are made."

Stone swallowed hard.

Was Arken right?

"I want you to meet with the Vile King," Joridd said. Both Stone's eyebrows shot up.

"Why?" Adler asked. "Sorry, not trying to argue with the king, just curious. What do we need to talk about?"

"Salus' offer," Stone said. "He gave me three nights to say the words three times, and he would show me the way to kill

Arken." Stone's hands squeezed into fists. "I still remember the words. *Arcanium Violiant.* He wanted the Majestic Wild's favor in return. I'd never sell out my friends to such a monster. And then he proved to be that... and more."

"He may have details that prove useful," Joridd said. "We've taken his tongue, but he'll be given chalk to respond. We've got those who will... incentivize him to talk... should he prove hesitant."

"Will he be put to death?" Adler asked.

Joridd nodded.

"His knowledge is too destructive to be allowed to remain in this world," Vandress said.

"I don't deny he should die," Adler said. "But the things in his head may be invaluable too."

Joridd's face twisted, and he looked down at his arm in the sling and bandages. "I'm losing my arm because of him. He is my greatest foe. Knowledge or not. I'm going to end his reign myself, after Vandress has squeezed as much from him as she can. His corpse will feed the crows and I'll sing songs of his end."

Stone did not argue. He saw the hatred in Joridd's eyes, and he looked at his arm as if for the last time. Remembering the way he saw Joridd fight for the first time, he knew he'd never have that ability again, if he was to lose it.

"Now," Joridd said, "if you will follow me down into the tombs. We will say our last goodbye, and then... the fate of the Worforgon will be decided."

Stone followed him as the Vlaer led them to the end of the long room, and down a winding stair. All of them followed the king into the torch-lit stairway down into the depths of the city. No one spoke as they followed their king, but Stone had this pounding sensation in his heart.

What if Arken's right? What if Joridd offers me another red stone? What would I do with it? I don't know... I deeply, sincerely, don't want to be anything like either of them. I don't want to rule. I don't want to be old and corrupt. I don't want to become anything like them. I just want what I've always wanted... to help my friends. And they need me now... more than any other time. I've got to be strong. I've got to figure out what to do to save them.

I've got to figure out... who I really am...

PART IV
SERPENTINE OF FROST

Chapter Twenty-Five

The crypt was shrouded in darkness. His boots splashed through the stagnant water that pooled from the rains during the battle. The air was old and musty in his nostrils. Torches echoed as they rumbled and crackled, hung along both sides of the Hall of Divinity with a high-arching ceiling of blocks of stone older than most things he'd seen in his short life.

Statues of proud kings and queens, and probably princes whose lives were cut too short, were arranged on both sides of the hall, twelve feet apart, in a hall that was only just that wide. A rat jumped over his foot; he felt its thick tail knock into his shin. Adler grabbed his arm and squeezed.

"I hate the underbellies of cities," he said, seeming to want to jump into Stone's arms.

"Me too," Stone replied. The hall reminded him of far too many times they'd been under cities, in very different circumstances. For a fleeting moment, he worried it was all a trick to try to throw them in some cell where they'd be forgotten, and the key tossed away in the slime of the hall's corners.

It reminded him of the catacombs of Verren, where they first met with the Mages of the Seliax to repair Marilyn.

"Eesh." Ceres squirmed in the cold as she rubbed her bare arms. "Reminds me of Atlius, gettin' Marilyn out of that cell." It was as if their minds were bound by disdain for such places.

A glowing haze burned up ahead, over the heads of the ones that walked before them. A burning silhouette like a powerful sunset. The corridor opened up to a much larger hall with dozens of people already in it. The floors had been swept away dry, and fresh banners hung straight from the ceiling—not an inkling of wind had ever found its way to this place.

It had been hours since they'd briefly met with the seven, and there they were—collected within themselves in the far corner of the room. Margaret bent her elbow to give a short wave. Stone waved back.

In the Hall of Divinity, with many more torches illuminating the walls and ceiling, Stone saw that it was different than any other place he'd seen under a city. It indeed felt divine, as if God had helped sculpt the figures into the rock on the ceiling. It was like a scene out of a painting, with cherubs with cute bottoms feeding grapes to bare-chested maidens and wild-eyed monsters with tridents cutting into other figures. It was something he'd like to lie on his back and admire with a bottle of dry wine—if the circumstances were far different.

At the center back of the chamber lay the queen's coffin, where Ghost still wept. It hurt him to see the fairy so devastated by the loss, for he too knew the pain it took. Every death of someone you loved like that took a piece from you—something you'd never get back. A living, breathing, smiling, laughing friend could have their light extinguished in an instant—and all that was left were the memories.

Behind the coffin stood King Joridd and Vandress together. Polav sat behind in the rows of chairs.

"Seems he won't be boring everyone through this one,"

Ceres said. Immediately to their right, with their backs to the wall beside them, were two men in the robes of Polav, who gave wicked glowers at her statement. Their scowls turned to surprise as she stuck her tongue out at them, turning away quickly to continue walking back toward the center of the room.

"Gotta love when she does that," Adler said, throwing his fist into his palm.

Stone snickered.

Corvaire and Marilyn stood in front of the coffin, waiting to welcome them. Corvaire and his sister had gone off to do their preparations before the wake. Stone wondered what they'd been out tending to. While the trio was off on their own, Ceres desperately wanted to know more about Drâon and Vandress, but those questions would have to wait until they had time together. There were so many other things to do before their departure to confront Crysinthian and Arken.

"Stone," Drâon said with an arm out to welcome them in. "How do you feel?"

Stone nodded. "I feel good."

Corvaire didn't give much of a reaction, but guided him to the casket and Joridd and Vandress.

Stone put the flat of his palm on the casket of fine wood. Ghost sobbed softly as she briefly brought her head up to look at him, quickly cradling it again as her shoulders bobbed.

"Never thought she'd react like this," Stone said. "I feel so bad for her."

Joridd groaned, acknowledging her grief.

"I feel like she didn't have to go," Stone said, bowing his head. "She didn't have to be one of the ones to go in the fight. There didn't have to be a needless fight at all. If they would've just stayed away…"

"She died doing what she loved," Joridd said. "She was

protecting her people. There's no higher honor—especially in this hall. Her legacy will rest strong."

Jarquiose rushed over. "We should prepare to begin."

He ushered Stone and the others to the front pew, front and center, only ten feet in front of the queen's remains. Vandress sat behind, a few chairs away from Polav, and Joridd remained standing.

He folded his one good arm behind him, as his pressed white shirt of linen warmed in the light of the torches. His braided black hair was pulled back tightly, with one braid hanging down from the front of each onto his chest.

The room hushed. As all sat, except a few of the Vlaer along the walls, that was when Stone noticed the medium-sized organ with pipes rising just above a full-grown man's height in the far back.

"Here we lay to rest Queen Bristole Velecitor," Joridd said in a powerful voice that resounded beautifully in the hall. "Born in the year three-thousand, three hundred ninety-five in her own city, she was raised by her parents Godin and Angeline along the south shore. Her father was a fisherman and her mother set to raise her and her two sisters. Bristole blossomed to become our greatest mother and protector."

He put his hand down on the casket and tapped two fingers on its delicate wood. "And she was a good friend."

"If you're here in this hall now, then she meant something great to you—more than just your queen, perhaps. We are here to pay our respects and say our final farewell. But her strong spirit will live on, within us and within the Divine City of Valeren for all time."

There were soft utterances of approval from the crowd.

"Farewell, Queen Bristole," Stone whispered to himself. "May you find comfort in your sacrifice. We won."

Ceres grabbed his hand, squeezing it tightly. Tears beaded in her green eyes.

"I didn't know her long," she said. "But she was kind of like a role model to me. Never dreamed a queen would be that regal, that strong."

He smiled and squeezed back.

"She'd be proud of you," he said.

"I miss my ma," she said with quivering lips. "I miss her so much."

Her head pressed into Stone's chest and he held her close. "I know... I know..."

Adler put his hand on her back as she sobbed.

"This is not the end," Joridd said in a voice that caused Stone's head to tingle from the inside. "For we all return to the earth, from where we were made. From dust to dust, ashes to ashes. Your spirit will flourish out into the world. It will feed those who need strength, courage, and power. Goodnight, sweet Bristole, may your passage be as pure as the light you created in all of us."

Ceres flipped to her other side and cried into Adler's chest.

Joridd bowed low, then pressed his hand flat against the coffin. He turned and sat as his fingers slowly slid along its smooth top as he did so.

The organ began with a long, bellowing low note. Then the player's fingers cascaded along the keys with a whimsical beauty. It was somber yet light, a perfect pitch for such an occasion as it rang majestically throughout the hall.

Vandress rose and walked to the front of the casket to pay her final respect. Others next to her got up to do the same, forming a line to the left. Her back was to Stone, so he couldn't tell what she did, but her posture sold her emotions as she wept.

Conrad was at the end of the line, after the other heads of the council. He gave a wink at Stone. Polav and a few of his cronies were just behind him—he didn't meet Stone's eye but fingered one of his thick rings on his plump fingers.

Marilyn and Corvaire got up, and Stone followed—Adler helped Ceres to her feet as she wiped the tears away.

She rarely talked about her mother. She must have been an extraordinary woman to have raised such a strong-willed girl. I would've liked to have met her.

Stone and they got into line just behind Polav. They inched their way to the coffin, and after Polav showed a gesture that made it look like he cared for the queen, causing Stone to roll his eyes, Marilyn and Corvaire held hands and put their other hands on the coffin together. Stone was still curious about their relationship with the queen—he knew Bristole knew them, and their mother especially, but wanted to know more. With the way that the two of them aged slower, there could be an interesting history there, he thought.

They stood to the side as Stone, Ceres, and Adler stood in front of it. Ghost floated up to Ceres' shoulder, sulking and looking down at her fallen friend. None of them knew what to say.

The only thing that came to Stone's mind was, "We'll finish this. You can trust us to finish this thing right."

"Aye," Adler said. "We'll handle it from here. Your people will be safe."

Ceres and Ghost cried, nodding, wiping away tears.

"Rest well," Stone said. "This is not the end."

He wasn't but a half step away when Stone found two emissaries in white robes standing before the three of them—Ghost still hung on Ceres' shoulder.

"Follow us, please," one said. His lean, wrinkled face was a ghostly white.

"This really isn't the time," Stone said, seeing Polav walking out the front entrance to the hall.

"Your presence is needed," the emissary said. "It's an urgent matter and must be attended to now."

"With Polav?" Adler rustled his sleeves down.

The ghostly man scowled as he watched Adler speak to him while not meeting his gaze.

"This way." The emissary stepped sideways, holding an arm out toward the exit.

"We're not going now," Stone said. "We have other matters to attend to now."

"This is not a request," the man snapped.

Ceres moved to lay into the man, but another man's voice called from behind before the words could leave her lips.

"They have arrangements with me," King Joridd said. "High Priest Polav can seek their council after."

The two emissaries looked to one another for what to do next.

"You heard your king," Marilyn said with her arms crossed and her expression sly.

They frowned, slinking away through the crowd and out the exit quickly, like two snakes slithering back into their hole in the ground.

"Haven't heard the last from him," Corvaire said. "He won't let you leave the city without him getting his word in. Remember, he worships the god. He doesn't want anything to question his rule or his church."

Why would he try to defend a god like that? Did he not see what I saw? Who would worship a being like that?

Conrad came over. "You as ready as I am to get out of this city?"

"What?" Stone's head jerked back to Conrad. "You want to leave? You just got appointed to a head."

"Eh," he said. "They can send me a raven if they need my vote while we're gone. I've seen enough politics for a lifetime already."

"If we're done here," Joridd said. "Then I'll take you down into the cells."

"We're going to speak with Salus?" Stone asked, itching his arm, trying not to look at Joridd's hanging in the cast.

He nodded.

"Let's go," Stone said. "I'm ready to hear what he has to say."

Chapter Twenty-Six

※※※

Dense, wet clouds became a thick fog—rolling through the city—or rather, the city rolling through them.

They held each other's hands tightly as they made quick steps through the roads, not hiding, but hoping not to be spotted.

Perhaps he was busy. Perhaps he wouldn't notice. Perhaps, he was away. But was there any real chance he wasn't looking? She certainly hoped there was at least a chance.

They wound around a corner—the two of them hand in hand. Rain that never had the chance to fall clung to their clothes, soaked their hair, and wetted their steps.

The city's white walls were darkened as the heavy fog strolled through eerily—not making a sound. A blue hue seemed to glow up through the wide stones that paved the city at their feet.

"I don't know why we're doing this," Gracelyn said, wiping her eyebrows dry with her free hand. "We don't even know if he's alive."

Rosen swallowed hard. "He's alive. For better or worse..."

"How do you know?" Gracelyn asked. She knelt behind the

corner of a building, looking out past the main courtyard with the white tree, flickering with dull firefly light at its tips.

"I just do," Rosen said, kneeling out behind Gracelyn to look past the courtyard.

"He hasn't moved," Gracelyn said, standing slowly, walking along the front wall of the building. Rosen followed.

Past the tree they ran, keeping the splashes under their boots as muffled as they could. Winding around the courtyard, they stopped at a spot between two buildings, walked halfway down it, bending over the waist-high wall, and looked down into the cloudy abyss.

Gracelyn gulped.

"Let's keep going," Rosen said, tugging her by the hand.

They popped back out into the misty courtyard and continued to the far side from where they'd entered. They stopped outside the one building that didn't have the warm orange glow of candles burning on the inside. Clicking the latch open with a twist of the squealing handle, the door creaked open.

A body lay on the floor in the shadows.

"Should we light the candles?" Rosen asked in a whisper.

Gracelyn shook her head.

"You sure he's alive?" Gracelyn asked as they both entered and stood over the body.

The large male frame was wearing a black leather shirt and pants, and his arms and legs were pulled behind him—tied in thick rope and cold steel chains. He lay on his side, twisted with his limbs behind him in a manner that would cause most men to panic and find madness. Worse than that though was the metal helmet placed over his head, tightly pushed on with three thin holes to breathe through, but no eye slits or other breaks in its heavy steel construction.

To his side was his black armor, cape, and hefty black sword.

Rosen tapped the body's shin with her boot.

It didn't move.

Gracelyn held her breath, but then said. "Hit him harder."

Rosen reeled her leg back and kicked into his shin, landing with a thud, jerking him to life.

He leaned into his knees and yelled behind a muffled gag. His wrists and boots twisted in their binds.

"Well," Rosen said, looking down on Arken as his chest heaved heavy, shaky breaths, "that solves that mystery."

"I'm going to take off his helmet," Gracelyn said, dropping to a knee.

Rosen clasped her hands together as she watched nervously, as if vipers would fly out from underneath with their fangs ready to sink in.

Gracelyn tugged at the helmet of thin, black metal, but it wouldn't budge. Arken seemed to yank from his shoulders, still to no avail. She went above his head, wrapped her fingers underneath the front and back of it, sitting on the ground, putting her foot on one of his shoulders.

She yanked it free with a grunt, and Arken's greasy black hair spilled out. It stank of old sweat. His eye blinked, trying to bring the room into focus. His mouth was gagged by a gray, brown-stained cloth.

"You sure about this?" Rosen asked.

"No," Gracelyn replied, but standing back up, reached down and untied it from the back.

Arken's lips flattened as he turned his head to look up at the two.

"Untie me," he growled, with black spit flinging from his lips.

"No," Gracelyn said. "We're here to talk. Don't expect anything else."

"You want to know about *him*."

The women both tensed at the shoulders at the way he said *him*.

"What do you know about him?" Gracelyn asked quietly, as if the volume of her voice had anything to do with a god's capability to listen.

"More than you, I take it," he said, half-smiling. "Free me, and I'll tell you what I can."

Rosen unleashed a hard kick with the toe of her boot digging into his stomach. "You're the reason my family is dead! They'd still be alive if it wasn't for you."

Before Gracelyn could restrain her, she grabbed his sword, pulling it toward her with its sharp point digging and cutting into the marble floor.

"You ended my whole world," she growled, with tears beading from her eyes. "I should kill you right here, right now."

Gracelyn grabbed her arms from behind.

"He deserves to die," she said. "But we need answers first."

"I didn't end your world," he sneered. "Look what you've become. I began your world. Look at you now. You're magnificent."

"Don't talk about me," she roared. "Don't you dare talk about me or my family."

"You're strong, Old Mother," he said, turning as much as he could onto his back, but his tied arms and legs caused an anguishing pain on his face. "But you can't kill me."

"What?" Rosen growled. "I'd cut out your heart and throw it from this place. With any luck, it would land in a volcano or the depths of the sea!"

"What do you mean?" Gracelyn asked, peering from behind Rosen. "She could cut you down right here, and this war would end."

"Stab me or do what you will," he said. "It would cause me great pain, but pain has become my ally. It hardens me—shapes me."

Gracelyn raised both eyebrows, and Rosen loosened her grip on the sword.

"I'll not give you the answers to that riddle," he growled, and then coughed, smearing black spit on the ground. "But your lover and I will meet to discuss that… in private."

"Lover?" Gracelyn said, grabbing the sword from Rosen's hands and heaving it over her shoulder. Her arms were shaking from its weight. "You just don't know when to shut your lying mouth, do you?"

"Enough games," he said, coughing and lying flat on his side again. "We have a common enemy. Let's not ramble on about trivial matters. You and I are the most powerful beings in existence, save for him…"

"How do you know he's not listening?" Gracelyn asked. Lowering the sword to let its edge hit the ground.

Rosen was shaking so much with rage she couldn't look at him—she was looking up at the ceiling with clenched fists.

"I don't. Do you?"

She shook her head. "Tell me how we can get off this floating rock."

He sighed. "There is no leaving this place."

"There has to be a way," Gracelyn said, gripping the handle of the sword tightly.

His one eye narrowed. "None of us will leave this place… alive."

"What do you mean?" Gracelyn asked, lowering herself to a crouch. "What do you know that we don't?"

His face turned mean and twisted. "Does the worm know why it's dropped into the water? It wriggles and writhes, but eventually it either drowns or becomes swallowed by the fish. There's no life ever after for the worm."

"You're calling us worms?" Rosen was glowing hot red from the freckles on her angry cheeks. "I'd rather be a worm than a blind follower of your cult. Murderers and zealots you are. You belong in the darkest flames of the Dark Realm."

"Yes, maybe," he said. "But so do those that did this to me and my people. I've lived lives worse than those of the underworld. There were tortures in my life that most would have gladly accepted death a thousand times. I know I begged for the release of death more than once, but my cries were never heard, and my anguish festered for years. That torture and pain created me. It has pumped my blood, nourished my body, fueled my rage."

"Lives?" Gracelyn whispered to herself.

"In the end, we're all worms," he coughed. "But some are strong enough to grow into serpents and snakes. The rest drown or get eaten."

"How dare you speak of the people you killed like that," Rosen said, shaking her fists in front of his face. "You have no respect for the living or the dead. You're pure evil. There aren't words for... *things* like you."

"And what would you do? Rosen Kalah? Daughter of Dranne?" His eye narrowed again, glaring deep into her. "Majestic Wild, Old Mother... you may wish for peace, but the time always comes when you three must make choices that define you, and change these lands, whether you want to accept that or not."

"I'll always choose what's best for the world," Rosen said. "I'm not perfect, but I'll always choose what I think will serve people the most."

"And if you must choose between two kings? Two queens? The north versus the south? The south versus the north? What would you do when all-out war hits the Worforgon for the hundredth time? Your decisions will cost lives in your generations-old age. You and I..." He was looking at both of them. "We're not that unalike. I've made many decisions I regret; years create that in us all. But I've always done what I deemed best to defend my people against the tyrants that killed my women, my babies. This isn't about us right now. Your parents died in this war I brought. But they killed my family too. Where's the vengeance for them? Where was Crysinthian when I needed him?"

"Don't say his name," Gracelyn said, looking out the window.

Rosen was sobbing and her fists were shaking, as she didn't know what to do with her rage.

"If we're to survive this," Arken said lowly. "Stone is our only chance."

"What do you mean?" Gracelyn snapped. "We need to get down there and help them. Not the other way around."

"Your bond is strong. He will come. Whether *he* knows it or not."

"How do you know this?" Gracelyn asked, her loose hair draping in front of her face. "What does he have to do with us being trapped up here?"

"I saw him, you know. We spoke. You should've seen the look on his face when I said your name. He would've driven his sword through my heart, could he have."

"You spoke to him?" Gracelyn said, shifting back.

"He'll come," Arken smiled. "What he does, though, that is yet to be seen."

"What riddles are you speaking?" Rosen said. "Out with it!"

"Who's the bigger threat?" Arken said. "The world isn't meant for us all to rule. *He* wants to recreate the world. *I* want to shape it, *you* want to save it. It cannot be all ways."

Rosen grabbed him by the neck, causing him to grin as she dug her claws in. "Don't be under any illusion you survive this."

He didn't respond, but just held that same thin-lipped smile. As she shoved his head back down.

"We're not going to get anything from him," Rosen said. "I don't know why we came here."

"We need answers, we need…" Gracelyn said, but in a flash Rosen had shifted, grabbed Arken's sword, hefted it over her body, and shoved it down into his chest. It sliced through the leather armor, broke through his chest bones, and struck through his heart.

Gracelyn stood with her arms wide and her fingers spread. Rosen hulked over his body as he winced in agony. His body convulsed and blood pooled on the ground. It was red.

Rosen heaved breaths, with tears running down her face.

"Th—There," Arken coughed, gurgling blood out the side of his mouth. "Do you feel your… revenge?"

"Just die already," Rosen said coldly.

"I—I told you," he grimaced in languishing pain. "You… cannot kill me."

Gracelyn's mouth hung wide open.

"Take the sword out," he coughed, wheezing through his chest. "Or leave me here to suffer. I don't care…"

Rosen turned her head over her shoulder. She raised an eyebrow. Gracelyn shrugged her shoulders.

"I'm not like you," Rosen said. "Whatever you say. I'm nothing like you." She pulled the blood-smeared sword from his chest, throwing it to the ground.

He inhaled deeply with a gasp. As if the air could finally return to his lungs. His face wrinkled, and he winced in pain. He laughed. A weak, wheezing laugh left his lips, and he rambled.

"What's he saying?" Gracelyn asked Rosen.

"I—I don't know. He's just mumbling. Like he's talking to someone," said Rosen.

He moaned, muttering nonsense, but in his ramblings, there were two words they could make out as a tear rolled down his cheek. They heard the words "Sorry, Timeera, sorry."

"Who's Timeera?" Gracelyn asked Rosen.

Rosen had a cold expression on her face. "Don't know, and I don't care. Let's get out of here."

She spat on him as he lay still, muttering nonsense and vomiting blood. They left the candle-less building as Gracelyn looked at him one last time before she left back out the door.

"C'mon," Rosen said from outside, waving her to follow.

"Why have you caused all this?" Gracelyn asked him. "All of this is because you didn't die. Was it worth it?"

Arken said in a faint voice, "Timeera…"

Gracelyn sighed, left the room, latched the door, and walked back out into the fog.

Chapter Twenty-Seven

The Vlaer led the way, behind and in front. A long line of soldiers and the seven walked down the dark, sharp-turning tunnels, dimly lit and smelling of old earth. They were taking no chances in the presence of Salus.

They'd left the Hall of Divinity from the rear, entering a labyrinth of tunnels beneath the city that made Stone wonder who they were created by, how long ago, and for what purpose? He took long strides in the dark while rats scampered ahead in the faint light. An unease flowed through him, not a nervousness though—more a worry that he wouldn't get the answers he needed. Even though the Vile King had lost his war, would he be stubborn enough to hold tight to his secrets?

Stone would find out soon enough…

Even Adler didn't speak as they made their way down what seemed to be miles of corridors. It gave them plenty of time to think. Joridd was with them, Vandress, too. Drâon and Marilyn walked just behind Adler. It was a procession of sorts. Stone knew Salus was going to die—that much the king had made clear, but he didn't know when, perhaps even Joridd didn't know. Revenge can be tricky like that. Put the marauding Vile King to justice? Or skewer him like a piece of meat and leave him to rot?

Those sorts of things and images darted through his head as he trudged through the underground, as if walking to another wake.

Where did Salus even come from? Was he born evil? No, that's not a thing. Where did all those mages come from? Magic is rare. How did he create such an army?

"When he dies, we may never know..." he muttered to himself.

"We're approaching him," Drâon said from behind, loud enough for them all to hear.

The path opened up into a wider corridor, with shackles hanging from nails dug deep into the stone walls. One of the Vlaer walked from torch to torch, sparking each of them alive. There were eight torches in the square room and a dusty, long table on one side. The seven went over, dusting the chairs off and sitting. Margaret stood, watching Stone, Ceres, and Adler.

"He's just down this hall," Vandress said, pointing down the dark corridor straight ahead. "Ready?"

"Who's coming?" Ceres asked.

"The seven have spoken to him," she replied. "Or attempted to. He wrote nothing for them, only stood there in silence. Joridd and I have tried to, but he either won't talk, or he's waiting for you."

"Guess we'll find out now," Ceres said, scratching Stone's arm. He took a deep breath.

"Let's do this," he said in as strong a voice as he could muster.

Do this and get on our way. Give me the answers I need, Salus. I go to fight my friends free from my enemy and a god. I need answers.

Joridd led them down the remainder of the hall, carrying a

torch in his one hand. Vandress was behind him, then Stone, Ceres, and Adler, with Corvaire and his sister behind. Everyone left remained in the large room with the dusty table.

There was no light ahead. It was so deprived of light that the torch was blinding if you looked too hard into it. Rats ran more readily along the corners of the walls by their boots, and a foul odor emitted from ahead—it was the obvious smell of feces.

Joridd suddenly stopped after only a few minutes' walk down the stretch of the corridor, sliding the handle of the torch into a holder on the wall. He put his back to the torch, staring at the iron bars on the opposite side. He stepped back to put his back nearly to the wall, with Vandress moving to his side.

"He's restrained," she said. "You can approach the bars, but be careful anyway. He may not have his words, but he's a bastard, nonetheless."

The trio approached the bars while Corvaire and Marilyn stood at their sides.

"Can't even see him," Adler said, tugging at the bars. "You in there?"

As their eyes adjusted, he came into the light with a few sweeping strides forward. His tan face and dark eyes were far more weathered than ever before, causing him to look years older. He'd become a frail old man. His slender, bony shoulder was knobby under the black robes and his thin fingers spiked out from his sleeve.

"An arm for an arm," Stone said, glancing back at the king, whose brow was furrowed and his teeth showed.

"You gonna talk to us or what?" Ceres snapped. "I've just about had as much as I can take of you, so let's get this over with, huh?"

Salus had a dead look in his eyes. His pupils moved to watch her, but his thin-lipped mouth didn't budge and his crooked nose didn't flinch.

"Pick it up," Stone said, shoving his arm through the bars and pointing to the tablet at the Vile King's feet, with chalk sitting atop it.

Marilyn tried to pull his arm back with a tug, but he kept his hand firmly through.

Salus smiled at his arm, and his chains rattled as he stepped forward. He was halfway into the twelve-foot cell, and his chains were nearly stretched taught. He bent down to pick up the tablet, and a rat ran right next to Corvaire's boot, which he didn't have time to notice.

Stone's mouth fell agape, and he tore his arm back through the bars to his side.

"What is that?" Adler asked.

The rat ran up to Salus, who untied the round scroll from its back.

"Shadow Scroll!" Marilyn shouted.

Stone summoned his Indiema as best he could as everyone around him readied their spells, except for Adler and the king.

In the scroll were flint and steel, which Salus quickly sparked to light, engulfing the scroll in what was doused in something strong. They burned quickly, and he blew the flames back, revealing the Shadow Scroll of dark parchment.

"Hold your spells," his voice echoed in the faint torch-lit cell.

Ceres, Marilyn, and Corvaire held their spells at bay, if only for a moment. Stone wondered if they should just let them fly and kill the old mage.

"I have no fight left in me. I have lost everything," he said. As the torchlight dimmed away, the iron bars disappeared, and all that was left in the room was all of them. "I'm not going to fight back. Kill me if you must, and I know these are my last days. I've come to terms with my death."

"The Shadow Scroll," Marilyn said. "How did you use it? That's Seliax."

He didn't show an expression on his face, but coughed into his hand. It was harsh and brittle. "The magics of this world are more closely related than we've all been led to believe. You used one of these in the past when your tongue was taken, did you not?"

Marilyn frowned, folding her arms.

"Then why now?" Stone asked. "What do you have to say?"

"Ah, the prophesied child," the Vile King slunk closer to him, causing the unseen chains on his wrist to snap tight. "The dead who will kill the Dark King. You've changed much, haven't you? I've enjoyed watching you grow—and turn into the soldier you are. All of the Worforgon has watched too."

"What do you want?" Stone asked coldly. "I'm going after Arken. I'm taking the fight to him this time! Now answer my questions or be done with this and be gone with you. The world will be better for it."

"Perhaps," Salus coughed again. "I know that one will." His chains jingled heavily as he pointed to Joridd.

"How do I kill the Dark King?" Stone knocked his fist into the unseen bars. "What were you going to tell me back then on the shores of the western sea?"

"You didn't heed my call," the Salus said in a coy voice. "You should've taken my offer. All this would have been avoided. Your queen would still be alive, and my people wouldn't have been murdered in cold blood by those dragons."

"They deserved their fates," Ceres snapped. "You invaded a city. You invaded Dranne with Arken too. You didn't think that might happen?"

"Yes," he said with a hiss, turning his back to them. "I remember Dranne as if it was yesterday. I'm sure you do too. Gained a Majestic Wild, but lost a few in the process, did you not?" He snapped back around, with his thin lips curled into a great grin, showing his reddish, aged teeth.

Stone didn't notice, but Corvaire and Marilyn both watched him, waiting to see what reaction he would muster.

His blood ran hot down his arms and pumped thick in his chest. The hairs in his ears tingled and tensed. He was so overcome with emotion; fueled by anger, taken by grief, and craving revenge.

"Life means nothing to you," Stone growled. "Especially a life of love and friendship. You take and give nothing back. Why would I have given you the friendship of the Old Mothers? You could've taken both my arms and legs and I still wouldn't lead them to you. Everything you touch turns to ash. You have no honor."

"You!" the Vile King shouted, pointing his shaking finger at Stone, "you could've averted all this! I would've used the Old Mothers to change the world in *our* image! I don't want to be king; I don't deserve this name given to me by your *royalty... Vile King...*" he spat into the darkness with disgust on his face. "We would've created a better world. But you... you ruined everything. Instead of me, you have two monsters to contend with. Arken is ruthless. You know him—he calls you to him as his own brother, as a rekindled son. Crysinthian, well..." his anguish turned to pleasure with a satisfying grin. "Good luck with him."

"You did this," Ceres barked. "Not us. Don't be mixin' that up in your demented head."

"He's not going to change everything," Salus said coldly. "He going to tear down the foundations of the Worforgon. No one will survive what he will bring. He's only here because you found the Adralite." He laughed suddenly. It was a full-bellied, exhausting laugh that made the Vile King cackle. "You didn't just find it... you carried it... you lost it... and you didn't use it!" His laugh echoed in the darkness and Stone's shoulders loosened and fell. The hot wind left his lungs.

What did I do? I created all this...

"Enough!" Corvaire's voice startled Stone back to life. "We're not going to stand here and wait for you to finish your farewell speech. Save that for the gallows and the priests. Tell us what you know. Tell us how to kill Arken. We'll deal with *the other* when the time comes."

"Arken…" Salus muttered in an exhausted voice. He knelt, collapsing to his side, then, sitting cross-legged, ran his hand over his bald head, scratching it with his sharp fingernails. "That man has endured more pain than any living soul in this world. Tamed the darkness, he did. No one alive can relate to what he's become. More than human…"

"What do you mean?" Stone asked, looking down at the frail man in the dark robes laying over his knobby knees.

"You still don't know?" he asked, twisting his head as he looked up at them. "Why do you think you awoke from that grave in the same year he arrived? Do you think it was chance? Coincidence? Fate?"

None spoke.

"You are more akin than you want to believe…" the Vile King snarled. "Arken beat death. So did you, aye? But while you overcame death… he survived death, bested it, controlled it. Death disavowed him. Death banished him to life. He found something in his torment, something in the east. Perhaps at the depths of the black ocean, or far off in his homeland. This I do not know, but what I do know is… he didn't completely leave the Worforgon with his banishment… he left something behind."

"What?" Marilyn asked. "What did he leave?"

Stone's fingers gripped the cold, unseen bars.

Salus clicked his fingers, snapping them to point to Stone.

Me? What does he mean?

All waited with bated breath for Salus to go on.

"Speak," King Joridd said in a stern voice.

"I'll betray Arken," Salus said, "if not only for lying to me and Paltereth at the gates. But..." His head cocked. "I want something in return."

Marilyn said, "You're in a cell waiting to be put to death. It had better be a simple request."

Stone glanced over his shoulder and saw Joridd shifting angrily.

"What is it?" Marilyn asked, hefting her crossed arms before her.

"Nothing more than a quick death. I may deserve the hate of every soul in this wretched kingdom, but I am human nonetheless... and I'm old. Don't burn my body, enough of my people have burned. I want to be buried or taken out to sea."

Joridd moved to speak, but Vandress silenced him with her arm over his chest, pressing him back.

"We will consider your request," she said.

"One more thing," Salus said softly. "I wish for you, Marilyn Corvaire the Conjurer, greatest of sorceresses, to be the one to do it."

She didn't move or speak, but stood in quiet contemplation.

Again, Vandress held Joridd's anger back.

"Why?" Adler asked.

"Even to my kind," Salus said. "We of the Arcane always admired the family of Darakon and their nobility. The Arcane and the Elessior are but two sides to the same leaf. If only by chance we ended up on different sides—different veins in the same heart."

"I wouldn't go that far..." Adler said snidely.

"These are my requests," the Vile King said. "Do these for me, and I'll tell you what I know. If not, then leave me be. I have much to think about before my time comes."

Vandress removed her arm from in front of Joridd.

"My king?" she asked.

Joridd looked to Stone for an answer, who nodded. "Very well," he said with a heavy exhale. "For as much as I want to cut the demon's head from his cursed body, I'll allow it. In the end, you'll burn in the depths of the Dark Realm either way."

"Well," Marilyn said. "Speak then. Tell us all you know about the Dark King."

Chapter Twenty-Eight

"Well, that was pointless," Rosen said, rubbing the new, bloody calluses on her hand; licking them clean.

"I don't know," Gracelyn said. "I don't know about much right now." They walked through the fog, back to the room Rosen had awoken in hours earlier.

Their steps weren't as light as before, and their voices rang louder within the walls and the thick air of the city that flowed through the clouds.

"He said he spoke to Stone," Rosen said, taking Gracelyn's hand with a soft touch as they walked side by side. "That means he's still alive."

"If he was telling the truth," Gracelyn said, squeezing her hand and then letting it fall from her fingers. "I feel like I should be able to tell with him, but I just don't know."

"Stone will come," Rosen said. "He'll come with Grimdore, Ceres, and Adler. I know it."

Gracelyn gazed up into the twinkling light of the specks of water that glimmered in the fog from the sun that felt so very far away.

"I just don't know what to do," Gracelyn said. "We are two of the Majestic Wilds. Shouldn't we have the wisdom and the answers?"

"Well," Rosen said, flicking a loose bit of skin from her callus away, "we are new at this."

"He said none of us are going to leave this alive." Gracelyn had both her hands up to the sides of her brow. "We need to get out of here."

Rosen sprang to life, grabbing Gracelyn and spinning her to her. "The Song of Dragons! Sing it! Grimdore will come!"

Gracelyn sighed. "I tried that, a few times before I found you. Either they can't hear or he's making it so nobody can hear it."

Rosen's expression soured, and she kicked a pebble.

"Where is he?" Gracelyn asked. "He just disappeared. Do you think he can hear us?"

"Don't know," Rosen said. "Seems like we're prisoners in this place."

"Our magic has no effect," Gracelyn said, holding up her palm before her—inspecting it. "Is he Wendren?"

"I think he's all of them," Rosen said. "He must've created the sets."

"I feel the only way off his rock," Gracelyn said, clearing her throat, "is to leap."

Rosen's eyes grew wide. "You're not serious, are you?"

"I—I don't know. I don't think so, but maybe the song could call them if we were far enough…"

"Stop it," Rosen clapped her hands, interrupting her. "They'd never make it in time."

"I don't want to die," Gracelyn said. "But you heard Arken. We're going to die here, and there's nothing we can do to fight back. We're defenseless, and I will not be tortured and murdered if I have anything to say about it. I've got family that needs me. Stone and the others need me too. I'm gonna go mad up here. That's torture enough, knowing that I'm helpless and that they need me."

"We'll figure it out," Rosen said. "There's always hope. They'll come when they can."

"I don't know if I want them to," Gracelyn said, folding her knuckle on his cheek. "What if it's a trap? What would he do if they came here? Who knows what he's capable of?"

"Nothing good anymore," Rosen said. "Pretty sure about that…"

They walked a bit farther, but nearly a street-length from the house they were going. Gracelyn nudged her to follow down a side road, less-lit, toward the edge of the floating fortress. Rosen followed.

Silently, they walked to the edge. Rosen put her elbows onto the ledge, letting her red hair waft past her. A break in the fog opened up, and they both looked down—hundreds of feet down until another swath of gray clouds flowed lazily along.

"Who do you think he was talking about?" Gracelyn asked, wiping away whipping hair from her brow. "Timeera. That a person?"

Rosen let out a puff from her nostrils and shrugged her shoulders.

"I wonder if he had children, if he had a wife," Gracelyn asked in a somber tone. "I know he and Seretha, and the others had relationships, but I wonder if he ever loved."

Rosen responded in anger, with flushed cheekbones. "Don't talk like that. Don't talk about him like he's a man. He's a thing, a tyrant. He doesn't deserve you even thinking about that."

"He used to be a great warrior," Gracelyn said. "From what the others said about him. I've always hated him. How could ya not? But looking at him in that room back there. I sort of felt… pity."

"Yeah, because he was hogtied like he deserved!"

"Yes, I agree," Gracelyn said, and she wanted to go on, but she forced her lips shut and exhaled. "You're right."

"Damn right I'm right. He's a monster. Period."

Gracelyn nodded.

They both stood there, feeling the cool air on their necks, wetting their eyes.

"How did we get here?" Gracelyn asked after a sigh. "How did we end up in this mess?"

A voice suddenly boomed, startling both the girls, who spun as if whatever was behind them with the voice was about to knock them from the walls of the fortress.

"You are the Majestic Wilds," he said. "That is why you are here."

His chiseled body was shirtless, tan, and muscular. His wavy silver beard blew against it as he hovered above the white stone ground. He wore a spectacular crown of gold and silver, with rubies inlaid into its upward spikes. His eyes glowed a lightning yellow and the white robes at his waist wafted as if in the sea.

It was the first time Rosen had seen him since he'd appeared on the battlefield at Valeren. She gasped, covering her mouth, and her knees wobbled. Gracelyn clenched her fists.

"You were listening then?" Gracelyn said, as Rosen's wavering hand delicately touched Gracelyn's forearm, in a meager attempt to get her to ease.

"I am everywhere," he said in a voice solid like granite. "I am everything, and everything is because of me."

"Then you know we wish to leave this place."

"That is not possible," he said, his arms hung at his sides strongly with long veins streaking like rivers down them.

"What do you want with us?" Gracelyn asked, taking two steps forward and looking up at the shimmering god. "You want us to just sit here while you come and go while our friends need us?"

He didn't respond. In fact, he didn't move. After a long couple of seconds, he wrinkled his nose and his brow furrowed.

"Let us go," Gracelyn said. "Do you want me to ask you? Beg you? What will it take?"

"You're here," he snarled, "because we are creating tomorrow. I am the seamstress, and you are the thread. We are above all that breathe, give birth, and die. I do not *need* you. But I cannot allow you to *be*—without me. As I said when you first awoke, request what you wish. It will be yours. Everything will be yours. You just need ask." He bowed his head, not low, but low enough that his long hair fell over his shoulders.

"I want to go!" Gracelyn said. "Get me off this rock or let me call my—"

A ribbon unleashed from his hip, flying like a zipping arrow at Gracelyn, wrapping itself around her mouth before she had time to put her hands up. It squeezed and pulled her violently back. She caught herself with her arms, slamming her elbows onto the hard stone.

"Gracelyn!" Rosen screamed, bending down, trying to yank the ribbon free. Gracelyn's eyes were wide with panic, breathing quick breaths through her nose.

"Crysinthian," Rosen yelled. "Let her go. Please get this thing off her. She can't breathe!"

"Let me be clear," he said, floating slowly toward them as the fog itself made way for him. "Do not speak to me so. I never ask. But I give, I love, I destroy. I will tear down the very mountains themselves if I see fit." He hovered just before them as his bare toes finally hit the ground.

Gracelyn's breathing slowed as she calmed, but Rosen looked up at the god with her mouth wide.

He leaned down to put his face before them. His strong

nose was only inches from them, and at his towering stance, he was bent low at his waist.

"Do not play the role of savior. I *hate* that." That word made both of them shiver. "You will do as I say, and if I ask you a question, you will give it honestly, but with love. I will not say this again. You two are the most powerful of creatures, but you are little more than ants to me. Together we will create a new world of peace…" He straightened back up, casting a long, wide shadow down upon them as the fog parted and the sun showed from behind him, creating a golden halo effect. "Or I will do it alone."

The ribbon fell limp, falling to Gracelyn's collarbone. She reached up, taking it down as it unwrapped from the back of her neck.

"I understand," Gracelyn said, holding it and rubbing its silky fabric with her thumb. He feigned a brief smile. "I do have one question though…"

The quick smile was washed from his face.

Rosen shushed her, but Gracelyn waved it away casually.

"So, you want us to help you create your new world? Okay, got it." She stood with square shoulders, brushing off her chest. "But why keep him? What's the point in keeping him alive?"

Rosen perked up, trying to keep in her smile.

"I do not need to explain myself or my actions," he said, folding his lean, brawny arms. "But I will, because I see the hatred in your eyes, and I understand that may be a question that you truly desire."

"He's the darkness," he said in a cold, icy tone. "King Arken Shadowborn has turned to something unworldly. He's wrought my lands in a manner I never thought possible. His soul has been twisted and warped, and he's grown strong— more powerful than any of my sons." An odd, proud look blossomed on his angled face. "He's an ingredient to a tonic I may use, or I may throw away. Tell me, my children, does it upset you that I keep him alive?"

Gracelyn hesitated—thinking hard before she spoke.

Rosen did not. "Yes!"

He paused as his eyes flickered yellow and gold.

"I think that is wise," he said finally. "Though bound and immobile…" His lightning eyes narrowed. "He's more dangerous than you can imagine…"

"Then kill him!" Rosen said. "If he's so dangerous, then why even keep him locked away? Just do it. Just run him through!"

The god's muscles tensed throughout his body, shimmering down his arms and stomach.

Gracelyn took a powerful step forward.

"I get it now," Gracelyn said, taking another step. "I see why you haven't killed him. It's because you *can't*… Can you?"

The god stood, unmoving, while the robes at his waist wafted in the cool winds.

"If he would've gotten the red stone, he'd be more powerful than you even…"

Crysinthian's face twisted in anger.

Gracelyn pointed down behind them, into the clouds below. "Stone is the only one who can kill him, isn't he? Not even the Great God Crysinthian can be rid of him?"

"Careful, Gracelyn," Rosen said nervously.

"Well, send us down there and we'll return with him," Gracelyn said. "We will bring Stone with us, and he can kill him once and for all."

"Children," he growled. "Children. Everything is black and white to you. There is no in-between. It's good and evil, oil and vinegar, life and death. I don't want him dead. He will serve a greater purpose than the long eternity after. You will too."

Gracelyn relaxed, with Rosen pulling her back.

The anger left his face, and an amused look shimmered in his eyes. "There's something I want to show you... come..."

He floated backward and then turned his back to them as he drifted back the way they came like the breeze.

"Should we?" Rosen whispered.

"I don't think we have a choice..."

They followed him the full length of the fortress city, a near replica of Endo Valaire, nearly twenty full lengths of road. It was where the entrance to the city was, where under the mountain of Elderon the sigil of the mystics was—the Artican.

"Look," he said, flowing past the edge of the city, looking down into the clouds.

They both walked to the edge, bending over a wall at their waists.

"All we see are clouds," Gracelyn said.

He didn't reply, but continued staring down.

They kept looking, and as if the clouds knew, they parted wide, showing a bright portrait of golden sunlight framed by the gray clouds.

Gracelyn squinted, Rosen too.

"What is that?" Gracelyn muttered.

"This is where I've been," he said. "This is what I've been working on. A new beginning, a new age, a new Aderogon."

"Oh my..." Rosen gasped.

Through the clouds was a new kingdom of sparkling, bright, new stone. It spread vast through the land, with high walls, growing to a single tower at its center like a mountain.

"Aderogon," Gracelyn said. "He's rebuilt the capital."

"*Not* rebuilt," he said. "Created anew."

Chapter Twenty-Nine

In the darkness beneath the great city of Valeren, each of them waited pensively. Stone's mouth smacked dry, his palms sweated, and he hardly noticed his head was fully between two unseen bars in the darkness of the Shadow Scroll's spell.

There was a rumbling overhead, something like the sound a heavy wagon would make as its wooden wheel fell into a pothole and broke.

"We agreed to your terms," Vandress said, "even with the king's spite. So, tell us… how do we kill the Dark King?"

"Stone is the key," Salus said with his head slunk, rolling it beneath his shoulders. "He has a power in him, unnatural, yet brilliant. The power of the Adralites is the rarest of all gifts, but he found something else in his exile. Even though he sought the power of the red gem here, he carries with him something similar—yet so mysteriously different."

"Enough of the riddles," Stone said, tugging at the bars. "Tell me what I need to know."

"How long were you down in that grave?" Salus asked, cocking his head and tapping his fingernails on the cold stone.

"Do you remember deep down inside you? Surely you didn't fall when Aderogon fell?"

"That was nearly a century ago," Ceres said, reminding Stone.

"I do not know where you came from," the Vile King said. "Since your rebirth, that is one thing I wish I had more time to discover. While I sent my mages digging through old scrolls and your libraries, Arken's arrival in these lands took the brunt of all of our attention." His cold eyes peered into Stone's. "Who are you? This… I do not know to this day…"

Stone closed his eyes, shaking his head.

Another dead end. How can nobody know?

"What about Arken, Salus?" Drâon asked in an impatient tone. "What is the connection they share? What did he leave here?"

"The Dark King, another name given by your idols and kings," Salus scoffed. "His does ring a bit true though, wouldn't you say?"

"You killed our friends," Adler said through clenched teeth. "You'd better start answering questions and not posin' more questions soon, old man, or I'll run you through myself."

"Three orphans," Salus laughed with a cough. "Three orphans to change our world. How poetic. Tell me, how confident are you that you can kill both Arken and Crysinthian? As I am not long for this world, I wish to know what and how you feel about the coming battle. I will tell you how to defeat Arken, but the Great God—that is out of all of my depth…"

"Salus," Marilyn said, calming herself. "Answer our question. Now."

He slunk back, shimmying to the back wall of the cell, with the chains sliding along the cold stone floor. He let out a deep exhale, looking longingly at her. An unusual look of admiration —or camaraderie—was on his face.

There was a muffled, shuffling sound above.

"Very well," he said, taking a deep breath. "Arken, as I said, never fully left these lands. He has an ability, something I've never heard of in anyone else—even to this day. And I don't mean that figuratively. He literally left a part of himself here."

Stone held his breath.

"For lack of a better word..." Salus said, almost proudly. "He broke off some of his essence, leaving it behind."

"Essence?" Stone muttered.

Like his soul? He can remove his soul? That doesn't mean I'm... actually a part of him?

"How is that possible?" Marilyn asked, with slight distress in her voice.

"Whatever kept him alive through that grueling torture he endured at the hands of your kings and queens, something split him. I don't know if that made him less of himself when he was cast away, back out to sea to die or not... But that is part of what recreated him. He's a broken man, in more ways than one."

"That cannot be," Drâon said. "Nothing can take a soul but the grasp of death itself."

"So, call him dead too," Salus said in a grave tone, and then pointed at Stone, turning his palm up with playful fingers. "In case you didn't realize it yet, Stone... that essence is in you."

"Liar!" Ceres shouted, echoing in the darkness. There was a loud boom overhead.

"Just because you don't want it to be true, doesn't mean I lie," he sneered. "They are of the same mind and flesh. But do not be mistaken. It wasn't Stone, or whoever you really are, that he passed it to. It was passed to and through you from someone else who had it before."

Stone shifted uneasily, fidgeting with his sweaty palms. Another crash overhead.

"What is going on up there?" Adler asked.

"You see, whatever separated from his body," the Vile King said, "dug its claws into the Worforgon out of a need for revenge. He wouldn't be taken away so easily. All of that betrayal in his mind and heart that occurred here, tore it from him, and it moved from body to body, mind to mind, heart to heart. Eventually ending up in you. And when the Dark King returned…"

"It awakened me," Stone said in a hollow voice. "When he returned—I returned."

Ceres laid her hands on his arm. "It's not true," she said. "It's a lie. Don't believe." But there was no truth in her words. He knew it. She was telling herself that she didn't help unearth another part of *him*.

"You didn't know," Stone said, patting her hands. "There's no way you could have known…"

"But…" she gasped. "I…"

"What does this mean, Salus?" Corvaire asked, after a deep sigh. "If what you say is true. Can it be parted from Stone? Taken from him?"

"From what I know," Salus said slowly. "You can die again. He cannot. The essence in you will travel to another, and another, keeping his hatred alive here in the Worforgon. So, wherever he flies, he will still be a part of these lands."

Stone swallowed hard, not wanting to believe it, but knowing at least part of what the Vile King was telling him was true. It was the only thing that made sense as to why he was still alive—breathing, talking, and able to fight again.

"If I can die," Stone snarled. "But he can't. Then how is it you said I could kill him? If I'm the only one, tell me how…"

Salus' gaze snapped at Joridd. "I can see the anger in his eyes."

Something boomed and shook the ground above, causing dust to fall onto Stone's head and shoulders.

"These are my final minutes," Salus said. "After I tell you that which you seek, the sword will come crashing down on me, will it not?"

Joridd growled, "It will."

"Then I suppose it is time to say my goodbye," Salus said.

"After you tell me how to kill him!" Stone said.

Salus lowered his head and mumbled to himself.

"Tell me how to kill him!" Stone shook the bars before him. "I need to know before anything happens... Tell me, Salus! Tell me!"

"You want to kill the unkillable?" Salus suddenly yelled, standing quickly. "You're going to have to do the unthinkable." He had a broad smile with his yellow teeth showing. "A part of yourself is going to have to die. That one part of you that you didn't know existed until now."

Another thundering boom crashed overhead.

"We need to get out of here," Adler said, drawing his blade.

"What do I need to do?" Stone yelled with dirt falling more onto him as the booms continued.

"Guards," Joridd yelled down the hall.

"You want to kill the Dark King?" Salus spoke as if only Stone could hear him. "Then you must—"

"Get back!" Marilyn yelled, pulling Stone away from the bars.

From above, the ceiling broke and crumbled, with heavy blocks falling into the darkness. The Shadow Scroll's spell dissipated and black scales and long teeth the size of a man's arm broke into the cell.

"No," Stone said, trying to break free of Marilyn and Corvaire, pulling him back. "No!"

The Neferian's teeth and mighty jaws chomped down onto the Vile King, at first at his waist, nearly completely separating it from the rest of his body, and then biting down again to get Salus' entire body into its giant maw.

"Get out of here!" Joridd said. "Man the Dead Bows! Man the Dead Bows!"

"Salus!" Stone yelled in anger. "Tell me how to kill Arken! You can't die yet! Tell me how to kill him!"

The Neferian's black head swallowed, glaring heavily at Stone with one raging eye of red and yellow, and then its black head tore from the gaping wound in the ceiling above, and Stone heard its mighty wings flap back up into the sky, letting out an ear-shattering roar as it left.

"No," Stone said, finally breaking free from his friends. He ran to the great hole above the cell, a full fifteen feet deep, which the dark dragon had torn through. He glared up at the sunlit sky with the silhouette of the Neferian flying off into the clouds. He clenched both his fists tightly, and that rage filled his chest and he felt the veins in his neck bulge.

He was so full of anger and hate, and a chilling thought ran down his spine. It was something so unsettling, it turned his anger into a bitter reality.

What if this part of me is him?

Chapter Thirty

"Kill it!" King Joridd yelled up into his city, but the dragon was already far off into the clouds. It wasn't Arken's massive red-headed beast, Vorraxi, but one of the other remaining three—Stone saw the long blue streaks down its back as it slunk off into the sky.

"Your highness," a guard yelled down. "It came from nowhere. We tried to push it back, but..." his eyes swelled with tears as he fought to keep them in. "It killed me' men."

Joridd bit down his anger, storming off down the hall back toward the seven. "How did this happen?"

Adler nudged Stone as they followed. "I think he's madder he didn't get to kill him than anything."

"Shh," Ceres said.

"How'd it know exactly where he was?" Vandress asked, as they emerged into the room with the seven and the Vlaer, who were all on high alert with swords and spells at the ready.

"It's gone," the king said with a grunt and a sigh.

The Vlaer sheathed their swords.

"How in the Dark Realm did it get him?" Joridd clenched his fist and his brow furrowed with a deep anger in his eyes.

The seven looked around with wide eyes, trying to figure out between them how it had happened.

"It came for him," Marilyn said, "to keep the Dark King's secret. It fulfilled its mission."

"That bastard," Stone said, knocking his fist into the table. "He was about to tell us. We were just about to hear his secret."

"You need to do the unthinkable," Ceres said softly. "He did say that. What would that mean?"

"The unthinkable?" Corvaire said, rubbing his chin.

"Well," Adler said, "whatever it is, it ain't gonna be good."

Marilyn wanted to shush him, but tended to agree with her restraint.

A soldier came running down the dark hall with a hand covering a small torch.

"What now?" Joridd grumbled.

"Sire," he panted. "News from Verren. A raven."

"Now?" Joridd said, grabbing the small scroll from the soldier. He inspected the seal. "Roderix." He looked up from the seal at Marilyn and Drâon. "He's alive and holds the city once more?"

"What's it say?" Drâon asked.

Joridd's eyes scanned the small scroll quickly. His eyebrows raised as he got to the end.

Stone's foot tapped as he waited, and Ceres' fingers fidgeted.

The king sighed, shutting his eyes hard.

"They know where Crysinthian has taken the Dark King and the Majestic Wilds."

"Where?" Stone asked.

"It appears," the king said, almost as if not able to believe his own words, "that the capital of Aderogon has been rebuilt."

"What?" Corvaire said. "Impossible."

"He indeed is the Great God," Marilyn said with a soft breath.

"It appears it's a fortress of white," the king said. "Like nothing else in the Worforgon. The Neferian rest there now, guardians of the god's new kingdom."

"We know where they are!" Stone said excitedly. "We need to go, now!"

"Not so fast," Marilyn said, touching his forearm. "A frontal attack on a fortress isn't anything to scoff at."

"It's not like it's gonna be any kind of surprise to him," Adler said. "He'll be expecting it."

Stone's shoulders hunched. "I don't care." His words were mean.

"You cannot be off yet," Joridd said. He sighed once more, as if running something through his mind, pausing and seemingly waiting for some kind of sign from Vandress next to him.

She closed her eyes and nodded.

"There is one more thing we must do before the battle begins," the king said.

In Stone's anger, he'd almost forgotten what Arken had said to him in the Dream World, but it sparked to life as soon as Joridd and Vandress seemed hesitant at that moment.

He was right. They're going to give it to me, aren't they?

"Boy, ol' priesty is sure to get pissy," Ceres smirked. "What's the one thing?"

"Follow me," Joridd said. "Only us."

They walked back out of the long room, leaving the seven and the Vlaer behind, who obeyed their king.

He walked first, followed by Stone, Ceres, Adler, Corvaire, and Marilyn, with Vandress at their tail. Every time Stone looked back, it seemed that she was watching behind them carefully.

Joridd led them through a series of tunnels, and the deeper into them they got, the more splintered they became. It was a labyrinth of dim halls, sludgy passages no wider than his shoulders, and the sounds of the city above trailed off—distant and hollow.

They came to a square room where they had to squeeze together, and Vandress was left in the corridor behind. There were six passages ahead, and Joridd hung his torch on the wall, clinking into the iron frame snuggly.

"No lights," he said in a soft voice. "Follow me and mind your footing. It will be dark and winding, so stay close together."

They didn't reply, but followed the king as he walked into one of the passages, looking no different than the rest. And it was dark. It was the kind of dark where a shimmer off the king's dark hair was a speck just enough to follow. It bounded up and down as he walked in the darkness, and Stone had to pay extra attention to which way he walked because the walls revealed to his fingers that there were more winding corridors to each side.

"How long did this take to build?" Ceres asked from behind. "How old is this city?"

Is this an older part of the city? From the time it was first built? Or was this dug after the city began?

"We are close," Joridd said, his whisper echoing behind.

Stone heard a flint spark and light flared before the king. It was just a candle he lit, but its glow felt like the sun's light after so long in utter darkness. It was so smoothly done with one hand; Stone didn't even notice.

How long had we been walking? I have no idea where we are or how deep we've gone.

The king turned to his side, holding the candle out to reveal a... dead end.

Stone leaned in to inspect the wall, and Ceres looked over his shoulder. Adler pushed his way through, pressing them together.

"What's there?" Adler asked, "we take a wrong turn?"

In the light of the flickering candle, Stone made out a pattern in the rock wall before them. To their sides, the walls were a chipped rock dug by axes long ago, but the dark wall before them looked different, as if a boulder had been placed there. He wiped it with his fingers. The dust brushed away, and he saw it reflect the light.

"There's something behind it?" Stone asked, wiping the dust on his pant leg.

"How do we get past it?" Ceres asked, touching the dark rock face gently.

"This hasn't moved for hundreds of years," Joridd said, holding the candle up. "No living thing has been beyond it for generations of kings and queens." He breathed deeply. "I wasn't sure if now was the time… but after much thought… I can't imagine a time more in need of what lies beyond."

"What is it?" Adler asked, with a look of awe in his wide eyes.

"A weapon." Joridd turned back and Vandress squeezed past Marilyn and Drâon, going in front of Stone.

"You sure about this?" she asked the king.

He nodded. "We're going in."

She took a deep breath, then looked back at Stone—she closed her eyes with a sigh. "I hope you are," she said to Stone.

Vandress pressed both her hands against the dark wall, lowering her head. A soft yellow glow lit between her hands and the rock. Golden flecks flowed from her fingertips into the rock, disappearing deep into it.

"I'm ready," she said.

Joridd put the candlestick on the ground and moved his hand between hers, placing it flat on the wall. The gold flecks drifted to his fingertips from hers.

As he spoke, his words were distinct and stern. "I am King

of Valeren. I open this door in the name of those before me. I command of you, let us pass."

"Now say the words," Vandress said.

He breathed hard from his nostrils. "*Ovictum Calla.*"

The rock broke like the sound of two slabs of granite slamming into each other. From their three hands, the rock wall snapped apart into three pieces, each with one hand pressed against one. The wall had broken with a deep 'V'-shaped break between the pieces.

"Help me with these," Vandress said back to them.

Stone went to the left piece, sliding his fingers into the crack as she and he pulled it to the side. Joridd pulled up on the center piece and Adler and Ceres teamed up on the right.

They pulled with great strength, and all together, they pulled the rock wall apart, sliding it into the walls at their sides, above and below. Beyond was complete darkness. Joridd walked through first.

The candle he held did little to light the way before them, and as Stone stepped through the entrance, the walls at his sides opened up greatly. They opened up so much, in fact, that he couldn't see any walls at all. He looked up and couldn't see a ceiling, either.

The air smelled stiff and musty, like nothing he'd ever smelled before.

"What is this place?" Marilyn asked as she walked through.

Stone was surprised to hear her ask that.

She doesn't know? I guess Corvaire doesn't either then…

"A long sealed-off hidden cavern," Vandress said. "Supposedly used to be a refuge in case of invasion when the city was very young."

"And can I ask why we are here, then?" Marilyn asked, as Joridd went to the left, finally finding the wall, inching along it until he found a torch, and lighting it with the candle. They all remained by the entrance, watching the torchlight slowly grow, revealing a wide room with a domed ceiling of stone—but they saw no far wall.

There was nothing in the long room, save for bits of snail shells and cobwebs hanging thick. The mere blow of their breath was enough to shake them from where they hung.

"No one has been in here in centuries, as the king said." Vandress brushed cobwebs to her side, knocking them from where they hung far above. They floated down like ribbons of smoke.

"It must be down here," Joridd said, leading the way with the torch.

It?

They all followed. Stone's heart raced, and he took eager steps forward. Ceres held his hand as they walked together.

"Who knows about this place?" Marilyn asked.

"No one," Vandress said. "Except us."

"Why?" Corvaire asked then.

"Only the kings and queens have knowledge of this cavern," Joridd said.

Stone eagerly listened as he brushed the long cobwebs away.

They walked through the darkness, letting the light of Joridd's torch propel them through the void. The tunnel took a turn downward, looking like a great wormhole dug deep into the earth.

"I only learned of it once the crown was bestowed to me," he said. "It was within the texts given to every new monarch."

"Then how did Vandress come to this knowledge?" Marilyn asked.

"Because I chose to confide in her," Joridd said gruffly. "Entering this place should not be weighed lightly. Only with the recent tidings in our lands would I ever have even considered coming down here."

"Because of *him*," Stone said.

"Because of both of them," Joridd said.

"Look," Ceres said. "Up there, you see it?"

Stone narrowed his eyes, scanning out to where she was pointing straight ahead.

He saw nothing at first, just an off-shade of black. As they slowly approached, though, the black turned to mute gray, and then a small dot of blue haze formed.

They approached with heavy footing, and their swords ready to draw. The blue haze grew the closer they got, and it turned different shades, with the lightest of the blues an almost white, cascading to an iceberg blue and then deep-sea colors at its edges.

When they finally stood before it, Stone was completely dumbfounded. He didn't know what to think.

A shimmering statue rested in the middle of the dank cavern. No dust or cobwebs littered its pristine lines, and its eyes were the piercing whites he'd seen from the gloom. Its head was above their heads, looking down. Its arms were firmly planted upon its base, with scales of silver and icy blue flowing up them. The scales on its back were stiff and mighty as they flowed down in waves from the back of its head to the wings tucked behind.

The statue stood eight feet tall, but looking around to its side, it went back at least twenty feet to the tip of its tail. Its teeth were sharply carved in its open maw and its talons dug mightily into its rectangular base. Each scale wasn't carved, but inlaid with shimmering jewels of so many varieties and shades Stone had no idea what to think.

"What is it?" Adler asked in a voice of awe.

"It's known to us as the Great Frost Dragon," Joridd said, standing with his shoulders back, admiring the statue, but also as if presenting himself to it.

"It's been called many things over the ages," Vandress'

voice was timid as if she was afraid. Stone had never heard her like that before.

This is the weapon? Arken was wrong. He let out an exhale of relief. *I don't want the power the Adralites hold. I just want to win this war.*

"In my circle of mages growing up," Vandress said. "We referred to him as Arran."

"Our mother told of stories of him," Marilyn said. "But called him Virranas, the Great Frost Dragon who created balance in nature—the protector. She used to sing a song that had him in it." She turned to her brother. "Remember?"

He nodded.

"Will you sing it?" Ceres asked. "I've never heard of him before."

She looked around, and Stone shrugged his shoulders, but Adler blinked and nodded.

"I have," Adler said. "Arran was what I heard him called. It was in a pub in Atlius long ago, late at night. Some boozed-up gypsy was singing songs about him. Figured it was just something he made up."

"Give me a minute to remember the words," Marilyn said, rubbing her chin. "I remember bits and pieces."

"I remember," Drâon said, clearing his throat.

The hairs on Stone's head tingled as his friend began to sing. His tone was low and deep, but heartfelt and soft. He sang with a sweet melody of a father singing their weary-eyed child off to a sweet slumber. Yet, it was powerful as a tale of a dragon should be—strong and terrifying. The song rolled as it captured them, seizing their spirits, as if time itself had slowed, and all that remained was a sweet father singing to his child.

THE WINDS SWIFT, they blew,
    Washed away the cold, wet dew.

· · ·

C.K. RIEKE

OF A MORN SO SOFT,
    With wicked dreams dreamt so oft.

THE LIONS, they crept,
    While the mice quiet, they slept.

WITH TOOTH AND CLAW, the lions did dine,
    The mice they shivered, quivered, and died.

THE LIONS GREW FAT,
    The deadliest of cats.

THEY STALKED, they sneaked,
    And in the night, floorboards creaked.

MICE NAUGHT WERE their only prey,
    For children, soundly at night, they lay.

LIONS IN THE NIGHT,
    They terror, they fright.

WITH SOFT PILLOWS beneath their heads,
    Sweet children sleep, with bellies fed.

THE LIONS' teeth do creep,
    While the children soundly sleep.

. . .

As the lion goes to feed,
    A blinding light does bleed.

The dragon with wings so blue,
    Arises, so beautiful, so true.

Virranas, the dragon as old as time,
    Spreads his wings, glimmering, flying.

The lions do flee,
    While the child rests with glee.

For no lion returns,
    While the dragon of frost burns.

So lay your head calm,
    For tomorrow will come.

With the sun's golden, warm light,
    And Momma will squeeze you tight.

Chapter Thirty-One

orvaire's head hung as the final words left his lips. The void of the cavern left a looming last echo of the last words of the song.

The torch crackled as King Joridd held it up to the statue of the Great Frost Dragon, by whichever name it was called. He held it high and low, as its light glowed off the jeweled blue gems that ordained its towering height.

They each crept in closer to behold perhaps the most stunning thing they'd ever seen, constructed by man. Stone wondered if it indeed was made by man, now that he knew the one god was real.

"How are we gonna use it?" Ceres finally broke the silence. "Can I touch it?"

Joridd nodded to her. And then raised the torch up before the dragon's head. "It holds the weapon, protects it. It's its guardian."

As soon as he said those words, Stone's stomach lurched up into his throat.

Ceres touched the statue with her eager, nervous fingers.

"It's cold." There was a chill in her voice.

"It hasn't been seen in centuries," Marilyn said. "What magic has kept it so pristine?"

Stone stood on his tiptoes to see what the torch was showering its light upon. The dragon's mouth was too high for him to see directly into.

"Need a lift?" Adler asked.

"I think I got it," he said. He reached up, with his fingertips six inches shy of the bottom lip of the open mouth.

"Careful," Ceres said. "Teeth look sharp."

He scanned both sides of the mouth and then leaped. Digging his fingers in between the teeth, holding onto both sides. He pulled himself up with a groan. His eyes rose over the bottom lip, the light of the torch nearly blinding to his side. Adjusting his eyes, squinting deep, and blinking hard, he looked into the dragon's open maw.

It was dark, and slid back into the back of the dragon's mouth, which was a full three feet in. The blue sparked a deeper shade of blue, like the waters of the Sonter. But then he caught a glimmer of color—a sparkling shade that didn't match the rest. At first, it reflected the light of the torch with an orange hue, almost mimicking a fire itself. As he pulled himself farther up, and more into the mouth—he saw it glimmered with a hue of red.

Deep inside the frost dragon's mouth, cradled at the back of its serpentine tongue... rested a red jewel.

"What is it?" Adler pressed. "What's in there?"

Stone propped his chest onto the bottom of the dragon's mouth and brought one of his arms up, shaking the cramp in his fingers away. His hand and arm slid into the throat of the dragon statue. With a solid stretch and a groan, his fingers clenched onto the jewel—which was no bigger than a thimble.

In the center, held tightly in his fist, Stone carefully exited himself from the statue, falling softly onto the rocky ground beneath the statue. He turned slowly, extending his hand, and all eyes were upon it.

He uncurled his fingers, and there were audible gasps, most noticeably, from Marilyn and Drâon.

"By all that's holy," she said under her breath.

Corvaire cleared his throat. "I always wondered why this was called the Divine City. Now I know."

"Hand it to me," the king said in a commanding voice. He handed the torch to Vandress.

Stone hesitated. He didn't know why, though.

He didn't want the power of the stone. But he didn't want to hand it away either. Joridd was the king after all, though, and a friend.

Stone took a deep breath and held his open palm out for the king, who plucked the jewel out like a piece of candy.

The king held it up to the torchlight, examining it as he turned it and it sparkled off its sharply-cut angles.

In a shocking move, the king threw it to the ground, hurtling it at great speed. Stone's mouth flung open, and his eyes widened as he moved to catch it. But the jewel fell to the ground, bouncing before it fell to a spot on its back on the flat rocks.

The king took his sword up from his sheath.

"Joridd, what're you doing?" Stone said. "We need that!"

The king slammed his sword down onto the small red gem, hitting it with his sharp Masummand Steel with wicked precision.

Stone's fingers were wide and shaking. He felt helpless as he watched the jewel break and shatter. He turned his head, looking around at the others to see what was going on. They looked as confused as he felt by their paled expressions.

The only one who wasn't… was Vandress. She looked as collected as if she'd just emerged from a bath. She withheld an amused smile as best she could.

"It..." Stone murmured. "It was a fake...?"

Her smile was shown with true splendor then.

"A good one at that," Vandress said. "Would've fooled me."

"Then... where?" Stone said. "What are we doing here?"

"There is a stone here," Joridd said, sheathing his sword. "And the Great Frost Dragon protects it."

"Where is it?" Stone asked, scratching his brow.

"There is only one way to get it," the king said. "At least that's what the ancient text said."

"What did it say?" Marilyn asked, folding her arms and shifting her weight to her side.

"The night I was crowned," he said, gently gliding his fingers down his arm still hung from the sling, "I was given the chest of ancient knowledge passed down from monarch to monarch. Inside were scrolls and texts for my eyes only. I ended up the entire night going through things written I could've never dreamed of. Some of the oldest information was carved into slabs at the bottom of the chest. Those were what I read first, and as soon as I read the one about this statue here, I didn't read another letter. I just stared out the window, down onto the city. It was far too great of a coincidence to cast aside."

"And?" Drâon said, rushing him to finish.

"I conferred with her," he said.

"Yes," Vandress said, putting her arms behind her. "Not only has it never happened in the history of these lands, and all the written texts, but it has only just passed now."

"What?" Stone asked. He didn't notice, but his foot was tapping fast.

"The stone is inside the statue," Joridd said. "And there is only one way to get in."

Joridd and Vandress both lowered their sights on Ceres.

"What—me?"

"This weapon is only to be used in the direst of emergencies," Joridd said. "It is the single most powerful weapon in the world. No king or queen, should they want to use it, had been able to, because the key to the lock is so rare that it never existed—until now."

Corvaire growled. "So, Arken was right when he said there was one here…"

"Yes," Joridd nodded. "Although I didn't know myself until just days ago."

"But the queen knew," Adler said.

"Yes," the king said. "Only she knew."

"So, what is it Ceres can do?" Marilyn asked. "And you are sure that this is the time to open the lock?"

"Vandress and I talked long about it," the king said, with the slightest of trembles in his voice. "We decided… if not now, then when? The Great God himself has stirred to life; threatening recreation and a new age of oppression. None are powerful enough to even disagree with him, let alone fight him."

"Are we sure he's not listening?" Adler asked, looking nervously at the walls.

"There are texts about him too," Joridd said. "I must admit, I did not fully believe he was real until I saw him before my eyes. But there are places the god's eyes and ears cannot pierce. This is one of those places. He cannot see where the stones are. They are like the bottom of the Obsidian to him, like an endless chasm."

"Did they give a weakness?" Corvaire asked. "A way to beat him?"

The king cleared his throat. "No. He is older than all the texts—perhaps older than written language. There is no way to beat him, other than becoming him."

Stone's jaw dropped.

"This is the only way," Joridd said.

Ceres brushed her hair back behind her ears, licking her lips. "What do I got to do?"

Joridd stepped back for Vandress to walk up to Ceres, reaching out and grabbing both of her hands. They stood there momentarily, Vandress holding her hands delicately between them. Her amber eyes glowed like a tiger's.

"A Majestic Wild must free the stone from the serpentine statue. Only she can decide to free the Adralite. But it is buried deep within the heart of the statue that no sword or spell can break—except one."

"What must I do?"

"Fire! No ice will break the Great Frost Dragon!"

Marilyn gasped with wide eyes. Corvaire crossed his arms and growled, shaking his head.

"How..." Marilyn muttered. "How would they know...?"

Vandress shook Ceres' arms. "You... are the only one who can free the Adralite from its resting place, since the beginning of time."

Ceres stood there with a paled expression. Stone didn't know what to say and Adler stood there with his arms crossed, staring blankly at her—but Stone could tell his brain was buzzing.

"Who could write this?" Marilyn asked. "Did the tablet tell how someone could know that Ceres would arise as an Old Mother of her set? This is far beyond coincidence."

"This is why I conferred with Vandress," the king said. "This not only has grave consequences, but for the first person with the ability to open such a weapon arising *just* after everything that has happened... it must have been designed this way by someone, or something, clairvoyant. That's the only thing I can think."

Ceres turned her head to peer over her shoulder at the colossal statue. It sparkled magically in the firelight.

Stone thought about how long this statue of the dragon

had sat there. *How many kings and queens had stood before it, puzzling over why they couldn't be the ones to open it—even if they wanted to? Surely, some were tempted by the power dug in deep within. Ceres is the only one in all the ages with the ability... but should she?*

"What say you? Old Mother?" Joridd asked. "If you wish to break the Great Frost Dragon, then we will give you the one spell that would break free the Adralite."

"I—I don't know," she said, looking up at the maw of the beast. Its teeth were shown, sharp and menacing as it loomed over them. "Stone?"

He sighed. "If we take the stone... we'll have to use it... can't risk Arken getting it... where we're going..."

"Crysinthian would take this one too," Adler said, "if he knew..."

"Maybe one of you should take it." Stone was looking at Drâon and Marilyn. "You've already proven your valor. Few would question that decision."

"There are those in the city above that would fight for the red gem," Drâon said. "It offers unimaginable power."

"It would not only be used against Arken," Marilyn said, scratching her cheek. "This would be used to fight against *his* rule."

"I trust you to carry the Adralite into this battle," Corvaire said, unfolding his strong arms and bowing his head slightly to Stone.

"As do I," Marilyn said, also bowing.

"I already lost one," Stone said in a solemn voice.

"That will not happen again," Marilyn said.

Stone's head sunk and his chin dropped to his chest. He couldn't hide his feelings.

"What's wrong?" Ceres asked. "You are deserving."

"I—" he struggled to say. His teeth clenched as he thought of it, yet it made him overwhelmingly sad.

"What is it?"

"I—what if he is a part of me? What if I'm like him? I can't use the stone. I could become… like him."

Ceres grabbed his chin gently, gliding his gaze to meet hers.

"You're not like him. Nothing like him! Get that through your thick skull."

"You're not," Adler said. "You're good. I've seen it so many times. Just because that spell spread him out and into you, doesn't mean anything. You're you, and he's him—completely opposite. That's why you're the one to do this. He fears you because he knows what you're capable of."

"He wants me," Stone nearly interrupted him. "He wants me to be by his side while he creates his world in his image. He wants me to use the Adralite and kill Crysinthian. He told me that. This is exactly what he wants…"

Chapter Thirty-Two

A stark silence filled the long cavern. Not a cleared throat, no breeze rustled, and the Great Frosted Dragon loomed large. Stone heard the crackle of the torch, and thick beyond was the unease and tension so taut if it were cut it would shudder the very walls of the hidden cave.

"He what?" Joridd finally asked. There was a sternness in his voice, and his body tensed visibly.

Stone's palms were drenched. He wiped them on his pants.

"I—I didn't tell you because…" he said, not knowing what to say next.

"The Dark King told you this would happen?" Joridd withheld himself from approaching Stone. Vandress scratched her arms, looking back and forth between the two. "Did you know of this?" He was looking at Corvaire and Marilyn, who didn't respond physically.

"We did," Corvaire said after a long pause of the king fuming through his nostrils.

"I didn't mean to hide it from you," Stone said. "I just… I guess I didn't want him to be right. Does that make sense?"

"It doesn't matter what he said." Vandress brushed her

dress back at her thighs. "What matters is what the scripture said. Whether he knew it or not is of little concern. This is destiny in our presence. We are merely the vessels of the freeing of the Adralite."

"It matters," the king growled. Suddenly, Stone knew what it was like for those invading mages to be face to face against the angry general.

"My king," Vandress said in a calm, soothing voice. "Direct your anger at the Dark King, and not our savior."

Stone wanted to crawl inside himself.

"He didn't want to say nothin' because we didn't know if it was true or not," Ceres said. "Might have changed this moment, and in the end, this may be what we need to win the war."

"King Joridd," Drâon said. "Teach Ceres the spell. We will have time to sort through this later." He paused; giving a deep sigh. "Gracelyn and Rosen are out there alone with them. This may be our best bet to save them. We must break the Adralite free and get the dragons back up into the air. The final battle is still ahead of us. Saving Valeren wasn't the end."

The king glared at him—then closed his eyes and took in a great breath, exhaling deep through the hairs in his nostrils.

"Very well," he said, pulling his shoulders back, but his arms relaxed. "Do it."

Vandress approached Ceres as the others gave them space from behind, far enough to be wary of the spell, but close enough to not miss anything.

The two women stood side by side, facing the dragon. The statue had stood longer than anyone knew, and this would be the last few moments of its existence. Stone noticed Adler rubbing his knuckles, bobbing slightly.

Marilyn had a look of sheer pride on her face, as if she'd raised Ceres from babe to the woman who stood before them.

Ceres had her hood pulled back and her golden hair fell

halfway down her back. She stood proud and true next to Vandress, whose jewelry sparkled along her arms in the torchlight. The king stood to the side, holding out the torch, causing the blue gems on the statue to shimmer like diamonds.

"You know one day you'll be teaching me spells," Vandress said in a soft voice, as if she were the pupil speaking to the master. It was almost bashful, yet playful. "You'll be young and beautiful, and I'll be old and wrinkled."

"If we live past this," Ceres said, rubbing her hands together, as if she were about to get into a fight with someone twice her size. She bounced up and down, cracking her neck. "And you'll always be beautiful."

"You better remember to say that to me when I need help getting up to pee," Vandress said, with her head cocked back, looking up at the statue, who seemed to glare back down at her.

"Deal," Ceres said. "I'm ready…"

"The spell is a fire spell that will come from deep within. It will be jarring, and you may feel faint, but you have to keep it going until it's complete. Any other besides a Majestic Wild would not survive."

Stone wiped the sweat from his brow, brushing his hair back, gulping deeply.

"I'll be fine," Ceres said in a reaffirming voice.

Those around them watched with pride and nervous tension.

"We've come a long way," Adler said. "Seems like only yesterday she cast her first spell."

Stone's heart swelled, and he could help but smile.

"The words are," Vandress said. "*Expulove Tormentum Aiges.*"

Ceres took one breath, shaking her arms out at her sides.

"All right. I got this. You've got this Ceres. You've got this… *Expulove Tormentum Aiges!*"

The air shook with violent light and heat.

White light overcame Ceres, and Vandress' hair and dress whipped angrily.

The fire of the king's torch extinguished.

Ceres screamed.

Stone brought his forearm over his brow but forced himself to watch.

His clothes singed, and heat radiated from Ceres' body.

Her scream echoed throughout the cavern as if she was giving birth.

The clothes burned from her body and her skin beamed in white heat.

Flames flew from her skin as they each were forced back.

The dragon beyond hummed and vibrated.

She screamed again.

"She's dying," Adler shouted. "We've got to stop this!"

"Let her do this!" Marilyn yelled over the raging inferno before them.

"No! She's got to stop! She's on fire!" Adler rushed to her, putting his own life at risk. Stone grabbed an arm, and Drâon grabbed the other while Adler fought to break free.

"Easy," Drâon said. "She knows what she's doing!"

The screams shook the cavern as the statue cracked down in the center of its face.

The flames erupted harder, sending them back as the heat was overwhelming.

Stone felt his eyelashes and eyebrows burn.

"*Ovalum Wendarum*," Vandress cast, throwing her arms up and sending up an orb of cold that bit Stone to the bone instantly. He, Adler, and Corvaire were thrown to the ground from the blast. Stone's elbow knocked hard into the rock, but that pain was nothing compared to the adrenaline that coursed through his veins.

Through the spell that caused snow to form with the sphere, Stone saw the shiver of heat beyond, and watched as the statue of the Great Frost Dragon cracked, broke, and flew backward; exploding into tiny pieces. Ceres' arms were out wide above her as pillars of flame tore out of them and down onto the statue.

He couldn't hear her screams, but the cavern shook so hard he thought it may come down on them.

In a flash of white light, the inferno beyond the ice spell died away to darkness. Vandress pulled her spell back into her and they were left in bleak, absolute darkness.

Stone was on his back, his elbow throbbed, and his skin stung from being burned and then hit with an extreme, high-mountain cold.

He heard the spark of flint and steel, and the sparks flung onto the torch at the king's feet. It lit, and he picked it up with his one arm.

The statue was gone, and as Stone got back to his feet and his eyes were able to focus on the soft light, he saw Ceres on the ground, naked and pale, lying on her side—motionless.

Adler and Stone ran to her.

"Ceres, Ceres!" Adler said, pulling her up between his arms and gently caressing her cheek with his fingers. "Wake up."

"She's breathing," Marilyn said, crouching and feeling her breath with the back of her fingers.

Stone took his shirt off and draped it over her.

She moaned—long and slow. Her eyes were closed; twitching, as if off in a dream. Her limbs were limp as Adler tried waking her. Her skin was pale, as Stone expected it to be blackened with soot and ash from the fires that consumed her, but she was unscathed—save for her clothes that were burned away to nothing. Her sword rested at her side, burning red.

In the commotion, Stone noticed the light of the torch fading and heard the sound of rocks being stepped through.

Ceres slowly opened her eyes... "Adler..." she groaned painfully.

Stone, seeing her awake, stood, following the torchlight. Joridd, Vandress, and Drâon were fanning out into the rubble. Stone followed.

The jewels under his boots scattered like deep piles of marbles as he bent over, looking into them.

"She all right?" Vandress asked next to Joridd.

While Adler was so concerned with Ceres' condition, Marilyn replied. "I believe so, or at least she will be. She's exhausted her Elessior. She'll need plenty of rest after this."

That soothed Stone's mind, as he dug his hands into the gems like splashing through water.

"Anything?" Joridd asked, giving the torch to Corvaire, so he could dig into the mound of blue gems himself.

Vandress was on her knees, swashing through the thousands of gems. "No."

Marilyn left Ceres' side, after removing her tunic and placing it loosely over her. Adler tugged it down onto her gently, even placing her arms through the sleeves of Stone's shirt. She appeared to be stirring back to consciousness.

Corvaire even was brushing away piles of jewels with his free hand. With the scattered, broken gems, the piles went back over twenty feet into the cavern.

"You did it," Adler said, cradling Ceres in his arms. "Rest a little while."

"A—Adler," she groaned. "I..."

Her head flopped to her shoulder, which he caught.

"Easy," he said, running his fingers through her hair.

Her eyes opened slowly, her normally mossy green eyes were dark, and her freckles were rosy on her flushed cheeks.

"I—" she moaned.

"It's okay," he said. "I've got you."

She lifted her hand, and her knuckles brushed against his neck, tickling him.

"Stone..." Her voice was weak and hoarse.

"He's here too."

"Stone," she said. "The stone... I've got it..."

She uncurled her fingers and his eyes went wide.

Resting within the cracks in the palm of her hand sat a sparkling, dark jewel—cut like a diamond in the shape of a teardrop. It was an otherworldly red, like that of a blazing sunset on a murderous eve.

His mouth slacked, but no words came out.

From behind, the mounds of blue jewels shifted as the others came to them.

"It is here," Vandress said in a voice of awe.

It sent shivers up Stone's spine hearing such a powerful sorceress as Vandress speak with a certain... terror... in her voice.

"Let me see it," Joridd said, as Corvaire held the torch brightly up before him as he leaned down to look into Ceres' pale, damp palm.

His strong fingers moved to pluck it from her, but they withheld it in a suspended pose, like a puppeteer unsure of the puppet's next move.

He glared at Marilyn, and then at Drâon, and finally at Stone.

The king stood back up straight, with his hand over his chest, wrapping his fingers around his other arm.

"It is yours to take," he said as if bequeathing a royal decree. "The jewel of the gods came to you once." He bowed his head slightly. "This time you've come to it."

"There is no other Adralite," Vandress said in a hollow, powerful voice that caused Marilyn to stir. "This one is named the Divine Stone, simply enough. The one that was rumored to rest deep within the Mountain of the Mystics was the Mystic Stone, but had never been found, until it appeared to you."

"How do you know this?" Corvaire asked. "From the chest of king's tombs?"

"Aye," Joridd said.

"So, this is it, then?" Marilyn the Conjurer asked. "Our last chance to save this world?"

"Aye," Joridd said.

Ceres reached up, holding the Adralite toward Stone.

"Here," he said, stronger than before. "Take it. It's yours."

Stone swallowed deep but tried to hide it. He collected himself to appear as strong as he could, as unafraid as he could, and as worthy as he could.

He bowed his head and knelt beside her. His hand hovered above hers, and then he delicately plucked the red, glimmering stone from her. He held it up with the flat of his hand, for all to see.

"We have the weapon now," he said coldly. "They took what has mattered most to us." He clenched his teeth and curled his fingers over the Adralite. "Now let's go take this fight to them. Gracelyn and Rosen... we're coming..."

PART V
THE ULTIMATE SACRIFICE

Chapter Thirty-Three

Sheets of rain poured down, clapping into the new stone blocks of the city, draining away into carved gutters. The rains poured out of slits within the walls, making the massive city look like a divine fountain. Heavy clouds rolled over as if foreboding the inevitable; the rise of the Crysinthian —in flesh and power.

The world was changing.

Gracelyn and Rosen peered down upon the newly erected city of white. Their clothes clung to their bodies and their hair stuck to their faces and heavy beads of rain trickled off the hair that wasn't.

The rolling fog turned to fervent rain with streaking, searing hot lightning in the clouds just above. The god had departed as quickly as he appeared, and as the two girls watched the shadow of the floating fortress overcome the city, the ground beneath their feet shook violently, as if the earth was breaking.

They clung to the wet stone walls, which attempted to slam into their stomachs from the sudden, jarring quake. The quake was brief, leaving a rumble beneath them that permeated all around.

"We... we stopped," Gracelyn said, eyeing the floating city's building, which remained unharmed.

"I think..." Rosen said, brushing the rain from her brow, "it looks like this is the crown to the new capital."

The city had peaked atop the center of the high, main tower of the rebuilt capital, and was slowly twirling above.

"So," Gracelyn sighed, "this is where he's taking us. Our final destination."

"Final?"

"You heard what Arken said." Gracelyn looked up into the rain as it fell in heavy drops, and she closed her eyes. She pulled her hair back and squeezed the water from it balled behind her. "*He* isn't going to let us survive this."

"I don't believe him," Rosen said. "Why would *he* do that? He's a liar and his words are meaningless."

"I do," Gracelyn said. "Arken is twisted, cruel, and many other things, but I believe Crysinthian has brought us here for a reason, and I don't like that reason; whatever it is."

"Um... Gracelyn...?" Rosen said, looking down at her arms which were coursing with spidery beams of light.

Gracelyn had the same. She swallowed hard.

In an instant, blinding light overcame them. They grabbed each other's hands, as if in one last effort to feel another human touch, if that was their end.

But it was not.

The overwhelming light that enveloped them zapped away like lightning being pulled back by a fishing line from the sky. They were rattled and shaking, and their teeth chattered.

They were both holding hands still, startled as to what had happened. Both the girls were freezing, but the rains had disappeared, and so had the clouds. The warm light of fire came into view as they struggled to realize what had happened, and that they were still alive.

Candlelight brimmed along long walls in the seemingly never-ending long hall they were suddenly in. There were hundreds of them. They lined unadorned walls of white, smooth, octagonal stones. Rushing over to a wall, they gathered up a couple of candles, trying to warm their shivering fingers.

They heard a commotion behind; something was scraping on the ground back where they were.

"It's Arken," Rosen said through chattering teeth.

They both inspected the long hall they were in with the twenty-foot-high ceiling. There were windows of clear glass high up with sharp points at their tops. Had there been sun shining on the other side, it would have lit the hall spectacularly, but there was only gloom beyond.

Then they heard a voice that made them both jump in fright. It was deep and filled the hall.

"You are cold, let me warm you," the god said.

Without the light or any sign of magic, their clothes were transformed. Before they could even blink, they were both wearing dresses that fitted nicely. They were tight at their stomachs, but not too tight. Their arms were left bare, and their skin and hair were instantly dry, without a drop of rain. The dresses weren't wide at the bottom and resembled something the women of the court would wear in one of the three kingdoms.

Gracelyn's dress was a cascade of different hues of blue, and Rosen's was of red tints. The fabric was soft, so soft that to the touch, it was softer than silk.

"Better?" he asked.

The god was standing above Arken, in the center of the long hall, with no doors in sight. Arken didn't move, as he was bound as he was before with his arms and legs tied behind him, but the helmet they'd removed was gone, and his mouth was gagged.

"Still alive, I see," Gracelyn said. "He wasn't lying about that."

Crysinthian, who towered above them all, stood with muscular arms and legs, looking down at the Dark King. His glare was cold and overwhelmingly powerful, as if he could rip the man in half with his bare hands.

The god wore his silverish, white robes that hung motionless from his muscular form. His wavy beard twitched, signaling his frown as he looked down upon Arken.

"Yes, he is still alive," the king said coldly.

There was a long silence, as the god seemed not in a hurry to speak, and the two girls didn't know what to say. Arken's one eye darted around the room, scanning for something, or just inspecting his surroundings.

Finally, the king spoke. "What do you think of it?"

"It's fancy," Rosen said. Gracelyn elbowed her in the side.

"It's the most splendid thing in all creation," he said. "Worthy of worship."

"This is Aderogon," Gracelyn said. "Why did you rebuild the old capital?"

"This is New Aderogon," he said, taking in a deep inhale through his nostrils. "This is the center of our new world."

"But why?" Gracelyn asked. "Why now? Why didn't you stay wherever you were? Life was fine here, until he came with the dark dragons..."

Crysinthian spoke in a flat, emotionless tone, as if a mountain itself could speak. "It was not... fine. My children are lost. They need a guiding light to steer them in my direction. I've returned to give them that. Order, balance, and fear will bring the change I desire."

"Who are you?" Rosen's voice cracked, trying to remain brave as she uttered such words. "Were you always... *you*?"

"I am time. I am the sky. I am the earth from which you nourish your body of flesh, and to which you return when you perish."

"What I mean to say is... were you always a god?" Rosen asked. "What came before you? Who made you?"

An angry flame burned in his eyes as tendrils of lightning zapped out of the crow's feet on his tan face.

"I have high hopes for you, Majestic Wild," he said, and then his voice grew dark and grim. "Do not spoil my taste for you. You will do much, and flourish like the most beautiful flower. But I am *him*, and I rage. Fear me, but love me, and I will shower you with love."

"So, what is it you want from us?" Gracelyn asked. "You don't intend to let us leave; I presume? You've refused, and here we are, still alive."

The god put his arms behind him, pressing out his chest, and looking up at the windows from which the storm continued from the other side.

"You... and the dragons... are the most powerful beings in all existence," he said. "The Old Mothers have always been protectors. Mostly, they sit up on their mountain in peace, but when the time comes, they must reveal themselves to shift the balance back to order. If the kings get too strong, you contain. If the meek get too bold, you retrain." His back was still to them as Arken shifted in pain on the floor—convulsing. He irked and winced behind his gag. "You will do the same for me."

"So, you want us to be your guards?" Rosen asked. "That's why you brought us all the way here?"

"Yes."

"What are you not telling us?" Gracelyn asked. "Why aren't you revealing what you really mean? Just tell us. If you're going to keep us here against our will, then speak plain."

He looked over his shoulder, with one eye glaring at them.

"You will not return to the mountain. You will not harness your power in the shadows any longer."

Gracelyn crossed her arms and Rosen's knee bobbed and her foot tapped, and she scratched her shoulder.

He turned, rising from the floor, letting his robes tickle the white stones. His strong arms, with long veins running along the muscles and down to his chiseled hands, were held out wide.

"You will become what no other of your kin have been," he said. "You will rule over man, not hide from them."

Arken's gaze shot at both of them, seeming to be waiting to see their reactions.

Neither spoke. They stood there in quiet contemplation. Gracelyn looked back at the god as much as she could, but then looked down at her feet. Rosen twisted back and forth at her hips, looking up at the ceiling.

"You will take the thrones of the three great cities of my kingdom, and when the third of you comes into existence, then you three will rule as my loyal servants… forever."

The two girls still didn't have replies. They didn't dare refuse, or they may face his wrath right then and there. After all, they'd been warned about refusing him before.

The voice that broke the silence wasn't from them, or him… but from Arken on the ground… he was… laughing…

Crysinthian's eyes blazed in fury and his silver hair waved behind him as if drifting in the sea, even though there wasn't a breath of wind. He glided over to hover over the Dark King as the candlelight flickered from the rage he emitted.

The gag vanished, and Arken spat up a dark spatter of what looked like a tarry, black blood.

"Do you have something you wish to say, worm?" Crysinthian fumed.

"You don't share power," Arken laughed. "At the first sign of anything you deem treason, you'll murder them in cold blood. Then another will take her place until you finally get what you desire—slaves."

The god seemed to consider the notion, not lashing out at the bound man beneath him.

"He doesn't have his sword," Gracelyn whispered into Rosen's ear. Rosen scratched her thigh.

"I don't agree with your terms," the god said, "but I don't deny your words. I am the one and only god, and I command loyalty and fealty. I will have no slaves, but I will abide no treason."

The Dark King winced in pain again and laughed once more.

"A slave is a slave. No matter what crown you put on their head, with how many jewels or how many attendants to wipe your ass, he'll use you until he doesn't."

The gag appeared again, wrapping tightly around his mouth, causing the black veins to sharpen in tone beneath his pale, scarred skin.

"What of the other kings and queens of the castles?" Gracelyn asked.

"They've failed me. King Roderix is a weak buffoon, and the new King Joridd is the servant of Queen Velecitor. She never bowed to me; I could feel her lies spread into the city like a sickness. They will both be... removed from their thrones."

"You're going to kill them, aren't you?" Rosen asked, clenching her fists.

Crysinthian lowered himself to the ground, stepping over Arken's body in a single, powerful stride. "Many will die." His voice was stark and icy. "But many more will be born into the new age. For the old age is done, and this is my new, the Age of Tranquility."

"If we refuse?" Gracelyn sneered.

"Then you die..."

Chapter Thirty-Four

As they emerged back out into the early evening dusk of the city, the faint, pale moon glowed through fast-drifting clouds. Winds rushed in from the north as they walked out of a hidden doorway that hadn't been unlatched in what seemed like decades by the rust and squeal of its hinges.

Stone had his hand in his pockets, needing the Adralite to at least be touching his fingers at all times. He scanned the alleyway carefully, looking up at the hanging clotheslines above and in the murky windows at their sides.

Drâon and Adler helped Ceres through the door, with her thin, pale legs showing from under the shirts that were wrapped around her waist. She sighed and moaned frequently, as she was still exhausted from the spell down far under the city.

Stone knew she'd need rest. But there was no time.

They knew where Gracelyn and Rosen were. He had the weapon—all that was left was to call the dragons.

"We need to get her to a healer," Vandress said, walking

behind Ceres and putting her hand on her brow. She carries Ceres' sword in her other hand.

"One night," Stone said, looking up to the sky and the clouds that were rushing their way out to sea.

"She's weak," Adler said, with his dirty hair sticking to his wet brow.

Stone turned back to them. They halted as he stood before them. He put a hand on Adler's shoulder, while Drâon gave him a curious look.

"She should stay. She can rest. I have it. I'll go."

"Don't be stupid," Ceres said, struggling to get to her feet on her own. "You've said some foolish things in yer' time. But that has to be the damned dumbest one yet."

"I can do this alone," Stone said. "No one else has to get hurt."

He heard a scuttling of paws on the far side of the alley. He spun quickly... and saw Mud running at him with spit flinging behind him as he ran. He sat before Stone, wagging his tail madly.

"See," she said. "Even he knows we're all stickin' together."

"I can't see you get hurt," Stone said, grabbing her hand. "I can't lose anyone else. You've already done so much. Adler, you stay and watch her. I'm the only one who is safe against him now. I'll use the stone and..."

"You're not the only one who's lost friends," Adler said. "We're not gonna lose you, too. Besides, someone has got to go who's got some brains. No offense, you're quick to the sword, but you'll need some real, quick... uh... *thinkers* with you."

Ceres rolled her eyes.

"I'm going," Ceres said. "Just need to get some clothes. I'll be fine." She waved for her sword, which Vandress handed to her. Her wrist drooped as she held the heavy Masummand Steel sword.

"You need rest," Stone said.

"You need to shut your mouth," she growled.

"I'd listen to her," Corvaire said, a trickle of worry in his voice.

"Let us move," Joridd said, throwing the torch to the ground to burn out. "This is not a place to linger."

They moved through the city. Soldiers quickly recognized their king and moved to his aid. Soon there was a squadron of soldiers in full armor escorting them toward Mÿthryn Palace, and to the house where Ceres could change.

Many eyes watched them in the streets. Perhaps they knew Stone would be leaving soon, off to fight the god who had come. The queen's funeral was over. A new king had been crowned, and in secret, he had the weapon.

It wasn't only watching eyes that just wanted a view of the man who was destined to kill the invading King of Dark Dragons, or the woman who'd saved them from the sorceress Paltereth Mir, but many glares swept back into the alleys, and the shadows.

In their haste, Stone had an eerie feeling that he was forgetting something. There was something left in Valeren left unfinished, but he couldn't think of what. They would need the dragons, and hopefully, Grimdore would come too from her rest in the sea. They'd decided the night prior that Ceres would be the one to try the Song of Dragons to see if their friend would come. If not, they'd fly upon the backs of the new dragons Zênon and Īzadan. Although only one person would fit on the smaller, slender green dragon. Zênon was much bigger, broader, and older and would fit more. Belzarath, their old friend, would carry as many as she could as well.

Their fleet was nearly ready.

They made their way to the house where Ceres normally rested her head. Vandress and Marilyn helped her up to her room. Adler went into his room to gather his armor; Stone did the same.

While they carried it down into the main room on the first floor, a knock came at the door. One of the soldiers opened it. Stone was relieved to see the Guild Master's warm smile as he entered.

"You're not leaving without me," he said as he and Stone embraced. "Can't stand this political drivel any longer."

Ceres was busy upstairs as they heard sloppy footsteps on the floorboards.

"We will retrieve our armor," Corvaire said, as Marilyn was next to him. "We will meet back here shortly."

Joridd sighed. "I will remain here, although I do not wish to."

"King Joridd will stay with the city," Vandress said, placing her palm on his arm bound in the sling. "When we return, he will appear... different."

"What do ya mean?" Adler asked with a worried look on his face.

"They're taking the arm," the king said. "Salus had one last laugh, didn't he?" An angry spark lit in the king's eyes. "Didn't get to get my revenge..." His teeth clenched. "That was taken from me."

"How'd Arken know he was there?" Adler asked, as if to himself. "How'd he know right then and there? Arken's holed up with Crysinthian all the way up in Aderogon!"

"We may soon find out," Vandress said.

"We will return," Corvaire said as he and his sister left the house.

This is it. We're finally getting ready. My heart is pounding!

"We're really going," Adler said. "Here we come, Gracelyn, here we come, Rosen!"

"I'm so sorry about your arm," Stone said.

The king groaned, looking down at the sling. "Yeah, looks like my days of hard fighting and training are behind me. The crown and my people are where my next battle begins. I've got her to look after me and Valeren." He winked at Vandress. "Could be worse."

They heard the floorboards creak overhead, as the footsteps made their way to the edge of the stairwell. Ceres grasped the handrail as she made her way down the stairs, moving both boots to one tread, then going down one by one.

Her ravishing blond hair fell out of the sides of her dark blue hood like a horse's mane fell down both sides of its strong neck. Silver armor, left for her in her room at the king's command adorned her chest. It was crafted with a white inlay of some metal that resembled the color of bone. At the center of the plate armor was fashioned the sigil of the Elessior—the Artican—two hands cradling three vertical spheres, the sun at the top, the crescent moon at the bottom, and the center resembling a piercing eye.

Silver gauntlets of dark gray were strapped to her forearms and pauldrons and grieves of the same metal fitted her well at the shoulders and legs.

"You look," Adler said with his jaw slacked, "ravishing."

She seemed not to notice his comment, waving away any help, and making her way down one step at a time. Her breathing was heavy.

Stone seriously worried about her going into battle in the state she was in. He rubbed his fingers together nervously.

Paying so much attention to her, he hadn't noticed that the king and Vandress were staring at the door to the house, or perhaps caring more for what lay beyond.

Then he heard it—there was a commotion going on outside, and shouting!

"What's that racket?" Conrad said, walking over and pulling at the latch. He fought to pull it open but couldn't. "It's locked." His dark eyes were wide.

King Joridd strode over angrily to the door. "Open this door at once!"

A man's voice spoke loudly from the other side. "We were told to lock it by the man of Darakon and his sister, the Conjurer."

"Open this door at once. This is your king!"

They heard the rattle of keys, and one quickly slid into the lock, popping it open.

"What's going on?" Ceres asked, halfway down the stairs, bending down to peer outside.

"Don't know," Adler said. "Some commotion... Corvaire locked the door. He locked us in..."

Joridd shoved the door open with his shoulder, knocking it hard into the soldier who opened it. Mud rushed in.

The king slid out of the room, with Vandress right behind. The Guild Master went out next, and Stone followed. What he saw took his breath away—and not in a good way.

Corvaire and Marilyn were still there, but both with their hands on the grips of their swords, and they were glaring out at hundreds of people surrounding the house—most of them wearing long white robes. They had swords, spears, and bows held out at the ready. They were in armor, and many were on rooftops. The sigil they wore on their armor and robes—the thin, golden cross—Stone had recognized many times before, and as he glared out at the round-faced man with the spectacles and tall hat of gold and seawater blue.

Polav...

There was a stark tension in the air, something that could be split with a sharp blade. The soldiers beside Stone were shifting uneasily, unsure about the entrance of the guards of the church. Some of the men holding out deadly weapons at them may be comrades, friends, or people they play cards with.

Bowstrings were drawn tight, and wobbly knuckles held arrows fixed in them, many of them aimed at Stone.

Mud whined at his side.

"Go get Belzarath, boy." Mud looked up at him, cocking

his head. "Mud, go get Belzarath." The black dog with the white spot over his eye took one brief look at the tense army before them and ran off into the darkness of a nearby alley.

"Polav," the king thundered. "What do you think you're doing? How dare you!"

Polav was behind a line of guards in fresh armor, seemingly unseen in battle. They held long tridents, and Stone wondered, *where were they in the battle?*

"This has gone on far too long, this charade," the high priest said. His dark eyebrows frowned down; his thin lips grew so thin they nearly disappeared. "Drop your weapons, return to the dwelling, and we will speak about what will happen next. There needs to be no fight."

"This is your king, you fool!" Vandress said, screaming with her arms out wide.

"You would not win this fight," Corvaire said coldly. "This is very unwise."

Stone was fuming with hot lead in his veins, but watched nervously at the bowmen whose sharp-tipped arrows were pointed at his friends. He touched the Adralite with his index finger—rolling it end over end in his pocket. Polav noticed this, raising one of his full, dark eyebrows, but didn't pay more than a second's notice.

"This is heresy," Polav proclaimed. "Crysinthian is and always will be our creator, our protector, our savior."

"He kidnapped our friends," Adler shouted in rage.

"*He* was here before, and *He* will be after. *He* is eternity," the high priest said, moving his hands out before him in a cross shape. He had no weapon visible to Stone.

"Alexander Polav," Joridd said, trying to calm himself. "You have one chance to walk away from this. One. Every soldier of the Vlaer will be here any second. You'd be a fool to match your swords against the magic here."

A smile rose on Polav's face. It was playful, but with a devious nature. "Your Vlaer?"

Instantly, Stone unsheathed his sword to the guards that stood next to him, most of whom were startled and pulled their weapons up over their heads, but there were four that kept their blades centered before them.

Polav growled, "He who is a pious man, will hold no man in greater esteem than Him. For he who loves *any* more than Him does not love Him at all, and is the same as a beast, knowing not what true love is."

"He's infiltrated the Vlaer!" Stone yelled.

Polav smiled again. "There's no infiltrated. There are simply wise, righteous men… and there are heretics."

Chapter Thirty-Five

❦

The king was speechless for the first time Stone had ever seen. Even in the fight against the invading mages, he always seemed to know what to do. Now... his own were raising swords against him.

This was more than betrayal. These were his brothers; his kin. Stone saw the fuel pouring into the flames of intensity in his eyes. Polav had taken away a part of Joridd's family.

Stone was still thinking about how their magic would crush Polav's forces before they could even release an arrow. Corvaire alone could decimate them with spells of his, like Bolt of Light, Storm of Thunder, or Storm or Wasps.

"Stand down and drop your weapons," Polav said angrily then. "This game is over, and has gone on far too long." He glowered at Stone.

The door behind slammed open. Stone and the others spun to realize Ceres wasn't even outside yet.

"You good-for-nothin' waste of air!" She fumed with fists balled at her side, stampeding through the soldiers. "You're gonna take his side? Didn't ya hear what he said? How many people are gonna die because he said so? He wants to make everyone his servants and slaves! You're dumb enough ta' think he's gonna treat you well because you're a suck-up? Well, you can suck on this!" She raised her middle finger at him.

The thick-necked, pale man's skin flushed red. His eyes squinted, although he was attempting to withhold his emotions by choking back his sharp tongue and wiping the sweat from his brow.

"And one more thing!"

Adler was gently trying to calm her and hold her back from walking straight up to the heavily guarded high priest.

"You should be thankin' us for saving your cushiony ass while you sat in your ivory tower, readin' stories and actin' like you know which end the shite comes out of! Crysinthian would be ashamed of your cowardice!"

"Enough!" he said. "You may use my name in vain, but I will not stand for you to even utter his name in such a tone."

"What're you gonna do about it?" she asked, ripping icy, blue flames into her hands.

"Me?" he grinned. "Nothing... But them... they aren't impressed..."

Stone's jaw slacked.

Polav moved to the side, revealing shadowy figures walking up from behind him. Stone recognized the faces, causing his heart to thump hard in his chest.

"Oh, no..." Ceres muttered, taking slow steps back.

Their faces warmed in the light of the road, but it wasn't their faces that necessarily sent shivers down Stone's neck. It was the number of them.

"The seven..." Vandress said under her breath. "All of them? How?"

"If you use your magic here," Polav proclaimed, sending echoes down the street. "Magic will be used against you."

Any glances or wandering stares from anywhere else on the

plaza vanished. The people of Valeren knew the destruction of magic; now more than ever.

"I'll say this again," the high priest said with sweat trickling down from under his pointed hat, "throw down your weapons. We only wish to talk this through. Violence has never been the way of the church, unless *absolutely* necessary…"

"We can take them," Joridd said in a cold, low voice to Vandress.

"But…" Vandress said in a somber tone Stone seldomly heard. "They're… they're our friends…"

"Nevertheless," the king said. "Total victory against the Dark King and the Neferian trumps alliances that proved to be broken links in the stronger chain."

Stone tapped his toe anxiously, not knowing exactly what was going to happen. Those bowstrings were still pulled taut after all, and the shining spears gleamed heavily.

"We must put our faith in Him once again," Polav said. "He will rid this world of Arken Shadowborn, erase his curse from our lands. Whatever His will thereafter is divine fate, and we will obey His wishes."

"You would willingly be his slaves?" Stone asked. "Where does it ask that in your books?"

"Not slaves… instruments. And I'm not here to barter with heretics and heathens. You were even once a man of the cloth, Joridd of House Boulme. Tell me, when did your faith waver and break so? Was it when you lost Helen? Was it when you lost your wife?"

Polav's expression was a practiced calm, a sheepish skin pulled over a wolf's ready fangs.

"Don't say her name," Joridd said. "You defile her honor by even mentioning her name here." His teeth gritted and the veins in his arm bulged, hefting the Masummand Steel sword in his hand.

"She passed far too soon," the high priest said. "She was a

sweet angel in this life. But her faith proved weak, in the end. That shouldn't have driven you closer to Him. We would have showered you with light and understanding, instead..."

"Stop this at once," Drâon shouted, startling soldiers on both sides. "Do not make this personal. He is your king, and any such insurrection is grounds for so many crimes I cannot state them all here." He then turned his attention away from Polav and spoke directly to the men and women around; the soldiers, the archers, and the seven.

Stone caught Margaret's glare. Her eyes wavered, and she looked at the brink of tears.

She's distraught. I can see the pain in her eyes.

"The only true crime is that of betrayal of the one God," Polav said.

"Yup," Adler said. "Gonna have to disagree with ya on that one. Lots of worse laws to break than that one..."

Polav disregarded his statement. "Well... then, here we are. I cannot allow you to lift arms against Him, from which you would surely perish, but spark the wrath of the great Crysinthian. You'd be inviting the wrath of our savior." He scowled. His look was cruel and menacing. His shoulders hulked underneath his robes, his eyes grew dark and powerful, and his words twisted and there was a long hiss when he said the god's name.

There it is. He's finally revealing his inner self. It looks as if he's about to transform into a demon. He's so wrapped up in hate and control he doesn't even look human.

He muttered something under his breath, making the soldiers in front of him shift in unease. Stone wanted to know what it was that he said, but there was too much space between them.

"We don't want to have to fight you," Marilyn the Conjurer said loudly, sending many in the seven to avoid her gaze. "But we will not hesitate to defend ourselves. We are going to

Aderogon—with or without your consent. Valeren has only one king, and he is not you."

Polav fumed red; raging mad.

Joridd turned to the soldier of the Vlaer standing beside him. "How many in number do we have?"

"Difficult to say," the soldier said in as hard of a tone he could muster. "Traitors within has never happened like this."

Joridd groaned. "We will deal with this… after I deal with him."

"It doesn't have to be like this," Margaret said, standing in the middle of the seven, who all watched her as she stepped forward. "We want the same thing. The Dark King must be stopped. We would go with you anywhere to rid the Worforgon of his madness. But you can't do this. You can't go after Him."

"He has our friends," Stone said. "They were willing to fight for you. They were willing to die for your city, which they've never even been to."

"You cannot go against God," Margaret said, with more passion in her voice. Stone started to realize her nervousness didn't match her conviction in this. "Even when it comes to the Majestic Wilds. He is the creator."

"He's a charlatan!" Adler poked the crowd. They moved angrily, wanting to lurch out, to attack, to hurt him.

Polav raised his hand to hold their attack at bay. More were joining their ranks from behind; sneaking through alleys, coming down from rooftops. They numbered two hundred already—and more were joining.

"What will it be?" Polav said. "I'm a patient man, but I don't abide insults, and I will not let this ruse go on any longer."

"What do we do?" Ceres asked softly.

"I'd love nothin' more than to cut his lyin' throat," Conrad hissed. "To go against his king so…"

"They are blinded in their faith," Marilyn said in a

soothing voice. "We all must admit that their god's sudden appearance has changed their belief drastically. They've foretold his becoming for how many centuries? Only to have him rise right now, and we go off to confront their savior."

Stone hadn't thought about it like that, and for a moment, he looked into the eyes full of conviction in the force before them. He thought about it—had his life been different—he very easily could be on the other side. But he wasn't. He stood with his friends, and he'd stand next to them until the bitter end. He had Gracelyn. He had Rosen. That was enough to make him fight.

Another dozen soldiers fell into the high priest's ranks.

One of the soldiers beside the king's hands shook, and he vomited.

"Sorry, my king," he said, wiping his lips.

"You're not the first to do that," Joridd said, with his gaze firmly fixed upon Polav. "And you won't be the last."

"You will focus your attack upon the seven," Marilyn said under her breath, only loud enough for them to hear. "I will cast Vines that Hold upon the rest. Vandress, if you'd be so kind as to protect us from those arrows..."

"Got it," Vandress said.

She's giving us a chance to not have to fight all of them... Clever. None of us want this to go this way. These are men and women of Valeren. They're good people, but they're just on the wrong side in this...

"Polav is mine," Joridd growled.

A king's vengeance. Not something I'm used to being on this side of. Much nicer.

Stone smiled wide. "We are with you, my king."

"Lay down your arms at once!" Polav screamed, with split flinging from his lips, and his words echoing down the alley. "Lay them down..."

His voice was cut short by a sound that even made Stone's heart stop. It filled the alley and sent all shuddering in fear, but everyone listened for the trail that would follow, signal the telltale sign of the Neferian… but there was no glass-breaking sound after.

The silhouette of the dragon appeared in the sky as she flapped her wings, rushing down into the city from the northern sky.

"Belz!" Ceres said excitedly.

Her magnificent white coat of ivory scales was shining in the last bit of sunlight, she'd washed in the fresh waters of the Forest of Parth. The gray webbing of her wings glimmered like silver and the dark horns on her head and back contrasted like obsidian stones. As she approached, Stone could see the fiery red in the center of her golden eyes.

"Belz?" Adler asked. "Never heard you call her that before."

"Just came up with it." She laughed. "Never been so happy to see her."

"Pretty sure you have," Adler jested.

"You sure you want to argue with me…" Ceres said, but her chipper mood was cut short but a sudden dull thudding snap of a huge bowstring.

The bolt ripped through the air, squealing its way at the ivory dragon.

"No!" Stone yelled, and Ceres cupped her hands to her mouth.

The Dead Bow's bolt blasted at her as she spun, tucking her wings in tight. It zipped just shy of the underside of her wing, and she let out a monstrous roar. She spread her wings wide again, flying down at them. Her serpentine eyes scanned the city for more bolts.

"Hold your fire!" the king yelled as loud as his voice could carry. "Those are for the Neferian, not our dragons!"

The soldiers beside him yelled out for them to cease fire,

whether it was to back up their king, or just for their own skins—Stone couldn't tell.

"I am your king! You will hold your fire immediately or you will be put on trial for treason to the crown!"

Another bolt soared through the sky at Belzarath, and Stone's heart again skipped a beat, watching in horror, not able to do a thing. The ivory dragon pulled her huge wings back, opening them wide, slowing her descent as the long bolt whizzed in front of her, flying off into the far distance.

"Enough of his madness," Vandress said, flinging her arms up into the air. "*Fridaras!*" Her icy spell shot at the speed of a hurricane wind at the tower where the soldiers were setting a fresh bolt.

The seven didn't hesitate.

As the icy touch of the spell crashed into the tower, freezing everything and everyone left upon its top, the thick bowstring may have tried to snap, but the bolt was frozen solid to the Dead Bow.

The seven's spells came in an array of blues and oranges as they whirled at them. Marilyn and Corvaire immediately shot up spells to deflect the incoming magic. Stone and Ceres huddled together with Adler.

"I can't believe they're attacking us," Stone said. "Just because they want to defend Crysinthian… They chose him over us? We fought together to save the city from Arken, and now they want us to stop? After we've come this far? Just when I think I'm understanding the world, then this shit happens. I don't understand."

"People are complicated," Ceres said. "And feeble… and petty… and stupid…"

Belzarath exhaled a plume of dragonfire into the air just before she landed, scattering the more unsure soldiers in the area and shuffling off into shadowy crevasses like crabs on the sands.

Past the raging sounds of the burning inferno, Stone heard the familiar barking of his best friend.

"Good boy," he said with a wide grin as he looked up at the panting dog's loving face, looking down at him over the white dragon's shoulder. "Good boy."

Belzarath landed heavily on the road, cracking the stones beneath her feet.

Vandress turned her spells against the seven.

"*Moltos Armos*," Marilyn said, casting out a misty red spell that enveloped the surrounding army, still scrambling with the appearance of the dragon. The crossbows the soldiers held smoked and cracked with a fiery light. The soldiers yelled and threw them to the ground. The bows they held did the same—some snapping in half from the fire.

"Up on her back!" Drâon yelled.

"No! No! No!" Polav blurted in fury. "Get them, take the beast down!"

Stone, ushering Ceres, Adler, and Conrad to the white dragon, saw Vandress behind a magnificent spell of a rainbow of shades of color. It was mesmerizing as the seven's spells poured into it.

"You coming?" Stone yelled in the chaos around.

The soldiers by them were huddled behind her spell, but the appearance of the dragon seemed to bolster their spirits as they yelled and held their swords with renewed vigor.

Corvaire pushed Stone toward the dragon. "She's not coming. Go."

"Vandress," Stone said with hollow words.

She turned and smirked. "Go," she mouthed.

"We will handle my city and these bastards," Joridd said. "Your fight is ahead. Mine and hers is here."

Stone heard the roars of two more dragons nearing Belzarath. Zênon and Īzadan were seconds away from landing beside her.

"But…" Stone said as Corvaire tugged him by the arm.

"We need to go," Corvaire said.

"We'll be fine," Vandress said. "Go!"

He reluctantly got upon the dragon's back alongside Ceres, Adler, and Mud. Corvaire, Marilyn, and Conrad climbed Zênon's massive wing and straddled his back.

"Let's go, Belz," Ceres said as she kicked her heels into the ivory scales. "To Aderogon!"

The dragons flapped their mighty wings, returning to the sky as the battle began below. The armies crashed into one another with the sharp, bright needles of swords clashing together. Joridd led the charge and Vandress fought the seven —her friends and comrades.

Stone felt anguish he couldn't help. He hated to flee. He wanted to fight. But he choked his feelings down. He watched the battle as it raged smaller and smaller as the clouds overtook them, eventually hiding the city from his view.

He sighed.

"Our fight is with him," Ceres said softly in the winds, clapping her hand on his thigh. "It's time we end this."

Chapter Thirty-Six

As Ceres sang the words, she could remember to the Song of Dragons, the smell of smoky dragonfire filled Stone's nostrils. He dug his fingers into Belzarath's thick, old scales, thinking so many things, his head felt like a bowl of mush.

How did the seven betray their friends like that? Or was it even betrayal in their hearts, for their belief was so blinding? How could Polav use the Dead Bows against the dragons trying to save them? What a fool he is. I hope Joridd sticks him right through the belly...

He thought about what lay ahead too...

What do I do when I see Arken? I don't know exactly. He says he wants me to kill Crysinthian... but there's only one way to do that, that I can see. Use the Adralite... but what if that makes me like them? I don't want that, not in a thousand years would I once want that...

I need to trust myself. And I need to trust my friends. That will be enough. It has to be enough...

"Damn it all to... how's it go? What're the words there?" Ceres cursed in the rushing winds.

"You'll get it," Adler said, with his hood flapping back behind him. "Just focus."

"Don't patronize me," she said, glowering.

"I—I'm not," Adler said with one palm raised.

"Keep trying," Stone said. "You'll get it." He didn't know if she would, at least not at the rate she was going, but he'd only heard the song a couple of times and never thought they would need it—he never imagined Gracelyn wouldn't be with them.

"Just focus," Adler said in a calm voice. "We need Grimdore."

"Ya don't think I know that?" Ceres said loudly, with fire in her voice. Adler shriveled to a shell of himself. "Of course, we need her. I don't see you tryin' to get her!"

"Point noted," Adler said coyly.

Ceres had her knuckles on her head, trying to think of the words, but Stone knew even if she knew them, Grimdore may not come. Her wounds were grave from the battle with the Neferian.

"You know," Adler said after a deep breath. "This is it…"

Ceres didn't respond. She was still stuck in her head.

"We may not make it out of this," he said, looking up at the light of the orange, setting sun off the bottom of the cotton-like clouds. The pale moon hung high above, ready to shine its light down upon them when the last light of the sun faded. "This may be our last night together."

"We've thought that before," Ceres finally chimed in. "And we were wrong before."

"We're going to face off against a god," he said. "This is different."

Stone was listening, thinking, not needing to respond. He knew Adler was right.

"I remember the first time I saw you two," he said, with a rare sincerity in his voice. He laughed. "Feels like that was ten years ago. You were like a newborn babe; Stone didn't know north from south. Now, look at you. Even used magic. Going off to fight for the future of everyone."

Stone smiled and nodded.

"And you, Ceres."

She still looked irritated at herself. But once he grabbed her by the hand, bringing it down from her head, her face sparked alive. Her mossy eyes grew wide, and her lips opened slightly. The freckles on her face deepened in color.

"The first time I laid eyes on you all that time ago in Atlius, I knew you were the one…"

"What're you goin' on about… you been hittin' the hard stuff again…?"

"Don't do that," he said, moving her hand in his. "I'm trying to tell you something."

"Why?" she asked softly, with her forest eyes still wide.

"Because I don't know if we're going to live long enough for me to tell you this, and I can't hold it in any longer…"

She looked as if the world had flipped upside down.

"I think I love you," he said.

He looked more nervous than Stone had ever seen him.

Ceres had a wide array of emotions painted on her face: anger, frustration, shock, and embarrassment were a few. Her cheeks flushed, and the moonlight touched its soft caress on them as her golden hair danced in the winds.

"I—I don't know what to say…" she muttered.

"You don't need to say anything," he said. "I just needed you to know. You make me feel like I have purpose, like me being here in this rotten world means something. I've never felt so high—or so low—since I've met you. You make me feel things I've never felt, and would never feel again if you weren't around." Stone smiled and simply watched as he petted Mud's neck. "I didn't really know what I was feeling until I saw you do what you did in your fight with Paltereth. I thought you were dead. I felt like I died too. I don't know what my life would be like without you. And I don't want to know."

"Why are you doing this now?" she asked, squeezing his hand with tears welling in her eyes, wetted with the reflection of the glowing white moonlight. "Why right now?"

"Because I may not have another time to do it," he said softly, his voice breaking with a quiver. "It has to be now. I'm sorry."

She looked as if she wanted to smack him. Her eyes darted around, looking as if she would run off into an alley if she could. But there were no alleys, no trees, no places to hide. It was just them.

"Oh." She sighed. "You're such an idiot." She shook her head with a faint smile. "You gonna kiss me or what then? Or do I have to do everythin' around here?"

He smiled wide. She spun on the dragon's back and fell into his embrace. Her face tilted up to meet his. Their lips pressed against each other's. He wrapped his arms around her, and she did the same.

She ran her fingernails through his wild hair as they kissed.

Stone's heart swelled.

They shared that moment in the vibrant moonlight for what felt like a long-awaited dream for Adler. It was a moment an oil painting master would spend a lifetime yearning for.

Mud even looked, cocking his head.

When their lips finally separated, they looked deep into each other's eyes.

"Well, if this is our last night on this earth," she said. "I'm glad I'm spending it with you."

"There," Stone said, pointing behind them. "There she is!"

Each of them turned to look, far behind Zênon and

Izadan, with Corvaire, Marilyn and Conrad noticing too… the great sea dragon was in the air, flying toward them.

"Wahoo!" Adler threw his fists in the air. "If that isn't a sight for sore eyes! Grimdore!"

The hairs on Stone's arms were straightening stiff. He was hollering and shouting too. Belzarath curled her long neck around, and her great ivory head with black horns hung over her wing, looking at the dragons trailing behind.

"Uh… Stone…?" Ceres mumbled, breaking their excitement into a scattered confusion. He didn't just feel the hairs on his arms standing straight. They actually were, and Adler's hair was lifting as if they were drifting in a clear lake. The winds suddenly and eerily stopped. Belzarath roared in anger, and Mud barked viciously all around them.

Corvaire and Marilyn were waving their hands above their heads toward them.

Stone looked overhead and saw the flicker of lightning in the clouds.

"There's no storm," he said, scratching his head.

"It's not a storm," Ceres said. "It's him…"

Stone's jaw slacked as he reached for his sword.

Suddenly, before he could draw it from its sheath, the light flooded down upon them, washing over every inch of their skin, and Stone felt it deep inside of him. It felt as if a warm death had filled him up to the brim. He was overflowing with light… and then there was nothing. Nothing but the golden light—pure, absolute, everything.

***

WIND. Biting, clawing, scraping. His hair whipped his face—he knew that feeling. His lips flapped. Tumbling. He felt the air hit his back, then rocked back into his chest and face. Wind.

He opened his eyes. Darkness.

Falling. Oh my god. I'm falling.

He was shocked alive, or rather awake.

"Stone!" he heard a voice call.

His eyes adjusted. And his first waking thought was... *Mud... where's Mud?*

It indeed was dark, but not the dark of an ancient cave, or a deep ravine. He could see the stars, and the clouds, and the moon above. But it was wet—he was wet. The rain had come.

How long was I out?

"Stone!" again her voice called. "Stone!"

Dropping at terrifying speed, his eyes finally caught the location of the faint voice. Ceres was calling upon Belzarath's back a hundred yards off. Stone's hope grew as the dragon flapped her wings, diving down at him. Her weight carried her down at ferocious speed.

His hood flapped at his neck and his normally pulled back hair was unraveled and whipped wildly in his descent. As the dragon approached, he checked for his sword, and sighed a breath of relief as he wrapped his fingers around its grip.

Belzarath came in as Adler reached his hand out for him. Adler held tightly onto a scale with his other hand, which Ceres clung to. Mud huddled tightly behind the back of the dragon's neck, digging his claws in.

"Grab on!" Adler yelled.

Stone's fingers stretched as far as they could.

"Almost there..."

"Gotcha!" Adler said as he clapped his hand into Stone's, grabbing with all his strength—which was quite strong!

Adler pulled him in as Belzarath spread her wings wide, slowing the descent. Stone fell onto Adler, nearly knocking the wind from both their lungs.

Stone choked, gasping for air. Ceres rubbed his back as the dragon leveled herself and they hung in the high air as the same moon glowed its light upon them in the rains.

"Wha—what happened?" Stone said between heavy breaths.

He saw Zênon flying to them, with Īzadan just behind. All three of their passengers were safely up on their backs. Stone breathed easy at that sight.

"Where's Grimdore?" he asked. "She was right there."

"I don't think she's here," Adler said, with his gaze firmly down beneath them.

"Not here?" Stone asked in confusion, with his head still thick with cobwebs. "She was just here."

"She's where we *were*, I think," Adler said. "We're not where we were... anymore..."

Stone had so many questions, that is... until he saw what everyone else was looking at below.

In the dark valley below, warmed only in the pale moon light, rested a place none of them had ever laid their eyes upon, even though they'd all been there before.

It sparkled as if created by starlight. It resembled opening a dark, briny clam to find a huge, magnificent pearl from within.

The castle was enormous, like nothing they'd ever seen. It towered almost as high as a mountain, and just as wide. It rose to a single peak, and above that was another, what seemed to be a city. Floating and spinning slowly around the top of the highest tower—there was no mistaking it...

"We're here," Ceres said in a low voice. "Aderogon. Crysinthian has brought us to his new kingdom..."

"We're here..." Stone mouthed the words.

Thunder struck in the northern field of the castle.

"This is it," Stone said. "This was where I was born. This is where I've come to battle to my death if it comes to that."

"We all have," Adler said, holding Ceres' hand.

Chapter Thirty-Seven

Time felt as if the minutes, seconds, and hours had halted for that long dream of a moment.

Belzarath drifted down in the rains, gliding back and forth as she growled low. The moonlight sparkled on the backs of her wings and made the black horns on her back gleam like dark glass.

"If a floating city in the air isn't enough to give you chills," Adler said, scratching his temple, "then that might do it."

In front of the front gates of the castle, which stood mightily, guarding a long platform of white with warm, orange fires burning along its edges, were the Neferian—all of them.

Belzarath's scales vibrated from her guttural rumbling within at the sight of them—apex predators with a deep loathing for one another. They'd killed Y'dran, and they'd killed the kin of the dark dragons.

The dark dragons, however, were bound in a way that made Stone's skin crawl.

"Have you ever seen anything like that?" Adler asked in awe.

"If I didn't hate them so much," Ceres said. "I might feel sad for them."

Before the long walkway behind the gate that served as a sort of entryway into the city were the four remaining Neferian. Their wings were spread wide behind their long arms—forced flat against the wet, muddy ground. Enormous spikes of metal had been driven into their wings and arms; blood poured into the puddles surrounding them.

Circular metal pieces were cut into the backs of their necks, legs and tails, with their tips deep into the earth—holding them down, and keeping them bound. Only the tips of their tails and the talons at their hands and feet were able to move freely. They were having their lives literally squeezed out of them. Their snarls were wheezy and raspy—a shell of their terrifying roars before.

Had this been Stone's doing, he would've been elated, but it only made him more worried for his friends as they flew down closer to the god.

Arken's dragon's crimson head was tied down directly before the gate to the white city. Vorraxi's red snout was only feet away from the gate, which was a huge sheet of iron that was pulled up high. His serpentine, yellow, piercing eyes glowered up at them as they landed at his side.

The three dragons fell softly onto the wet ground, splashing into murky puddles as they did so. They got down from her back, and Marilyn, Corvaire, and Conrad came up to them as the three dragons sniffed and growled at the helpless Neferian.

"This certainly is something…" Drâon said, eyeing the dark dragons spread across several hundred yards. Their backs were so high that Vorraxi's spikes along his spine were thirty feet high, Stone thought. The metals that bound them were as thick as his torso.

"We should just kill them here and now," Adler steamed.

"Don't disagree with ya, boy," the Guild Master said. His

short, wavy silver hair was stuck to his wrinkled face and his wide shoulders showed their muscles from under his wet linen sleeves.

Stone walked up to the side of the huge Neferian's maw, touching it with the tips of his fingers as Vorraxi fought to break free of his bindings, but they would not budge.

"Come," he heard a voice call from within the city gates. He knew what that meant. It was time.

"We should wait for Grimdore," Ceres said, shaking her head.

"She's a day behind us," Marilyn said as she grabbed her by her shoulders, leading her toward the gate.

Stone walked under the enormous gate, with spikes dripping rain from twenty feet up. They splattered onto his head and loose, long, black hair. He brushed it back, feeling his widow's peak, reminding him that Arken had that same feature on his head.

Once past the gate, with the others following him—the dragons too—he began walking up a set of two dozen stairs that led to the wide, long platform of perhaps three hundred yards.

He made his way to the top, and once his eye-level topped the stairs, his heart pumped hard in his chest. He could feel it in his neck and arms, and his stomach squeezed.

At the center of the platform was the god—the Great Crysinthian. He resembled a statue carved of hard marble—constructed as a part of the new city as its centerpiece. He wore robes of silky white, with long hair of white on his tan skin—all unfettered or dampened by the rain. Hanging from his muscular chest, dangling on a golden chain, rested the Divine Stone, the Adralite.

To his sides were two faces Stone hadn't seen in far too long—Gracelyn and Rosen. Both were adorned in intricately woven dresses Stone had never seen. Gracelyn in a glacier-blue, and Rosen in maroon-red.

Gracelyn's eyes went wide, and she ran to him with her arms out. She was half the stretch down the walkway, but she was pulled back instantly without Crysinthian even lifting a finger. Tears wetted her eyes. Rosen shifted nervously from side to side.

Stone topped the platform and took forty steps onto it, spreading his feet wide, with all his friends and dragons behind him.

It's time.

Before the towering god was Arken, on his knees with his arms bound behind him. His greasy, long black hair stuck to the sides of his face and his pale, veiny, scarred face winced in pain as he glared with his one eye at Stone. His wide, gray sword lay on the white ground before him.

Two rows down, nearly the entire stretch of the platform was possibly the entirety of the Runtue in the Worforgon. Over a hundred of them were bound and gagged, shackled in place as if the platform had been constructed for this moment entirely.

They were in drab garb, tattered and frayed clothes hung underneath their gray, stone-like armor. Their golden gauntlets carried less of a luster than normal. What surprised Stone most about them—and perhaps it was just because of how subdued they were and open to inspection—was that they seemed to be a wide array of people. Some had blond hair and fair skin, some had red hair even. He always felt as if they resembled Arken—but these men and women did not. They felt more… *human…* than before.

"Come forth," Crysinthian said with his strong, bare arms reaching out to the sides from under the white silks. Stone swallowed hard, took a deep breath, and walked forward. He made a special note to not reach into his pocket.

The Adralite is the last resort. You can't let him know you have it... or it's all over.

Arken coughed as Stone and the others walked between the rows of the people of the Runtue. Their glares were heavy, but Stone couldn't tell who they resented more, him or the god.

Stone stopped ten feet in front of Arken, with Crysinthian seemingly eight feet tall, just behind.

"Stone," Gracelyn said with a whimper.

"It's all right," he said with his hands hanging at his sides. He didn't reach for his sword or the red gem.

"Welcome to the new capital of the Worforgon," the god said as if proclaiming one of his most proud creations. "Welcome to... New Aderogon."

"Let them go," Stone growled with his hair falling in front of his face.

"The Majestic Wilds are a bright part of my new future," Crysinthian said. "Their roles are great, and so shall be their wealth... and power."

"I said," Stone said, with icy blue flames ripping into his hands, "let... them... go..."

"Do not be mistaken, mortal," the god said, lifting his chin up, as if in amusement. A slight smirk crossed his face, but his eyebrows lowered. "You are not in a place to make even requests here, now or ever."

Ceres reached out and put her hand on his back, making him feel as if he wasn't alone.

Belzarath, Zênon, and Īzadan stood behind, snarling and fuming smoke from their toothy maws. Mud growled as the hairs straightened on his neck.

"We are with you, Stone," Drâon said.

"Aye," Conrad said.

"We believe in you," Marilyn the Conjurer said.

"Let them go," Stone said, slowly drawing his blade from

its sheath with a sharp metal ring. The blade of the Masummand Steel sword glowed in blue flames.

Crysinthian gritted his teeth.

"I could rip your heart from your chest with not even a beautiful word from my mouth," the god said.

"Then do it," Stone said.

The god fumed in anger with his silver hair lifting from his shoulders.

"That's what I thought…"

Crysinthian's hair fell back to his shoulders, and the heaviness in the air calmed.

"He can't kill Arken," Gracelyn said, touching her face, looking down at the Dark King from behind.

"The time has come," Arken said, with black blood trickling down the sides of his mouth. His voice was cracking and breaking. On his knees and slumped over—he looked old and weathered. Stone didn't feel remorse for his torment—Stone remembered all too well the ones who'd lost their lives from his madness.

"You've come home, Stone," the god said. "What a perfect place to finally find the answer you most desperately seek."

Stone held his gasp back. The blue fires sparked alive on his sword. His Indiema blossomed from those words.

Does he know… who I am…?

"You're no ordinary son of the Worforgon," the god said in a strong, powerful voice. "You must feel it… deep down inside? You do? Do you not?"

"I've seen him…" Stone said. "But I don't know who I am. Tell me if you know. Tell me… my name…"

"Be careful, Stone," Ceres said. "Remember what he is…"

Crysinthian glowered at her.

"I will tell you what you wish," the god said, raising his head once again. Gracelyn and Rosen both looked up at him.

"But there is something I ask of you. That is the reason I've brought you here. Surely you know what I will ask of you…"

Stone hefted the sword in his hand, feeling its weight. He felt the magic stream from his chest, down his arm, and into the cold, exquisite steel. He glared angrily at the Dark King, tied in thick chains before him.

"Yes, I know…"

"You, Stone," the god said, with everyone around them waiting in bated breath, "are of powerful, royal blood."

Stone's mouth fell open and his sword nearly dropped from his hand.

"You weren't buried here for no reason. Aderogon was your home. You were raised here, trained with the sword here, and you died here."

Stone's heart raced so fast he felt light-headed. His entire world was focused on the god's mouth and words.

"Your name is… Gogen. You were a prince of this city when I created it, and it stood as a beacon of hope and worship for me."

Gogen… my name is Gogen. I've waited so long… so long to hear that…

Stone's eyes watered and his hands trembled.

"You're the son of Gogenanth and Queen Harima. She was killed by Vendrix Soloras, a mediocre sorcerer, when the insurrection came, and so were you. Your body was buried, and your kingdom burned. You rested for years until, by chance, you awakened, and Ceres happened to hear you in your coffin. Fate was on your side that day. Everything about you has led you here, to this very moment. Prince of Aderogon, welcome home."

Chapter Thirty-Eight

"Home?" he mouthed the words. "I have a home?" He envisioned the man's face he'd seen before; the gray streaks in his black hair, his broad nose, and his deep eyes. The face appeared as his own in a pool not so long ago, when they first summited Elderon, and had seen him in the Dream World since. "Gogenanth... my father's name is Gogenanth... and... and I had a mother... Queen Harima..."

His Elessior kicked in his hands, sending flames dripping to the ground. Lightning crashed far off and thunder rolled on endlessly.

"Why tell me this now?" he asked.

"To create, one must destroy," the god said. His eyes burned with lightning and his words were powerful like rock. "He cannot exist in either of our worlds, and you must be the one to destroy so that *I* may rebuild."

"This world you wish to rebuild... I need to tell you that not all is bad or lost. There are good things in this world." He looked over his shoulders to Ceres and Adler—who stood on opposite sides of him, both with their Masummand Steel swords illuminated in the moonlight.

The god didn't respond but stood as if in contemplation.

"He..." the Dark King coughed, hacking up dark bile onto his chin. "He knows... he just doesn't care..."

Again, the god stood motionless, as Gracelyn and Rosen stood beside him nervously. Their magic had proved useless against him, and they had to stand there, fidgeting with longing eyes. They wished to join their friends but could not.

"Ask him," Arken said, angling his head up sideways to look at Stone. "Ask him!"

The words startled him.

"What are you going to do?" Stone asked forcefully.

"Look all around you," the god said. "Perfection, every inch of it. This will be my new home, and I'll watch and listen. I will be the eyes, and I will be the ears."

"What are you going to do with the people?" Stone guided him.

Crysinthian's brow furrowed. "I saw what you did in the Divine City. You betrayed the call of my followers, my most devoted."

"To come here," Stone said, cutting through his words.

"To kill him," the god said coldly as the rains intensified, biting onto their shoulders and heads. Thunder crashed to the south.

"Yes," Stone said. "But once he's gone, then what? Tell me."

The others behind stood in the rain, waiting eagerly too for the god's plan. The dragons lowered their heads with their devilish eyes glaring like the predators they were at the god, the Dark King and the Runtue.

The god put his long, muscular arms behind him, puffing out his chiseled chest.

"The three great cities will return to the earth, and new

ones will be erected. They will be clean, and their people's minds will be pure, cast away of doubt and free to worship me. The Majestic Wilds will have their place as the queens of Verren, Dranne, and Valeren. And you, Stone, will be the commander of my armies."

He wants me on his side, too? What an awful thought… surely killing innocent men and women who don't believe in his way…

"Do you see?" Arken asked with a hiss in his voice. "He will kill far more than I ever have. He's going to kill everyone! Who's the evil here? Ask yourself that. You know the answer."

The god's foot moved like lightning, barreling into the side of Arken's head, nearly knocking it from his shoulders.

Arken fell to the cold, wet light stones with a whimper. He sounded like an old, beaten down man.

"What of people like Alexander Polav II?" Stone asked. "He going to be in your royal court?"

"He will be rewarded for his faith, and legion," the god said. "You will have to set your feelings aside. You will be comrades at the dining table in my house. This will not be bartered or discussed. You will do these things. Do not mistake free will to be existent in my wishes. You will slay Arken Shadowborn, ridding him and his soul from this world. Then I will create peace."

Stone gathered his courage; every scrap of it in his being. He gazed angrily at the god before him. "No…" he said slowly.

The god's eyes beamed in fury. His hand moved quickly before him. Mud yelped by Stone's feet. He looked down and his heart sank. Mud was on his side, panting heavily, drawing in quick breaths in and out. He cried in pain.

"Leave him alone!" Stone yelled.

"Stop it!" Ceres screamed. "You're hurting him!"

"Pfft," the god sneered. "Pathetic. You show your weakness for an insignificant animal who matters in not one ounce of importance in my world—save that he may prove to be nourishment for the worms and crows."

"For all your power," Stone said. "You lack some of the most important things in humanity. Love. Compassion. Empathy. All you know is control. You're the weak one. All alone in your white tower. You're sick. Look all around you. This is not the Worforgon, you are not the Worforgon. We have Arken here. We have the Dark King helpless, and the Neferian too. I can end this war." Lightning struck behind them with a crash. "Let me finish this war, end this death and pain, and you can go back to where you were. Others will still worship you—more now than ever before. Live up in the sky, watch your creations with glee. Love will thrive again and be given a fresh start. The world doesn't have to be filled with bitter kings and queens. It can be good. It can be better."

There was a long pause, as Arken got back to his knees, waiting too for the god's response.

Crysinthian crossed his arms over his chest, folding his chin down, letting his wavy, dry beard flap over his arms.

"You've made me realize something," the god said. His words carried weight and were strong. "I don't need you for my new world." His eyes flickered and Stone fell to his knees as if strong ropes from underground hooked him, pulling him down. His knees knocked hard into the rock, and he winced in pain.

"Stone!" Gracelyn said, lighting the air with blue magic, forcing it at the god, but he merely waved it away, without even a glance in her direction.

The god took a lumbering step toward Stone, inching his way closer to Arken. "You *will* do as I say. You *will* kill Arken Shadowborn. And then… I *will* kill you…"

"Over our dead bodies," Drâon Corvaire said, walking between Stone and the god. Marilyn the Conjurer and Conrad Galveston gathered at his sides. They looked as powerful as they ever had before to Stone. Lightning cracked from Corvaire's body, and flames poured through Marilyn around her robes of dark red. Conrad held his sword keenly before him.

"When you die," the god said. "Your line will be broken. No kin to the Conjurer, and your son created his own demise... leaped from a window, did he not?"

"Stop it!" Rosen screamed. "You monster."

"The line of Darakon will be gone forever..." then suddenly the god's eyes beamed. "No, there is something stirring back in Valeren... yes... a seed has been planted."

A seed? Did... did Corvaire get Vandress pregnant? I... I can't let Corvaire stand against the god alone. I've got to help, but I can't move!

Drâon didn't respond, but Stone could feel his tenseness.

"I don't need you. I don't need any of you," Crysinthian said. "It will just be me and the Majestic Wilds, and if they don't obey, then away with them, and new ones will come to me. Every new generation of them will spawn until I find the ones that will bow down to me. I grow tired of your insolence. I don't need any of you!"

"And we don't need you!" Stone said, standing tall behind his friends, walking forward, pushing between Corvaire and Marilyn, whose eyes were wide, and their mouths were agape. Crysinthian took a half step backward.

"No," he mouthed. "It's not possible..."

Stone had the Adralite in his hand seconds ago. He fiddled with it, letting it roll around in the cupped palm of his hand.

But there he stood, against the god's will, with the red gem still tucked away.

He didn't know how he was doing what he was doing, but he glared in anger at the god, who looked like he'd seen a ghost... perhaps that wasn't too far off from the truth.

"By my beard," Corvaire gasped.

"What in the Golden Realm?" Marilyn said, covering her mouth and stepping away from Stone.

"Hello," said an enchanting, wispy voice. "My old friends."

Stone saw they were staring behind him, and when he looked over his shoulders, his head spun. He didn't know if he was in a dream, or this was real life.

"It can't be," Crysinthian said, glaring past Stone.

Adler was speechless as the three women walked from behind Stone, all with their hands placed upon his back and arms.

"We cannot allow you to ruin this world," the tallest of the three women said. Her skin was a cool blue, casting an angelic glow from it. Her eyes were wise and serene, but he couldn't feel her touch—he couldn't feel any of their touches—but he felt their power coursing through his body. *Raw, pure, light power.*

"What have you done?" the god roared in anger at the Dark King beneath him. "What dark magic is this?"

"It's the Worforgon, herself, bringing back balance," Arken said in a cold glower. "Something so powerful as yourself cannot exist alone, there must always be… another…"

"Seretha…" Marilyn reached out her shaking hand to touch her long-lost friend. "Gardin, Vere my friends… how are you here?"

"We've come to your aid from the light," Seretha said. "We heard his call from the everything, and we came."

Crysinthian roared in anger and slammed his foot hurtling into Arken's side, causing him to cry out in agony. His back streamed in cracks and pops. He lay motionless on the ground, wheezing and moaning.

Stone held his sword before him, its shining light-colored steel ablaze in icy blue flames. Seretha stood behind him, draped in thin robes untouched by the rain. Her pale, hairless head reflected the moonlight.

Vere stood to his right, with her long blond hair flowing dry down her back, and Gardin stood behind his left shoulder with her glacier-blue piercing eyes glaring at the god.

"You died," Crysinthian said. "I saw you burn. How have you returned? I demand you tell me what this is…"

"He really can bring people back," Stone said, looking down at the Dark King, whose back appeared to be broken and his face wincing in pain with his cheek flush against the wet stone. "He wasn't lying…"

Every one of the Runtue watched in awe at the three new appearances before them. Mud itched his ear.

"Go back to the Golden Realm whence you came…" the god exalted, echoing into the storm.

"Stone," Seretha whispered in his ear. "We can protect you from him. But we cannot help you defeat him."

Stone's heart sank. He felt the weight of the Adralite in his pocket again.

I don't want to use it. I don't want the curse, but if I must, then I must…

"But there is one who can," Vere whispered into his ear after.

"What?" he whispered back, knowing full well the god could hear them.

Gardin pressed her lips by his other ear. "The Majestic Wild of fire. She's the one." Stone's head turned sharply toward Ceres. "Her magic is wild. She is free. This world has never seen what she possesses. She is the balance."

"Ceres!" Stone yelled as he leaped and ran to her.

A beam of pure white, roaring, thunderous light poured out of his fingertips. The light was coursing through him from his arm raised at Ceres.

Stone ran and leaped, but he watched as time slowed. He wasn't going to make it. He was too far. The light was moving too fast, and Ceres was so caught off guard, she wasn't able to move her lips fast enough to cast a spell, or move her arms quick enough.

No! Not her. Don't take her! Please, anyone, hear me... no...

But he saw something dark streak from the corner of his vision. It flashed in a long, dark streak. Its body was elongated, flying at speed faster than any human could move. It rocked into her, and Stone saw its huge, glassy black eyes as it flew into her side. She fell to the ground with the thing on top of her. The bolt of white from the god crashed into its side.

Stone was in shock, and all watched as Ceres looked up at the one who saved her life.

The god's bolt rocked into the side of the Skell, who hovered over Ceres. His long, frog-like legs bending back over hers as his side smoldered into golden ash that blew away. His dark eyes narrowed on her, and his wide, thin lips smiled.

"Mogel," she murmured. "You... you saved me..."

A tear fell from his eye, hitting her chest.

The golden ash quickly overcame him as it flew away in the storm.

"Friends..." he muttered as his legs blew from his body. "You are, Mogel's friends..."

Those were the last words Mogel ever uttered before he drifted off into the Golden Realm. He was gone.

Chapter Thirty-Nine

S tone's mind whirled.
Mogel's... gone? After all we've been through... good and bad... he's gone?

He walked between Ceres and Crysinthian, while Arken cocked his head—glaring up at the three resurrected Majestic Wilds in their transparent, foggy state of being.

"You don't care about life," Stone fumed. "You just want to kill all that doesn't obey and recreate until you get those who do. You're no god. You're a demon!"

Seretha, Gardin, and Vere stood behind him, releasing their touch from him, but leaving him enveloped in that same misty, blue magic.

Adler helped Ceres to her feet. Her face was flush, smudging the golden ash between her fingers.

"He was an insect." The god glowered. "A mistake."

"The only mistake was you coming back," Stone said, pointing his long sword at him as it danced in wicked flames.

"Fire Majestic," Gardin said softly. "While Crysinthian created the Elessior, the Arcanica and the Seliax—you were not born of any of these. Nature found a way."

"What do you mean?" Ceres asked. Crysinthian's ear tweaked.

Vere added, "Virranas has returned the balance."

"You, Ceres," Seretha said. "You are the balance."

"That means?" Ceres asked, glaring at the god.

Marilyn grinned wildly. "That means… go get 'em!"

Ceres walked out between Stone and the phantom Majestic Wilds. Her hands sparked alive in burning-hot fire.

Crysinthian did not know fear, Stone thought, for he showed nothing resembling that on his face or posture. His eyes lit with frightful lightning.

With a flash of motion, his huge, muscular body shifted to the side, letting loose a thunderous bolt of white light at her. It crashed into her with a blinding, ear-splitting explosion, causing Stone to get to a knee to avoid being blown back.

When the light faded, Ceres remained standing there, with a fiery half-sphere before her. She brushed a trickle of white flame from her shoulder.

"Infernus!" The fire erupted from her fingertips, whirling into a searing funnel of screaming hot fire. It shot into him with wicked ferocity. He felt the heat by the way he turned his back to it, covering his face.

The red-hot fire burned his silken robes, singing its tips and blackening his tan skin.

She ended her spell, letting the fire flicker in her hands, and all watched carefully as the god heaved angry breaths from behind. He stood back up, turning to face them once again with a face twisted in fury.

Arken was slowly crawling away, as best he could with the injuries he had.

Mud barked at the god with his paws wide and spit flinging from his snout.

Crysinthian fumed, but didn't seem to know what to say.

"End this madness," Corvaire said. "Return to your sky.

Leave us be. We need no more bloodshed." He glowered at Arken as he sniveled away. "At least not with you."

Gracelyn and Rosen were both tiptoeing to the sides, separating themselves from the giant god between them.

"How dare…" the god said slowly and with deep hatred. "You attack me? I am no mortal that you can dismiss as some villain. I am the world." His biceps and forearms bulged, growing to twice their thickness. "I am power." He grew another two feet before their eyes, and his feet spread naturally apart as they slid on the wet stone. Thunder crashed all around them. "I am everything."

"You've become more than the Worforgon needs," Seretha said softly. "You swing the balance too far. Your power is not needed here… anymore."

"Vile witch," he snarled, his normally perfect face of tan, unblemished skin, and perfect silver hair—twisted and darkened. That was when Stone noticed that the raindrops were hitting him, and sticking! His hair was wet and stuck to his skin, and it dripped off his beard onto his barrel chest. "The Worforgon was done with you. Why have you returned? There is no need for your false words here. This is my house. This is my fortress. It's mine. It's all mine!"

The whites of his eyes flashed, and the darks darted to both his sides, and Stone's heart sank as he attempted to run at him, but Adler held him back.

Crysinthian reached out with both his arms like tree trunks and grabbed both Gracelyn and Rosen, wrapping his enormous hands around their waists.

"No!" Stone screamed. Corvaire, Marilyn and Conrad all were stuck in a moment of dread.

Belzarath roared, slinking her enormous neck and head over them, glaring down in wild, predatorial anger at the god.

He lifted them both up as they fought to break free—

hurtling spells of flashing light at him, but he didn't flinch as they flew into his face.

"Is this what I must do?" he said as lightning sizzled through the dark clouds above him, and above his floating, twirling, gigantic fortress. "I must end the line of Majestic Wilds? You were to be my greatest creations. You were to share this world's splendor with me. Instead... I will end your line forever."

"Ceres," Stone said. "You have to stop him." The lightning grew above, collecting in a giant orb far over them. "You are the only one who can. Believe."

She stepped forward, with wind ripping her hair to her side. Red fire tore down her arms as she raised them at the god.

In his rage and conjuring, he did lower his gaze upon her, and a smirk crept up on the side of his mouth.

"All three at once." His angry words shook the ground beneath them, causing it to split and break. "A fitting end, as I send you to the Dark Realm!"

Seretha, Vere, and Gardin floated to Ceres, clasping their hands upon her.

"You will do no such thing," Ceres said through clenched teeth, and her fire consumed her.

"Excindier!" The fire shot from her in a giant wave of scorching heat. Stone leaped back as the spell hurtled at the god.

From above, Stone saw the fire grow. Three dragons' heads hung above, blasting their own dragonfire upon the god. The amalgamation of fires twisted and twirled into each other, rushing into the god as blue, delicate flames lapped upon Gracelyn's and Rosen's skin.

The god roared as the flames hit him, causing him to stagger back. He did not release his grip, but as his roar intensified—so did the great orb of light above.

He spoke in words that shook the very earth and broke the ground—echoing for miles. "I will not have this... not in my world... I am the one... I am true... I am death!"

The orb of light shot down at terrifying speed, like a great bolt of lightning, but one hundred times thicker and brighter.

The horrifying explosion sent Stone hurtling back. He felt the fires burn his skin, and the heat from the lightning heat his metal armor to a searing, untouchable hot. Mud cried out as the two flew through the air backwards.

He fell onto his side, knocking his knee and elbow on the ground, eventually stopping by the brunt of crashing into Belzarath's claws.

He coughed, drawing in smoky air from his burned clothes.

"Mud?" he fretted. "Mud, where are you, boy?"

He was so disoriented from the explosion that in his fogginess there were so many others to worry for, but all he could think about was the dog.

"Mud? Where are you?"

His eyes blurred from smoke, and he wiped the tears away, desperately seeking out his dog.

Mud cried behind the dragon's claws, as Belzarath growled low. Zênon and Īzadan both snarled above in the misty, gray air above.

Stone ran to him, cradling his furry heat in his arms. There were burned patches in his fur on his neck and side, and the dog panted with his tongue falling from the side of his mouth. His canine eyes looked up at Stone and he winced in pain, crying.

Stone petted his head. "It's gonna be all right. You're going to be fine."

The dog's tail wagged, and Stone laid his head gently on the ground. "Rest," Stone said, standing back up, grabbing his sword back up in his hands.

"Protect him," he said to the ivory dragon above, and he

walked forward into the smoldering smoke before him... disappearing.

"Ceres, where are you? Call out to me! Ceres?"

"I—I'm here..." her voice called out.

He followed it to her, falling to a knee as she lay resting in Adler's arms. "I'm all right," she said through the pain in her twinging face. "Fucker packs a damn punch..."

"Gracelyn!" Stone shouted, desperately wanting to hear her voice. "Gracelyn!"

"Stone!" He heard her cry back. A relief washed over him, letting out an exhale that lifted a deep worry from within.

He suddenly heard the dragons shift, though, curling their necks back and snarling loudly.

A dragon roared. Not the dragon he expected, though. Its long, deafening roar cracked with the sound of shattering, breaking glass.

"No..." he muttered.

Belzarath and the others spun with their long tails hovering above Stone's head as the smoke cleared.

"Gracelyn!" he yelled; his head still whirling.

"Stone!" she yelled back.

He ran to her voice as she called. It mattered not to him who he ran into through the smoke. As he ran forward, her voice grew louder, and his heart hummed.

Then, only feet from him, he saw her. Her eyes beamed and her face glowed in a radiating smile. They ran to each other and wrapped their arms around each other tightly—they embraced one another so strongly they may have been trying to make it so they could never be separated again.

She pulled back, and Stone saw Rosen was just behind her. "He's stunned, but Arken's gone. We couldn't see him after."

"Hopefully, he's dead and gone," Rosen cursed. "But we're probably not that lucky..."

The Neferian roared—two of them this time, and Belzarath and the others roared back.

"We need to regroup," Stone said. "Come, we need the others."

She grabbed his hand, and he led her back through the dissipating smoke.

"Over here," he heard Conrad's voice call.

They followed the voice and found Ceres, back to her feet, being helped by Adler. Corvaire, Marilyn, and the Guild Master stood closely by with uneasy looks on their faces. The phantom Majestic Wilds loomed silently behind. Stone drove his hand in his pocket to make sure the red gem was still where it needed to be.

Ceres is the key. I just need to keep this safe. Then when the battle is won, I'll return it to Valeren, or destroy it. No one needs something so powerful... the Worforgon doesn't need anything that powerful...

As the smoke thinned, the first thing Stone made out was the Great God. He stood with his barrel chest bared, with his silken robes tattered and burned, wafting; blackened and frayed at his belt.

His divine face was stoic, yet there was something different he was hiding. He was lost in thought, a deep contemplation.

"Mogel," Ceres said. "He saved me. In the end... he sacrificed himself so that we have a chance."

"The little bugger ended up with us," Adler said. "Killed Kellen he did, and now this. In the end, he proved me wrong."

"Going to have more time to reminisce after this is over," Drâon said. "It's good to have you two back." He feigned a smile.

"Seems it's not only the god we have to worry about, though," Conrad said, looking to both sides of the long, white walkway. As the smoke cleared, the winds blew in from the top of the fortress like crisp mountain winds, and the rains continued to beat down upon them—another stark reality set in.

The rows of Runtue that were being forced to watch the execution of their king... were removing their gags with their freed hands.

"Arken's people and Neferian are free," Corvaire said. "But... where's Arken?"

Stone glanced around desperately, as Crysinthian still stood watching the aftermath of his collided attack with Ceres. His infinite lightning eyes were fixed upon her—and hers upon him.

"What do we do?" Rosen asked.

"Support Ceres," Marilyn said without hesitation. "Protect her at all costs."

"Seretha," Stone said, "don't protect me. Keep them all safe. Don't worry about me."

Seretha sighed with an ethereal groan. "You don't seem to understand how and why we are here."

"What do you mean?" His eyebrow raised.

"Why are you here?" Drâon added.

"We were returned to this world by Arken," Seretha said, with Vere and Gardin standing like statues on both sides of her. "We have limitations on what we can and cannot do."

"You don't have free will?" Marilyn asked.

"We remember all from our past lives, but with our return at his command, we can feel him deep within us. He still calls us."

"What does he say?" Gracelyn asked, not seeming to want to hear the answer.

"Protect Stone, and protect the Majestic Wilds, but not the Fire Majestic—until the Great God is dead. That is all."

"How did he do this?" Marilyn asked forcefully, taking a strong stride at them. "Tell me. How does he have this power? How has he found this dark immortality?"

Seretha sighed in a wispy voice. "He found something. Something long-forgotten, something in his time floating endlessly upon the waves of the sea. He has a power thought long lost over the ages. But he found it, or rather... it found him."

Chapter Forty

Angry rains pounded the cracked, long platform that led to the god's newly erected city. Lightning crashed all around, sizzling the air and barking loud echoes of thunder from the depths of the dark sky above.

Crysinthian glowered at Ceres with a guttural anger.

Ceres stood with fists swirling in furious fire, staring back.

"Where's Arken?" Stone asked in the rain as the Runtue stirred back to life, unbound and shouting war cries as they regrouped.

"What do we do?" Adler asked, scanning the area and the reformed army of Arken's men and women. "Get back to the dragons?"

"No," Gracelyn said. "The dragons will defend us from the Neferian as long as they can. It's Crysinthian, who is the most pressing right now. We need to aid Ceres, however we can."

"Protect Ceres," Corvaire said.

"Aye," Conrad growled.

They huddled into her, forming a ring around her; swords drawn, magic spewing from their arms, and Mud ran between Stone's legs—barking madly.

"Crysinthian is more powerful than you," Seretha said, "but you are the only one in these lands that can cause him harm."

"Then I'm gonna do some hurtin' on this bastard," Ceres stirred, shaking her fists.

The Runtue had their weapons at the ready, and many whistled for their horses, making Stone worry they were nearby. Arken's warriors greatly outnumbered them, but at least they had magic, Stone knew, reassuring himself that they could hold their defenses long enough for Ceres to figure something out.

Crysinthian stood in harsh silence, standing like a great statue of old. "He have any weaknesses?" she asked.

"No," Gardin said coldly.

"Well," Ceres said. "Let's see what we can do."

The Runtue crept into them.

The dragons flapped their wings, returning to the sky.

Vorraxi ascended the stair with his huge, blood-red scaled head snarling. The three Neferian behind took to the sky.

"Infernus!" Ceres hurtled a ball of twirling fire at the god.

His wrist flicked, and the ball ricocheted to the side, flying into a pack of Runtue, erupting into a fiery explosion that caught their skin and clothes alight. They hollered screams as the others ran to them, trying to extinguish the magical flames.

Crysinthian snarled. His face twisted in anger.

She shot another blast of fire magic at him. Again, he flicked it to the left side of the walkway. The Runtue bolted from its collision into the wall, cradling the platform. It exploded in a huge eruption of flame, shaking the ground.

The god fumed. "It isn't worth just killing you. I want to savor this one." His lightning eyes gleamed a hot golden hue. "I'd torture you for eternity. I'd pull out fingernails and toenails one by one. I'd unleash parasites that would rot your flesh and cause endless hunger."

"Well," she flicked her hair over her shoulder with a kick of her neck, "one of us is gonna die today. So that ain't gonna happen..."

"They approach," Conrad said, pointing his sword out at the dozens of Runtue that crept in. "Stay in tight to her, but don't let them get in a spit's reach!"

"What about that one?" Adler asked in a nervous voice that broke. He was motioning toward the approaching red-headed dark dragon, which was looming over them, not far off.

"That one," Conrad said. "I'm not so sure of..."

"Drâon," Marilyn said. "At my side, we will hold off the beast."

"Sure wish Vandress was here," Adler gulped.

"I still can't see him," Stone said in a frustrated voice. "I can't find Arken!"

Marilyn and Corvaire rushed to Ceres' back, and to where Vorraxi approached. Their magics surged all around them—Marilyn with the red heat of the Sonter Set, and Corvaire cast the golden light of the Primaver.

"You're an abomination," Crysinthian growled, lowering a shoulder and hulking like a beast at her. "I carefully created the Elessior and its sets ages ago. Not once... not *once* has my creation been bastardized like you are... standing before me like a cancer."

"I'm here because you've become evil," she shouted in the thundering storm. "You're no god. You're a demon, comin' to kill everyone and everything eventually—because no one's gonna bow down to you when they see what you really are!"

He took a thunderous step forward. "They all bow... eventually..."

"Stay back," Conrad yelled to the incoming Runtue.

"Use Storm of Wasps," Marilyn said to her brother. "I'll cast Searing Flesh."

"It won't hold him back," Drâon grumbled to her.

"Well, we can't do nothing!" Marilyn shouted.

Roars erupted overhead as the dragons and Neferian swirled viciously into battle, clawing, biting, and mauling each other. Vorraxi snarled as the smoke poured from his huge nostrils and corners of his mouth.

"Everything has always been in its place," Crysinthian said. "I even created the Seliax as a beautiful counter magic to the Elessior. Growing in bleak shadows and blossoming with venomous poisons, it brought the balance back to the strength of the animal kingdom and the grand elements themselves. I gave the Seliax to those who wrought wicked magic, to give a brimming source of magic in the most powerful of all my creations—death."

"You didn't create death," Ceres barked back. "You're no god. You're just somebody who found an Adralite a long time ago. You were probably a fisherman, I bet, maybe a cobbler..."

"You dare call me a *man*?" Crysinthian raged, pausing the incoming Runtue and even the red-headed, enormous Neferian. The platform rocked from his voice as he took another fuming step forward.

"You're no man," Ceres said with her own rage showing from the furious magical fire in her arms. "You're a coward."

Pillars of pure, blinding white light poured from his hands into the ground, permeating the cracks that splintered their way down the long walkway to the city behind. An energy buzzed from beneath heavily.

"I created you," he snarled. "I watched your parents birthed from their mothers' wombs. I watched them die. I'll watch you all die."

She clenched her teeth, heaving her magic into swirling swaths onto the ground. They were only twenty feet apart, and the rains themselves fled the area between them, spitting away to the sides.

"He will attack soon," Seretha whispered.

"You must attack first," Gardin whispered.

"You will not survive his onslaught," Vere said in a ghostly breath.

"This world is mine," he said, taking another step forward as the platforms hummed with pure power and light pouring out of the honeycombed cracks. "Your 'Dream Walking world' is mine. You... are mine."

"I belong to no one," she yelled. "Especially not to you! Infernus!"

Her arms shot at him. The fiery light dazzled in a swirling eruption of heat at him. The flames ripped the air like razors and the heat nearly sent Stone flying back.

The god crossed his forearms before his chest as the fire hit him like a lightning strike upon the mountain itself. The impact was deafening. The explosion knocked them all to the ground as Stone could feel the vibration move through his chest. The Runtue were shot back, and even Vorraxi moved his long neck and armored head to the side.

Ceres leaned forward with her hands before her, ready to defend herself, watching the smoldering god before her. The smoke rippled off his body and singed clothing. The rains returned in sheets as the spells dissipated.

The god stood angrily, but eerily calm.

"Look," Adler gasped, getting back to his feet. "Is that... blood?"

The god's eyes widened as he put his fingers to his cheek and saw the fresh blood on them. A sharp cut lined from his nose nearly to his ear. It was a scratch to any man, but to him, it caused gasps all around.

"I see you're not so god-like after all," Ceres gawked. "That's for letting my parents die."

A mad look drove through the god as his brow furrowed,

his face twisted in rage, and his powerful hands were lifted over his head.

"I'll burn everything you've ever touched to the ground, you worm, you insect!" His voice raged over the thundering storm. Even the dragons above ceased their ongoing battle to glare nervously at the mad god. "I'll tear down the foundations of this world! I'll burn everything you've ever loved! Burn it all, burn it all to the…"

There was a flash of shadow at his side.

Stone swallowed hard. *No… It can't be…*

The god crashed his hands down to his side, but the swift shadowed hand moved too quickly.

Stone watched in dread as the red gem was yanked from Crysinthian's neck, breaking the gold chains, and shoved into the shadowy figure's scarred mouth.

Crysinthian's hands crashed into the figure with the thick leathery cape, but where they'd normally cripple their victim, blasting him away to a puddle of broken bone and bloody organs… they hit into him like a mountain colliding with another mountain.

A thick blade burst through Crysinthian's chest, washed in fresh red blood. Crysinthian clasped his hands onto the sword, cutting his fingers. His eyes were wide, and his teeth gritted looking down at the sword protruding from his chest.

The Dark King behind him rose, taking his knee up, placing his boot heel onto the god's back, and shoved him forward. Crysinthian fell forward onto his knees, off of the blade still fixed in Arken's grasp.

The Great God fell to his side, curling up into a ball as the blood poured from his chest, falling into the cracks upon the platform.

None spoke. Not even a dragon snarled.

Arken Shadowborn stood with his legs spread wide over the god beneath him—his sword dripping in blood.

Stone slid his hand into his pocket slowly.

"The Great God of the Worforgon is dying," he growled, with black bile seeping from his lips. "With that, my revenge is final. You watched as they tortured me. You watched as they killed my children! You did nothing while they murdered my friends and family. Now watch as I take away all that is most precious to you... your power..."

The Runtue knelt all around, bowing to their king.

"It's over," Arken said, slowly looking from the fallen god to Ceres and the other Majestic Wilds. "I've taken his bite... but I cannot end his life... even with my power..."

"What are you saying?" Ceres asked. Her face was pale and her voice cracking, as if scared to know the answer.

"You, the Majestic Wilds," he said proudly. "You must be the ones to kill Crysinthian."

"Seretha?" Stone asked. "What does this mean? Has he done what I think he's done?"

Seretha sighed, lowering her head. She then raised it back with her eyes glowing a sad blue hue. "He has replaced Crysinthian as the god of the Worforgon. He has consumed the Adralite. But a god cannot kill a god. What he says is true. You three... you must be the ones to kill Crysinthian."

He did use the Adralite... oh no... what torture will the world endure under him...

"Kill... Crysinthian?" Gracelyn said in shock.

"I used to pray to him," Rosen said with saddened eyes. "Every night before bed, we'd pray to him to keep us safe."

"Did he do it?" Arken said coldly. "Keep you safe?"

Rosen gritted her teeth at him. "You killed my family, not him!"

"Oh?" Arken asked. "He didn't save them. He could've. Just like he could've saved mine..."

Stone wanted to think what Arken was saying wasn't true... but he knew the real truth. All the rot in the world, all the pain

—wasn't all because of the Great God, but he could have stopped it.

"My mother might still be alive," Stone muttered. "Lucik, Hydrangea, Y'dran... so many. Millions have died terrible deaths because you didn't do anything. It sounds like... you even enjoyed it."

"You..." Crysinthian coughed. "You have no way of even dreaming what real creation and destruction is like... life welcomes death, and death welcomes life... that is the cycle."

"The cycle is over," Arken said in a wicked growl, with his chest out, his shoulders wide and his brawny arms gleaming. "Your reign is over..."

Chapter Forty-One

"Do it..." the Dark King growled. "End it."

"How?" Rosen asked, sending a shiver down Stone's spine. "Even if we wanted to."

"You must do it together," Arken said proudly. "Punish him, as he's punished so many others."

"What if we don't?" Gracelyn asked in that commanding voice Stone had heard her use so many times. The Dark King glowered back. "What if we don't want to?"

"Do you understand what I am?" he asked, raising his hand before his face, twisting his fingers in circles, staring at them himself. "You know of what I've become?"

No one answered. Perhaps they were scared to—if they said the words aloud, then that might make their worst fear come true.

"I'll snap your necks," he hissed, "and wait for new Lilatha—Old Mothers like you to do my bidding. This is not a request." Black oozed from his mouth. "You will do what I demand, and I shall let you live. I've been betrayed once by your kind; I will not abide another betrayal..."

Seretha and the others swayed in their ghostly shapes, not whispering a single word.

"Has he become too powerful to stop?" Corvaire asked, scratching his temple. Sweat beaded on his brow and his black hair whooshed in the winds.

"He is new to his new power," Seretha said coldly.

Stone swallowed hard.

"But…" Seretha said. "The prophecy holds."

Gracelyn took strong steps forward. Her dress of a dozen shades of brilliant blues slid behind on the cold, cracked ground.

"We shall do what you ask," she said in a loud voice for all to hear. Crysinthian glared up at her with an unfamiliar look in his infinite eyes—fear. "Come." She turned and held her hands out for Ceres and Rosen. "It is time the old god became just that."

Stone wanted to shout out to her to stop. He wanted to tell her to wait; to think about things. They couldn't just do the Dark King's beckoning, just like that. They needed time… and all those thoughts slowed to a crawl when she coyly winked at him, then nudged her head toward Seretha.

Time…

Ceres and Rosen walked with an uncertain hesitation—looking at one another and looking behind.

"Do it," Adler said, surprising Stone, but then he noticed his own wink toward Stone.

"Come, sisters." Gracelyn held out her hand for the women to grab. As they grasped her hands, she whispered to them in a voice Stone could only just hear. "Slowly."

Arken stood tall and proud. Even if he did hear her words, the fact that she'd agreed to kill his foe seemed to be enough to make him care for little else.

Gracelyn said loudly, "What must we do?"

His voice boomed. "Cast your spells together upon him, unleash your wrath. He will not die easily. But he will."

Stone took an eager, sly sidestep closer to Seretha's phantom blue silhouette.

"Tell me what I must do," Stone said in as soft a voice as he could muster. Corvaire, Marilyn, Conrad, and Adler's ears snapped to attention.

"*Coronus Fridaras!*" Cold ice erupted from her hands onto the god, still on his side, clutching his chest, gushing with fresh blood. He yelled out in pain, shaking the ground.

"The prophecy calls for the dead to aid in the King of Dark Dragons' end," Seretha whispered.

"*Fridaras!*" Rosen said, sending blasting ice onto the god's body, which turned a glacial blue.

"You can still defeat him," Vere said, "but you must do something that will break your connection to him. It must sever it forever."

"What must I do?" Stone asked, clenching his back teeth—feeling the anxiety ripping through him.

Gardin glared at him with her ghostly eyes. "You must kill… what you love most in this world."

"Infernus!" Ceres said, casting wicked flames upon the god who screamed in agony. The fire roared into the ice as it cracked and snapped like a great ice cap breaking into the sea.

"No," Stone gasped. He turned his head to look at Gracelyn as she poured her magic onto Crysinthian.

Adler's head hung with his hair covering his eyes. Corvaire's shoulders slumped, and Marilyn covered her mouth with wide eyes.

Conrad growled, "I'm so sorry, boy…"

"I—I can't," Stone said, glancing around quickly in panic. "I can't do that. I can't…"

"You must if you wish to defeat your greatest foe," Seretha said. "To save this world, you must destroy your own."

"It's the only thing that can break away the part of him that is in you," Vere said.

Crysinthian moaned as the complete magic of the three Majestic Wilds poured into his body, casting out a glowing orb of tulip oranges, sunrise golds and sunset reds. The Runtue watched eagerly, many clapping their hands to their hearts. Many shed tears. Their revenge was at hand, and almost complete.

Stone heard a voice in his head. At first he thought it was Seretha beside him, but then he saw her lips weren't moving.

Remember what I said Stone, a god cannot kill a god...

She glanced down at his pocket, and his lips separated, as he slid his hand slowly out and to his side.

I can't use the Adralite... I need to remain mortal for this fight...

She nodded, seeming to hear his thoughts back to her.

Corvaire and Marilyn seemed to notice something was going on but said nothing.

"There must be another way," Marilyn said finally. "That can't be the only way."

"The boy must kill what he loves most," Seretha said. "That is the only way."

"The world will plunge into darkness," Vere said. "Far worse than the world Crysinthian created, or a new era will begin, one created in light and love."

"Can't he take me instead?" Adler asked, rising from his kneeling position. "He could kill me. Wouldn't that be enough?"

The three phantom Old Mothers shook their heads.

"It must be her," Gardin said. "Stone must kill Gracelyn."

Stone's head filled with pain, remembering the feeling of losing Lucik and Hydrangea; the same feeling he had when he thought Marilyn died. Mud whimpered at his side.

"Are you sure?" Stone asked.

All three nodded. If they had tears, it looked as if they'd be crying. Gardin's bottom lip quivered.

"Arken!" Stone said in as strong a voice as he could muster. His throat scratched, and every glare shot at him.

The Majestic Wilds halted their spells and turned back to him.

Stone strode forward with his Masummand Steel sword dripping with rain, glimmering in powerful moonlight.

Crysinthian collapsed to his side as his head knocked on the wet stones.

Arken's one eye narrowed and his lips curled down.

"I'm not done with you," Stone said as the Runtue shuffled back to their feet and Vorraxi snarled behind. The three dragons and three Neferian above hovered in the dark sky.

"The lost boy," Arken snarled. "Finally has a name and wants to get into a sword fight."

Stone took another stride forward, holding his sword with both hands; its tip pointed at the Dark King.

"Tell me," Arken said. "Did he give it to you?"

Stone's brow furrowed. "No."

"I don't believe you. You wouldn't face me if you didn't have the Adralite…"

"He offered it… but I turned it away."

"Liar."

"I don't need it to beat you."

"Liar! Fool!"

"You're the fool," Stone said. "You think by killing Crysinthian that anybody will listen to a lying word you utter? You're no leader. You're no king! You're a usurper. You're an imposter. You're a rat."

"I'm no Dark King, as your people named me," Arken roared. "These are not *Neferian*… they're the Legendary Wyverns of the Bright Isles, and I am King Arken

Helmhammer of the Runtue people. *Shadowborn...*" He spat. "Now I am divinity incarnate, and you will bow before me!"

"I'll never bow to you," Stone said. "Murderer!"

"Yes, you will..." the Dark King fumed.

What do I do? I can't kill her just to kill him. I can't live without her. He sighed. If I have to do it, then I have nothing to live for... That's it, then.

This will be my final battle. If this is to be my fate, then I forfeit my life if I have to forfeit hers.

I don't want to be a part of a world this cruel, but I can help create a better one...

"Arken," Stone said. "We need to finish this. You and me."

"Then come," Arken said, hefting his massive, thick sword at his side. The heavy rains pelted his two-horned curling helmet, and his long black hair snaked down the sides of his pale, scarred face. "I offered you to be a part of it . . . You could've helped me construct my beautiful new world, but instead... you chose the Dark Realm. Raise your sword against me, and meet your fate..."

Stone walked down the platform toward him.

"What're ya doin'?" Ceres asked.

Corvaire, Marilyn, Adler, and Conrad followed him, and the Runtue closed in. Vorraxi drew forward, awaiting his king's command.

"The only thing I can," Stone said, as lightning struck beyond the fortress. Thunder roared through the air.

He walked up and stood beside his friends—Ceres, Rosen, and Gracelyn. Crysinthian moaned at his feet. Arken stood but ten feet away.

"Where is the Adralite?" he demanded.

"Where it belongs," Stone replied.

"Where?" Arken growled.

"Stone, what are you doing?" Gracelyn asked softly.

He turned to her, holding his hand out. He could barely

handle looking into her delicate yet powerful hazel eyes. Her thick brown hair cradled her innocent face.

"Stone?" she asked again.

"I—" he muttered. "I know what the rest of the prophecy is… Seretha told me…"

His head sank, and he lost all strength in his arms.

"Stone?" Ceres asked with an eyebrow upturned. "What are you saying?"

"What did she say?" Rosen asked, raising her hand, inches away from covering her mouth.

"They told me what I have to do to end this, and fulfill the prophecy." His lip quivered, "but I don't know if I can…"

Gracelyn reached out, touching his chin and pulling his head up, forcing him to look into her overwhelmingly beautiful eyes.

He wanted to crawl inside himself. His stomach twisted in painful knots and his heart pumped so quickly he felt as if it may explode.

"It's not fair," he cried. "It's not fair."

Gracelyn sighed, reaching down and grabbing his hand, squeezing it tight. Her skin was warm and smooth. Her hair smelled of lilacs and her touch calmed him, and his shaking breath turned calm.

"I can't live without you." He blinked heavily, with tears rolling down his cheeks.

"Oh no," Ceres gasped.

"I understand," Gracelyn said, squeezing his hand tighter.

"I—I can't do it," he said, feeling her heartbeat connect through their touch.

Their hearts beat together.

"You can, and you must," she said with her powerful, wise voice. "End this madness. Give the people a future worth living in, a future worth fighting for."

Stone's lip quivered and tears streamed down his face. "I can't live without you."

"You have to. They need you."

"I need you," he said. "I don't care about anything else."

"Stone, listen to me. You have to stop this. You have to be brave." He choked up, sobbing heavy tears. "You're the only one who can end this. If I have to forfeit my life, then so be it. Just remember, though, I'll never leave you." Tears streamed down her face in the storm. "Don't you ever forget me. Because I'll always be with you."

Ceres, Rosen, Adler, and Marilyn were all sobbing. Corvaire glared devilishly at Arken, who didn't say a word, only staring at the two.

"I love you so much, my Stone," she cried.

"I love you," he cried.

She pulled herself up to his lips, pressing them together in one last kiss.

He felt all the strength in his body fade. The sky turned to infinity, and time stopped. There was just her and him. The bond of their love held them together like two stars stuck in the sky; majestic, forever.

He'd never felt this way about anyone. It was the most painful thing he'd ever felt.

As they kissed, the world slowly turned upside down, and nothing made sense. Everything he thought was true, was betraying him. Even his hatred for Arken didn't seem enough to do what he needed to.

Her lips drew away from his. "It's okay," she said in a whisper.

"I—I can't," he said. "I'm not strong enough."

Her other hand grabbed the blade in his hand, drawing blood, which trickled down the blade.

His eyes shot wide.

"You have to," she said. "It's the only way."

"I don't want to lose you," he cried.

"You won't." She winked. "I'll always be with you."

"No…" He could barely see her through his wet eyes.

"It's okay," she said in her powerful voice. "It's going to be all right…"

"Gracelyn," he sobbed. "I… I…"

"Stone, do it!" she roared.

She angled the tip of the sword to her breast.

Heavy sobs carried into the surrounding air.

He took a shaky breath.

"For a brighter future," she said, shutting her eyes and sending long streaks of tears down her face. "I give my life."

He swallowed hard, feeling the blood rushing down his arm into his hand, tightening the grip on his sword.

"It's all right," she whispered. "It's going to be all right."

"Gracelyn, I—" he breathed.

"I know, Stone. I know… you've given me everything you can. Now… do this one more thing for me…"

"I love you," he said. He felt strong, yet delicate touches on his back. He looked around and saw their heavy gazes upon him.

They didn't say a word, but he felt their pain and he felt their power.

"Do it," she said.

Corvaire put his hand on his back, sighing deeply.

"Do it," she said. "I love you, Stone."

He cried, "I love you too."

The muscles in his arm tensed, thrusting the sword forward. It broke her breastbone and pierced her heart.

Her eyes went wide, and her breath left her open mouth. Her eyes were welled with tears. She fell to her knees. He took his hand from the sword and caught her. He never felt such guttural pain before.

. . .

"Gracelyn, Gracelyn," he sobbed into her, driving his head into her neck.

"It's—all right…" Her voice was weak. "It's all going to be… all right…"

Her head fell back.

"Gracelyn…" he cried into her. "I can't do this alone… I can't do this without you…"

Chapter Forty-Two

The two lay in the thundering storm, in the pouring rain in the center of the army of the enemy. Monstrous dark dragons waited for their moment to kill, to feed... Stone's army was outnumbered ten to one, and while Stone's heart and soul were withering in pain... Arken... laughed.

Stone pulled his sword from Gracelyn's chest, and it erupted in magical blue flames.

Arken's hearty laugh filled the air all around them. Vorraxi roared with smoke pouring from its red maw.

Stone had never felt a fire within him like he felt right then. It was as if a hot coal furnace powered him, driving him. The only thing he saw in his blazing rage was the Dark King before him—laughing.

"Stop it," Rosen cried, her fists shaking in rage. "You monster!"

"I couldn't have planned this better if I tried." Arken loomed large and powerful over them as blood mixed into the puddles of rain at their feet.

Stone suddenly felt something behind him, pushing

forward. He moved to the side, and his anger abated for a split second, but his sadness was overwhelming.

Seretha flowed past him, with Vere and Gardin behind her. They approached the new god, hovering over Crysinthian's body—lying motionless on the cold ground.

Arken's laugh faded to a hollow echo. Vorraxi snarled, slinking his huge head closer.

"What?" Arken spat. "Your time is done here. You've done as I beckoned you to do. Begone!"

"We will return to our rest." Seretha's voice was cold, snapping like ice, but full of wisdom. "But before we go, we wanted to return your gift to us, with one of our own…"

Arken's expression darkened, and his eyebrow raised. "What could you possibly give me that I do not already possess?"

"You believe us to the be the ones who betrayed you," Gardin said, her tone grave and deep. "You started your long-lasting war because of us."

"You *did* betray me. You betrayed my trust!" Arken snarled. "There was a part of me that even believed that I loved you. But then you turned your backs on me. When I needed you most, you left."

"We did not betray you then." Vere's words were magical in their essence, and frost rose from her lips. Her glare snapped cold. "But we do now…"

"What?" Stone muttered.

"Begone!" Arken roared, raising his sword at them.

"You may have summoned us for your purposes," Seretha said. "But we are not through with you. You took our lives. You betrayed us!"

"Enough! Back to the Dark Realm with you!"

"You see," Gardin said, turning to the side, revealing Stone behind her. "Stone has almost completed the prophecy."

Arken gritted his teeth, and his thick cape whipped in the wind.

"He has separated himself from you by killing Gracelyn," Vere said. "You feel it, don't you? You've lost part of yourself."

Arken's gaze shot around at them, as if trying to reconcile something within himself.

Seretha's voice was stark; jarring even. "You can feel it, can't you?"

Arken's mouth moved, but no words came. He didn't know what to say.

"I'm free of your wickedness," Stone growled. "We are nothing alike. Never were. You're evil, and I'm going to cut your head off for what you've done."

"You are wrong, Gogen," Arken said flatly. "You may have cut the bond that bound me back to my lands, but nothing can hurt me now. Every ounce of pain that existed in me is gone—taken from me as I was resurrected to the god you see before you."

Stone dug his boots in, moving his sword over his shoulder —ready to strike like the asp stalking the mongoose.

"You may have consumed the Adralite," Seretha said, with a long pause. "But that does not make you invincible. You *will* feel pain again. I promise you that!"

Stone shot through her, dissolving her essence into a mist behind him. Gardin and Vere dissipated into the air as well, and Stone's sword shot like lightning at the god, dripping in icy, blue flames.

Stone moved with unnatural speed, catching even the god off guard. His sword thrust forward, then twisting at his hip, he arced the sword around in a spiral, slashing at the god's arm.

Arken snapped his thick, gray sword into position as Stone's sword slammed into it with a sharp ringing sound.

All behind him prepared to enter the fray as the dragons roared.

Arken's menacing glare shot into Stone, and Stone's hatred steamed right back at him.

"You cannot hurt me," Arken hissed. "Why do you fight?"

"Because... I hate you!"

"Argh!" The Dark King winced as he looked down at his leg, and Stone pulled his sword back—readying another blow. At Arken's ankle, Mud's teeth sunk in, pulling at him with his tufts of thick hair standing up straight on the back of his neck.

"Always was fearless," Stone growled. He pulled his sword to his left with both hands, and with all his might, thinking of Gracelyn dead behind him, he swung his Masummand Steel sword at the Dark King.

Arken pulled his sword in to parry. The dog bit hard at his ankle, and Corvaire, Marilyn, and Ceres cast a dazzling bombardment of magic into him. The Dark King was fraught from the onslaught of spells, and Stone's sword crashed into Arken's armor, cutting through, sinking into the side of his abdomen.

The god's yell was guttural, emerging from the furthest depths of his rage and anger. Red blood rolled down Stone's sword as he pulled it free, slicing farther through Arken's tough skin.

Arken dropped to a knee, while Mud still tugged at his other leg. Stone pulled back to swing again.

The Dark King said nothing, but had the fury of the gods in his eyes.

"He can be hurt," Marilyn said. "Stone, you can kill him!"

Arken finally found his voice. "My Runtue, kill them! Kill them all!"

The Runtue flew into position. They were skilled warriors and moved like the wind. They ran in from all angles, and Vorraxi took to the sky. Stone moved to strike the god, but he swatted Mud away with a whimper.

Before Stone realized what was happening, Arken's arm

raised above his head, and his giant red-headed Neferian clasped onto his arm, pulling him up into the air. Vorraxi was flying him up high, toward the circling fortress above the white city.

Stone looked around for what to do, but the Runtue warriors flew into him with a powerful, skilled attack—instantly putting him on the defensive—parrying blows and finding his feet beneath him.

You can't get away from me so easy, Arken. This isn't over!

But something wasn't right. Something was amiss. Their numbers weren't right, and in his sword fighting, he glanced back up at the Neferian carrying his master up into the air... and there was something—someone—hanging from his long, spiked tail... *Corvaire*...

"Drâon!" Marilyn yelled as she cast bolts of magic at the invading army.

The Runtue attacked from all sides, with bloodlust streaming in their veins. They were at their moment of victory. They let out animalistic grunts as they swung their heavy weapons at them. Their yellow teeth shone in the moonlight and rain and sweat dripped down from their brows and muscular arms. They fought with a barbaric abandon. They were fighting for their new king. They fought for their new home.

Adler and Conrad fought off many of the invading men and women as Marilyn, Ceres, and Rosen cast spells all around them, pushing the army back. Stone swung his sword in such a flashing array of movements that he would've impressed himself had he had time to think.

All that rushed through his being was pain, rage, and an urge to get up there and finish the fight—once and for all.

"Belzarath!" he yelled with all the breath in his lungs. "Come, girl, come!"

The three dragons whirled around in the air, battling the

Neferian. They snapped their jaws and flapped their powerful wings, breathing deadly fire and slashing and clawing at their hated foes.

"Belzarath, come!" Stone yelled, but there was no call back.

"She either can't hear me or can't come," Adler said, slashing wildly at the Runtue, who fought just as fiercely.

"They're closing in," Conrad said with the wrinkles on his face tightened as he fought. "We need to get out of here, or to higher ground!"

"Easier said than done," Adler said in between slashes.

"Corvaire's up there alone!" Ceres said. "We need to help him!"

Rosen, with both hands full of sea-blue magic, said, "I think we're the ones who need help!"

The encroaching army closed in tighter, and Stone found he was nearly back-to-back with the others.

Think, Stone, think. What can I do? What can I…?

Then they heard the sound… it was one of the most beautiful sounds Stone had ever heard… It was the blow of a clear, vibrant, triumphant horn calling from the near distance.

The back ranks of the Runtue snapped their gaze west—down toward the stairs that led to the walkway.

The attacks continued upon Stone and the others, but he felt new strength in his arms and legs. He pushed one back with a solid boot in the chest and cut halfway through another's neck, sending him almost instantly to the afterlife.

"What is that?" Rosen asked in a bright, yet baffled, voice.

It was then that Stone saw the colors of the banners that came upon the platform—they were rose red and sunflower yellow.

"Verren!" Adler shouted. "Verren has come to fight at our side!" He shook his fists.

"Commander Rourke," Stone said, seeing his face in his

helmet at the front of their legion as they ran at the Runtue with weapons shining in the moonlight.

Then he heard the familiar roar Stone knew, like he knew his right hand.

He looked south, and in the dark sky he saw nothing. But then, through the rain and the gloom, he saw a light glow high in the clouds.

"How has she made it this far?" Ceres asked. "It should've taken her another day, or more."

"I get the feeling," Stone said. "That's one of those things we may never get an answer to."

"Grimdore the Sea Dragon," Conrad muttered, as if speaking of an old tale come to life. "I'll never be sad to see that beast as long as I live."

Marilyn cut in, "Which may not be too much longer if you don't get your sword up. This fight isn't over!"

The fighting continued, and both sides took quick casualties. But the cries and moans of those dying were drowned out by the roaring battle and the terrifying dragons battling in the sky.

Grimdore approached quickly with a speed none of them had ever seen her fly at. Her wings stretched wider, and her scales had extra luster. Her white horns had grown, and she looked more radiant than any of them had ever seen.

The great sea dragon landed behind them, and they all readied to get on her back.

But they quickly stopped by a gathering of pale blue light before them. It was Seretha.

"These are my last fleeting moments in this world," she said in a ghostly voice. "But heed my words."

"What is it?" Stone asked impatiently, wanting nothing more than to run up the dragon's wing and get quickly into the air.

"You must face the Dark King Arken alone," she said. His heart sank.

"What?" Ceres steamed. "What do ya mean? He needs us!"

"All will die at the god's hand," she said. "If your friends accompany you, then they go to their deaths. You must do this alone. You are the only one who can face him now."

"Alone?" he said in a hollow voice.

Seretha nodded. "Alone."

"Nonsense," Adler said. "I'm getting up there too."

Marilyn forced her arm in front of his chest as he barreled forward. "This is Seretha Valair's word. She is one of the greatest of all the Lilatha. I'd listen to few in this world. If she says this is the way… then I trust her."

"But Gracelyn is dead because of him!" Adler said with eyes full of tears and hatred licking his words. "Corvaire's up there! He's up there all alone!"

"My brother can handle himself. But we must do as she says."

Adler was raging and his eyes grew thick with tears. "No. I can't let him do this alone."

Stone went to him and wrapped his arms around his friend. "I'll do it. I'll do it for both of us."

"You better," Adler said as his tears rolled onto Stone's shoulder. "I'll be pissed at you forever if you don't."

Stone pulled away. "I'll get him. I'll finish this. Even if I have to do it alone."

The rest of them looked longingly at him as he walked up the dragon's wing. Seretha watched him, bowing her head one last time.

"Get that son of a bitch," Ceres groaned.

"Come back to us," Rosen said softly. "Kill him for what's he done."

"Get 'em, kid," Conrad said, nodding his head.

"You can do this," Marilyn said. "You have to."

"For Gracelyn," Stone said as he kicked Grimdore's back and watched his friends' faces for possibly the last time. Seretha vanished one last time as they shrank away, and the teal dragon soared up toward the spinning fortress above the city.

It doesn't matter if you survive this. You've had a good life, full of love you could have never dreamed of. He forced me to kill that love. If it takes everything I have... everything... I'm going to kill him for that.

Chapter Forty-Three

The winds and heavy rain pounded onto his face, sending his loose hair flapping behind. His hands clung to Grimdore's scales—thicker and denser than before. She let out a monstrous roar as their gaze hovered above the horizon line of the floating fortress.

Buildings of white lined long roads—but they all converged at the same spot at its epicenter: the white tree with the firefly lights. The tree looked like a shrub compared to the size of the red-headed dark dragon.

Vorraxi snarled, raising its long neck up high and spreading his huge wings behind long arms out wide. Grimdore shot forward like the sea winds themselves. Vorraxi lowered his head, snarling with long yellow teeth and glowering with his small, fiery yellow eyes fixed upon them like a tiger's.

Grimdore roared hot from deep within, nearly burning the insides of Stone's legs.

They flew in at frightening speed, and in the flash of the city beneath, Stone saw Corvaire lying on his side by the tree.

"You take care of Vorraxi," Stone called out to Grimdore. "I'll settle this."

Stone leaped from the dragon's back, sliding down its slick side as if he'd done it a hundred times before. He kicked off the bottom of her side, flying down the fifteen feet, landing with a hard splash of rain upon the white stone—he rolled over his shoulder, drawing his sword as he came back to kneel.

Grimdore crashed into Vorraxi at lightning speed, causing a boom that shook inside Stone. Both the dragons roared as they fell onto the northern part of the fortress. Like the wild beasts they were, they clawed and bit at each other. They fought with a hellish hatred for one another.

"Where are you hurt?" he said, knowing Corvaire was ten feet back by the tree—but his gaze was fixed upon *him*.

"I'm fine," Corvaire groaned as he rose to his feet. He was cupping his side with his hand—blood flowing down from it.

Stone knew that wasn't the case, but he could deal with it... after he dealt with *him*.

"It's time to end this," Stone said with the muscles in his arms and legs throbbing in hot, pumping blood.

"Yes," Arken hissed. He stood tall and proud, without tending to his deep wound, which Stone could see was still cut into the gash in his pale-skinned side. "Once you are dead and gone from this world, my revenge will be complete."

"You wanted me to lead your army," Stone snapped. "Glad you realized I'd never join you."

"As much as I enjoyed watching you kill her," Arken said with a half-grin. "You cut that part of you away that brought you to me. So now my new power can't harm you, but it matters not. We were like kin. Now we are nothing."

"Good." Stone pictured the face of his father he'd seen those few times, in that pool of water the first time, and in the Dream World those times after. He gathered all the Indiema he could muster. Sky-blue flames erupted up his sword. "You sure you can fight still?"

"Don't worry about me, lad," Corvaire grunted through his

teeth. "Got more than enough to send this devil back to where he came from."

Arken's hand rose to the front of his huge two-horned helmet, removing it from his head—tossing it away as it slid along the wet white stones. Lightning crashed past the two dragons, engulfed in a horrendous fight. He drew his thick cape off, casting it to the side. He grasped his sword in both hands.

The Dark King's black hair was down and snaked down his pale, scarred face and streamed down his shoulders. The same widow's peak as Stone's cracked down his forehead and his one eye glared heavily upon them.

"The time for words is done," Arken sneered. "You two are supposed to be the best swordsmen in the Worforgon. Let's see how much merit there is in those words."

"This is for Gracelyn," Stone said bitterly and in stark anger.

"This is for Timeera," Arken growled through yellow teeth.

Stone shot forward, Arken too, with Corvaire just behind. They were twenty paces apart under the white tree with the firefly lights as the dragons destroyed the fortress city in their destructive wake.

Roaring red and orange dragonfire mixed with beaming white-hot dragonfire as the city crumbled.

Arken's sword crashed in with frightening speed, and Stone was forced to defend. The Dark King's sword flew in over and over, and Stone managed to quickly keep the attacks at bay, while Corvaire lumbered in.

Drâon joined the battle with his sword moving through the air with as graceful a skill as Stone had ever seen him fight with. Perhaps his injury wasn't too great…

Stone's Masummand Steel sword hummed as it zipped through the air, colliding with Arken's and ear-piercing shudders that echoed throughout the city. Ocean blue flames dripped down with each collision, and Stone's heart pumped hard.

Corvaire lunged heavy blow after heavy blow upon the god, as Arken fought back the two men, making Stone take unwanted steps backward.

They fought for what felt like days, with Arken slowly pressing forward until Stone and Drâon's backs were nearing the tree.

"I lavish this," Arken said in a heavy, gravelly voice. "This is to be my crowning moment in this world. Killing you, Stone, will make me invincible... forever."

"You're not invincible yet," Stone said, holding his sword up with one hand, blocking a blow from the Dark King, and with his other, thrust it into Arken's wound. "We may not be able to use our magic on one another..." He twisted his hand into the cut. "...but I sure as hell can make you bleed!"

The god snarled in pain, grabbing him by the wrist, pulling his hand out.

"That's it," Drâon pressed. "He's weak. This is it!"

"Weak?" Arken fumed, and heavy winds spun around them. "You call me... weak?"

With a mighty blow, Arken swung his thick sword at Stone. The force was so great it knocked him to his knee.

"Weak?" Arken snarled, with black bile and red blood trickling from his mouth. "Me? Weak?"

His hand shot out, grabbing Corvaire by the throat.

"Weak?"

No... Don't!

Corvaire's eyes snapped with flickering lightning as Arken picked him up by the neck, leaving his boots dangling in the air. The Dark King kicked Stone in the chest so swiftly Stone couldn't block it—knocking him to his back.

No!

Arken squeezed Corvaire's throat as Corvaire tried to mutter the words—but nothing came out.

"Son of Darakon," Arken hissed. "Your kin's days in my world are done. Your sister and your unborn child will lie beneath the ground by your son. I want you to know this, so that even in death—there is no hope for you."

"Drâon!" Stone yelled, rushing back to his feet.

Corvaire strained and fought, slamming his sword at Arken and trying to get his hand from his neck, but Arken's sword was too swift, and he too strong.

All hope washed from Stone as he watched helplessly as the sharp tip of Arken's sword drove through Corvaire's stomach, cutting through thick armor and into his soft flesh.

Corvaire gasped for air, wincing in pain.

Arken dropped him as he crashed back into the tree. Blood poured from his stomach from the wide wound and his mouth turned red as he muttered gargled words.

Stone ran to him, "Corvaire... Corvaire... no..." He pressed his hands hard down onto his wound... not knowing what else to do. "Tell me what to do. Tell me what to do to help you... I—I can't lose you. You need to stay awake. I need your help still."

Corvaire's eyes rolled back, drifting in and out of focus.

"Drâon... you need to fight. You need to stay with me."

Corvaire's hand rose and touched Stone's cheek. Stone's eyes welled with tears.

"You—you've got to finish this," Corvaire's voice was distant and weak.

"I need you with me," Stone cried. "I don't know if I can do this alone."

A stern look focused into Corvaire's hazel eyes. "Listen to me, Stone, and remember these words." He grabbed the back of Stone's head, threading his fingers into his hair. He pulled and pressed their foreheads together.

Stone shook with sadness and the tears streamed down his cheeks as the rains poured onto them.

"You are not alone..." Corvaire said faintly as his fingers lost their strength. "You never were... and you never will be... alone..."

Corvaire's head fell back onto the tree, and his eyes closed one final time.

Stone's head fell to his, and he sobbed. He sobbed harder than perhaps he ever had. It was too much for him to bear. His whole body ached with sadness. His hands trembled and his heart felt as if it had been ripped from his chest. He did the only thing he could think to do.

He stood.

He turned to face his enemy.

He took his sword up in his hand.

"No more," he said, with his words twisted in rage. "No more death. Never again from you."

Arken shifted to his side, arcing his sword down at him from over his shoulder.

"Then end it... if you can..." he said.

Stone burst forth. His mind raced, and his feelings for Gracelyn and Corvaire made his sword feel as if it weighed no more than a thimble.

The Masummand Steel sword that Seretha had made for him so long ago flew through the air in fanning streaks of reflected moonlight. The blade hummed with a vibrant, violent magic. The sword yearned for Arken's blood as it sliced through the air, each time being parried by Arken's sword, which was four times the size.

Arken's eye grew as the storm that was Stone's attack was overwhelming.

The Dark King, the new god, was pushed back as he took a lumbering step behind him. His eye narrowed and the veins in his arms bulged as their thunderous blows broke the ground beneath them.

Thick, monstrous lightning zapped down into the city to the side, illuminating the dragons as they tore at each other. Thunder roared as the two ancient beasts cut deep into one another, erupting blazing dragonfire upon the other.

Stone's sword crashed onto Arken's as he was berating him with blows with both hands from over his head.

Arken's strength didn't diminish, but his anger flourished.

"How… how is it you can match me?" Arken snarled. "I have consumed the Adralite. You are mortal…"

Stone thought of the Adralite in his pocket, and with Gracelyn and Corvaire gone, it was the first time he thought of using it to enact his revenge.

He remembered Seretha's words though—a god cannot kill a god.

"I don't need anything to beat you," Stone growled. "Your destiny had led you to this moment, and mine, too. I had to kill the one I loved most to rid the world of you, and that's exactly what I plan to do!"

He rose his sword high over his head as Arken drew deep, worried breaths.

His sword crashed down onto Arken's, chipping this thick sword in the center. Arken didn't seem to notice, but Stone drew back his sword quickly, erupting its steel in brilliant, crackling blue flames.

He drove it down again onto the Dark King's in the exact same spot.

The seconds felt like minutes as he slammed his sword onto Arken's—over and over.

Stone's teeth gritted. The whirling in his head vanished to a strict tunnel vision upon his foe. His hands clasped his sword like a tree growing from two boulders.

Again and again he poured every ounce of strength he had

into the overhead blows. Arken winced, falling to a knee, and his sword breaking.

"Argh!" the Dark King howled.

"There's no one to help you now," Stone screamed, raining down blow after blow. "There's nowhere to run. It's just you and me."

"Vorraxi! Come to me!" His words echoed throughout the heavy storm.

The great red-headed Neferian roared and thundered his tail into Grimdore, pushing her back just enough to break free from their battle above. He spread his huge wings and flapped them, flying at the two. White-hot flames fumed out of the sides of his mouth.

I need to end this. I need to kill him before his dragon gets here... I need...

He brought up his sword again, readying all his strength in his arms.

In the sky, he heard a glass-shattering roar. Stone spun to see Grimdore had flown above Vorraxi. Her curling horns curled longer, her teal muscles tensed tighter, and her great wings spread broader.

With flashing speed, she flew into Vorraxi, sinking her claws deep into the back of his neck. Her wings spread wide, slowing his descent, and she bit down hard into the center of his long neck.

The Neferian roared in anger, twisting its colossal head back. White flames shot from his mouth, blasting away.

From beneath her maw, the golden dragonfire exploded from her mouth—still clamped down onto him.

Vorraxi roared so loudly, it surely echoed for many miles in every direction. It broke and shook, shuddering in vicious waves. Stone cupped his ear, freeing one of his hands from his sword.

Grimdore bit down harder, lurching her teeth from side to

side as the muscles in her neck tensed, jerking at the dark dragon's neck.

Vorraxi shot an enormous plume of white dragonfire to the side again, not able to angle his head around enough. His claws ripped helplessly through the air. His mad wings flapped wildly, but Grimdore's weight proved too much for him to escape her grasp.

The sky glowed a brilliant golden color as a great explosion of dragonfire ripped from her maw, hiding away their fight, but leaving a long roar of hers lingering long. The golden fire grew so bright it cast a white, blinding hue.

Stone and Arken looked up at the dragon battle as the light of her fires slowly faded.

Silhouetted against the dark clouds beyond, Grimdore looked as majestic as anything Stone had ever seen. It was like something out of a painting of a tale long ago.

She flapped her wings, and as she lifted her head to roar up into the air, the body of Arken's Neferian tumbled. It fell toward the fortress at a heavy speed, and its head fell separately.

Grimdore roared a victorious, ancient, primal roar that celebrated her victory over her greatest foe.

"No…" Arken muttered.

"Grimdore!" Stone shouted.

In his celebrating, Arken returned to his feet like an asp slithering back up with its head and its fangs flashing.

He slammed his fist into Stone's stomach, knocking the breath from him. He kicked him onto his back like a snake's flashing strike. Arken drove his half-broken sword down onto Stone as Stone rolled to his side, gasping for air.

The sword's tip drove into the white rock, and he pulled it back quickly for another stab.

As Arken thrust his sword down again onto Stone, he knocked the Dark King's sword aside as he rolled back to his other side. As Arken's sword cut into the rock, Stone arched his sword around, slicing into the back of Arken's boot. Its fine steel was so sharp it cut through not only the metal in the boot, but sliced the tendon in the back of his ankle.

Arken roared and Stone got to his knees and jumped.

He leaped onto the Dark King, who fell back from his injuries.

Stone fell on top of him.

Each of them held the other's sword hand in their free hand, and they were left snarling face to face at one another on the ground.

"I hate you for what you've done," Stone raged behind clenched teeth.

"I loved you like a son," Arken growled. "But you betrayed me. They always betray me."

"I never betrayed you," Stone said with adrenaline pumping through his veins. "You don't see it, but you're evil. You're a plague that blackened our lands. You're a disease that needs to be wiped out."

Stone slammed his forehead into Arken's nose, stunning him, but making the Dark King glower in rage. Blood poured from his scarred nostrils.

He crashed his head into his again, twisting his nose to the side.

"I'm no more a curse than you," Arken said. "Look around you. Everything that follows you dies. Everyone that shows you love sees only pain and grief. We're more alike than you want to admit. You see... even if you cut yourself from me, you can't hide who you truly are... you're a killer. You're a murderer. You're a villain."

Stone smashed his head into Arken's nose, shattering it. Arken gasped in pain, and Stone felt his strength break for a fleeting moment.

He pulled his hand free from Arken's grasp, rising up with

both knees spread over Arken's chest. He spun the sword around, angling its tip down and gripping it with both hands.

He drove his great sword down, plunging it into the Dark King's chest.

Arken's eye went wide, and his mouth flew agape. Black bile oozed from its sides as his face paled and he glared into Stone's eyes.

Stone heaved heavy, labored breaths—hulking over the sword that stuck through Arken and into the white rock below.

"It's over," Stone said between breaths.

Arken's gaze soured, and his voice grew cold. "Not yet, it's not..."

That's when the world swirled black. An immense, all-consuming, empty black...

Chapter Forty-Four

The familiar emptiness clicked into him as if waking from a nightmare.

He knew this place.

His hands were before his face, inspecting them to make sure they were his own.

It was the kind of black you might see in a cave where the eyeless creatures slumber and eat. It was the kind of black you might imagine the lands of purgatory to hold.

"The Dream World…" Stone said slowly, taking in a deep breath. "Why have you brought me here?"

"B—Because," Arken's voice crept out of the shadows. "This is where I go to die."

"Then die!" Stone's fists clenched, and he thought of his friends lying in the rain while their blood cooled and their faces blued.

Arken emerged in the darkness, as if lit by a beam of white light from a new crack in the cave above… as if someone had driven a pickaxe through a mountain somewhere up there.

His body seemed frail… helpless. He wore no armor, nor his helmet of curled horns. His bare, white chest was pumping blood from his beating heart through a gaping, deep cut in the middle of his sternum. He had blackish bags under his eye and where his other used to be. Slumped back against a boulder, he indeed looked like death's grasp wasn't long off.

Stone strode up to him, but he had no sword in his hand, nor magic in his veins.

Arken coughed, with bile and blood running down his chin onto his chest. The cough was raspy, and his breaths wheezed.

"How did you cheat death?" Stone asked bluntly. "How did you bring back Seretha and the others? How did you survive all those years after being torn apart?"

Arken coughed again, appearing many years older than only moments ago. The wrinkles were deeper on his face and the scars sagged.

"You know…" he said hollowly, "the things we do for love…"

Stone lunged forward and grabbed Arken by the throat, squeezing. His throat was slippery, but Arken let out a long wheeze as he did so.

"Don't you say her name…" Stone snarled. "Don't you dare…" His voice broke and his lips quivered.

"Timeera was her name," he said, and Stone loosened his grip, pulling his hand away, and falling to his knees just feet before the Dark King. "I loved her more than life itself. I would've done bad things… terrible things just to have one more day with her… one more minute even."

"You did… You did do terrible things."

Arken's focus was fading. He didn't have long, Stone thought.

"How did she die?" Stone asked reluctantly.

"I killed her…" Arken's head was rested upon the boulder behind, but he jerked it up with a moan, resting his chin on his chest. He clenched his black teeth. "I killed her, and for my sin… I was cursed with this life."

"Cursed? How?"

"I found it in the sea. Cast away, drifting for countless ages... It was there the whole time, in the waves of the Obsidian. Waiting for someone like me to find it at just that time, in just my situation? I do not know, but I found it... or it found me..."

"What? What did you find?"

"A gem."

"A gem? What kind of gem?"

"That kind of gem." Arken pointed to Stone's pocket.

Stone slid his fingers into it and pulled the Adralite out. He let it rest in the middle of his hand.

"Magnificent." Arken's dark eye gazed upon it. "So, you did have it."

"Yes. But I didn't need it to beat you."

"No... no you didn't." Arken hacked up blood, clutching the hole in his chest.

"You didn't find this in the sea," Stone said. "You didn't have the power Crysinthian did."

"It wasn't an Adralite. I needed the Adralite to become strong enough to kill Crysinthian, but in the end it didn't prove to be enough, did it?"

"No. Ceres refused."

Arken's head fell back, and he moaned.

Stone reached out and grabbed Arken's head, pulling it up to look into his eyes.

"What gem did you find in the Obsidian Sea?"

"A... a black gem. Cut like a diamond. Black as coal. It floated on the water. I was at the absolute brink of death. My arms and legs were gone, I was mutilated, and all there was was pain. I was burned from the sun and my tongue was like bark. I lay on a boat only big enough to push off into the sea to cause me further torture."

He groaned, wincing in pain.

"I rocked the boat as best I could with what I had. I wanted all the pain to end. I was going to fall from the boat, if not to at least taste the wetness of seawater on my tongue, but to fall to the depths of the ocean so my pain would cease."

He looked up above him.

"I couldn't even do that. I couldn't even get out of the boat. I cried for days. I cried for my Timeera I'd lost. I cried for my people who were killed because I lost my war. I cried because everything I had was gone, including my body. There was nothing for me."

Lowering his head, his eye squinted and his eye focused on the Adralite in Stone's hand. Stone wrapped his fingers around it and tucked it behind his back.

"The gem just appeared one night."

"What? What do you mean?"

"I was in my throws of exhaustion and agony, when I turned my head and there it was. I didn't know what it was, and I've spent years trying to find out. I don't know why I moved toward it and grabbed it with my teeth, but for some reason I took it into my mouth and swallowed it. Maybe I thought it might kill me. Maybe I thought it might save me. It had been so long since I tasted hope, I didn't even remember what it was like. So... I slept... I believe I slept a long time."

"You don't know what the gem was?"

"I came to call it... the Black Phoenix stone."

"Because it brought you back to life?"

"See?" Arken said with a snicker. "We aren't so different after all."

Stone glowered but didn't want to waste his breath arguing. "What of Timeera? What happened to her? Why'd you kill her if you loved her so much?"

"That... Stone... I'll take to my grave. That and all my treasured moments with her. She was ravishing, you know... simply ravishing. Like an angel."

Stone pictured Gracelyn's face in the light of a sunset he'd seen so many times, and so few... he choked down his tears.

"Why'd you bring me here?"

"Because, Stone..." Arken's tone was dark and grim. "Because I don't plan on going into the darkness alone!"

The light of steel flashed. Stone tried to fly back, but the Dark King's movement was too swift, and the dagger's blade ripped through the air, diving at Stone's neck. Stone couldn't get his arm up in time, and the world slowed, and time stopped.

The dagger was mere inches from his neck, when all of the sudden Stone heard the thick clap of skin hitting skin hard.

He looked at the tip of the dagger, which hung less than an inch from where his neck meets his collarbone. Arken's mouth opened as he looked up at the man who had caught him by the wrist.

The strong, muscly hand squeezed Arken's thin wrist. Stone's eyes glided up the veiny arm of pale skin with black and silver hair. The man was standing, with broad shoulders beneath his linen shirt of white, and gray hair was pulled at the back of his head. His nose was broad and his eyes wise and full of a loving light.

"No," Arken hissed. "This isn't how this is supposed to go. You shouldn't be here!"

"F—Father?" Stone muttered.

"Hello, son," the man said in a warm tone.

Stone couldn't hold down his tears anymore. He sobbed into his arm; he could barely stand to look at the man towering over both of them.

"You've done well," the man said in a low voice. "This is the end of the journey. You've grown so much since I've seen you last. You're a man now."

"I—I've lost so much," Stone cried. "I—I killed her, father.

I killed her... I don't know how I can go on like this. I'm afraid this feeling I have won't ever go away..."

"Stand up, my boy." He put out his free hand for Stone to take.

Stone wiped his tears away as best he could, and he took the man's hand.

"You know what must be done," the man said. His tone was serious, and he scowled at Arken. "Take it."

Stone looked at Arken, and his blood boiled. His arms were hot with thick blood pumping down them. His hand grabbed the dagger from his hand, hefting it up—feeling its weight and its cold steel slick wet from the sweat of Arken's hand.

"For all the wrong you've done in your miserable life," Stone said. "I still feel pity for you for some reason. You lost your way so long ago, and you don't even seem to see it."

"You're alive because of me," Arken said, with split flying from his lips. "You should be thanking me for you being here. You should be on your knees, begging for my love. You should be..."

Stone drove the dagger through Arken's eye, piercing the back of his skull. He gave the blade a quick twist, just to be sure.

The Dark King's mouth moved, but nothing came out.

"I should be what?" Stone asked, pulling the blade from Arken's head. Arken fell roughly to his side. Stone let the blade fall from his fingers as it fell into the darkness.

The black swirled around them, but Stone looked up into his father's eyes. "I know your name," Stone said with tears streaming down his cheeks. "I know my name."

Gogenanth smiled wide. "I'm coming for you, boy. I'm coming..."

The light of the moon faded back into focus, and Stone found himself standing before the Dark King, dead. Red blood washed into heavy rainwater beneath him.

He turned and ran to his fallen friend.

In the pouring rain, he knelt beside Corvaire, placing his sword back in his hand and clamping it to his chest.

Grimdore walked through the city, hobbling with her huge body. She limped heavily on one side, shaking the ground as she approached. Both her wings were tucked in and appeared injured. She had huge gashes on her neck and face.

"Oh, girl…" he said as her head curled down to see Corvaire's body propped up against the white tree with the firefly lights. "I couldn't save him. I'm so sorry…"

She whimpered, smelling his body with her huge nostrils. She moaned low, as if beginning a somber song for the other dragons.

"Come," he said. "Let's take him home…"

As Grimdore brought them down back to the walkway that led to the palace of New Aderogon, every single pair of eyes watched them descend.

The Runtue watched eagerly, most of them bound with their hands tied behind them, and the three Neferian growled as they flew in—yet they weren't flying in swiftly for an attack. They were cautious, weary of Grimdore, it seemed.

Stone saw Ceres and Adler holding each other as they gazed up at Corvaire's motionless body being carried down by Grimdore's claws.

She set his body down carefully next to Gracelyn's. Crysinthian lay unconscious beside her with a pool of blood beneath him.

Stone sat upon Grimdore's mighty back, and he got to his feet. Standing tall, he raised his sword above his head in the moonlit storm.

"The Dark King is dead!" he yelled as thunder boomed from the north, beyond the city. "The war is over!"

The droves of men in the army of Verren erupted into victorious shouts and hollers. They laughed and clapped and hugged each other.

But Ceres, Adler, Rosen, Marilyn, and Conrad didn't celebrate. They didn't even raise a fist, instead they all went over to Corvaire's body, and they knelt and each of them placed their hands upon him, and they cried. Mud whimpered beside his body.

Stone leaped down from Grimdore's body as the Neferian landed in the field just beyond the city wall.

Commander Rourke went to greet him, but he bowed and stepped back and away.

Stone went to his friends, kneeling between Ceres and Adler.

They didn't say a word, but Stone let his emotions give and his soul finally feel the pain it needed to. Ceres and Adler cried beside him, and Stone looked over at Gracelyn's face as she faced the sky with her eyes closed forever.

The pain was so deep, and the hurt so great, that Stone felt he may not survive the grief. It was as the eternity of death had washed into him like a wave, filling him from his heart to his toes.

"You did it, Stone," Conrad finally said, forcing a smile, but biting back his own tears. "You did it."

Stone nodded his head, choking down tears. "Not at no cost though…"

"It was just their time," Marilyn said. "Death comes for us all someday. They died heroes. Mogel even, in the end, gave a warrior's death to save his friends.

"It hurts so bad," Stone said. "I'll never get to see her again… I'll never get to tell her I love her, or dance with her."

"Oh, Stone," Ceres said, pulling his head into her chest as he cried. He heaved forced breaths as he shed heavy tears.

A chill filled the air, and he could see his breaths from his nostrils. He sniffled his nose and pulled his head back from Ceres. Wiping his eyes, he watched as the rain had turned to…

"Snow?" Adler said softly.

Grimdore growled, and Belzarath, Zênon and Īzadan came flying in, landing behind them.

Even the Runtue and the army of Verren were shuffling around, caught off guard.

"Are we under attack?" Conrad asked.

"Oh, my…" Marilyn said with shock in her voice.

Stone looked up as the sky filled to a majestic, icy blue and white, powerful light glowed like a moon hung directly overhead.

Its body had appeared from nowhere, and trailed out at least a full mile long. It hovered without flapping its wings and it had a great beard and mane of white flowing down its gleaming blue scales. Its eyes were pure, divine white, and they were glaring down upon them.

"The Great Frost Dragon," Stone murmured. "It can't be…"

It slithered slowly in the air, hanging above them like a cloud.

The dragons bowed their heads low, and Stone was shocked to see the Neferian do the same.

"What does it want?" Rosen asked.

"Is it trying to say somethin'?" Ceres asked.

"I don't know…" Marilyn said.

Something occurred to Stone.

He dug his hand into his pocket and pulled the Adralite out. He stood up, holding the red gem up for the Great Frost Dragon to see. He cupped it in both hands above his head.

"Great Frost Dragon," he said. "Great Arran, or Virranas.

Take this Adralite as a gift. Take it from this world. Upon the fortress above lay Arken Shadowborn. He consumed one and a black gem, too. Here lays Crysinthian, one who used its power. Take these away from here, please. Take them as a gift. We don't need them. We don't want them."

Arran's head glided close, inspecting the Adralite. The head of the dragon was one hundred times the size of Grimdore. Its scales were taller than a man and there were thousands of them. Its almighty eyes glared at it, and Stone watched in awe as the Adralite lifted from his hands, spinning slowly, letting the cool light of the dragon flicker off it.

"Look," Conrad said, pointing to Crysinthian's body as red light glowed from his chest. An Adralite crystallized on top of his chest, and it spun up too.

The red gems floated so high that they faded into the blue mist that enveloped the dragon—disappearing.

Arran groaned from deep within, and it sounded like a mountain was cracked in half. It flapped its wings that spread a half mile across, gliding forward. They all looked up at its underbelly as it glided silently past, like a ghost as it flew.

Nearly everyone who watched mouths were open in awe as the dragon flew past overhead, and as it had nearly flown completely over, Stone felt his sadness return as the dragon was leaving.

Marilyn turned her attention away from the southern flying dragon and back to Stone. She wrapped her arms around him.

"I'm sorry," she said, as Mud nudged his muzzle on his leg.

Just as the dragon was about to fly past them and disappear into the night sky, the tip of its tail flew low, and upon the bottom of it, a single drop of blue liquid fell from it like a single drop of rain.

Stone watched as the shimmering drop fell a dozen feet, and it splashed onto Gracelyn's blue dress on her chest, soaking into the cloth.

He watched her lifeless body and her pale skin as the light of the blue dragon faded and the moonlight and rains crept back in.

"I can't believe they're gone," Stone cried. "I can't believe…"

He pulled away from Marilyn, and Mud cocked his head.

Stone took a slow step toward her.

"Stone?" Adler asked.

He thought he saw it, but he couldn't be sure.

Come on, please be true… please…

Gracelyn's nose twitched.

Stone collapsed onto her.

"Gracelyn, Gracelyn. Wake up… please wake up…"

Her eyelids twitched and her eyes flickered.

Ceres and Rosen gasped audibly.

"Wake up, baby," Stone said eagerly, with his eyes full of tears. "Wake up. You're all right. It's okay now."

"St—Stone?"

"It's me, I'm here." He smiled wide and laughed.

"Stone…" she said, pushing herself up from her elbows. "What—what happened?"

"He's gone," Stone said. "It's finally over."

Crysinthian stirred, mumbling something. Gracelyn looked at him, but then looked to her other side.

"Oh no," she breathed. "Corvaire… no…"

"He did it to save me."

"I—I don't know what to say," Gracelyn said.

"You don't have to say anything. Just kiss me."

He wrapped her tight in his arms, with the warmth returned to her body, and they pressed their soft lips against each other's.

Stone wished that moment would never end, and he'd never need to make another wish again.

"Excuse me," Commander Rourke said as the metal in his armor clanked as he came forward.

"Yes, Commander," Stone said. "I thank you for your help in the battle."

"An honor," Rourke said. "What is it you wish for us to do with the prisoners?"

Stone looked to Gracelyn, and she nodded for him to stand up.

"You're not gonna ask your king?" Adler said brashly.

"All respect, sir," Rourke said. "My orders are to leave none alive. But... after seeing you fight... We will do as you wish."

Stone looked to his friends for the answer, but each of them gave him a look of trust: with a nod, a grin, or a bark.

He stepped out before Crysinthian, after helping Gracelyn to her feet, where she embraced her friends—partially still in shock.

"People of the Bright Isles. I offer you a choice." His voice was loud and clear. "Return to your home. Take your wyverns and return to your families. Your war here is done, and your king is dead. Learn to live a life without war and revenge. For if you wish to find that here again, you forfeit your lives, and I'll happily send you to the Dark Realm myself."

The Runtue looked around at one another, some even scowling at Stone. They spoke a language he didn't understand, and didn't care to.

Finally, one stepped forward, with many swords drawn in his direction from the army.

"What do you say?" Stone asked.

The man cleared his throat. "We accept," he said in a heavy accent.

Over the next ten minutes, Rourke's men freed the remaining living Runtue as they mounted the three Neferian. They quickly flapped their wings and made their way back to the sky, flying east as the rains finally slowed.

"What do you think, girl?" Stone asked. "Think you got it in you to get us back to Valeren?"

Grimdore snarled and lowered her neck.

The commander squared up to Stone as they were about to get back up on the dragons.

"This world and its kingdoms owe you a great debt," he said, bowing. Every soldier also bowed—there were hundreds of them.

"You owe me nothing," Stone said. "I just want to live a quiet life now."

"Good luck doin' that," Adler scoffed, and Ceres elbowed him in the side. "Hey! We all know it's true. C'mon, really? I can't be the *only* one…"

"You're an idiot," Ceres smirked and kissed him.

"Until we meet again," Stone said as they mounted the dragons. Grimdore carried Corvaire's body, and Belzarath carried Crysinthian's as they flew south. Gracelyn sat in front of Stone as he wrapped his arms around her waist, and finally he felt as if he was home.

PART VI
THE RETURN HOME

Chapter Forty-Five

They arrived in Valeren in the early evening light of the second day. The air was cool and damp, and the city smelled of fresh bread and warm chimney smoke. Thousands were filling the streets as the dragons returned.

The light of candles and lanterns behind glass windows all around the vast city warmed Stone's aching heart.

Grimdore landed in Gambry Courtyard, with the other dragons behind. King Joridd and Vandress, along with all the Vlaer and most of the heads were awaiting their arrival. Ghost fluttered with her sparkling wings over the king's shoulder.

She laid Corvaire's body delicately on the ground before them, his body wrapped in blankets. Belzarath released her grip on Crysinthian's body as he rolled onto his back with a low grown.

Vandress covered her face and snickered.

King Joridd stood proud and tall and had a wide smile with his white teeth showing.

"His arm," Gracelyn whispered.

The king approached with bandages at his shoulder, where his arm used to be.

"Come, come," he said warmly. "Come down."

Stone embraced Joridd, and he could feel the king's body tighten when he glared at the body wrapped in blankets.

Joridd pulled him back, looking him proudly in the eyes. "We must celebrate. He would've wanted that."

"Yeah, maybe," Stone said with a brief laugh. "But all I really want right now is a full belly, some dry wine and a soft bed."

"Something sweet," Ceres asked. "For the love of all that's holy, I'd kill for a tart, or some chocolate."

Vandress walked to Marilyn, bowing her head. She was wearing a lavish purple dress with gold trim and her bracelets on her arms clanked together.

"I feel for your loss, my condolences," she said.

Marilyn sighed, "Thank you. He cared greatly for you, too."

Vandress' eyes welled with tears.

Stone felt a rock form in his stomach, thinking of what may be developing inside her.

"We'll hold the funeral tomorrow midday," the king said. "Make the preparations." Jarquiose nodded and made his way back toward Mÿthryn Palace.

"What of the rat, Polav?" Ceres asked.

"He's deep in a secure cell," Vandress said. "He's awaiting trial."

"And the seven? Margaret?" Marilyn asked, fidgeting with her fingers.

"That..." the king said. "Remains to be seen. With the turn of events at the Battle of the Dark King... things we've had word of from Verren... there's no god for them to be worshipping..."

"What does that mean?" Stone asked.

"It means," Vandress said. "We're hoping there's a chance some of them can repent and repay their betrayal. If not, though… then so be it."

"I see," Marilyn said.

"How are you, Stone?" Joridd asked Stone. "I want to hear about it in due time, which we have now. But how you doing, son?"

Stone thought of his father.

"I'm good," he said, looking at Gracelyn, who smiled widely. "I'm doing just fine."

"Well, be off to rest," the king said. "Big day ahead tomorrow."

Ghost flew over to where Corvaire lay, and moaned, landing on his chest and sobbing gently.

"Going to miss him dearly," the king said. "One of the best warriors I've ever had the pleasure to fight alongside. Good friend too—a rare thing to find like that."

"I know what you mean," Stone said, looking at Ceres, Adler, and Rosen.

"Now, let's be off," the king said. "Follow me."

Stone went over and rubbed Grimdore's snout as she rumbled from deep within.

"Go rest, girl. You've earned a long slumber. Come back and see us someday…"

Grimdore flapped her wings, rushing squalling winds down upon them. She rose to the air in her majesty and flew off to the southern sea. She soared with the sort of splendor that can be heard in songs of old and told in long tales from triumphant legends. The other dragons flew into the forest as she slipped into the dark seawater.

Joridd led them to their house where the fight had taken place in front of when they left.

The Vlaer opened the door for them, bowing their heads.

The hearth was roaring with warm fire. There was an

array of fresh meats, cheeses, fruits and breads with desserts, fresh water, beer and wine.

They ate together at the table in a night filled with laughter, tears, warm memories, and sad ones, too.

Mud snored by the fire as Marilyn, Conrad, Ceres, Adler, Rosen, Gracelyn and Stone all raised their mugs to their fallen friends.

After a few hours, Gracelyn took Stone's hand and pulled him away from the tables. The others said their dear good nights as he followed her up the stairs.

They slipped behind the door, letting it creak behind them.

They kissed as if there wasn't a promised tomorrow.

"I love you so much, Stone."

"I love you," he said.

They slipped their clothes off, pressing their two nude bodies together. Falling to the bed, he let the backs of his fingers trail down her body.

"I thought I lost you," he said. "I thought I'd lost you forever."

"You won't ever lose me." She grinned. "Now stop jabbering and kiss me."

That night, under a full moon behind slow-drifting clouds, the waves of the sea rolled onto the shores of the Divine City of Valeren—a city that had finally found peace—and Stone got the first deep, restful sleep he'd gotten in a very, very long time.

On a warm, breezy day in the year 3477, the son of Dyandra and Monte Corvaire was laid to rest. During the ceremony, there were many in attendance. Stone learned that the day he fell, and the day that the Dark King died, was Drâon's birthday. He turned fifty-six that day but looked no older than thirty-five.

The sigil of their family blew behind the closed casket: a bird of black feathers perched upon a branch with an oak branch and a sword behind. It was sewn specifically for the funeral.

Marilyn was dressed in a black dress with a dark gray overcoat. She sat in the front seat between Stone and Vandress. King Joridd led the ceremony. He had a crown of gold with red rubies and emeralds with tall, sharp peaks.

There was no mention of God.

For most of the ceremony, Stone was tuned out. He listened to Joridd tell tales of his triumphs in his days: hunting down a rogue group of soldiers of Valeren who raped and killed those most vulnerable, helping to apprehend a sorcerer that was plaguing the city of Dranne from its sewers, and finding and helping Stone on the mountain of Elderon.

Stone thought mostly of why the Great Frost Dragon resurrected Gracelyn, but not him.

Earlier in the day, he'd expressed his frustration with Marilyn, but she told him not to fret about it. She told him to be grateful for what he did do.

When the ceremony was over and the trumpets blew, the lines of hundreds of chairs shuffled and their wood creaked as the crowd rose—many stood in line to pay their respects.

Marilyn, Vandress, and Stone were the first to say their goodbyes.

Marilyn the Conjurer was strong in her respect, sniffling but muttering soft words to her fallen brother.

Vandress, however, was overtaken with grief. As Ghost lay at the foot of the coffin, as she'd slept there the whole night before, Vandress collapsed onto the coffin of white wood, heaving with tears and deep sobs.

Stone, Gracelyn, and Marilyn lent their strength to her as they placed their hands on her back as she cried.

Marilyn led her away gently.

"I'll miss him too," she said.

To the south, there was a sudden stir of the soldiers. They formed long rows, and a horn blew from the tower above the seaside entrance to the city. King Joridd rushed with his Vlaer to their ranks. Stone and the others followed.

"What is it?" Joridd asked the soldiers.

"Creatures coming in from the sea," one of the soldiers said with urgency.

"Creatures? What creatures?" the king demanded.

The Vlaer shifted their focus behind, and Stone drew his sword to face whatever it was they saw. Mud turned, but once he saw the creature, he sat on his side and scratched his ear. Stone sheathed his sword.

A pair of black-eyed, wide-mouthed creatures with thin frames, human-like arms, and long legs bent back with high knees approached. Each of them carried a chest of dark wood with heavy locks. Both of them had dark hair, unlike Mogel, and were much smaller in frame.

"Skells," King Joridd muttered, sheathing his sword. The Vlaer still wielded theirs.

"King Joridd," one of the Skells said.

He nodded, but said nothing.

"Our people are here, coming upon your southern shore," the other said with his voice trembling.

"What do they want?" the king asked.

"They've come to take us back to our land in the east. If you allow us to take our leave…"

"You've been here?" Stone asked. "The whole time?"

"Mogel was our champion," one said with his chest out, but sadness in his voice. "He was the greatest of us. He brought us here so that we might find wealth to feed our people: grow crops, purchase livestock, provide for our young ones."

"Mogel betrayed Stone," Joridd said with strong words.

"Yes." They both bowed their heads. "It was a great burden upon him. He spoke kindly of Stone, Ceres, and even Adler. He called them friends to us, as close as friends can be between one of us and your kind."

"Calling someone friend doesn't give them the right…" the king said.

Stone cut the king short with a delicate wave of his hand. "We forgive him. He did us a great service with his sacrifice."

Both Skells looked somber, with tears in their huge, black eyes.

"Yes, we saw," one said.

"You saw?" Adler asked.

"Where he went, we followed," the other said. "We were charged with being his protectors. In that charge, we failed him in the end."

"He bade us to stay at bay, stick to the shadows when you confronted the Dark King and the divine one. He will be missed."

Joridd thought hard about their request.

"What's in the chests?" Ceres asked.

They unlocked the chests, opening their heavy iron locks. The light of the setting sun sparked a warm gold hue off the thousands of coins within.

"We offer this to you," one said. "If not only to let us leave your lands, but to pay for his mistake. The Lord of Atlius paid greatly, but Mogel looked at it later as blood money… and he was not deserving of it."

"Stone," the king said. "I leave this for you to decide."

Stone went and knelt before the two Skells, closing the chests with his hands. "Take this to your people, and don't tell them of your champion's mistake, tell them of his triumphs.

He saved Ceres so that she could take on the god, Crysinthian, which led to the freeing of all the people of the Worforgon. He did a great deed, and he was a hero worthy of song and legend."

They both wiped their tears away. "Thank you, thank you, great Stone."

Stone and the king led them to the shore, dividing the lines of soldiers.

As Stone and his friends looked out at the dozen ships of great length and sturdy build, he looked into the dark eyes of the many who came from their far-off land. The ships were of a dark-amber wood and their sails were a fine material that resembled silk.

The two Skells bowed and carried the chests to where the Obsidian met the sandy beach. Another pair of Skells leaped from the ship and met the other two with weary, darting glares at the hundreds of soldiers on the beach.

"Tell your people," Stone said. "Your champion Mogel was a friend, and a hero to our people. We will remember him fondly."

The two new Skells nodded with smiles.

The four of them muttered a language Stone didn't know, and they hefted the chests onto the lead ship.

As the Skells rowed their boats away and the wind caught their sails, Stone realized his words were true: he would remember his times with the Skell as good ones, and in the end he was a hero.

Chapter Forty-Six

"Are we sure about this?" Adler muttered with a nasty bitterness.

Two days had since gone by, with Drâon laid to rest and the Skells returned back to sea.

"It's what those at the council deemed to be his punishment," Gracelyn said. "We must respect that."

"I could think of lots of other things that seem more fitting," Adler growled. "Lot more violent."

"I agree," Conrad grumbled.

The Vlaer unlocked the shackles that bound the former god's hands from behind.

Crysinthian looked worn down, haggard, and defeated. He looked back at them with bloodshot eyes—glaring back at Stone with a sort of hatred and a longing for pity.

No one spoke to him as he staggered away from the city. His white robes were frayed, and his once silver hair was matted and darkened with dirt. His stature was gone—he looked like nothing more than an old beggar.

As he cried, walking off straight out of the city out into the open world of the Worforgon Stone had lots of strong emotions wash over him—anger for those whom the god hurt, bitterness that he or Ceres wouldn't be the ones to end his reign, and indeed pity for the broken god.

What worse fate could there be for the one with infinite power that had been prayed to for generations of man? A finite, mortal life seemed like a proper punishment in the end, and Stone agreed with that.

Adler, however, didn't understand—and perhaps never would.

Crysinthian walked off into the sunrise, and Stone didn't know if he'd ever see him again. He didn't care to, but he hoped he'd suffer. He didn't want him tortured, but he wanted him to know what it felt like to be hungry—truly hungry. The kind of hunger that made men cut into damp logs to eat creepy crawlies. He wanted him to know true cold—the kind of cold where not sleeping under a leafy tree in cold, pounding rain was nearly enough to make a man go insane. He wanted him to know loss—loss like Stone had felt.

"While you're here," the king turned to them. "I thought you'd like to know that construction of statues will be underway soon in Gambry Court. While the statues of old that were destroyed will be restored—I've ordered monoliths of Drâon, Lucik, Hydrangea, Y'dran, and even one of the Skell."

Rosen's lips quivered as she grasped Gracelyn's sleeve.

Stone nodded. "I know your sculptors will do wonderful at honoring their memories."

"I hope you plan to stay here a bit, Stone," Joridd said with his arm out to his side, gliding it up toward the city gate. "This could be a home to you. Valeren will always have its gates open to you."

Stone nodded, grabbing Gracelyn by the hand. "I appreciate that."

"We will have much to go over in the following days," the king said.

"Like what?" Ceres asked, rustling her fingers through her hair.

"I've been in contact with the rulers of Verren and Dranne," the king said, eyeing Stone to gather his response.

"And?" Marilyn asked, standing with her shoulders back and the golden sunlight glowing around her silver hair, making it dazzle like a wild mane.

"The monarchs of the Worforgon wish to ask of you one thing," he said, as Vandress folded her arms and stood at her king's side.

"And what's that?" Adler asked, fiddling in his pockets and rocking on his heels.

"We wish to restructure a part of the security of the Worforgon, if the Majestic Wilds see fit to it."

"Don't be so mysterious," Vandress said.

Stone didn't mean to, but he was glancing at her belly. "We would ask for the Majestic Wilds, for the first time," he said, "to watch over the three kingdoms—with us, but separate."

"What do you mean?" Gracelyn asked.

"We invite you to make homes in the great cities, one of you in each, to help us watch over our people, and help create our new world."

"You want us… to help you rule?" Ceres asked with an eyebrow raised.

"We want the people to know you, see you, and feel safe knowing you're there. You don't have to live there all the time." He winked. "Just keep homes there, after all—you do have dragons to fly around on."

The three girls looked at each other, thinking it over without saying a word.

"We'll think about it," Gracelyn said.

"Excellent," the king said, bowing his head as the Vlaer made their way back into the city as Crysinthian turned to a tiny speck on the horizon.

"One more thing," Vandress said as she scratched her cheek, and the bracelets on her arm fell to her elbow, jingling.

"Marilyn," the king said in an authoritative tone—full of pride and awe. Stone suddenly noticed Jarquiose rustling behind the king.

She nodded. In the light of the warm sunrise, she looked like the strong mother Stone wished he could have had. She was everything that a mother should be—brave, loving, protective, powerful, and gentle.

"Marilyn Corvaire," Joridd's voice was courtly, and Vandress suddenly knelt. Stone's jaw dropped.

From behind the king, Jarquiose presented the king with something draped in a velvet maroon cloth. It fit widely into the king's hand, and once rested there, Jarquiose pulled the top of the cloth from it, revealing to them all a tiara of gold branches, with silver leaves, inlaid diamonds by the dozens, and a single ruby the size of an apricot at its center.

"Stone…" Ceres muttered, tugging at his sleeve at the elbow.

He looked down to see them all kneeling, except Marilyn. He knelt quickly.

"For your bravery and valor," the king said. "The Worforgon and its kings and queens owe you a great debt. You've proved your heroism more than any man living, and for that, I present you with this…"

He raised the tiara. "Marilyn the Conjurer, with this crown, I bequeath you the first of your title, and for whom this crown was built. You are henceforth known as, for the rest of your days, and all the days you bless these lands with your great presence—the first High Priestess of the Worforgon. May your magic protect us, may your strength shine a warm light of hope in the darkness, and may your heart guide us through good times and bad. You, more than any, can help make these lands a place of peace and prosperity. Will you accept this title, this crown, and this responsibility?"

Marilyn smiled, warming Stone's heart, and Gracelyn squeezed his arm tight. "I do, and I'm honored." She bowed her head, and the king slipped the tiara onto her silver head as the sunlight glimmered off of it like rays from the Golden Realm itself.

"Excellent," the king smiled wide, and Vandress clapped. Stone heard more applause, and he looked up to see the heads on the wall above clapping too. The remaining Vlaer around knelt, bowing their heads, and Marilyn folded her hands over each other. She looked like a queen as the city of Valeren paid its respect, welcoming a great source of strength and power to its arsenal.

"Congratulations," Vandress said, walking over to her and embracing her. "Your brother would be so proud."

"I like to think he would," Marilyn said. "I'll do my best."

"That will be more than enough," the king said.

They each got back to their feet.

"Seems like as good a time as any," Conrad said, taking them all off guard.

"Huh?" Adler moaned gutturally.

Conrad put up his fingers to his mouth, whistling loudly as it rang out in the open, damp air.

Seconds later, men in hoods flooded out of the city gates, hundreds of them.

"What's this?" Adler asked with his eyes wide, taking a stuttering step back.

The Assassin's Guild poured out of the city, standing in lines behind the Guild Master, who unsheathed his sword.

"Kneel," Conrad said with his beady, dark eyes staring seriously at Adler. All playfulness was gone from his being, washed away like the tide. There he stood, like a king in his own right to his people, as Adler knelt, unsure of what was happening.

"Adler Caulderon," he said, placing his blade on Adler's shoulder. "Son of the Guild. Through the courage you've shown in battle, the strength of your character, and your defeat of the great Neferian, I, Guild Master of our order, honor you with this…"

Stone could see Ceres' eyes watering, and Adler's hand was tapping nervously on his thigh.

"I promote you to the title of Lord of Shadows." His sword's blade lapped over to his other shoulder.

Adler bowed his head, and his fingers stopped fidgeting.

"Lord of Shadows," Ceres mouthed silently.

"That's third in command," Gracelyn whispered into his ear, sending a darting smile across his face.

Adler! Lord of Shadows! Incredible! I've never been so proud!

"I know you will lead in great honor," the Guild Master said. "And I'm proud of you, my boy."

"Thank you," Adler said. "That's a great honor. I will do my best."

Conrad said then, "Up to your feet, boy, we've got some celebrating to do!" The Assassin's Guild erupted in cheers from behind. Stone was amazed by the ability of the Guild to congregate in the daylight, perhaps for the first time in history.

"It pays to help save a city, I suppose," Ceres said.

Their ranks pulled Adler in, clapping him on the back, shoving ales into his hands, and welcoming him back.

Stone was brimming with pride—his friend had grown so much since he first met him, and he didn't know a more deserving person for the job. And it'll be good to keep his *active* mind busy, Stone thought.

"There's another thing," the king said, pulling them away from the celebrations behind. His voice was softer than before. They walked a ways away, huddling together.

"What is it?" Marilyn asked, with Vandress, Ceres, Rosen, and Gracelyn waiting with Stone.

The king looked over his shoulder, with his black braids flapping back over it. "Below the city…" Stone noticed what resembled a slight gulp in the king. "The statue of the Great Frost Dragon… It's returned…"

Stone gasped, "What?"

"Yes," he said, as they each looked at each other nervously. "But… there's something else."

"What is it, Joridd?" Gracelyn asked.

"I—I had a dream," he said. "Last night, I saw him. Arran appeared in my dream. He hovered over me, gazing down into my eyes as I lay in my bed, and he spoke to me."

"What did he say?" Stone asked quickly.

"He said… the Adralite rests within the statue… and the key to opening that is a Majestic Wild, but no ordinary one. It must be one with the gift of thunder and lightning."

Gracelyn smirked. "A gift for a future generation, perhaps when it's needed most."

"Hopefully, that isn't for a long, long time," Rosen said.

"An Old Mother from the Primaver Set," Vandress said, seemingly just hearing the dream for the first time. "Arran really is the balance of nature, isn't she?"

"She?" Ceres asked in surprise.

"What?" Vandress said. "You don't think the god of balance and order would be a man, would you?"

"No, no, I wouldn't."

They all laughed heartily.

"Well," Ceres finally said. "What do we all do now that the war is over and Arran watches over the stones?"

"Well," the king said. "The mages still have the Ring of Fog, which sits well with none of us. Maybe we'll start with that after we rebuild the city."

"What of New Aderogon?" Stone asked.

"Looking for a new house?" Ceres asked with an elbow to his side.

"We've yet to decide," the king said. "For now, it's guarded so as to not be used. In time, we will figure out a plan for the city. Without Crysinthian and his power, though, the white stones of the city have already lost their luster, and a layer of dust is settling in."

"And the Neferian?" Rosen asked.

"Gone," Joridd said. "Flew off to the Bright Isles like they said they would. Without Arken, hopefully, they will find peace in their lands. With Grimdore and the other dragons here, and Arken dead, I don't think they'll be returning anytime soon."

"I certainly hope so," Ceres said.

Rosen looked shy, twisting at her hips with her hands behind her. "Do you think… with Crysinthian gone… do you think there's a Golden Realm and a Dark Realm still?" Her question was directed at the king, but all thought hard about that. "Do you think Arken went to one of them when Stone killed him?"

"What do you believe, my child?" Joridd asked.

"I—" Rosen's eyes watered. "I just want to believe my family is up there, looking down on me… I hope they are proud…"

Ceres wrapped her arms around her. "They are, sister. They are."

"I hope Arken rots in flames down there," Rosen cried into Ceres' shoulder. "I hope he pays for what he did here."

"We all do, Rosen," Marilyn said. "We all do…"

Chapter Forty-Seven

※※※

Five days later.
Far north of Valeren, over the sharp-peaked, sweeping Androx Mountain range, and past the deep, lush Everwood, Stone and Adler had made their way back to where they first met—Atlius.

The air was crisp, and the heavenly sun warmed what its rays touched from over the eastern, rolling plains. Coffee filled their bellies, and sandwiches were packed for lunch. Mud slept in the corner of the burnt-out room's second floor.

Stone wore a loose-fitted white shirt, smudged with work from the day prior. His gloves were rough leather, something he and Adler had picked up from the market in Atlius when they arrived, two days before.

The Majestic Wilds had decided to separate, at least for now, if not to appease Joridd, but to see what a world with them more involved in the cities may look like. Rosen went back to Dranne upon Īzadan's back. Gracelyn went to Verren on Belzarath, which was closest to her home anyway, and Ceres was to stay in Valeren.

Stone and Adler took Zênon up to Atlius—to finish something Stone promised himself he'd do—if they made it to the end of their journey.

What once was Serenity's Pub and Tavern, where they were attacked, and where Marilyn met—what they thought—was her end, Stone and Adler laid out their plan to rebuild the burnt-out building.

The building had been roped off, squatted in, and left to rot. Stone offered to rebuild it for the old Matron, which she declined, but graciously took a hefty sum for Stone's guilt in the form of tandors.

So, they decided to rebuild it together, and own a little tavern themselves—as long as Adler promised to drink under his allotted daily limit. He'd have to go elsewhere to indulge further. Stone doubted he'd live up to that, but a promise was a promise.

Stone yanked on an upright beam of wood, sticking up through the floor. It was black and had been soaked with rainwater. It crumbled through his fingers, but didn't budge at its base.

"You've got to use some muscle," Adler said, coming over and pushing and pulling it with Stone. It still didn't budge. "Hmm, we might need to rethink this."

"I'll get the saw," Stone said, taking his gloves off, brushing them off, pulling his pants up, and adjusting his belt.

Outside the burned-out tavern, in the early morning light, no one had yet come to see Stone and Adler. It got to be worse after lunch, when dozens came to come and meet them, shaking their hands and thanking them for what they did. So early mornings were best when stuff needed to get done.

Stone went down the stairs, into the bar and eating area where his tools were. He dug into his leather bag of tools, pulled out a pry bar, and picked up a saw that lay next to it. He went to head back upstairs, but from outside he heard the all-to-familiar grumble of a larger dragon. It was Zênon.

He knew the aged, gray-scaled dragon was roads away, off in the large square where he could fit—so Stone ran out the door as Adler sprinted down the stairs for the same reason; Mud leaped down the stairs after them.

They rushed through the door but didn't have to make it to the square to see what the old gray dragon was growling at.

High above, in the blue sky, lined with thin strips of scant clouds, a dragon of enormous size was descending toward the city. Zênon flapped his wings and flew over to them.

"What is that?" Adler asked, shielding the sun's rays from his eyes as he inspected the dragon.

"Easy," Stone said, laying a hand on Zênon's claws beside him. "It's no Neferian."

"Looks like there's riders, though," Adler said. "Three? Maybe more?"

"It's bigger than Grimdore and Zênon," Stone said. "It's almost as big as Vorraxi was."

"Where'd it come from?" Adler asked. "Who else has a dragon?"

Stone's chest swelled with nervous, tense energy. He swallowed hard.

Adler seemed to notice something was off, glancing at Stone. "You're paler than usual. You all right? What's the…?" His words trailed off as he looked up at the splendor of the dragon as it came down quickly with its underbelly showing. From there, they could see its massive curling horns, and gray body with red streaks running from its head to tail. "Oh…"

The dragon flowed down from the sky as gracefully as they'd ever seen a dragon fly. It soared down with the sort of majesty an angel would glide down from the Golden Realm with, only much, much more terrifying.

Stone covered his mouth, standing with his eyes wide and his heart thumping in his chest as the dragon landed.

Zênon sniffed hard through his huge nostrils, but ceased his growls, and didn't take his eyes off the dragon that was larger than he.

As the three descended from the foreign dragons' back, Stone immediately recognized the man's face. He choked down his tears.

"The widow's peak," Adler muttered. "Is that…?"

The wide-shouldered man with silver hair pulled back behind his widow's peak clapped his boots down to the road first. His tunic of tan linen wafted in the winds, and Stone sensed grains of sand trickling off it.

After, a woman with auburn skin, bronze eyes and tattoos down both her long arms followed. There was a third woman that remained on the dragon's back as if taking in the moment.

Stone didn't know what to do, so he did nothing. He couldn't move, he couldn't speak, he only stood there, overtaken by emotion.

Mud ran up to the man as he approached with a huge, broad-curved sword sheathed at his side. The man patted his head as Mud smiled excitedly.

The man and woman walked up to Stone, standing a body's length away. The man looked down at Stone, examining him as he stood petrified.

Then a warm smile lit his face.

"Son, is that you?"

Stone erupted into tears, biting his lip, and nodding eagerly.

He couldn't say a word.

"I never thought I'd see you again," Gogenanth said as he walked up to his son and wrapped his arms around him. "I thought you were dead."

Stone felt as if he could melt in his father's arms, but he also felt a feeling that he could only describe as *coming back home*.

"F—Father," Stone cried. "You came. Just like you said you would."

"I'm here, son. I'm here."

After a loving moment, Gogenanth pulled away gently as Stone wiped his tears. Adler wiped a few away too.

"I'd like to introduce you to a couple of important people to me." Gogenanth pulled the silver-haired woman close. "This is my wife, Ezmerelda."

"Pleased to meet you," she said. "I've very much looked forward to meeting you. I've heard a great deal about you."

"Nice to meet you too." Stone smiled. "This is my best friend, Adler."

She nodded.

Gogenanth whistled back to the dragon. "Girl's got a mind of her own," he grumbled. "Kera! Get down here. I want you to meet."

The woman snapped alive at the whistle, as if she was in a trance at inspecting the city and the gray dragon beside him. She leaped down like a cat, barely making a sound as she landed twelve feet down. Walking up, Stone noticed she had a sort of aura about her he couldn't place. He'd never really seen or felt anything like her presence before.

"Kera, this is my son," Gogenanth said.

"Pleasure," she said.

Her eyes were wild and mystical. They were a pale gray that made her look ancient but within the body of a woman in her late twenties, perhaps. She had pale skin and the same widow's peak as Stone. Her long black hair flowed down the entire length of her back, even with her hair pulled up.

"Nice to meet you," Stone said, still unsure of what was so different about the girl.

"She's the one who told me about you," Gogenanth said.

"You?" Stone said. "You... knew about me?"

"I felt your awakening," the woman said. "All the way in the sands of the Arr, I felt you stir from death."

"That's... impossible," Adler said, scratching his cheek.

"I wouldn't go on throwing that word around with her," Ezmerelda laughed. "You have no idea what this girl can do."

"Apologies." Stone bowed his head, as if unsure what he should do.

"I should be bowing to you," Kera said. "You saved your people. You rid the world of your god."

"I—I..." Stone fumbled his words.

"How'd you know that?" Adler asked.

"Kera has a... complicated relationship with gods." Gogenanth laughed. "We've got plenty of catching you up on those things to do."

"I guess you do," Stone said.

"Listen," Gogenanth said in a serious voice, reaching out and touching Stone's arm. "I'm sorry I haven't been there for you. I'm sorry you had to go through all this on your own."

"I wasn't," Stone said, nudging Adler.

"I know." His father nodded to Adler. "I only wish I could have been there for you when you needed me." His own eyes watered. "I would never have left all those years ago—had I known."

Stone cried again.

"I buried you," Gogenanth said. "My sweet boy. I buried you in the dirt and I left you."

"You didn't know," Ezmerelda said, laying her head on his shoulder. "You couldn't have."

"You're here now," Stone said. "That's enough. That's more than enough. And you were here. I saw you. Somehow, you came to me when I needed you."

Gogenanth looked over to Kera and grinned.

"You are full of surprises," Adler said. "Ain't ya?"

"Are you a Dream Walker too?" Stone asked her.

"I'm not sure what that is," she said. "But I've got a *gift* for these sorts of things. I did what I could to help re-unite you two. But it's tricky crossing seas, even on Herradax's back."

"Herradax?" Stone mouthed the word. "She's magnificent."

"The Arr?" Adler asked. "What's it like?"

Gogenanth and Ezmerelda both looked to Kera.

"Dry," she said. "Buts it's getting better now."

"Getting better?" Stone asked.

"Again, long story," she said. "Had to deal with some things. It's better now, though."

"That's about as simplified as you could make it," Gogenanth said with a laugh.

"I'd like to go there someday," Adler said.

"Me too," Stone said. "It'd be nice to get a break from all the attention for a while."

"We can take you there," Kera said, as a wind blew back, catching her long hair and whipping it over her shoulder.

"But first," Gogenanth said. "Let's spend some time here. I haven't been here in ages. It'd be nice to get to see these mountains and streams a bit first."

"Looks like there's some work that needs to be done, too," Ezmerelda said, looking up at the burned-out building beside them.

"Yup," Stone said. "That's our project."

"Looks like you could use a hand," Gogenanth said.

"Boy, could we," Adler said.

"I look forward to spending time with you," Gogenanth said, brimming with love. "I want to get to know the man my son turned out to be."

"You know he met a girl?" Adler said.

"A girl?" his father said with a wide grin.

"He's going to propose to her," Adler said, forcing the words past Stone, trying to shush him.

"Well, we will need to meet this woman, Gogen," Gogenanth said.

"You will," Stone said eagerly, but then he scratched his

arm. "Actually, Father, I think I'd rather stick with the name Stone."

"Oh," his father said, wide-eyed and apologetically. "I see. Stone it is then."

"Is this real?" Stone asked as they began walking back to the tavern. "Or is this all another dream? It seems too good to be true."

"It's as real as anything," Gogenanth said, grabbing Stone by the shoulders and facing toward him. "For if it's a dream, then I don't want to wake."

"It's been so long," Stone said. "I didn't know who I was for so long."

Gogenanth pulled him in again, embracing him with his powerful arms. He smelled of dragonfire and tobacco. "It has been a long, long time. I have so much to tell you about who you are, where you came from, and what has happened since."

"Father…" Stone said with a smile and tears in his eyes. "I want to know *everything*…"

The End.

Author's Notes

Here again.
 End of an Era—again.

As I sit here typing this on my Bluetooth keyboard on my phone watching the Atlantic Ocean's waves roll in, from an Airbnb in Lagos, Portugal... I'm pretty fucking excited. Fair late warning—if you know me in my author's notes, I speak more like myself, which isn't as PG-13 as the books.

I'm here with my wife and her best friend for a late celebratory trip for my 40th birthday.

I'm not necessarily excited about turning 40, but things are turning to the up and up.

But it hasn't been that way completely—never does.

During the writing for Riders of Dark Dragons, I believe it's been like a 4-year process? I actually remember writing the first chapter fairly well, a man escaping from being buried deep in the ground, but needing help because he couldn't do it himself. There was far too much weight burying him down—Ceres had to save him.

AUTHOR'S NOTES

I remember the first dragon's appearance and Mud coming in bravely.

During those years, we all know the not-so-fun pandemic that popped up and affected everyone differently. I'm not going to drudge on about it, but I did experience true anxiety for the first time in my life. Anxiety attacks aren't really something I would wish on my worst enemy—and I didn't do all that much writing for the better part of two years.

If you're struggling with them—best thing I can suggest is that therapy, cutting back on alcohol and caffeine, and getting out of shitty, stressful jobs did me wonders, and now here I am… no pills, just waves.

While writing War of the Mystics, I traveled to Vegas for my second writer's conference—already planning on attending this year too!—I've had a couple of sad losses in my little family.

We're a dog family. We lost Chops while I was in Vegas. He was a ten-year-old pit we rescued and he went downhill very quickly in the week that led up to Vegas. My wife Rachel told me to say an extra long goodbye to him before I left (just in case), and I'm sure glad she did. He was gone too soon. It was hard.

Three weeks ago we lost Olive, our three-legged, one-eyed cocker who was nine. To be honest, we got more years out of her than I thought we would, but I felt cheated because we could've gotten so many more out of Chops. Olive loved nothing more than to lay around, eat, beg to get pulled up onto the couch, and go on strolls in her stroller.

Harvey is my baby boy, a thirteen yo-cocker back at home with Rachel's parents, and I'm going to squeeze him so hard when I get back.

Life happens, and the good times outweigh the times with the bad. So we're going to probably foster some dogs when we get back.

One of the reasons I'm so excited was because this trip came at the perfect time to where I got to write the words 'The End' on Riders. It's sent off to Tiffany before the trip so I had the stress-free trip to chill, refill the creative well, and brainstorm the next series.

Jet lag can be a real bitch.

I laid awake in bed in the dark the other night until five a.m., needing to get up at eight to get on the bus that came here from Seville, Spain. I love to travel, and speaking Spanish, I love Spain. It sort of spins my brain into overdrive. So while I lay awake, my mind kept developing some ideas for the new books: characters, magic, world, and all the fun stuff.

I'm gonna plot it out a lot before I start getting the chapters in and may watch some of Brandon Sanderson's lectures on YouTube as some reminder guidance. But my drive is kicked back into gear after my long layoff, and I'm ready to hit the gas!

Riders really was an expression of what I wanted to do during the pandemic, get my ass on a dragon's back, learn some powerful magic, and save the world from all the shit going on. But I didn't do that, Stone did. And writing the last scenes in War of the Mystics was just about as much fun with writing as you could imagine. I was writing until my fingers hurt, and while at my day job cooking, my mind would keep the story moving—so much so that my notes keep growing because I didn't want to forget what someone was going to say, or how the action was going to move forward.

Spoilers, but you probably already read if you're to this point, but god damn I hate spoilers, and spent time avoiding all human contact and internet scrolling during certain seasons of Game of Thrones.

I always knew Corvaire wasn't going to make it. I always dreaded the thought of it because he was such a rock to Stone, Adler, and Ceres. But hey, I gave you twins of his so he isn't completely gone from the Worforgon, right? I mean, who wouldn't want to spend their time sleeping with a beautiful someone on the nights before the possible end of the world? Sign me up!

That was really tough to write, but actually, the part that made me most emotional to write was when they laid their hands on his body. That shit always gets me. Like when Aragorn makes everyone bow to the hobbits, damn I might cry now! Nope, holding it back. Deep breaths. Hold it in. Okay.

In the beginning, I wasn't sure if Stone and Ceres were going to end up together, so their kiss was a sort of test run, just to see what spark happened. I thought it was a really cute, precious moment. I mean, I kissed my friends when I was young and drunk, and we didn't end up getting married. But once Gracelyn came into the story—I knew.

He had a pretty deep fascination for her right away. But man, did she have a lot going on in her world. I think it took her some time to warm up to even be able to feel those kinds of emotions.

And as much as I'm on the fence about writing their story more—it is absolutely heartbreaking to me to think of him growing old, while she says the same age. He'll die while she surely is tormented by his loss. But also, there's so much there because who knows what kind of growth a fully-fledged Majestic Wild can go through. It would be so interesting to see what that would do to her. She could evolve into something so special with that sort of loss.

I refuse to write Mud's death. Flat. Out. Refuse. I'm not putting another dog I love down. He lives forever! I don't know how... but that dog never dies! If you tell me differently, then you're a liar lol.

Adler and Ceres are together, kind of a no-brainer. I loved their relationship from the start, and it's not so different from some of the marriages I know, partly part of my own too.

I loved writing the fall and rise of Marilyn. She'll prove to be a great aunt, no doubt. Lead the Worforgon into a great future, even though nothing is perfect. There's always sure to be trouble, and those Mages of the Arcane are still out there somewhere.

Gogenanth, for my big readers, will understand my world through his arc pretty well. Planned that pretty much from the beginning. Powerful yet sensitive, courageous yet troubled—he's no stranger to loss.

Does anyone enjoy seeing Kera again? Might even have a gray hair on her head...

Loved the villains, and loved writing Arken but didn't want him to have too much of a redemption story. Bad guys don't always regret their bad. Even til the end, he thought he was doing good. Loved Salus and Paltereth, loved Mogel and even Ghost I thought brought a good spirit of life when things seemed bleak.

What a promising start to a new era in the Worforgon. No gods, clean slate, good Majestic Wilds spread out to help build peace. What more could you ask for? Having Lucik and Hydrangea around would surely make the world a better place, but that's life, especially in wartime.

Well, cheers, friends!

Thanks for taking this journey with me. It's always been my dream to be a storyteller. Even when I was young I wanted to be a chef, novelist, and film director. Went to film school but my screenwriting course was what really kicked my passion for writing into motion. Turns out that screenwriting teacher ended up winning an Oscar for screenwriting, so who knows, maybe someday I'll direct a movie too.

You never know what the future holds, so grab the wheel when you can, and enjoy the ride as best you can.

The sea and trails are calling me. What's calling you?

C.K.

About the Author

Having grown up in the suburbs of Kansas, but never having seen a full tornado or a yellow brick road, he has been told more than his fair share of times while traveling, 'You're not in Kansas anymore.' He just responds, 'Never heard that one,' with a smile.

In the 'burbs' though, he found my passion for reading fantasy stories early. Reading books with elves, orcs and monsters took his young imagination to different worlds he wanted to live in.

Now, he creates his own worlds. Not so much in the elves and orc vein, but more in the heroes versus dragons one- there's a difference, right?

Yes, he grew up with The Lord of the Rings and tons of RA Salvatore books on his shelves, along with some cookbooks, comics, and a lot of video games too.

Other passions of his are coffee, good beer, and hanging around the gym.

To find out more and learn about what he's working on next please visit CKRieke.com.

C.K. Rieke is pronounced C.K. 'Ricky'.

Go to CKRieke.com and sign-up to join the Reader's Group for some free stuff and to get updated on new books!

www.CKRieke.com

Printed in Great Britain
by Amazon